W9-BLH-075
WITHDRAWN
No longer the property of the
Boston Public Library.
Sale of this material benefits the Library

Much Ado
About You

Also by Eloisa James in Large Print:

Duchess in Love
A Wild Pursuit
Your Wicked Ways
Potent Pleasures

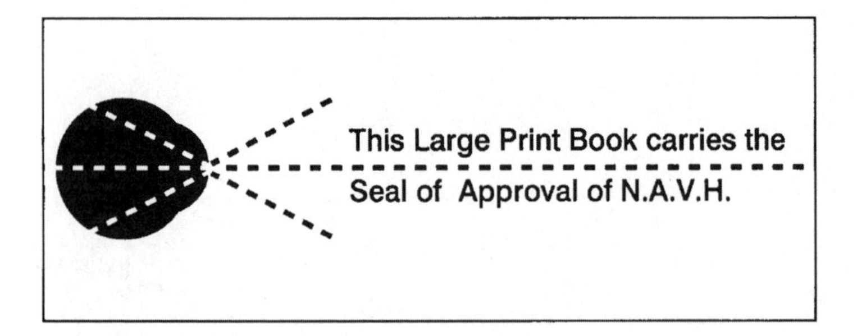

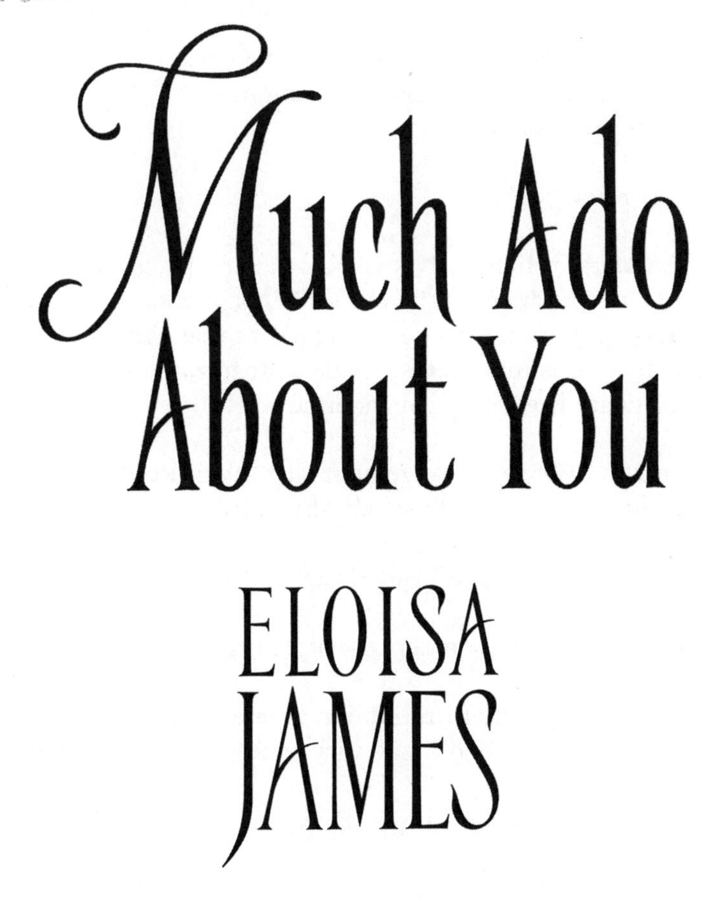

Thorndike Press • Waterville, Maine

Excerpt from A.S. Kline's "How Many Kisses: For Lesbia" appears courtesy of Poetry in Translation (www.tonykline.co.uk/)

This is a work of fiction. Names, characters, places, and incidents are products of the author's imagination or are used fictitiously and are not to be construed as real. Any resemblance to actual events, locales, organizations, or persons, living or dead, is entirely coincidental.

Published in 2005 by arrangement with Avon Books, an imprint of HarperCollins Publishers, Inc.

Thorndike Press® Large Print Basic.

The tree indicium is a trademark of Thorndike Press.

The text of this Large Print edition is unabridged. Other aspects of the book may vary from the original edition.

Set in 16 pt. Plantin by Minnie B. Raven.

Printed in the United States on permanent paper.

Library of Congress Cataloging-in-Publication Data

James, Eloisa.
Much ado about you / by Eloisa James.
p. cm.
"Thorndike Press large print basic" — T.p. verso.
ISBN 0-7862-7441-7 (lg. print : hc : alk. paper)
1. London (England) — Fiction. 2. Orphans — Fiction. 3. Sisters — Fiction. 4. Large type books. I. Title.
PS3560.A3796M83 2005
813'.54—dc22 2004029219

Much Ado
About You

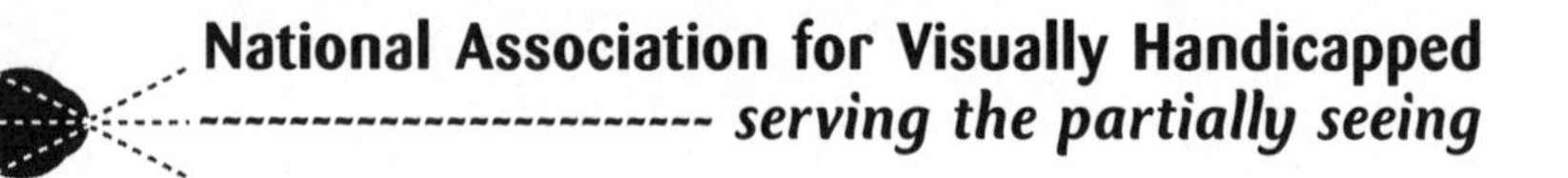

As the Founder/CEO of NAVH, the only national health agency solely devoted to those who, although not totally blind, have an eye disease which could lead to serious visual impairment, I am pleased to recognize Thorndike Press* as one of the leading publishers in the large print field.

Founded in 1954 in San Francisco to prepare large print textbooks for partially seeing children, NAVH became the pioneer and standard setting agency in the preparation of large type.

Today, those publishers who meet our standards carry the prestigious "Seal of Approval" indicating high quality large print. We are delighted that Thorndike Press is one of the publishers whose titles meet these standards. We are also pleased to recognize the significant contribution Thorndike Press is making in this important and growing field.

Lorraine H. Marchi, L.H.D.
Founder/CEO
NAVH

* Thorndike Press encompasses the following imprints: Thorndike, Wheeler, Walker and Large Print Press.

Chapter 1

September 1816
Holbrook Court,
seat of the Duke of Holbrook
On the outskirts of Silchester

In the afternoon

"I am happy to announce that the rocking horses have been delivered, Your Grace. I have placed them in the nursery for your inspection. As yet, there is no sign of the children."

Raphael Jourdain, Duke of Holbrook, turned. He had been poking a fire smoldering in the cavernous fireplace of his study. There was a reserved tone in his butler's voice that signaled displeasure. Or perhaps it would be more accurate to say that Brinkley's tone signaled the disgruntlement of the entire household of elderly servants, not one of whom was enchanted by the idea of accommodating themselves to the presence of four small, female children. Well, the hell with that, Rafe thought. It wasn't as if he'd *asked* to have a passel of youngsters on the premises.

"Rocking horses?" came a drawling voice from a deep chair to the right of the fireplace. "Charming, Rafe. Charming. One can't start too early making the little darlings interested in horseflesh." Garret Langham, the Earl of Mayne, raised his glass toward his host. His black curls were in exquisite disarray, his comments arrogant to a fault, and his manners barely hid a seething fury. Not that he was furious at Rafe; Mayne had been in a slow burn for the past few months. "To Papa and his brood of infant *equestriennes*," he added, tossing back his drink.

"Stubble it!" Rafe said, but without much real animosity. Mayne was a damned uncomfortable companion at the moment, what with his poisonous comments and black humor. Still, one had to assume that the foul temper caused by the shock of being rejected by a woman would wear off in a matter of time.

"Why the plural, as in rocking *horses?*" Mayne asked. "As I recall, most nurseries contain only one rocking horse."

Rafe took a gulp of his brandy. "I don't know much about children," he said, "but

I distinctly remember my brother and me fighting over our toys. So I bought four of them."

There was a second's silence during which the earl considered whether to acknowledge the fact that Rafe obviously still missed his brother (dead these five years, now). He dismissed the impulse. Manlike, he observed no benefit to maudlin conversation.

"You're doing those orphans proud," he said instead. "Most guardians would stow the children out of sight. It's not as if they're your blood."

"There's no amount of dolls in the world that will make up for their situation," Rafe said, shrugging. "Their father should have thought of his responsibilities before he climbed on a stallion."

The conversation was getting dangerously close to the sort of emotion to be avoided at all costs, so Mayne sprang from his chair. "Let's have a look at the rocking horses, then. I haven't seen one in years."

"Right," Rafe said, putting his glass onto the table with a sharp clink. "Brinkley, if the children arrive, bring them upstairs, and I'll receive them in the nursery."

A few minutes later the two men stood in the middle of a large room on the third floor, dizzily painted with murals. Little Bo Peep chased after Red Riding Hood, who was surely in danger of being crushed by the giant striding across the wall, his raised foot lowering over a feather bed sporting a huge green pea under the coverlet. The room resembled nothing so much as a Bond Street toy shop. Four dolls with spun gold hair sat primly on a bench. Four doll beds were propped atop each other, next to four doll tables, on which sat four jack-in-the-boxes. In the midst of it all was a group of rocking horses graced with real horsehair and coming almost to a man's waist.

"Jesus," Mayne said.

Rafe strode into the room and stamped on the rocker of one of the horses, making it clatter back and forth on the wooden floor. A door on the side of the room swung open, and a plump woman in a white apron poked her head out.

"There you are, Your Grace," she said, beaming. "We're just waiting for the children. Would you like to meet the new maids now?"

"Send them on in, Mrs. Beeswick."

Four young nursemaids crowded into the room after her. "Daisy, Gussie, Elsie, and Mary," said the nanny. "They're from the village, Your Grace, and pleased to have a position at Holbrook Court. We're all eager for the little cherubs to arrive." The nursemaids lined up to either side of Mrs. Beeswick, smiling and curtsying.

"Jesus," Mayne repeated. "They won't even share a maid, Rafe?"

"Why should they? My brother and I had three nurses between us."

"Three?"

"Two for my brother, ever since he turned duke at age seven, and one for me."

Mayne snorted. "That's absurd. When's the last time you met your wards' father, Lord Brydone?"

"Not for years," Rafe said, picking up a jack-in-the-box and pressing the lever so that it hopped from its box with a loud squeak. "The arrangement was just a matter of a note from him and my reply."

"You have never met your own wards?"

"Never. I haven't been over the border in years, and Brydone only came down for the Ascot, the Silchester, and, sometimes, Newmarket. To be honest, I don't think he really gave a damn for anything other than his stables. He didn't even bother to list his children in *Debrett's*. Of course, since he had four girls, there was no question of inheritance. The estate went to some distant cousin."

"Why on earth —" Mayne glanced at the five women standing to the side of the room and checked himself.

"He asked me," Rafe said, shrugging. "I didn't think twice of it. Apparently Monkton had been in line, but he cocked up his toes last year. And Brydone asked me to step in. Who would have thought that ill could come to Brydone? It was a freak accident, that horse throwing him. Although he was fool enough to ride a half-broken stallion."

"Damned if I thought I'd ever see you a father," Mayne said.

"I had no excuse to say no. I have the substance to raise any number of children. Besides, Brydone gave me Starling in return for acting as a guardian. I told him I'd do the job, as soon as he wrote me, and no bribe was necessary. But he sent Starling down from Scotland, and no one would say nay to adding that horse to their stables."

"Starling is out of Standout, isn't he?"

Rafe nodded. "Patchem's brother. The core of Brydone's stable is out of Patchem, and those are now the only horses in England in Patchem's direct line. I'm hopeful that Starling will win the Derby next year, even if he is descended from Standout rather than Patchem himself."

"What will happen to Patchem's offspring?" Mayne asked, with the particular intensity he reserved for talk of horses. "Something Wanton, for example?"

"I don't know yet. Obviously, the stables aren't entailed. My secretary has been up there working on the estate. Should Brydone's stable come to the children, I'll put the horses up for auction and the money in trust. The girls will need dowries someday, and I'd be surprised if Brydone bothered to set them up himself."

"If Wanton is for sale, I'm the one to buy him. I'd pay thousands for him. There could be no better addition to my stables."

"He would do wonders for mine as well," Rafe agreed.

Mayne had found a little heap of cast-iron horses and was sorting them out so that each carriage was pulled by a matched pair. "You know, these are quite good." He had all the cast-iron horses and their carriages lined up on the mantelpiece now. "Wait till your wards see these horses. They won't think twice about the move from Scotland. Pity there's no boy among them."

Rafe just looked at him. The earl was one of his dearest friends, and always would be. But Mayne's sleek, protected life had not put him in the way of grief. Rafe knew only too well what it felt like to find oneself lonely in the midst of a cozy nursery, and cast-iron horses wouldn't help, for all he found himself buying more and more of them. As if toys would make up for a dead father. "I hardly think you —"

The door behind him swung open. He stopped and turned.

Brinkley moved to the side more nimbly than was his practice. It wasn't every day that one got to knock the master speechless with surprise. "I'm happy to announce Miss Essex. Miss Imogen. Miss Annabel. Miss Josephine."

Then he added, unable to resist, if the truth be known, "The children have arrived, Your Grace."

Chapter 2

The first thing Teresa Essex noticed was that the Englishmen were playing with toys. *Toys!* That fit with everything they'd heard about Englishmen: thin, puny types they were, who never grew up and shivered with cold during a stiff breeze.

Still, they were only men, if English versions of them.

Tess hadn't been much over sixteen years old when she realized that men's notions of toys were flexible. With a glance at Josie and a touch on Imogen's shoulder she brought her sisters into a straight line. Annabel had already fallen into place, her head tilted just so, the better to allow the beholders to appreciate the sheen of her honey-golden hair.

These Englishmen looked even more shocked at the sight of the four of them than was usual. They were practically gaping. Quite rude, really. They weren't exactly the spindly-legged, sickly creatures she would have expected, from what was said about Englishmen. The one of them looked like a fashion plate and had a wild mop of black curls that she supposed must be fashionable. Not that he was a dandy. Dandies didn't have that faintly dangerous air. The other was tall, with a bit of a gut and a messy shock of brown hair falling over his brow. A lone wolf, perhaps.

"Well," she said finally, when no one spoke, "we are, naturally, sorry to interrupt you both, especially when you were so gainfully occupied." She gave it just the faintest stress. Just enough to let them know that they were not merely pretty Scottish lasses, to be shunted off to the back room and ignored. They were ladies, after all, whether they wore unfashionable clothing or not.

The elegant one bowed and came forward, saying, "What a delightful surprise to meet you, Miss Essex. All of you."

There was something odd about his voice, as if he were having trouble not laughing. But he kissed her hand with all the adroitness of a courtier.

Then finally the big one, the lone wolf, shook himself, for all the world like a dog coming out of a puddle, and came to her side as well. "I apologize for my impoliteness," he said. "I am Rafe Jourdain, the

Duke of Holbrook. I'm afraid that I mistook your ages."

"Our ages?" Tess let her eyebrows ask a delicate question. Then, slowly, the implications of the gaudily painted room and the clusters of toys sank in. "You thought we were still *children?*"

He nodded, standing before her now, bowing again, the easy sweep of a man who has spent his lifetime in the highest echelons of society, even though he (apparently) didn't bother to brush his hair. "I offer you all my heartiest apologies. I was under the erroneous belief that you and your sisters were quite young."

"Young!" Tess said. "You must have thought we were mere babes in arms!" Because now she had taken in the presence of a nanny and four gaping young nursemaids in white aprons, the rocking horses, the dolls. "Didn't Papa tell you —"

But she broke off. Of course Papa hadn't told him. Papa had likely informed him of Starling's age, and Wanton's stride, and what Lady of Pleasure liked to eat before a race, but not the ages of his daughters.

Their guardian had taken her hand and was smiling down at her now, and her heart warmed despite her resentment. "I'm such a fool that I forgot to ask your father. And, of course, I hadn't the faintest notion that my guardianship would be needed. Will you accept my deepest sympathies for your loss, Miss Essex?"

Tess blinked. His eyes were a curious color, sort of a gray-blue. And kind, for all he looked like a wild man of Borneo. A dash of hope mixed with the bleak feeling of defensiveness in her chest.

"Of course," she said. "May I introduce my sisters? This is Imogen," she said, turning to her sister. "Imogen is just turned twenty." There were moments when she thought that Imogen was more beautiful than Annabel (and that was really saying something). She had their mother's sleek black hair and her laughing eyes, but that mouth — only Imogen had a mouth that took such an exquisite curve. Sometimes it struck men like a blow in the stomach; it was rather interesting to watch the duke blink and recover.

Imogen, of course, never paid any mind to the effect she had on men because she was in love. She did smile at the duke, though, and gave a pretty curtsy. When their father had a bit of money, he usually remembered to hire a governess for a time, at least, and so they all could put on dandified manners when required.

"This is Annabel," Tess said, putting a hand on Annabel's arm. "Annabel is the eldest after me; she is twenty-two." If Imogen paid no heed to men, Annabel must have toddled out of her nurse's arms knowing how to flirt. Now she gave the duke a rosy-lipped smile that spoke of innocence and something else; she pitched her voice to the tune of an unheavenly appreciation. Her simple greeting sounded like honey with an edge of lemon.

The duke showed no sign of turning weak at the knees. "Miss Annabel," he said, bringing her hand to his lips. "It's a pleasure to meet you."

"And Josephine," Tess said. "Josie is fifteen, and still in the schoolroom."

Tess noticed that the duke was already smiling at Josie, which was a sign of his good manners. She loathed it when men acted as if they were stuck by glue to Annabel's side and only gave Josie the scantest glance.

"I'd rather you didn't kiss my hand," Josie said briskly.

"May I introduce a friend of mine?" the duke said, acting as if he didn't hear Josie's comment, although he made no effort to kiss her hand. "Garret Langham, the Earl of Mayne."

Annabel gave Mayne a blithely appreciative smile, as if she were a four-year-old being handed a piece of birthday cake. There was nothing more to Annabel's taste than a man in possession of all his limbs *and* a title.

Mayne smiled back with something of the same admiration, although Tess thought that his emotion likely had little to do with Annabel's forefathers.

The gentlemen completed their greetings, and the duke turned back to her. "Miss Essex, since none of you are likely to have interest in these —" he waved his hand — "these playthings, shall we retire to the public rooms? I'm afraid that my housekeeper will likely need a short period of time to ready bedchambers for you, but I imagine your maids will assist."

Tess felt a blush rising up her collarbone. "We haven't brought any maids with us."

"In that case," her guardian said without even blinking, we can employ these four young women for the purpose, if that would be acceptable." He indicated the four nursemaids, still lined up against the wall, their eyes wide as ha'pennies. "I'm certain the housekeeper can train them in their duties readily enough."

"You're in need of a chaperone," Mayne

put in, with a slanting glance at the duke. "Now that you're no longer running a nursery. *Tonight,* Rafe."

Clearly the thought hadn't crossed their guardian's mind. "Dammit, I'll have to write a note to Lady Clarice," he said, running a hand through his wild hair, "and ask her to pay me a visit. That's if she'll come after last time; I think I was a trifle rude to her."

"In your cups, were you?" Mayne asked.

A wry grimace curled their guardian's mouth. "I threw her out, with luck not bodily. Can't really remember." He suddenly realized that Tess and the girls were all staring at him and gave them a smile that hadn't a whit of remorse in it. "Now my wards will think I'm a sot."

"To know you is to love you," the earl said, throwing him a sarcastic grin. "My dear Misses Essex, the evening when your guardian isn't clutching a bumper of brandy will be the day hell blooms with roses."

"Lady Clarice's land runs parallel to ours," Holbrook said to Tess, ignoring his friend's comment. "I daresay if I send a pretty enough note, she'll forgive me since we are in desperate circumstances. You can't possibly spend the night under my roof without a chaperone."

But Mayne wasn't to be silenced. "The lady's a widow, and she has an eye for your guardian," he told the girls. "I do believe she's hoping that one day she'll find him so deep in his cups that he doesn't notice that she's calling the banns. It's too bad for her that Rafe doesn't show his liquor."

"Nonsense," the duke said gruffly, sweeping his hair about so that he looked even more of a lunatic.

"Doesn't bother her that she has ten years on Rafe," Mayne continued blithely. "Lady Clarice has an optimistic soul, for all that her own son is almost Rafe's own age."

"Maitland is considerably younger than I," the duke said rather curtly.

"He's in his twenties," Mayne said, "and that makes Lady Clarice at least five years older than you."

Tess felt rather than heard an agitated little sound from Imogen, at the same second that her own heart sunk. They were hoping to wean Imogen from her hopeless adoration of Lord Maitland, and finding him next door wasn't the best start. "Are you by any chance referring to *Draven* Maitland, Your Grace?" she asked, obedient to an imploring glance from Imogen.

"So you know Maitland, do you?" It didn't look to Tess as if their guardian thought much more of Lord Maitland than she did. "Likely he'll accompany his mother then. I'll ask them both to join us for supper. Perhaps you and your sisters would like to take a short rest before the evening meal?"

"That would be pleasant," Tess said. Imogen was grinning like a fool. Tess saw the duke's eyes take in her grin, but he said nothing.

"The rose suite will do until your chambers are readied." Holbrook held out his arm, and Tess took it, rather awkwardly.

The Englishmen were so unlike what she had expected! They were — formidable. But Englishmen weren't supposed to be formidable. Everything she'd ever heard about English gentlemen suggested that they were willowy creatures, liable to sneeze and blow away. Oh, there were exceptions, of course. Lord Maitland, for one, had a sturdy enough figure.

Their new guardian didn't fit the mold either. He was not ducal in the least. He wasn't dressed in satin or velvet. Instead, he was wearing trousers so old that she could see the seams on the side, especially where they strained over his belly, and a white shirt that didn't have a bit of satin on it. Its sleeves were even turned up, as if he were about to set to work in the stables.

There was nothing aristocratic about his voice, either. It was nice enough, but gruff and brusque. And he had lines around his eyes, for all he couldn't be more than thirty-five. Dissipated, that's what he looked. Not a womanizer: Tess could spot one of those a mile off, and though he looked at all of them with interest, there wasn't a spark of appreciation of their womanhood in his eyes.

And yet, for all that wild hair and dissipated face and ancient clothing, for all of that — he wasn't frightening.

Tess felt a hard knot in her chest begin to loosen, just a trifle.

This burly man who had hired four nursemaids for four little girls and was never without a bumper of brandy . . . he wasn't someone to fear.

Tess looked down at the worn linen of his shirtsleeve and said, "I want to thank you, Your Grace, for accepting this guardianship." She swallowed, but it had to be said. "My father was an improvident man, and sometimes he traded upon acquaintance in a way that must create a burden."

He looked genuinely surprised. "Don't

think twice about it, m'dear."

"I'm quite serious," Tess persisted. "I —"

"So am I," the duke said. "I must be named guardian in at least twenty wills, Miss Essex. I am a duke, after all, and I've never seen that I had a reason to refuse such a request."

"Oh," Tess said, shocked to the bone. It seemed her father wasn't the only man to take advantage of a slender acquaintance with Holbrook.

He patted her hand, for all the world as if he were a middle-aged uncle. "Not to fear, Miss Essex. I'm certain we can figure out this guardianship business amongst us. It should be an easy enough business to find a governess for young Josie. Finding a chaperone that we can bear to live with might take a bit more thinking. But there's nothing to worry about."

To Tess's mind, worry had been her sole emotion of last few months, most of which had been occupied by squabbling over the possibility that their guardian was a reasonable, kindly man versus a half-cracked horseman. And to each and every nervous question Tess had said stoutly, "I'm certain he will be an estimable gentleman. After all, Papa chose him with careful forethought."

Lord knows that wasn't the truth. On his deathbed, Papa had grasped her hand, and said, "Not to worry, Tess. I've an optimal man to look after you all. Asked him just after poor old Monkton up and died last year. I knew Holbrook years ago."

"Why has he never visited, Papa?"

"Never met him again," her father had said, looking so white against the pillow that Tess's heart had clenched with fear. "Not to worry, lass. I've seen his name mentioned time and again in *Sporting Magazine*. He'll take good care of Wanton, Bluebell, and the rest. Said he would. Wrote me as much. And I sent him Starling to seal the bargain."

"I'm sure he will, Papa," Tess had said, putting down her sweet, feckless Papa's hand with a loving squeeze since he seemed to have drifted off to sleep. So this duke would take good care of Papa's beloved horseflesh — but what of his daughters?

He opened his eyes again though. "You'll be right and tight with Holbrook, Tess. Take care of them for me, won't you?"

She picked up his hand again hastily, trying to force back the tears crowding her throat.

"Feel as if I'm looking at you through a snowstorm," he had said, his voice just a whisper of sound.

"Oh, Papa," Tess whispered. "I do love you."

He shook his head, obviously gathering himself. "I'll be seeing your mother, I've no doubt." There was a little smile on his face. Papa was always very good at looking forward to a happy event. Sometimes she thought he was happier in the week before a big race, when he had something to anticipate, than when he'd won a race. Not that he won very often.

"Yes, Papa," she whispered, brushing the tears away as they coursed down her cheeks.

"My lass," he said, and she didn't know whether he was talking of her or her mother. Then, "Don't forget that Wanton likes apple-mash." And, again, "Take care of them for me, Tess?"

"Of course I will, Papa. I'll inform His Grace immediately on our arrival about Wanton's weak stomach."

"I didn't mean that, Tessa," her father said, and this smile was for her, not for her mother. "Annabel's too beautiful, you know. And sweet Josie." There was silence for a moment, then he said, "Maitland's not right for Imogen. Wild thing, that boy."

There were tears running down Tess's wrists.

"You're . . ." His voice faltered, then he said, rather dreamily. "Tess. Those apples . . ."

But he had gone to sleep, then. And though she and her sisters had told him of the stables until they were hoarse, and Josie had brought a bowl of steaming apple-mash into the bedchamber, thinking it might arouse him, he didn't wake. After a few days, he slipped away in the midst of the night.

The funeral passed like a gray dream. Their plump cousin, who had inherited the estate, appeared with a clucking wife and two maiden aunts in tow; Tess did her best to make them comfortable in a house that hadn't even one decent feather bed. When the duke's secretary finally arrived to announce their fate, she managed not to scream questions about his master but waited patiently. When that secretary spent the first full week of his visit arranging for their father's horses to be sent to England with all possible comfort, her questions seemed unnecessary. The horses left long before they did. Could their unknown guardian have made it clearer where his priorities lay?

So even as she reassured Josie, and told Imogen to stop talking of Draven Maitland or she would strangle her with the only ribbon Annabel had left, Tess had worried, and worried, until the lump of grief in her chest seemed to turn to permanent stone.

She'd just as soon have nothing to do with a horse-mad male, ever again. It was galling to find that their futures were utterly dependent on just such a man. It made her think fierce thoughts of her darling papa, and *that* made her feel guilty, and guilt made her feel irritable.

Looking at the Duke of Holbrook now, there was no question that their guardian was indeed horse-mad. With that hair and clothing, he was probably garden-variety mad and no need for the adjective.

But he was kind, too. And not lecherous.

He didn't seem to have their father's easy way of ignoring their comforts. He certainly had no obligation to invite them to live in his house, nor to treat them like real relatives.

Perhaps she'd been too hasty. Perhaps — just perhaps — all men weren't mad in the same ways.

Chapter 3

A few hours later, Tess lay under the damp cloth that the duke's housekeeper herself had placed over her eyes. The faint smell of lemons drifted to her nose. She could hear the sounds of a large household around her. It wasn't the echoing, empty sound of her father's house, marked only by the harsh rap of boots on the bare floor (Papa had sold the carpets long ago), but a faint hum that added to the smell of furniture rubbed with lemon oil, and sheets dried in the sun, and a mattress that had been turned once a season.

"It's time for a family council," said a cheerful voice. The side of the bed dipped as Annabel sat down.

Tess lifted up the cloth over her eyes and peered at her sister. "I only just lay down," she objected.

"No, you didn't," her sister retorted. "You've been lying there like a plum pudding under a steaming cloth for at least two hours, and we must talk before dressing for the evening meal. Here come Josie and Imogen."

The girls climbed up onto the bed, just as if they were in Tess's bedchamber at home, where they'd spent many an evening curled under the covers so as to stay warm, talking endlessly of their future, and their papa, and their horses.

"All right," Tess murmured, yawning.

"I shall marry him," Annabel announced, once they were all settled.

"Who?" Tess asked. She put the cloth on the bedside table and pushed herself upright against the pillows.

"The duke, of course!" Annabel said. "One of us must become the duchess obviously, since he doesn't seem to have one at hand. Duchess of Holbrook. The man isn't married, although —"

"Holbrook may well be promised in marriage," Imogen pointed out. "Look at Draven." Lord Maitland had been promised in marriage for two years or more, without showing the slightest interest in progressing toward the altar.

"I doubt it," Annabel said. "And if not, I shall marry him. That way, my husband can give each of you excellent dowries. Perhaps you won't marry as well as I, since there are only eight dukes in all England, not counting the royal dukes. But we shall find titled men for each of you."

"What a sacrifice," Josie said acidly. "I suppose you read all of *Debrett's* in order to discover the names of those eight dukes?"

"I shall steel myself to the task," Annabel said. "And mind you, given our guardian's looks, I do consider it a sacrifice. The man will be positively potbellied before he's fifty, if he doesn't watch out."

Imogen rolled her eyes, but Josie leaped in before her. "Sacrifice, Annabel? You'd marry an eighty-year-old man if you could make yourself a duchess! *Your Grace!*" she added for good measure.

"I most certainly would not!" Annabel retorted. Then she laughed. "Well, only if the man was very, very wealthy."

"You're naught more than a money-grubbing flirt," Josie observed. "And who's to say that this duke is any richer than Papa was? After all, Papa was a viscount, but his title was naught more than tin when it came to his pocket!"

"If Holbrook has no money, I shan't marry him," Annabel said with a delicate shudder. "I'd rather slay myself than marry a man as out at the elbows as Papa was. But don't be foolish, Josie. Look at this house! Holbrook is obviously deep in the pockets."

"Don't be disrespectful of your father," Tess broke in. "Annabel, truly, the duke may well be affianced, and it would be best not to think in such an improper fashion of the man who was kind enough to agree to be our guardian."

Annabel raised one eyebrow and took a small mirror from her reticule. "Perhaps I'll make him regret that arrangement, then," she said, rubbing her lips with a scrap of Spanish paper that she'd bought in the village before they left Scotland.

"You're revolting," Josie said.

"And *you're* a squib," Annabel said. "I'm being practical. One of us has to marry, and immediately. Imogen has been telling us for two years now that she means to marry Maitland, and Tess has never made the slightest push to marry anyone — so that leaves me. One of us has to marry and take the others to her house. That's what we always said."

"Tess could marry anyone she chose!" Josie said stoutly. "She's the most beautiful of us all. Don't you agree, Imogen?"

Imogen nodded, but she had her arms clasped around her knees, and she was clearly paying not a whit of attention to the conversation. "She may marry anyone, other than Draven, of course," she said dreamily. "Just think, I might see him in a matter of hours . . . minutes really."

Annabel ignored her comment, which was pretty much the way the girls had acted every time Imogen mentioned Maitland's name for the past two years. "I agree with you as to Tess's beauty," she told Josie, "but men aren't prone to marry penniless girls who show no interest. Yet *I* am interested in marriage. Very interested."

"In the institution, not the man!" Josie retorted.

Annabel shrugged. "Imogen is romantic enough for the rest of us. It's Papa's fault. He made me keep the books for all these years, and now numbers float before my eyes every time I think about matrimony."

"He didn't precisely *make* you keep the books," Tess put in, a trifle wearily. She was tired of defending their father from Annabel's charges, but Josie took any criticism of their papa very badly. There was no way to sugarcoat the fact that their papa had discovered Annabel had a gift for figures at age thirteen and dumped the entire financial accounting of the estate on her slender shoulders.

"The important point is that I shan't be keeping books any longer. I don't want to think of numbers, or bills, or unpaid accounts ever again in my life. Thank goodness, men are silly enough to overlook my lack of dowry."

"You could try for a little modesty," Josie needled.

"You could try for a little maturity," Annabel retorted. "I'm not being immodest. I'm simply being practical. One of us must marry, and I have the attributes that make men dazed enough to overlook lack of dowry. I'm not going to pretend to possess ladylike virtues that I don't have in front of you three. It's too late for that. If Papa truly wanted us to think like ladies, he wouldn't have trained us to do exactly the opposite."

"Papa did wish us to be ladies!" Josie protested. "He taught us to speak just like English ladies, didn't he?"

"Poppycock," Annabel said, but there wasn't any real spite in her voice, just an amused acceptance. "Josie, if Papa had given a fig for his daughters' futures as ladies, our lives would have been quite different. For one thing, he wouldn't have pissed in the chamber pot right there in the dining room."

"Annabel!" Tess said. "Keep your voice down."

But Annabel just grinned at her. "Don't worry," she said. "I fully intend to counterfeit every ladylike quality that exists, until at least a week after I convince some bacon-brained peer to marry me and hand over his pocketbook."

Tess sighed. It wasn't easy to be an elder sister to Annabel, with her startling tawny hair and brazen belief in her own magnificence. The problem was that she and Imogen truly did look like the princesses in the fairy tale "Snow White and Rose Red."

"Well, you needn't set your cap at Holbrook," she said. "I don't think he'd make the best husband in the world."

"If he's rich enough, he's good enough. Frankly, I can't marry just anyone," Annabel said. "I've very expensive tastes." She hopped off the bed and examined herself in the glass. "I may never have had a chance to indulge those tastes, but I'm certain they'll be expensive when I do indulge them. I have no objection to considering the Earl of Mayne if he shows as much depth in the pocket as our guardian."

"You're being shocking for the mere sake of it," Tess said.

Annabel ignored her, as she had ignored every piece of advice that directed itself toward proper ladylike behavior. "The duke is a better bet. Higher title, and all that. I shall reel him in," she announced, "then I shall go directly to London. From the day I am married, I shall wear nothing but silk next to my skin."

"There's a word for women like you," Josie observed.

"And that word is *happy*," Annabel said. It was hard to offend Annabel, even though her smallest sister devoted herself to the task. Annabel was too — Annabel. Too sure of herself, too glowing, too sensuous, too loving. Too desired. "I can hardly believe that we have finally found our way out of that backwater and almost to London. I don't mind admitting that there were times that I despaired. Papa's schemes, after all, never came to anything, for all he kept promising that he'd take us to London for the season."

As far as Tess could ascertain by staring in the mirror, she and Annabel certainly looked like enough to be sisters, but their effect on men was utterly different. Something about Imogen and Annabel drove men into imbecilic paralysis in their presence, and whatever it was, she, Tess, didn't seem to have it. They were all beautiful, thanks to their mama, who had been the most lovely debutante in London until she threw herself away on a horse-mad, bankrupt Scottish viscount. But Tess never reduced anyone into stammering silence the way Annabel and Imogen did.

Tess sometimes thought the problem was that she not only looked like their mother but that she remembered her. Annabel would never speak of their mother, and Imogen and Josie had been too small to have clear memories. But Tess remembered. And remembered. And somehow since Papa died, it was all wound up together in her chest . . . missing her mama so much that her chest hurt, then missing her father with the same pulse of pain.

"Now, if I marry the duke," Annabel said briskly, "one of us ought to marry that earl our guardian has so kindly provided."

"Better the earl than the duke," Imogen said. "I don't think Holbrook has combed his hair since last Tuesday. Not that I'm marrying either of them."

"I'm too young to marry anyone," Josie said with satisfaction. "And even if I weren't, the Earl of Mayne would never want to marry someone like me. There's something rather arrogant about him, don't you think?"

"What do you mean by *'someone like me'*?" Tess asked. "Because you are beautiful, Josie. He would be lucky to marry you."

"A plumpy partridge?" Josie said, and there was a hint of shame in her voice.

"Papa meant it as an endearment, not as a description," Tess said, cursing her father silently, then instantly following the impulse with a silent prayer for forgiveness.

"Did you hear His Grace mention that he would ask Lady Clarice to be our chaperone?" Imogen said, abruptly changing the subject back to her favorite topic of conversation. "Lady Clarice is Draven's mother. His *mother!* We are bound to see him often. And if she likes me . . ."

"The fact Maitland's mother exists does not alter the fact that his fiancée exists as well," Josie noted.

"I can tell that Draven's heart is not engaged in the match," Imogen said with an edge to her voice. "Just consider, he's been betrothed for over two years without progressing to the altar."

"I hate to be dour," Annabel said, "but there's likely a great deal of money involved in a breach-of-promise suit. Maitland has never been one to consider money as other than fodder for his stables. Do you really think he would choose you over his stables?"

Imogen opened her mouth, and then lapsed into silence.

"Enough," Tess said, sitting up and pushing back the counterpane. "We must dress for supper."

"I'm merely going to the drawing room briefly to meet our chaperone," Josie said. "Then Mrs. Beeswick is going to serve me a comfortable meal in the schoolroom. I've been there while you were sleeping, and it's all books. Lovely books!"

Tess gave her a hug. "That's splendid, darling. And the duke told me that he'd find you a governess directly, so perhaps you could even start lessons in the near future. It would be nice if one of us were learned. Imogen, you mustn't let Lady Clarice have even a hint of your *tendresse* for her son."

"I'm not stupid!" Imogen clambered off the bed. She'd left her hair down, and it swept behind her in a great swirling gleam of black silk. "Just don't ask me to marry anyone except for Draven. Not the duke nor the earl. I'm quite certain that —"

"Oh, no," Josie moaned. "Can't you just accept the fact that Maitland is unavailable, Imogen?"

"I don't agree," Imogen said stubbornly. "Don't you remember the time that I managed to fall out of the apple tree at Draven's feet, and he picked me up?" She shivered. "It was lovely. He's so strong."

"Yes, but —" Josie said, but Imogen overran her.

"I thought I might not see Draven until we traveled to London, but here he is living down the road, and his mother is to be our chaperone." Imogen's eyes were glowing with fervor. "Obviously, it's fate! We belong together."

"I think we've neglected the possibility that she injured her head in that fall," Josie said to Annabel and Tess.

Tess sighed. It was obvious to everyone that Draven Maitland didn't really give a pin for Imogen, and it was equally obvious that Imogen wouldn't countenance marrying anyone other than Maitland. Either she or Annabel would have to give Imogen a home until their little sister finally gave up her fruitless adoration.

"Our marriage was fated in the stars!" Imogen announced, looking dramatic as any heroine in a melodrama.

Annabel was standing before the glass, pulling her honey hair in a great mass over her shoulder. "Darling," she said, giving Imogen an amused glance, "you keep your idea of how marriages are made, and I shall keep mine. From everything I've seen, the best marriages are those between practical persons, entered into for practical reasons, and with a reasonable degree of confidence in compatibility."

"You sound like a solicitor," Imogen said.

"An accountant," Annabel responded. "Papa made me into an accountant, which means that I can't help looking at life as a series of negotiations, of which marriage is the most important."

She smiled at herself in the glass and twisted her hair into a great shining pile on her head. "Do I not look like a duchess?" She struck a pose. "Make way for Her Grace!"

"Make way for a goose!" Josie said, and then shrieked and ran for the door as Annabel made a swipe at her bottom with the brush.

Chapter 4

Imogen's hands weren't shaking. She was quite proud of that. Any other girl would be trembling like a leaf under the circumstances: she was about to meet her future mother-in-law for the first time, and perhaps see Draven too . . .

She brushed her hair until it crackled, and pinched her cheeks until she looked feverish, and then practiced demure smiles in the mirror. There was no reason to be nervous, given that fate had obviously brought them together. She practiced her smile again. She must use just the right smile when meeting Draven's mother: a smile that was not grasping, socially aggressive, or any of those undesirable qualities. She had decided to aim at adorably shy and very young.

It took a while (adorably shy not being one of Imogen's natural characteristics), but finally she was fairly certain of success. If she merely curled up the very edges of her mouth and let the smile tremble on her lips, she looked positively Juliet-like. Thirteen at the most.

Josie stuck her head in the door just as Imogen was practicing a deep, yet bashful, curtsy before the mirror. "One can be certain," Josie said in her customary acerbic tone, "that your darling Maitland will be out at the racetrack. So you might as well save your adoring glances."

Imogen didn't bother telling Josie that she had already figured that out herself. If a race were being held within fifty miles, Draven wouldn't be at home. He wasn't the sort of man to hang around his mother's apron strings, not an out-and-outer like himself.

"I truly don't see what appeals to you about Maitland," Josie continued disagreeably.

Imogen turned back to her mirror and dropped another curtsy. It was no concern of hers that her sisters were unable to see Draven's manifest virtues. Why, he had so many that it was hard to catalog them; they were jumbled in her mind. Of course, he was handsome, with a rakish air of danger. He drove his horses to an inch, and he always looked as if he should have a whip in his hand, even when he was in church. Just thinking of him made her feel giddy with pleasure.

"It will do you no good to snip at me," she told her little sister, sweeping past her out the door. "Someday you'll understand love, and until then, we need not discuss the subject."

It felt as if they had been sitting in the drawing room for hours before the door finally swung open, and Brinkley announced, "The Lady Clarice Maitland."

In the doorway was a lady dressed in the very first stare of elegance, her head cocked to the side and her hands making all sorts of elegant circles before she even said a word. Her nose had a narrow, chiseled look that was echoed by her high cheekbones. She looked coiffed, sharp-tongued, and inexpressibly expensive.

"Holbrook, *darling!*" she trilled, sweeping in the door before the butler. "You needn't announce my son, Brinkley, we're positively members of the family."

The man who stood at Brinkley's shoulder made Imogen's heart stop in her chest for a full second before it started beating again.

He was singularly beautiful, with his wide square jaw, that little cleft in his chin, his almond eyes . . . She stood up, but her knees felt weak.

"Remember, the man is betrothed!" Tess

whispered, as they moved forward to curtsy before Lady Clarice.

Of course, a distant acknowledgment was all that Draven deserved. He *was* promised to another, no matter how many four-leaf clovers and stars she'd wished upon in the past two years, since she first caught sight of him. She could feel her mouth spreading into a smile that hadn't even a shadow of demureness about it.

"You caught me in the nick of time," Lady Clarice was shrilling as she held out her hand to be kissed by their guardian. "I was just off to London to see my mantua-maker when I received your summons. Luckily, I judged your state more desperate than mine! And *these* must be your wards."

Lady Clarice was wearing a dress more gorgeous than any garment Imogen had ever seen. It was fashioned of twilled sarsenet in a rich crimson with three rows of ribband trimming shaped into small wreaths along the hem.

They were all wearing horrid mourning gowns, of dull bombazine with only a narrow strip of white lace lining the neck, and that the gift of the seamstress in the village, who said that she couldn't see her way to sending them off to the wilds of

England without a bit of trimming, and never mind that they couldn't pay.

Lady Clarice had lace flying from her hair and trimming her hems and her reticule, but she had a sharp face to go with all that decoration. Imogen blinked, pushing away that thought. She was Draven's *mother.*

As she and Tess sank into deep, demure curtsies, Imogen looked at Draven's boots. Even his boots were beautiful, of a rich, brown leather that looked as shiny and perfect as himself.

"Allow me to present my ward, Miss Essex," the duke was saying, "and one of her sisters, Miss Imogen. We are all tremendously grateful for your assistance."

Lady Clarice peered at them as if they were curiosities in a traveling circus. "I can't imagine what your father was thinking to send you here without —" she half shrieked, and then paused as a thought apparently strayed into her mind. "But of course, your father is no longer of this world, is he? Then he isn't thinking about chaperones. Best leave that to the living!" She beamed at them.

Imogen opened her mouth and shut it again. She would have to meet Draven's eyes in a moment. He was *betrothed,* she told herself again. He had told her in as many words that they had no future together. But then —

"Where are the other two girls? You did say four, didn't you? Holbrook," Lady Clarice screeched, "do you have four wards or not?"

The duke started visibly and turned back from greeting Draven. "There are indeed four of them," he confirmed, running a hand through his hair.

Tess beckoned to Annabel, who was standing to the side of the room flirting with the Earl of Mayne, and then to Josie, who was hiding behind the piano.

"Just look at these four young ladies!" Lady Clarice cried, once they were all standing in a line. "Exquisite! You shall have no problem whatsoever firing them off on the market, Holbrook. I would say that we can achieve *at least* a lord. Perhaps even higher, dears, perhaps even higher! One must think of these things in a positive light. Of course, there is some work to be done," Lady Clarice continued, without seeming to draw a breath. "Their gowns are abhorrent, naturally. There is *mourning*, my dears, and then there is *mourning*, if you understand what I mean. But the Scottish have no concept of dress and never have. These days I won't even approach the border. Why, my hair quite stands on end at the thought!" She patted her gingery ringlets happily.

Josie curtsied and slipped back behind the piano, where she was pretending to shuffle through sheet music. But given that Papa had never had the blunt to hire a musical tutor of any kind, Imogen — if no one else — knew that was a mere pretense. She only hoped that the duke wouldn't think to ask Josie to play them something.

"A diet of hard-boiled eggs and stewed cabbage should trim your little sister's figure," Lady Clarice whispered loudly to Tess. "I was *just* the same when I was her age, if you can believe it! But look at me, I managed to catch a baron! You may not be able to look quite as high as that, but I think a lord is not out of possibility! Even the chubby little one should be able to make a good match, with the help of a *modiste*."

Tess's eyes narrowed and her mouth opened, but Holbrook was there before her, suddenly sounding quite ducal. "Josephine has a figure that many a young lady will envy."

Lady Clarice gave him a liquorish smile and giggled. "Quite right, Your Grace. You mustn't lose hope of firing off all four of them. There are men who prefer a poke pudding, as they say!"

Imogen could feel her spirits lowering. The hope that perhaps Lady Clarice would allow her son to marry for true love withered. Lady Clarice looked as if she hadn't yet learned the meaning of the word *love,* and she certainly wouldn't encourage the emotion if she had.

"But I must introduce my son!" Lady Clarice said, dragging him forward. "Although, darling girls, I must warn you that my darling is promised to another." She giggled shrilly. "We'll do our best to find you someone just as suitable, however. Miss Essex, Miss Imogen, may I present my son, Lord Maitland."

Imogen curtsied, as did Tess beside her. She felt a delicate wash of color rise up her neck.

"We are acquainted with Lord Maitland, Lady Clarice," Tess was saying rather coldly. "He is — was — a friend of our father, Viscount Brydone."

Imogen knew her sister thought Draven was dissolute, and all because he was dashing and funny and too handsome for his own good, as their nanny would have said, back when they had a nanny.

Draven bowed, quite as if he had never shared a bread-and-cheese supper with them — and he had, time out of mind, because he was as horse-mad as her papa.

"I have known the Essexes for some two years, mother," he said, but his eyes were holding Imogen's. Her heart fluttered as if it were a bird caught in a cage.

"What? Oh!" Lady Clarice laughed. "You must have met each other when darling Draven hunts in Scotland, is that it?" Something guarded entered her tone. Lady Clarice was no fool, and the Essex girls were astonishingly lovely.

Tess caught Lady Clarice's inflection and felt a wave of panic. If Lady Clarice even caught wind of Imogen's abject devotion to her son, she might refuse to chaperone them, and then what would they do?

"I race in Scotland, not hunt," Draven told his mother. He was bowing over Imogen's hand now, and Tess noticed with a sinking heart that he was looking at her sister with some semblance of the passion with which she looked at him.

"I do believe that my son has a remarkable seat on a saddle," Lady Clarice said, not seeming to notice (to Tess's relief) that Annabel had rudely wandered off without bothering to curtsy and was now standing far too close to the Earl of Mayne and giggling so hard that her curls bobbed around her shoulders like corks caught in a backwash. "Not that I can swear to this, because I abhor the out-of-doors." And, when Tess looked confused, "Fresh air, Miss Essex! It's ruinous for the complexion to attend those races, I assure you. I only do so under the strongest duress. Of course, my son loves my company so much that it means the earth to him if I do watch one of his horses sail to victory. So I sacrifice . . . I sacrifice . . ."

My complexion is clearly ruined, Tess thought to herself. Their father had been dragging them to races since they were able to walk.

"But I have ever encouraged dear Draven to follow his own delight in these matters," Lady Clarice was saying. "I *do* like a man to have an occupation. Far too many gentlemen of my acquaintance sit about all day and never rise from their chairs at the club. They end up with very ill manners, I assure you. And it causes" — she lowered her voice "— a certain spreading in the derriere, if you follow me!" She trilled with naughty laughter. "Although I shouldn't say such a thing to you, an unmarried girl, for all you are a bit long in the tooth! But not to worry, dear, Holbrook will put you on the market the very first *day* that you're out of blacks."

"Now, Duke," she said, turning from Tess without pausing for breath. "What are we to do? I mean, I am more than happy to chaperone your darling wards for a day or so, Holbrook, but London calls. My mantua-maker beckons. *Allures* me!" she said with a giggle. "So I ask you, Your Grace, what are we to *do?*"

Their guardian didn't even blink, so he must be used to Lady Clarice's style of conversation. Not having had that pleasure herself, Tess could feel a headache coming on. She felt a light touch at her elbow.

"Would you like to take a turn around the room, Miss Essex?" The Earl of Mayne stood smiling at her.

"I would," she said, "but —" And she looked helplessly to where Imogen stood talking to Lord Maitland. Surely it wasn't her imagination that there was something overfamiliar in the way that he smiled at Imogen, something complaisant in the way his fingers sat on her bare arm, just above her elbow.

The earl followed her glance. "Rafe," he said in a pleasant, low tone that cut through the shrilling hum of Lady Clarice's speech, "our guests are likely famished. Shall we adjourn to supper?"

Their guardian promptly towed Lady Clarice out of the room, her stream of gently vindictive conversation fading as they turned the corner into the dining room.

"Imogen!" Tess said, trying to sound commanding yet not motherly. Then she turned to the earl and put her hand on his arm.

He looked down at her for a moment, and Tess saw a smile lurking somewhere in his eyes. Then he took her hand and raised it to his lips. "If you insist," he said softly.

Tess blinked. Could he be starting a flirtation with her?

But the next second Mayne was making smiling remarks about there being no need to attend to protocol amongst close friends and deftly bearing Imogen out of the room.

"Miss Essex," Lord Maitland drawled, turning to her and putting her hand to his lips.

My goodness, Tess thought rather bewilderedly, this hand has been kissed more in the last hour than in my entire life.

"Josie!" she called, luring her little sister

out from the piano, "you may retire to the schoolroom now."

Maitland may have been wild, but he wasn't rude. As Josie reluctantly approached, he bowed. "Miss Josephine, you look particularly exquisite this evening," he said.

"Cut rope!" Josie snapped at him.

"Josie!" Tess cried, aghast.

"Oh for goodness' sake," Josie said. "It's only Maitland." She rounded on him. "You can save your faradiddles for others. You should know that I'm not the person for that sort of foolish talk!"

Tess felt a reprimand coming to her lips, and then bit it back. Josie was obviously on the point of tears. She must have heard Lady Clarice's comment about a cabbage diet, and Josie was extremely sensitive about her figure.

But before Tess could decide what to say, Maitland tucked Josie's hand under his arm, and said, "Do you know, I've a question you may be able to answer. Perfection, my chestnut filly —"

"I remember Perfection," Josie interrupted, a bit curtly. "She is a trifle long in the haunches."

"I don't agree about her haunches," Maitland said with unimpaired good humor, beginning to walk Josie toward the door. "However, she seems to be suffering a bit of tenderness just behind the saddle."

"Have you tried Goulard's lotion?" Josie asked, her complete interest turning to Maitland. Their father had appointed Josie to make up ointments for the horses's various ailments, and what had begun as an onerous task had become a true interest.

Tess had to admit that Maitland could be quite beguiling when he put his mind to it. Not that it was of the least consequence.

Still, there were moments in which she could see why Imogen loved him quite so passionately. He was pretty enough, with his cleft chin and rakish eyes. But he was not only horse-mad, he was gambling-mad. Everyone said that he couldn't turn down a bet, not if it were for his last farthing. Maitland would eat in a ditch, were there the chance of a race afterward.

Just like Papa.

Chapter 5

Supper

Tess found herself to the left of the duke, with Lady Clarice seated to his right. The long table glowed with dishes of a deep maroon, with gold bands around the edges. It was set with such an array of silverware that each plate looked as if it had a small shining fence laid on three sides. The silver caught the light of the candles and cast gleaming sparkles on people's hands.

Suppers during Tess's life had consisted of two courses at the very most and, in one of their papa's dry spells, perhaps merely a thin slice of fowl. But on this occasion the courses came and went with bewildering speed. A tall footman with his hair caught back in a bag kept whisking away her plate before she had even tasted it and replacing it with another. And then, just after she would try the new dish, it would vanish. The footman had removed little pastries bulging with chicken and lobster before she finished one, then a turtle soup briefly appeared, and now they were all contemplating sweetbread pie.

The sparkling drink in their glasses was champagne. Tess had read about champagne but had never seen it before. The footman poured her a second glass. It was entirely delectable. It fizzled on her tongue and seemed to increase the pleasure of the moment immeasurably; Tess even found herself forgetting the fact that she and her sisters looked like so many black crows perched around the table.

"Miss Essex," her guardian said, when Lady Clarice finally turned to the Earl of Mayne, "it is truly a pleasure to have you in my house."

Tess smiled at him. The duke's slight air of exhaustion made him quite appealing, and the way his hair fell over his eyes was a welcome contrast to the faultless elegance of his friend, the Earl of Mayne.

"We are tremendously lucky to be here, Your Grace," she said, adding, "rather than in your nursery."

"Your claim to luck is generous, given that your father's death has brought you to me."

"Yes," Tess said. "But Papa was bedridden for some time before he died, you know. I do believe that he is happier where he is. Papa would not have been content had he been unable to ride."

"I understand that Lord Brydone simply did not wake up, due to a head injury," the duke said.

"He did wake several times," Tess explained. "But he was unable to move his limbs. That would not have been a happy circumstance for him."

"No, I can see that would have been difficult for one of his temperament. I have vivid memories of my first meeting with your father. He had a horse running at Newmarket, years ago. I was a mere stripling. His jockey was lamed in an earlier race so your father leaped onto the horse and rode it himself."

"I would guess that the horse didn't win," Tess said, smiling at the image of it. That was just like Papa — both in the bravado and in the foolishness.

"No. No, he was far too heavy to win. But he had a wonderful time, nonetheless, and the entire crowd was howling for his victory."

"Alas, Papa rarely won," Tess said recklessly, feeling as if the champagne had loosened her tongue a bit. "I feel — I feel quite ashamed that he asked you to be our guardian, a man who scarcely knew our family. It's altogether too much to ask of you, Your Grace!"

But he was grinning at her. Really grinning! "As I told you earlier, it's a pleasure. I no longer have family of my own other than my heir, a second cousin who's more trouble than he's worth." He looked around. "And I have no plans to marry. So this house and everything in it . . . no one is enjoying it except me. I much prefer it like this."

Tess looked down the table at her sisters, trying to see it through his eyes. Annabel was sparkling, her eyes alight with the pure joy of flirting with the Earl of Mayne. Imogen was glowing with a more subtle happiness; her eyes drifting to Lord Maitland's face, then jerking away. Tess only hoped that Lady Clarice didn't notice.

"This is what the dining room was presumably like when my parents were alive," the duke said. "I'm afraid that I've become something of a solitary man, without realizing it. I must say, I am enormously pleased to find that my wards are of an age to converse, rather than lisp nursery rhymes."

"Why did you —" Tess asked and hesitated. Was she right in thinking that proper English ladies didn't ask personal questions? But she had to know. "Why did you say that you'll never marry, Your Grace?"

Then she realized that he might guess that they had discussed marrying him, or even think that she had the ambition herself. "Not —" she added hastily "— that I have any personal interest in the question."

But Holbrook was looking at her with all the oblivion of an older brother. It was clear that he had never even considered the possibility that he might make her, or one of her sisters, for that matter, a duchess. Annabel would have to look to one of the other seven dukes if she wished to be a duchess. Or perhaps — Tess looked down the table again and caught Annabel laughing at the earl — perhaps she could simply turn to their guardian's friend.

"There are a few of us who eschew the whole process," Holbrook said. "And I'm afraid that I'm one of them. But it's not due to misanthropy, Miss Essex."

"Do, please call me Tess," she said, drinking a bit more champagne. "After all, we *are* family now."

"I would be more than pleased," he said. "But you must call me Rafe. I loathe being addressed as Your Grace. And may I say that I am tremendously happy to have acquired a family?"

She smiled at him, and there was a moment of perfect ease between them, as if they'd been siblings for life.

"I've never had a sister," he said, nodding to the footman who wished to refill her champagne glass. He was drinking a large glass of something golden and quite without bubbles. "I believe it's quite a different relationship from that one has with a brother."

Their *Debrett's* may have been two years out of date, but it did list the duke's brother, with a little note, "deceased," beside it. Tess's champagne sent tingling chills down her throat; the very idea of losing one of her sisters was inconceivable. "I know that you once had a brother," she said rather haltingly. "I am sorry, Your Grace."

"Rafe," he corrected her. "To be honest, I think of myself as still having a brother. He simply isn't with me any longer."

"I know just what you mean," Tess said impulsively. "I keep expecting Papa to walk in the door. Or even my mother, and she's been gone for years."

"A maudlin pair of us, then," he said, his eyes twinkling.

But Tess could see the sadness at the back of those gray-blue eyes, and felt a sudden surge of liking for their unkempt, rather lonely guardian.

"Now tell me what it's like having sisters — and so many of them," he said, drinking from his glass again.

"Sisters are very good at keeping secrets," Tess answered. "My sisters and I keep reams of them amongst ourselves."

"Of what sort, pray?"

"These days, they are mostly to do with matters of the heart," Tess said, wondering if perhaps she had had rather more champagne than was entirely wise.

"Ah," he said. And then: "Should I be expecting a group of Scottish suitors to arrive at my doorstep, then?"

"Not for me, alas," Tess said, devoting herself to a piece of plaice in a delicate cream sauce. "In fact, not for any of us. Papa had great plans, you see. Once he won a truly large purse, he was going to bring us to London for the season. He wouldn't listen to the suits of local gentlemen."

"If you'll forgive the impertinent question, did any of you ever develop an affection for any of these suitors? For surely they existed, your father's permission or not."

"Here and there," Tess said airily, "one developed a *tendresse*. But it was a bit difficult, you understand, due to Papa's strictures as concerned the local nobility."

His face was alive with interest, which was a heady pleasure for Tess. When was the last time that someone besides her sisters showed an interest in her opinions?

"Did *you* ever gain acquaintance with one of these inappropriate men? Is that one of your many secrets?"

"If I tell you," she said with a small hiccup, "you must needs tell me a secret as well."

"The only problem will be thinking of one," he said, "for I lead a tediously proper life. So is some Scottish lad fair slain for love of you?"

"I did fall in love once, with the butcher's boy," she told him. "He was called Nebby, and he was truly an enchanting young man although not precisely eligible."

"I should think not. What did Lord Brydone do on learning of this remarkable attachment?"

"My father encouraged it," Tess said, giving him a small grin.

Rafe blinked. "Really?"

"He thought it was a most useful connection, because Nebby brought me cuts of meat as a sign of his affection. We were," she added, "both eleven years old, and so my father had little fear of permanent affection between us. The truth is that Nebby cast me off, married at a young age, and is already the father of two spanking young future butchers."

"Young Nebby was the last to have captured your affections?"

"The very last," Tess nodded.

Rafe had managed to shovel down his supper, whereas she kept forgetting and allowing the footman to take away untouched plates of food. He touched his glass of golden liquor to her champagne. "I believe that you and I are of a type. Untouched by matters of the heart."

"Alas," Tess said. "Love doesn't seem to be my forte. I find courtship rather tedious, if the truth be known." Then it occurred to her that he would likely take that news with dismay, given the idea that his guardianship extended until she married. "Not that I am averse to the idea of matrimony," she hastened to tell him. "You needn't worry that I shall plague your household forever; I fully intend to marry."

"You relieve my soul," Rafe said, laughing.

"Now," she said, leaning toward him, "you'll have to tell *me* a secret. I would like to know what's turned you into such a misanthrope about marriage."

"Why on earth would you be interested in such a triviality?" Rafe asked. Unless he was much mistaken, his new ward was just a tiny bit muzzy on champagne. Likely a guardian wasn't supposed to allow his wards to become chirping-merry. Perhaps he should substitute lemonade for champagne? But he loathed a hypocrite, and he had no intention of giving up his brandy. He drank half the bumper on the thought.

Tess was talking, and he pulled his attention back to her with a jerk. "Because if you don't, I'll allow Annabel to continue in the mistaken belief that she could become Duchess of Holbrook with a mere crook of her little finger."

His eyes widened, and he looked down the table. At that moment, Annabel looked up and smiled. There was nothing overt about her smile. She was, quite simply, one of the most beautiful women Rafe had ever seen, with her buttery hair that gleamed with the dull gold of old silk in the candlelight, her eyes tilted slightly at the corners, marked with sooty eyelashes. Even in drab mourning clothing she was formidable.

But he hadn't the faintest inclination to marry her, magnificent or not.

"She would make a lovely duchess," her sister told him.

Rafe narrowed his eyes at Tess. "I see you have some of your father's bravado." There was Annabel, glowing like a piece of expensive jewelry, down the table. And then here was Tess. Her clear blue eyes had the same tilt as her sister's, but they spoke of intelligence, courage, and humor, rather than pleasure. "You have no plans to become a duchess, do you?" he asked, wondering as he said it whether the brandy had gone to his head the way the champagne had to hers.

She shook her head.

"*You* would really terrify me," he said frankly. "In fact, should you have made up your mind in that direction, I might have had to flee to the North Country."

"A remarkable compliment," Tess said. "I think I would be more moved by it had you not mentioned the prospect of flight."

Just then Brinkley entered the dining room and stooped at Rafe's side. "Mr. Felton has arrived from London," he said. "He has agreed to join you for supper. I suggest that we place him beside Miss Essex."

"A friend," Rafe explained, turning to Tess. And then, to Lady Clarice, "Yes indeed, Mr. Felton. We were at school together, although that was many years ago now."

"Not *so* long," Lady Clarice said archly. "You're not more than your midthirties, Your Grace, and I won't have you pretending to be an elder statesman!"

Tess blinked. Perhaps the earl was right, and Lady Clarice pictured herself a future duchess. Well, if Annabel rushed to imagine herself in the position, why should not every widowed or single lady in the vicinity?

She caught the duke's eye. He gave her a crooked smile as he leaned closer to Lady Clarice, who had declared the need to tell the duke something tremendously humorous that happened at the last Silchester assembly.

A footman began placing a setting to the left of Tess. She finished her plaice, listening to Lady Clarice prattle to Rafe of an agreeable interlude in which a dear, dear friend of hers had quite lost the anchoring on her bodice whilst in the midst of a crowded room, or so Tess understood. From Lady Clarice's relish in repeating the episode, one grasped immediately the idea that the friend in question had neglected to put on sufficient undergarments.

Then the door opened again, and Brinkley ushered in Rafe's new guest. It must be the champagne, Tess thought rather foggily, a second later.

The man who entered the room after Brinkley looked like a fallen angel. The candelabra on the table bounced light from his sleek hair, off his austere face, off the severe line of his nose. He was wearing a black coat with velvet lapels. He looked every inch a duke, every inch a patrician, a wealthy creature of privilege. And yet there was a sense in which he was like one of her father's stallions: large, beautiful, a man who dominated the room merely by entering it. A man whose eyes showed a combination of restraint and a faint boredom, a sleek man.

A rather terrifying fallen angel, really.

Chapter 6

Lucius Felton was, like most men, enamored of habit. When he journeyed to the Duke of Holbrook's house, as he did every June and September to attend the races at Ascot and Silchester, he expected to find the duke sprawled in a chair with a decanter at his elbow and a copy of *Sporting News* in the near vicinity.

Sometimes the Earl of Mayne joined them; either way the talk circled comfortably around horses and brandy. All tedious subjects such as women, financial affairs, and family were avoided, not from some trumped-up idea of secluding themselves from the world, but because those subjects *were* tedious. By their advanced age of thirty-some, women had proved to be (except in certain circumstances) fairly wearisome companions.

Money came to all three of them with supreme ease, and money is only interesting when it is in short supply. As for family . . . since his own had eschewed contact with him for years, Lucius viewed the turmoils of other people's families with some, if lethargic, interest. But after Holbrook had lost his brother, they had stopped discussing family as well.

Thus when Lucius descended from his carriage at Holbrook Court, he viewed with some severity the butler, who conveyed to him the news that the duke had unexpectedly become guardian to the four nubile young daughters of Lord Brydone, and with even less pleasure did he receive the news that Lady Clarice Maitland and her devil's spawn of a son were at the table. The presence of Mayne was the only mitigating light in this dismaying turn of events. Mayne must be planning to run his filly Plaisir in the Silchester Gold Plate, which would provide a good opportunity for Lucius to test the paces of his own Minuet, running in her first race.

But as Lucius pulled on a clean shirt in the chambers assigned to him (not, he noticed with disapproval, the room to which he was accustomed because *that* apparently had been given to one of the nubile young misses), he rather thought that he might skip the Silchester and leave his stable master and jockeys to do the job on their own. He had several sweet deals brewing in the city. And if the duke's house was no longer a bastion of male comradeship and comfort — and the presence of females had undoubtedly changed it to something more starched-up and far less comfortable — he might as well abandon his intent to attend the race and return to London in the morning. Or at least to the estate he owned an hour or so from here. He hadn't visited Bramble Hill in some four months.

His manservant Derwent bustled in the door, having obtained a bowl of shaving water from the kitchens. Derwent had taken this news even more poorly than had his master; the company of women was distasteful to Derwent at the best of times, and the presence of so many marriageable ladies in the house had thrown him into a flurry of acid comments.

"Apparently they haven't a stitch to their backs," he said, brushing up a warm froth of soap, preparatory to shaving Lucius's face. "One can only guess at the endeavors the poor duke will have to go through to hoist *four* females onto the market, and none of them marriageable in the least."

"Are they unattractive, then?" Lucius asked, gazing at the ceiling so that Derwent could shave his neck in a clean stroke.

"Well, Brinkley didn't describe them as strictly unattractive," Derwent said, "but they came with only one or two garments and those most repellent, if you can believe it. And Scottish, you know, without dowries. The accent is fatal on the market. The poor things would have to be very lucky to take."

Derwent gazed anxiously at his master. One didn't have to think hard to realize that the Duke of Holbrook would be desperate to bestow his wards on all and sundry . . . including his oldest friends.

Felton was lying back calmly, but Derwent had a sense of doom. Doom. His left eye was twitching, and that always signaled an unfortunate turn of events. His eye had twitched unmercifully the day that the Duke of York fell off his horse in the midst of a victory parade two years previous; and then there was July of last year when the master entangled himself with Lady Genevieve Mulcaster. Derwent had been unable to see to his left side for a month and was nearly struck down by a wagon and four horses on High Street.

"Finished?" his master asked, opening his heavy-lidded eyes.

Derwent jumped, horrified to find that his hand had paused in midair, thinking about the travails of marriage. Goddesses, that was how Brinkley had described Holbrook's young wards. He sniffed. Goddess is as goddess does, and no woman could *do* well enough for the master. He patted Felton around the chin with a soft towel.

Lucius stood up and began tying a neckcloth in deft folds. "I'm considering skipping the Silchester races," he told Derwent. "Under the circumstances."

"Precisely!" Derwent agreed. "The circumstances will be difficult indeed for the poor Duke of Holbrook. We would do better to leave immediately. I shan't unpack your bags, sir."

Lucius threw him an amused look. "I'm not in the market for a wife," he said gently. "I consider myself able to resist the charms of Rafe's wards for a night or two."

"I would never venture to comment," Derwent said with an air of studied carelessness, as he helped Lucius shrug into an evening coat of superfine wool.

"Good," Lucius said. But then he relented. "Still, I thought it kind to divert you from such wholly unpleasant and unnecessary thoughts, Derwent."

"Very kind," the valet said with dignity, opening the door. "Extremely so."

"I am quite certain," Lucius added, "that should I become ensnared in the parson's mousetrap someday, it will not be due to the presence of a few inexperienced Scottish lasses left without friends and family and thrust on the kindness of poor Rafe."

"Without a doubt, sir," Derwent said. His left eye was twitching like murder.

His master peered at him. "Are you quite all right? Your eyebrow appears to be developing a life of its own."

"Yes, sir. I am quite all right." And Mr. Felton left, for all the world like a lamb to the slaughter.

Derwent went over to the mirror and picked up the silver bowl of spent shaving water. But his attention was caught by his own appearance in the glass. His eye was twitching something mortal; the price of being a sensitive soul, as his mother always said. But his mustache was so fine as to draw attention away from any particular element of his face. It swept out from his mouth and ended in an innovation all Derwent's own: a waxed spade shape on either side.

Alas, Lucius Felton was resolutely conservative when it came to dress. No mustache. No facial hair whatsoever, as a matter of fact. The most he would allow his valet to do was to sleek his thick blond hair back from his face in a style that was most severe.

Derwent sighed. It was his fate to be an *artiste* in the service of a man with no sense of fashion.

And now, possibly, Felton would take a wife. Wives meant the end of pleasant jaunts hither and yon, as the race season dictated. Domestic life! It was enough to drive a man to tears.

Lucius strolled after Brinkley into the dining room, hoping against hope that Rafe wouldn't see fit to place him next to Lady Clarice. The very idea of Clarice Maitland made the hair stand on the back of his neck.

He found Rafe seated at the head of the table, looking much the same as usual. His neckcloth was tied in a careless knot, his hair stood straight up in the back, and there was a glass of brandy in his hand.

But the rest of the table — Lucius almost stopped flat in his tracks. Derwent had said Rafe's wards were not unattractive? *Not unattractive?* A woman with hair of a deep golden color looked up and smiled at him . . . and the smile was enough to make him bolt the room. And there was a dark-haired, dark-eyed one, with the expression of a passionate saint, one of those early virgin martyr types whose face burns with emotion. He just caught himself from stepping backward.

"Lucius!" Rafe called, beckoning to him.

He walked over, calculating how soon he could leave. It was a good thing that Derwent did not plan to unpack his valises. The last place he wanted to be was amidst a nest of marriage-minded young ladies: he had enough of that on his rare appearances during the season. "I am very sorry to disrupt you, under the circumstances," he told Rafe. "I would not have intruded."

Now that he was closer, Rafe didn't look precisely the same as usual. For one thing, he appeared to be sober, rather than jug-bitten. And for another, there was a faint but distinct look of panic in his eye. The man would never escape without marrying one of these women, although the poor old duffer was so slow on the uptake when it came to women that he had probably only just discovered that fact.

"I'm extremely pleased to see you," Rafe said. There was no doubt he was sincere: of course, drowning men always hoped a friend would throw them a rope. Or, in this case, Lucius had to suppose a wedding ring would offer the desired salvation.

Rafe turned to the young woman seated to his left. “Miss Essex, may I present an old friend of mine, Mr. Felton?”

Miss Essex was presumably the eldest of Rafe’s four new wards. Lucius hadn’t seen her at first. She was not in the least like that sensual, glowing sister down the table, nor like the black-haired passionate one. Oh, she was beautiful: brandy brown hair, cheekbones that the harshest sunlight couldn’t diminish. But it was her eyes, tip-tilted at the edges, serious, intelligent, dark, and sweet in her gaze . . .

She was smiling at him, and he was standing like a lummox without speaking. He bowed. “Miss Essex.”

“How very nice to meet you,” she said, holding out a hand. The ruffle at her wrist had been darned; at least Derwent’s information about the girls’ lack of dowries was correct, even if his assessment of their marketability certainly was not.

“I am truly sorry to hear of your father’s death,” Lucius said. “I met Lord Brydone a time or two and found him a gallant and merry-hearted gentleman.”

To his horror, Miss Essex’s eyes took on a little glimmer. “We are —” She paused.

"Papa was an excellent rider."

"Lucius, do have a seat. Brinkley has laid a place next to Miss Essex," Rafe said. "I shall introduce you to everyone else after the meal."

"I shall take it quite amiss if you do not personally greet *me* before seating yourself," Lady Clarice thrilled from the other side of the table. "*Dear* Mr. Felton, how are you?" She held out her hand with a positive smirk of greeting.

Lucius gritted his teeth and walked around the table, kissing a hand that was thrust in his face with arch command.

Sure enough, Lady Clarice launched into her favorite topic without waiting for breath. "I met your dearest mother at the Temple Stairs just the other evening," she said, watching him like a hawk from behind her fluttering eyelashes. "We were both on our way to that production of *All for Love* everyone has been talking about. It was utterly lackluster, not that it signifies. But the poor woman, *how* Mrs. Felton has aged — so thin, so melancholy, so pale! Perhaps you have visited her recently?" Her voice trailed off suggestively, even though she knew perfectly well that hell would freeze over before he darkened his parents' door.

Lucius bowed again, saying nothing. If his mother was pale, it must have been from an attack of distemper.

But the loathed Lady Clarice wasn't done yet. She grabbed his hand and clung to it. "From what I hear, Mrs. Felton hardly leaves her bed. If only I could impress upon you the grief that assails a mother's heart when her child strays from her side . . . the anguish is like no other!"

Lucius sharply withdrew his hand and bowed again, to make up for it. As he straightened, he caught Miss Essex's eyes, across the table. She looked faintly surprised. Even though he'd long ago stopped caring much for his reputation amongst the *ton*, he felt a pulse of rage. Damned old hag, airing her ridiculous ideas about his family to the whole table.

"Lucius is rather old to be tied to his mother's apron strings," Rafe said, his normally lazy tones carrying a sting. If anything, Rafe loathed Lady Clarice more than Lucius did, since in the past year she had demonstrated a fixed determination to become the next Duchess of Holbrook, and nothing short of assault had dissuaded her of the notion.

"Tied to one's apron strings — well, I should hope not! My own darling son is a man grown, and wouldn't countenance my interference. But" — Lady Clarice reached for Lucius's hand again, but he nimbly avoided her — "a mother needs to see her son occasionally, if only to revivify the wellsprings of her heart and being!"

Lucius opened his mouth to utter some commonplace, but Rafe nipped in. "Why, Maitland," he said, looking down the table at Lady Clarice's hell-raker of a son, "I had no idea that you were such a *useful* chap. Here you've been running about resuscitating your mother's wellsprings when we all thought you were doing little more than following the races!"

Rafe's comment was intolerably rude. It was intolerably drunken. It also gave Lucius time to retreat back around the other side of the table and sit down beside Miss Essex, revising his initial assessment of Rafe as sober: in fact, the man was utterly cast-away. Awkward, what with his wards at the table, but not unexpected.

One of Maitland's qualities, however, was that he didn't take offense quickly — a trait that had probably kept him alive during a lifetime crammed with well-earned insult. He merely laughed at Rafe's jibe and returned to regaling the bottom of the table with a story about the horse called Blue Peter, whom he'd just won in a wager. "His hocks are just right, squarely set, beautiful knee, facing square. He's young still, but he'll take a good fifty starts for me, and win a number of those!" His eyes were shining. He leaned toward the black-haired sister, the only one showing any real interest in his tale, and said, "For tuppence, I'd race him this year, though he is a yearling. He never puts a foot wrong, flies along as sweet as a flea on a duck's back."

"What a charming analogy," the blond sister put in. The sharp irony in her voice made Lucius raise an eyebrow: all that honeyed lushness hid an intelligent mind.

Maitland didn't even spare her a glance, just kept his eyes on the passionate black-haired sister. "A yearling beat a three-year-old at Newmarket Houghton last spring."

"At what weight?" the blond sister asked skeptically.

"Five stone," Maitland said, finally turning to her.

The passionate black-haired missionary was nodding as if stars were circling Maitland's head. In fact, it seemed to Lucius even after only a few seconds' observation that Lord Maitland was the likely object of that sister's particular religion. An odd choice at best, and one that would cause Rafe considerable trouble, if it went beyond calf-love.

"Charming," the blond sister said. "I suppose I have never considered you in the role of an innovator, Lord Maitland. I was under the impression that racing yearlings was not an accepted practice."

Lucius swallowed a grin and turned back to Miss Essex, who was talking to Rafe. She was wearing one of the most awful garments he'd ever seen, a shapeless black thing that made her appear to have a gorgeous bosom — and a stomach exactly the same size. The dress went out below the collarbone and just forgot to go in again.

She had a slender white neck, though . . . and slender shoulders too: he could just see their outline through the dull fabric. And from what he could see, her bosom appeared to be real, although the stomach was just an illusion. Under that black cape of a dress, she was —

She turned from Rafe and caught him looking. Her eyes flared. "I gather you are particularly close to your mother?" she asked sweetly.

A faint smile curled Rafe's mouth. An English miss would never broach such a topic with him, not even in a fit of pique.

He was far too big a fish to risk offending; all he'd had from young ladies for years were buttery smiles. "Alas, my mother and I have not spoken these nine years," he said. "That circumstance makes our *closeness* debatable."

Miss Essex drank the rest of her champagne. "I would venture to say that you are in error," she said, in a conversational tone. "My parents are both gone, and I would give much for a chance to speak to either of them — just one time."

Her voice didn't shake, but Lucius felt a pang of acute alarm. "Ah, but it would be different if we shared mothers," he said quickly.

"Why so?"

" 'Tis my mother that chooses not to speak with me," he said, and wondered at himself. Most of the *ton,* Lady Clarice amongst them, believed the shunning went the other direction. It must be something to do with Miss Essex's dark eyes. They gazed at him with such curiosity that it was hard not to answer, even though he routinely avoided questions about his parents with dexterous efficiency.

"How could you know after nine years?" she asked. "Perhaps she is longing to see you. If she is bedridden a great deal of the time, I'm certain that you don't have opportunities to meet accidentally."

"We live merely two houses apart. If Mrs. Felton had the inclination to see me, it would be a moment's work to send me a message," Lucius remarked.

She looked shocked at that. An innocent, this Scottish girl. Probably she would be a huge success on the market: there were few enough ladies with her beauty combined with that bone-deep sense of honesty.

"Two houses apart? And you don't speak?"

"Precisely," Lucius said briskly. "But surely you are correct. Perhaps one of these days we shall meet accidentally, and all will be well." He wasn't going to tell some chit of a girl that he had bought a house in St. James's Square precisely so that such meetings would happen. He had never told a soul how many times his mother had indeed accidentally encountered her only son . . . and let her gaze slide away as if she'd encountered a particularly repellent rodent.

Miss Essex appeared the stubborn sort, though, and leaned toward him to make another comment. Luckily, Lady Clarice commanded both their attentions.

"My son's *lovely* future wife will be visiting us tomorrow," she was saying. "I am persuaded that you know her, Mr. Felton, since you are quite cultured, are you not? Miss Pythian-Adams is quite the most cultivated young lady of the hour. Apparently the Maestro of the Opera House remarked that Miss Pythian-Adams has a voice to rival Francesca Cuzzoni!"

"I'm afraid that my reputation for cultivation must have been exaggerated," Lucius said, as a footman placed turtle soup before his place.

Tess stole a glance at him. Mr. Felton clearly considered their conversation about his family to be over. She didn't believe for a moment that his mother didn't wish to effect a reconciliation: the poor woman probably dampened her pillow every night, longing for her cruel-hearted son.

One only had to take a look at the line of his jaw to know that Mr. Felton's pride was as fierce as the north wind. If he inherited that trait from his father, it was no wonder the family was split asunder.

Then Lady Clarice's voice caught her attention again, and Tess realized with a shudder that it was *Imogen* who was receiving the brunt of Lady Clarice's description of her son's betrothed. Lady Clarice must have caught the glances that

Imogen kept sending Maitland.

She had captured the attention of the entire table now, although her comments were still markedly addressed to Imogen. According to her future mother-in-law, Miss Pythian-Adams had the most superb carriage, the most intelligent mind, and the most exquisite sensibilities of any living young woman.

"She sounds charming," Imogen said, clutching her glass so tightly that Tess hoped it wouldn't break.

"Oh, she is," Maitland put in. "Miss Pythian-Adams is quite, quite charming. Any woman with five thousand pounds a year is, by definition, a dazzler."

There was an unholy edge to his voice that made Tess uneasy. Surely that wasn't an appropriate thing to say about one's betrothed?

"Dearest," Lady Clarice said to her son, "that was unworthy of you. While it is true that Miss Pythian-Adams is quite fortunate in having such a generous dowry — left to her by her maternal grandmother, the Duchess of Bestel — your lovely fiancée is far more than merely an heiress. Miss Pythian-Adams is *cultured* in every way. I declare, I have been all a ruffle, thinking what I can do to keep such a cultivated young lady amused during this visit! It's not as if I could teach her a new tatting stitch, after all; she has had her sketches of the Roman Coliseum printed in *The Ladies' Magazine*."

Imogen was holding up remarkably well. "What an honor," she commented, taking a deep draught of champagne.

"I don't suppose you had superior tutors in the art of sketching up in Scotland," Lady Clarice commented kindly. "Miss Pythian-Adams combines true ability with the very best instruction. I've heard her sketches compared to those of the great Michevolo himself!"

"I believe you may be referring to Michelangelo," her son put in. He was getting a tight-lipped look that reminded Tess of the petulant tempers he indulged in when his horse didn't perform as he wished at the track.

Mr. Felton leaned slightly toward her, and said, "Alas, it appears that the course of true love is not quite smooth."

"A cliché," she told him.

"I didn't say that it *never* runs smooth," he said. "But I stand corrected, Miss Essex, and shall quote you no more Shakespeare." His eyes had a wicked twinkle to them. Probably because Mr. Felton's place had been added later, the footmen had placed his chair at an improperly close distance to her own. She felt as if his hard physique was positively towering over her. The sensation was not quite pleasant: it was rather unnerving, in fact.

Tess pointedly turned her gaze back to Lady Clarice, who was still talking of Miss Pythian-Adams's visit. "She must see the ruins at Silchester. After all, it is one of the very finest Roman ruins, and so close to here. I'm quite certain that she will be able to regale me with its provenance and — and all manner of interesting facts about it!"

Her son cut in with an acid comment. "I suspect *you* are no bluestocking, are you, Miss Imogen?" he asked. "There's nothing more tedious than a woman with her nose in a book."

Tess was certain that Mr. Felton was still looking at her; it was as if she could feel his eyes on her face. She turned her head and was instantly caught by his gaze. His eyes were indigo blue and curious, with something so intense about them that she felt it almost like a blow.

"I'm afraid that my sisters and I have had little opportunity —" Imogen began.

"Of course not," Lady Clarice broke in.

"Raised in the backwoods of Scotland as you were. Why, it's not fair even to compare a young lady with Miss Pythian-Adams's refinement and — to be frank — her advantages to a young lady of Miss Imogen's background." She beamed at Imogen, although to Tess's mind there was something of the cat's greeting to a mouse in her smile. "You are a perfectly charming young lady, my dear, and I cannot allow my son to slight you in this manner."

"Lady Clarice," Rafe said, his voice only slightly slurred, "I have heard the most extraordinary rumor about one of our neighbors. Now surely you can tell me the truth of it . . . is it indeed the case that Lord Pool has embarked upon elk farming?"

But Lady Clarice was not to be deterred by such a weak ploy. She gave him a stern glance and returned to the fray. "You see, Draven," she trumpeted to the table at large, "it wouldn't do to slight this sweet child by implying that anyone in the *ton* might compare her to Miss Pythian-Adams. We are not so unkind, not at all! We in the *ton* accept every gentleman or lady for what he or she is, and we do not judge on the opportunities he or she may not have had."

"That is very kind of you, Lady Clarice,"

Imogen said bravely, into the curdling moment of silence that followed.

Draven Maitland stood up with an abrupt scraping of his chair. "If you'll excuse me," he said through obviously clenched teeth, "I needs must garner a bit of culture before I grow a day older. Perhaps I can find myself an opera singer."

And with that extraordinary bit of impudence, he smashed his way out of the room.

"One might suppose that he meant that to be a cutting remark," Mr. Felton said to Tess, imparting to this quite reasonable assessment a degree of disdain that would have made her curl up like a hedgehog had it been applied to her.

"Perhaps Lord Maitland had an urgent appointment," she suggested with no conviction.

He threw her an amused glance. "As I understand it, his mother holds the purse strings and has selected a cultivated bride in an effort to overcome the influence of the turf. One can only assume after this display that he doesn't agree with her tactics. Or," he added thoughtfully, "one might conclude that cultivation is wasted on the man."

Lady Clarice was gently patting her

mouth with a handkerchief. "My son," she said, in a clear, carrying voice, "has an artistic temperament. I'm afraid that sometimes his nerves get the better of him. But I expect that marriage to Miss Pythian-Adams will calm his tempestuous nature. *She* understands the artistic nature since she has one herself."

Suddenly Rafe leaned in Tess's direction, and said, "You four already know Maitland, don't you? That's right . . . you said — no, Imogen said . . ." His voice trailed off as he looked down the table at Imogen. She was looking quietly at her plate, but there was a little smile playing around her mouth that *said* volumes.

Tess couldn't think what to say.

Rafe blinked at her. "I gather that your sister Imogen was not competing with Annabel to become a duchess?"

Tess bit her lip.

"Damnation, if this guardian business doesn't look like more work than I anticipated!" Rafe muttered.

"Mr. Felton, why are you visiting the depths of Hampshire?" Lady Clarice asked. Her customary arch tone was a little strained — one must suppose that she felt the stress of her son's departure — but she seemed determined to avoid comment on it.

Mr. Felton put down his fork. "There is a race at Silchester in a few days. I intend to run two horses. I generally bring my horses down a week before a race and allow Rafe's stable master to baby them."

"Rafe? Rafe?" Lady Clarice said querulously. "*Oh.* You mean His Grace. I am afraid that I simply cannot accustom myself to the easy manners of this generation."

"I'm afraid it is my idiosyncrasy rather than Lucius's lack of manners," Rafe said. "I abhor being addressed by my title."

"Lucius? Ah, our dear Mr. Felton," Lady Clarice said.

Tess watched, rather surprised. She had formed the impression that Lady Clarice would have nothing to do with those who were untitled.

Rafe bent his head close to hers. "Lucius is blessed with an income the size of the Prince Regent's. There's always the chance that she'll be led astray by his estate and let go her dreams of being a duchess."

"Stop funning!" Tess whispered. "She might hear you!"

"The excitement of being able to make sisterly confidences has likely gone to my head," Rafe told her, not even bothering to hush his voice.

"That, or the brandy you've tucked away," Mr. Felton put in.

So Rafe was drinking brandy! He had finished the glass given him when they sat down, and he was well near down in the next glass. But to Tess's mind, the only sign that their guardian might be the slightest bit daffy was that his voice was even more growly than earlier, and he'd stopped flinging back the hair from his eyes. Instead, he just sat back, long legs spread before him, a lock of brown hair over his forehead, pushed back from the table in a most unducal fashion.

Lady Clarice leaned closer to him and smiled in a way that set Tess's teeth on edge. "You poor man," she cooed. "You're holding up under the strain of this invasion of females *so* well."

"Females never bother me," Rafe growled, "only ladies."

Tess swallowed a grin.

"Do you know your guardian well?" came a voice from her left.

"Not well," she said, turning reluctantly to Mr. Felton. "I gather you have been friends for years."

"Yes."

Tess could see out of the corner of her eye that Rafe was waving his glass in the air, just a trifle unsteadily.

The butler, Brinkley, was making his way toward the top of the table with a decanter in hand and a disapproving expression on his face.

"He handles his liquor well," Mr. Felton said coolly, "but you might as well understand immediately, Miss Essex, that Rafe is not one to greet the evening without a copious draught of brandy."

Tess's eyes narrowed. Felton's voice had the slight edge that she recognized; just so did the local nobility talk about her father's ever-failing stables. It made her bristle all over. "I myself find abstemiousness remarkably tedious," she said, picking up her champagne and finishing the glass.

"Your guardian will be euphoric to learn of your compatibility." Felton was obviously the sort of man who thought a sardonic expression was good enough for all occasions. He was overly large as well. Why, he must be all of fifteen stone and it looked to be pure muscle. He likely rode a stallion. Even his shoulders were a third again as wide as their guardian's.

Thanks to being reared in a house cluttered by gear and periodically swept by groups of horse-mad gentlemen, Tess could spot a horseman at ten paces. When the dibs were in tune, and the horses were running sweet — well, then a horseman's life was beautiful. But when a horse had to be put down, or the downs were too mired for galloping, or —

She shook off the memory of her father's fits of despair. The shortest way to inoculate herself against this Adonis — nay, *any* man — was to ask him about his livestock. There was nothing more tedious than a man in the fit of equine adoration. "Do you have a large breeding program, sir?"

"Small but select. I fear I give my stables far too much importance in my life."

Precisely. "I would adore to hear about your stables," she continued, giving him a dewy-eyed glance. Now he would launch into a fetlock-by-fetlock description and —

"Seven horses," he said. "Would you like them categorized by color, by year, or —" and he paused — "by gender?"

"By all means, use whatever convention you wish," Tess retorted, forgetting to look dewy-eyed.

"The females first, then," he said. "Prudence is a filly of two years: nicely built with a graceful neck. Chestnut. Her eyelashes are so long that I wonder if she can see to race."

Tess blinked. His descriptions were certainly different from her father's, which would have run along the lines of the filly's parentage, markings, and breeding. She doubted Papa had ever noticed a horse's eyelashes in his life.

"Minuet is a filly too," Mr. Felton continued, his eyes on Tess's face. "She's a beauty, sleek and black, with one of those tails that flows behind her when she runs, like water going downhill. She's a thief, and likes nothing better than to steal a bit of grass or corn."

"Do you allow her to eat grass, then?" Tess asked.

In reply, he asked, "Did your father have a specific eating program for his horseflesh?"

"They were only allowed to eat oats," Tess said. "Oats and apples. We used to make apples into apple-mash because the horses got so tired of plain apples. Papa was convinced that apples were key to good digestion, and that would make the horses run faster."

Lucius thought that diet was absurd, if not abusive. Miss Essex might have agreed; she had lowered her eyes and was picking at her food with all the interest of an overfed sparrow.

For his part, Lucius had now distinguished Rafe's wards one from the others. Annabel sparkled; she dazzled the eye and ear with her honey voice and honey hair. Imogen was like a shock to the system. Her beauty was paired with a pair of eyes so ardent that he was uncomfortable even looking at her and felt more than grateful that he wasn't Maitland. That much emotion directed across the table must make a man queasy.

But Miss Essex — or Tess, as Rafe was calling her — had as much beauty as the other two, and it was paired with a dry sense of humor that hid itself behind propriety. He couldn't quite decide whether her humor or her mouth was the more remarkable. She had the look of the others about her; the sisters shared retroussé noses, high cheekbones, pointed chins, and thickly fringed eyelashes.

But Tess's mouth was unique. Her lips were plump and of a lush, deep red. But the outrageous detail, the thing that made her mouth like no mouth he'd seen before, was the tiny, scandalously sensual black mole that marked just where a dimple might be. Hers was a hussy's mouth, though not that of a common dasher. No, obviously virginal and obviously proper Miss Essex had the mouth of a woman who would become *coquette* to a king, a mouth by which a courtesan could make herself celebrated on two continents.

Lucius shifted in his seat.

Thank goodness Derwent hadn't unpacked those bags. He was no sacrifice to be offered at the altar of Rafe's obligations to his wards. Although, in the presence of Miss Essex, one could almost imagine —

Lucius came to himself with a start. What in God's name was he doing? Hadn't he decided, after last year, to forgo the dubious pleasures of marriage?

He didn't have enough to offer a woman, and especially a woman like this. She was laughing again, a husky laugh that didn't belong to a virgin. The very sound sent warning prickles up his spine.

He turned away.

Chapter 7

Late that night

"I've quite made up my mind to marry him," Annabel said. She was curled up against one of the posters of Tess's bed, wearing a chemise so worn it had been consigned to bed clothing. She tugged the chemise over her bare toes: none of the sisters had owned bed slippers for years.

For once, Josie didn't respond with sarcasm. "I suppose you mean the duke?" she asked. She was curled against the opposite bedpost, a blanket pulled around her shoulders. She had clearly had a good cry after supper, but everyone was tactfully ignoring her swollen eyes.

"I think you could do better," Imogen put in. She had burrowed straight into Tess's bed and was curled like a sleek little cat against the pillows. "Our guardian obviously drinks more than he ought, and he's lost his figure. To be blunt, Holbrook is a sot."

"That's extremely harsh," Tess objected.

"But while I hate to disappoint you, Annabel, it is my definite opinion that Rafe does not mean to marry."

"I was referring not to our esteemed guardian, but to the Earl of Mayne," Annabel said. "After watching Holbrook single-handedly empty a decanter of brandy, I decided I want a husband who is not yet pickled."

"Tess, don't you think that Mayne deserves someone nicer than Annabel?" Josie inquired innocently.

"Extremely unkind of you," Annabel said. But she was grinning. "Believe me, Josie, if Mayne turns out to be as rich as our guardian, I will be kind to him all day. Why wouldn't I? The only thing that makes me crotchety is poverty. Well, poverty and Scotland."

"I miss Scotland and —" But Josie broke off and swallowed.

"You can't honestly say that you miss Scotland," Annabel said. "Not that soggy old house and the way it smelled like peat every time it rained. Have you ever seen a counterpane as lovely as this one?" She smoothed the fabric with her hand. "My sheets are as fine as silk itself. I've never seen the like in my life. And look —" She gestured upward.

All four sisters obediently stared up at the midnight blue canopy that graced Tess's four-poster.

"No water blotches!" Annabel pointed out. "The roof doesn't leak."

"We don't know that," Josie objected. "There's another floor above us, you know."

"As there was in the bedchamber I had at home," Annabel argued. "Not to mention the attic above that. But there wasn't a room in Papa's house that didn't have watermarks on the ceiling, even so. Sometimes I thought the nursery had a regular sieve for a roof. And why Papa never —"

"Don't say anything mean about Papa!" Josie said. Her lips set in a firm line. "Don't you dare!"

Annabel reached over and tweaked her little sister's toe. "All right, you little termagant, I won't."

"He's not here to defend himself," Josie said, her voice arching high in a way that obviously embarrassed her. "I wish he were here. He would have laughed himself blue in the face over Lady Clarice."

Imogen smiled faintly. "Hush about my future mother-in-law." But somehow the ancient jest that she would marry Maitland someday fell flat now that they'd actually seen the man in England, and met his mother, and heard of his engagement from lips other than his.

Tess bit her lower lip and scooted over a few inches so that she was sitting just beside Imogen. They had always known Imogen's love for Maitland would come to nothing, but it was so hard to tell her so.

She met Annabel's eyes and saw the same awareness in her eyes. Imogen would never be able to marry young Lord Maitland, with his driven, ambitious mother and his oh-so-dowried fiancée. Not that he showed any particular desire to marry Imogen, if he were free. Other than giving her a few scrawled notes and one kiss, he had never —

Imogen interrupted her thoughts. "He behaved badly at dinner because he is distraught," she said fiercely. "He doesn't wish to marry Miss Pythian-Adams, no matter how cultivated she is. I think he is beginning to love *me*."

"One would have to suppose that he's hiding his emotion, if that's the case," Josie said, in her usual blunt fashion. "What on earth did Maitland do at supper?"

"He was overcome with emotion and left the table," Imogen said. Her eyes were teary now. "Obviously his mother has chosen his bride. It's just like *Romeo and Juliet* when Lady Capulet was determined Juliet should marry Paris. And *Pyramus and Thisby* too. Wasn't Pyramus's father determined to marry him to someone he abhorred?"

"That must have been before Thisby was eaten by a lion," Annabel said. "I'm so glad that I'm not the type to be overtaken by passion. I have the greatest wish not to be munched by a wild animal. The whole business of love seems not at all in my style."

"I wish I were like you," Imogen said. She stared up at the canopy, her eyes a little teary.

"It's much more comfortable this way," Annabel said, patting Imogen's foot as if to encourage her in the pursuit of logic. "I have no expectation of love and every expectation of making a worthy marriage. I assure you that life is truly relaxing when there is no expectation of heartbreak."

"I suppose I shall just have to — to resign myself to a loveless life," Imogen said in a rather choked voice.

They were all silent for a moment. Imogen had been so long possessed by the idea of marrying Draven Maitland that it was hard to imagine her no longer in love.

No longer scribbling Imogen Maitland on every piece of discarded foolscap she could find. No longer studying etiquette books so that she would know the proper precedence of all the Maitland relatives.

"I'm sorry that we nurtured the hope," Tess said, stroking Imogen's hair. "We shouldn't have let you dream for so long."

"I do feel as if I've been living in a dream," Imogen said, her voice a little choked. "Why did he kiss me, that time? Why did he — does he — look at me, in such a fashion? He must know that he cannot excuse himself from his engagement."

Tess cleared her throat, trying to find a way to answer, but Imogen leaped in before she could formulate a thought.

"And don't tell me that he merely wanted to dally with me in an improper fashion, because he didn't! He didn't! He never once tried unseemly behavior. And yet — and yet, all last winter, and the winter before, when he was in England, he must have known full well that his mother would never allow him to marry a penniless Scot. He could not help but be aware of her — her enthrallment with his future bride!"

" 'Twas wrong of him," Annabel ventured.

"Perhaps he couldn't help flirting with you," Josie put in. "Romeo was beside himself with passion, even though his family would never have agreed to the match."

But Imogen pushed herself higher up against the pillows. "If Draven loved me as much as Romeo loved Juliet, he would declare himself," she said flatly. "He may be miserable affianced to Miss Pythian-Adams, but he isn't truly fighting his mother on the issue. He — he let Lady Clarice rattle on and on about Miss Pythian-Adams through the meal. Any fool could tell that she was warning me off. In truth, I think he may have reacted with anger not to his mother's assault on me but because he was irritated with her for other reasons."

"True enough," Tess said, putting her arm around Imogen.

"At first I was happy when he was so rude to his mother," Imogen continued. "But then I realized that he was just baiting her. He didn't really mean to defend me, did he?"

"There will be someone else, someday," Tess said after a moment, rocking her against her shoulder.

"No, there won't," Imogen said, wiping

tears away with the linen sheet. "There won't be, not for me. If I don't marry Draven, I'll marry no one."

Imogen hadn't braided her hair for bed yet, and it tumbled past her shoulders, sleek blue-black as a raven's feather, her eyes a stormy blue slanting under perfect eyebrows. She was too beautiful and too dear to spend her life grieving over an irresponsible, uncaring boy.

"Then you'll come and live with me and my fabulously wealthy spouse," Annabel said, smiling at her. "We'll spend all our days dressing in silks and dancing all night. Who needs a husband?"

"I'll marry no one," Imogen repeated, taking a deep breath. "It's just the sort of person I am."

"Then that's settled," Annabel said briskly. "I know you all think that I am jesting about the earl, but I am not. Frankly, I'm concerned that Holbrook may be ill prepared to bring us into society. I doubt he has ever been to Almack's in his life. I would be surprised if our guardian knew the names of a tenth of the society matrons in London. How are we to depend on him to launch us properly on the season?"

There was a moment of silence. For all

Tess's newfound fondness for Rafe, she felt the truth of Annabel's assessment.

"My maid reports that Mayne is quite unattached," Annabel continued. "He is clearly a man of taste and breeding. He does not drink to excess. He can bring us into fashion, allowing the rest of you to find appropriate husbands."

"What of plain Mr. Felton?" Tess asked.

"Not good enough for any of us," Annabel said. "Just listen to all those things that Lady Clarice said about the importance of titles. I do believe she indicated that not one of us should look below the level of a baron."

Josie said the very thing that Tess was thinking. "Now who's the naive one?" she asked jeeringly. "A title will not keep the house warm, or so you said yourself. I'm guessing that plain Mr. Felton is worth more than the duke and the earl put together. Do you know who he has in his stable?" Her voice hushed. "He bought Pantaloon last year. And he has Royal Oak."

"Pish-posh," Annabel said. "That's enough to convince me to pass him by, were he the Golden Ball himself. I've no wish to marry a horse-mad man and watch him liquidate his estate to buy a poor, swaybacked mare that couldn't win the Derby if she tried."

Josie's voice was needle-sharp. "I hope that is not an interpretation of Papa's buying practices, Annabel."

But Annabel was off to bed. "It's merely a statement of fact," she said, pausing at the door. "I want a man who will think about buying me rubies, not about paying a thousand pounds for a horse. And I do believe that the Earl of Mayne is just the man for the purpose."

"Did you like him, then?" Tess asked curiously, hugging her knees. Sometimes her younger sister seemed so much older and more worldly than she herself was. The earl rather frightened her, to be honest. It was something about how polished he was: polished and large and exquisitely dressed.

But Annabel grinned wickedly, and there wasn't a shadow in her eyes. "I looked him over quite closely," she said demurely. "Before *and* behind. He will do."

"Annabel!" Tess squealed.

But she was off through the door, and the only thing they heard of her was an echo of laughter.

Chapter 8

Quite late that night

"The man who marries your eldest ward gets Something Wanton? In truth?" Mayne exclaimed.

"There were only four offspring of Patchem in all the British Isles," Rafe confirmed. "And my lawyer just told me that each of my wards has one of those horses as her dowry. Something Wanton, as the eldest Thoroughbred, is Tess's dowry. The other three are foals — two fillies and a colt."

"A horse as a dowry," Lucius commented. "A peculiar provision. This Brydone must have been an eccentric man."

"He could have ordered the horses sold, and the proceeds converted to a dowry," Rafe said. "But the will very clearly states that the horses are the dowry. I can only gather that he wanted his children to marry men who were as mad about horses as he was."

"There's nothing to stop a man of poor moral character from marrying one of the girls, and then selling the horse at auction," Lucius pointed out. "Any of the four would bring at least eight hundred guineas at Tattersall's. And since Something Wanton almost won the Ascot last year, he'd fetch even more."

"The lucky man is not allowed to sell his wife's dowry for a year," Rafe said, looking back at the documents in his hand. "But, of course, you are right."

"Something Wanton!" Mayne said. And then, with a broad grin: "Were you gentlemen aware that I am looking for a wife?"

"I will confess that the thought had occurred to me that perhaps I could persuade you or Lucius to marry my eldest ward," Rafe said. "Teresa — Tess — is a beautiful woman."

"Exquisite," Lucius said briefly.

"You and she would be perfect for each other," Rafe said, looking at Lucius. "She's remarkably intelligent, and unlikely to serve you up tantrums. And you haven't, as far as I know, any serious female interest at the moment."

"This is a most improper conversation," Lucius observed.

"Oh, don't be so damned gentlemanly,"

Rafe retorted. "If you don't want to tie the ribbon, just say so."

"You're in luck, Rafe," Mayne said, leaning back in his chair. "I'm considering it. But in truth, what is there to consider? She's good-looking — not as gorgeous as Annabel of the golden curls, but pretty damn beautiful. My sister is forever nattering at me to find a wife. And here is a perfect wife: beautiful and endowed with a horse." He swallowed another gulp of brandy. "She'll need a bit of training in social niceties; those girls don't seem to have spent overmuch time with a governess, but if she's that intelligent, she'll catch on quickly. I'll do it."

Rafe narrowed his eyes. Mayne had been possessed of a wildness ever since he was rejected by a countess whom he wished to make his mistress. "Do you think to love her?" he said, finding the words queer on his tongue, even as he said them. But he *was* a guardian now; presumably this was the sort of question guardians asked prospective spouses. Or brothers asked men who wished to marry their sisters.

"Love . . . that I doubt," Mayne replied, peering at the wallpaper through the golden film of brandy clinging to his glass. "But there's no need for love between us. I shall be faithful and if not, discreet, and Tess shall probably be faithful, and if not, discreet. We shall enjoy each other's company on a regular basis until I am pitched from a horse into a ditch somewhere."

"Precisely as her father did," Lucius put in, a warning in his voice.

"Most likely."

"Or shot by an irritable husband?" Rafe inquired.

"Always a possibility." That prospect didn't seem to bother Mayne either.

Rafe stared at him. He didn't know how to help his old friend, who appeared to spend all his time flitting from the bed of one married woman to another. Mayne never stayed long enough to break a heart: that was all that could be said of his nighttime activities. He was getting an edge, a sharp, twisting tongue, and a dissolute gleam in his eye that Rafe didn't like.

And had no idea how to solve.

"If you hurt her," he said, surprising himself yet again, "I'll do you an injury, Mayne, for all you're my friend. I know you think I'm a lazy —"

"Lazy?" Mayne interrupted, arching a mocking brow. "No. Just slowed to a genteel stroll by brandy knees."

"You know what I'm saying." Rafe

turned to Lucius again. "Are you quite certain that you don't wish to make an offer for Tess's hand?"

"I would almost venture to guess that you're showing prejudice against me," Mayne interrupted, turning his glass again and again in the golden light.

"I am," Rafe confirmed. "I think that Lucius would make Tess an admirable husband."

"Stubble it!" Mayne said sharply. "I've offered for her, and Lucius doesn't want her. Let's leave it at that, shall we? Why don't you start brokering the lovely qualities of whoever's next in line? Imogen is a raven-haired beauty. You do have three more girls to get off on the market, Rafe. No rest for the weary."

"Why are they all unmarried?" Lucius asked. "It seems peculiar, given their ages. There's three of them in their twenties: virtual spinsters, from an English point of view."

"The Scots are all gelded," Mayne said. "I loathe the entire country."

"Perhaps there were deaths in the family that postponed their debut?" Lucius asked, ignoring Mayne. "When did their mother die?"

"My understanding is that their father

never had the money to bring them out," Rafe said. "According to my secretary, Wickham, the estate is in a terrible way. Wickham stayed for a few days helping the new viscount, who'd been living off in Caithness and hadn't seen the estate in Roxburghshire for years. Apparently it was grim. All unentailed land that might have brought in rents had been sold years ago. The house was a monstrous pile, and falling about their ears. The new viscount was beside himself when he found that the horses were willed to the girls: all the money made on the estate in the past ten years had been poured into Brydone's stables."

"Brydone spent *all* his blunt on horses?" Mayne asked.

"He wasn't niggardly with the girls. It's just that there wasn't anything to give, unless he were to sell one of his horses. From what Tess told me at supper, it seems he was counting on some big purse to bring them to London for a season."

"And until that moment arrived, his four daughters were left to molder unmarried in a tumbledown house?" Lucius asked.

"He undoubtedly didn't live up to your standards of gentlemanly behavior," Rafe said, draining his glass. He had a fierce headache coming on. Too much brandy: one of these days he was going to have to give up the drink, for all it made life tolerable. The splitting headache seemed to come on earlier and earlier.

"Any number of men will line up to take the other three off your hands," Mayne pointed out. "By the time the season opens, they'll be out of mourning. I got the impression that Maitland is taken with Imogen. He's got plenty of blunt."

Rafe shook his head. "The marriage to Miss Pythian-Adams was set up years ago. What's more, Maitland has run untamed ever since his father died, and lately he's gone from bad to worse. He's mad for racing and belts neck-or-nothing all over the countryside at all hours of the day and night. He'll find himself planted, one of these days."

"Not a bad way to go," Mayne said idly.

"Don't be a fool," Rafe snapped at him. "If you're to marry Tess, you'll have to mend your ways. No more endearing yourself to married ladies and risking your neck."

"I vow to be a model husband," Mayne said, and there was such a deep strain of tedium in his voice that Rafe narrowed his eyes.

But Mayne continued. "I've given up married women, hadn't you noticed?"

"No," Rafe said bluntly.

"Well, I have." He didn't look up, just kept flipping a quill over and over in his long fingers. "Lady Godwin — and I never *had* her — was the last, and that was all of four months ago. So Tess will have me all to herself, such as I am."

"That's not a bad bargain," Rafe said, his deep voice falling into the silence. "For all you seem to be inclined to think it so, Garret."

Mayne looked up. "You know I loathe my Christian name, dammit."

"Using it always wakes you up," Rafe said. "Now you're awake, I'll have you ten to a hundred on a game of billiards."

"I'm off to bed," Lucius said, stretching.

"Here's hoping you find a chaperone by Sunday," Mayne said to Rafe. "I'll have to elope with Tess if Clarice Maitland remains in the house long. The woman gives me hives."

"I'll send a note to my aunt Flora," Rafe said. "She lives in St. Albans. Perhaps she could be here as early as next week."

"So I have your blessing, then?" Mayne demanded. "I'm to start my courtship tomorrow?"

"Unless you think it better to wait until Tess is out of her blacks," Rafe said.

"Can't," Mayne said briefly. "The Lichfield Royal Plate is in a month. If I'm to race Something Wanton —" He shrugged.

"An unseemly reason to rush posthaste into marriage," Lucius remarked.

"Gentlemanly rubbish," Mayne said, draining his glass. "You remind me of all the sanctimonious bastards wandering around London, forever hinting that I'm a loose fish and not daring to say so to my face."

"And aren't you?" Lucius asked, his voice controlled.

Mayne considered it. "No. I'm lecherous, and I sleep — have slept," he corrected himself, "with a good many married women. But I'm not an ugly customer, although I'll be damned as to why I have to defend myself to one of my oldest friends."

"Perhaps because you're planning to marry a woman simply to get your hands on a horse and race it at the soonest opportunity," Lucius said.

"There's nothing irregular in that. Marriage is nothing more than a trading of assets, and Tess will receive far more than a horse from me. And I might say, Lucius, that all this talk of civility from you is hard to bear."

Lucius's jaw set. "Why so?"

"You're not exactly a slave to society yourself. You more than dabble in stocks; you damn near control the English markets. There are those who would think my irregular courtship is nothing to some of your irregular financial maneuvers. Lord knows, no one bred with a silver spoon is supposed to engage in anything resembling commerce."

"I gather you agree with my parents' estimation of acceptable activities," Lucius said. There was an ugly moment of silence, and then Mayne sighed.

"I don't give a damn what you do with your pennies, Lucius, and you know it as well as I do. And you've never given a damn whose bed I frequented either. So why are you suddenly making me feel like the devil's spawn when all I've done is declare an intent to become respectable?"

"At least you've both kept your figures," Rafe said morosely, ignoring the rage that had sliced through the room in the last moments. "My closest friends are a lecher and a merchant, but at least they —"

"A charming threesome, we," Mayne broke in. "A drunkard, a lecher, and a merchant. The flowers of English society. At least we inherited our sins honestly . . . from our forefathers."

"My mother would not thank you for that reminder of my father's birth," Lucius said wryly. "She decided long ago that my head for figures must have come from his side of the family."

"Your mother's a fool," Mayne said, but without venom, turning up his glass for the last drops of brandy. "You're the best of us, even if your father's inheritance was his face and not a fortune. Ah, well, at least *I'm* reforming! First marriage, then children, and before you know it, I'll take up my seat in Lord's."

Rafe doubted that. But it was true that Tess could hardly hope for a better match in a worldly sense, which was precisely the sort of things guardians were supposed to pay attention to. "It can't be a public wedding," he said. "She's still in mourning."

"Strictly special license," Mayne said. "My uncle's a bishop, y'know. He can give us the license *and* do the ceremony, right here. You have a chapel, don't you?"

"All right, but Tess has to agree. I'm not forcing her into a marriage that's too hasty to feel comfortable."

Mayne gave him a faint smile. "That

shouldn't present a problem. God knows I've had enough experience making women love me. I'd give it two days at the most. A few compliments and some poetry should do it." He said it without boastfulness, simply accepting of his own place in the world and his own skills.

Rafe hesitated. "No improprieties until you're married." It came out more harshly than he intended.

Mayne looked surprised. "I wouldn't think of it. She's to be my *wife*."

"I only said it because we haven't a proper chaperone," Rafe said, feeling rather embarrassed.

"You know," Mayne said, "my sister Griselda has been staying at Maidensrow, just a few miles down the road. Why don't you ask her to play your chaperone? The life of a giddy widow leaves her plenty of time to put your wards through the season, and she's always been fond of you, Rafe. She'll give the girls a bit of town bronze, and it would make my wedding less of a nine days' wonder."

"If you think she would be agreeable," Rafe said, "that would be most helpful. Aunt Flora wouldn't be any good at advising the girls in matters of dress. Since she never married, I'm not sure she'd be the best at that sort of business either."

"My sister excels in such matters," Mayne said. "I think it must be a requirement for young widows that they spend most of their time matchmaking while vigorously resisting a return to the state themselves. I shall send a messenger over first thing in the morning. Griselda's dress sense is only matched by her curiosity, so I would guess that she will join us as early as luncheon tomorrow. Perhaps I shall have all this courting finished by the time she arrives."

"In that case," Rafe said, "I wish you luck."

"I'm off to bed," Lucius said quietly.

"Can you put off your return to London?" Mayne said, looking up at him. "I'll like you to stand with me at the wedding. I swear I'll have the business in hand by a week at the most."

Lucius hesitated, and then: "Of course."

Rafe followed Lucius to the door, but, seeing nothing in his shadowed eyes, closed the door behind him.

Chapter 9

The next morning

Tess had never been stupid about men, only surprised by them. It didn't take her long to discover that the Earl of Mayne had decided to woo her. In fact, she knew the moment she looked up from the breakfast table, where she was buttering a crumpet and wondering when her sisters would appear, and the earl prowled in, bearing all the signs of a man on a quest.

Her first thought, that he must be looking for Annabel, was dispelled by the way he lushly declared himself, "Enchanted — no, *enchanté!* — to see the exquisite Miss Essex," making no mention of her sister whatsoever. After that, the only question was whether he wished for her hand — or something else.

She finished her bite of crumpet as he swept himself into the chair next to her, looking fearfully elegant all in black with white at his throat. But he was looking at her. And that look — there was no mistaking it.

"Good morning, sir," she said, giving him a smile calculated to encourage. There was no need to be abrasive until she learned his objective. Lord knows, she had plenty of practice rebuffing horse-mad Scots who thought a penniless viscount's daughter would trade her respectability for a few fine gowns.

"Miss Essex," he said. And even if she hadn't already cottoned to his intentions, the way he rolled the sound of her name — as if he owned her already — would have alerted her.

Of course, there are suitors, and there are suitors. Some come with spots, and some come with earldoms, and one clearly doesn't reject the latter candidates. Especially if their profiles were Romanesque and more than acceptable, and their chins neither weak nor receding. In short, there were no excuses for lack of courtesy, even if one did find the gentleman rather unsettling. Tess put down her crumpet and prepared to be courted.

Mayne took his cue immediately. "You look even more exquisite in the morning than you did last night," he told her, picking up her hand. His hair was a perfect tumble of curls; one must suppose that he wished it to look that way.

He seemed to take her silence as all the encouragement necessary. "I trust I don't offend if I mention what beautiful eyes you have, Miss Essex. They are a truly extraordinary color of blue. One would expect a darker hue, but they are a stronger, clearer shade, the color of lapis lazuli, perhaps."

Tess was conscious of a strong wish to finish her breakfast. It was not that his compliments were without interest, but they didn't seem to assuage her hunger. "You are too kind," she said, extracting her hand and picking up her crumpet again. Now she thought of it, Annabel would not be pleased. Tess had the distinct impression that under her sister's funning the previous night was a firm decision to marry the earl, who now showed every sign of wishing to marry the eldest Essex sister instead.

The earl glanced at Brinkley, who was busying himself at the side table. "I realize that this is a most unconventional request, since we are unchaperoned —"

Tess's eyebrows rose involuntarily. Could it be that the earl was going to make his offer here and now? After all, if she didn't have an excellent memory, she might well have forgotten his name altogether. Which is to say that they had the slimmest of acquaintances.

But he was only asking her to accompany him on a walk in the gardens. They would be unchaperoned, since Lady Clarice never rose before noon. "We shall stay well within view of the house," he assured her.

Tess didn't bother telling him that she and her sisters had spent their childhood walking about the estate just as they pleased; their governess (when they had one) could hardly chaperone four girls at once.

"I'd be pleased to," she said, realizing a second too late that her tone was lacking in a certain enthusiasm.

"Unless you would rather stay inside the house. Rafe won't rise for hours: he generally nurses his head in the mornings." The earl had witch black eyes.

"Why do you call him Rafe?" Tess asked. "I was under the impression that English gentlemen never used Christian names in reference to each other."

"Rafe won't countenance being known as Holbrook," Mayne replied. "He has only been the duke for five years, since his elder brother died."

"Oh," Tess said, seeing immediately. "It's as if he had to step into his brother's name as well as his title."

Mayne nodded, but just as Tess began thinking that perhaps he wasn't as brittle and fashionable as she would have guessed from his manners, he bent his head to her hand and kissed it again. The repetitive hand-kissing was giving her quite a sympathy with Josie's churlish refusal to be kissed the previous afternoon. Thank goodness she hadn't been working with the horses for a good year or so; at least her hand was sufficiently white and soft to warrant so many intimate touches.

Sure enough, when he raised his head, the trace of sympathy she'd seen in his eyes when they were talking of the duke had vanished. Instead, he looked at her as if she were an exquisite cravat that he had quite decided to purchase. He must have been looking for a wife before they even arrived at the house, given his precipitous decision to court her. Could one imagine that the arrival of *four* marriageable misses had driven him to distraction, and he simply chose the eldest, without pausing to ascertain her suitability?

"I find it is dangerous to spend time in your company, Miss Essex," he said.

"No doubt that is a disagreeable sensation," Tess told him.

He looked faintly surprised, but regrouped. "Not at all," he assured her. "One feels, always, a kind of exquisite twinge in the presence of a woman of your beauty."

"A twinge?" Tess asked, raising an eyebrow. Really, he made her sound like a case of jaundice.

The earl seemed to have realized that the conversation had gone astray. He pressed her hand and raised it to his lips again. "True beauty always brings a bit of sadness to the heart. One feels the same looking at the great marbles of Greece and paintings by the Italian masters."

"I haven't had the pleasure." Tess withdrew her hand. She was wishing rather desperately for the solitude of her own chamber. "I do believe that I have a touch of a headache," she said, standing up. "I must postpone our walk, my lord."

Again, he surprised her. There was a flash of amusement in his eyes. He might be a rake, but at least he had a sense of humor.

"May I bow, if I *don't* kiss your hand in farewell?" he asked, and that was definitely laughter in his eyes. "I can certainly sympathize, Miss Essex. We English are outrageously overformal."

Apparently, he saw her as some sort of untutored country miss, shaken by kisses to her hand and likely to be thrown into a positive twitter by an elegant bow.

He bowed. She watched. Then she let a deliberate sardonic edge creep into her voice. "How kind of you," she said. "I learned so much from this brief encounter. I can only retreat to my room and study how to raise myself to the level of such elegant discourse."

Truly, she didn't even care if he was left with his jaw hanging. He was too beautiful for his own good. Probably he was used to women throwing themselves at his head, the way Annabel had done the previous night.

Well, perhaps he would be put off by her gaucheness and shift his attentions to Annabel. She turned and walked out.

Left to his own devices, Garret Langham, Earl of Mayne, collapsed back into his seat and stared at the coddled eggs Brinkley had placed on his plate. Miss Essex didn't like him much. She was remarkably beautiful, with deep chestnut hair and lips of deep rose that looked as if they were curved to smile, even when they compressed with a faint disapproval.

The lady wasn't pleased with his particular brand of civility. Not that he could blame her. Ten years of making himself beloved by every eligible young matron in London — and the only qualification for eligibility was a husband who looked able to hold his firearm at thirty paces — had polished his phrases to a high gleam. He was tired of them himself.

For a moment he wondered whether such flummery simply didn't work with unpolished girls from the Scottish countryside. But no. He had seduced matrons far younger than Miss Teresa Essex. Though not — he admitted rather reluctantly — more beautiful.

Unbidden, the picture of an overly slender blond countess, her head a sleek cap of wispy locks, clothed in fabric so light that it floated around her body came to his head. He narrowed his eyes and clenched his jaw. Countess Godwin had no interest in his company. He had made a fool of himself over her. Enough.

He wrenched his thoughts back to his future wife. He had to marry. His sister told him that daily. He was all of thirty-six and in need of an heir. It all just seemed so . . .

final. So tediously final. Yet Miss Essex was lovely. She was intelligent too, intelligent enough to be unimpressed by his practiced compliments.

If their union was unlikely to be passionate, well, she came along with a horse named Something Wanton, a horse who had come close to winning the Ascot just the year before. At least he was assured of a passionate attachment to that horse.

Who could want anything more?

Chapter 10

Afternoon

"A *modiste* will arrive just after nuncheon tomorrow," Rafe said to Tess, catching her on her way up the stairs.

"Oh, you needn't," she said, feeling a tinge of embarrassment. Of course he must have taken one look at their wretched wardrobes and realized they were in desperate straits.

"Nonsense." He looked up at her with a grin that made him look suddenly much younger. "You're my new sister, remember? I can't have my new sister dressed in bombazine. I can't stand the stuff. It reminds me of the cook we had when I was growing up: a fearsome lady likely to employ her ladle on a young lad's head."

"Ouch," Tess said. She agreed about the bombazine, but it was humiliating to be penniless.

"And you're past the first three months

of mourning," the duke continued. "You needn't wear unrelieved black. On quite another subject, Lady Clarice has inquired whether you and your sisters wish to join her in an excursion to the Roman ruins at Silchester tomorrow morning. Miss Pythian-Adams will join us here until we find another chaperone. So if you wish to investigate the ruins, this would be an excellent opportunity."

The very idea of Lord Maitland's cultured fiancée was disheartening, but Tess knew that Imogen would insist on attendance in the off-chance that Draven Maitland would accompany the party. "That would be very kind of Lady Clarice," she said, with just the tiniest wrinkle of her nose.

"I saw that," Rafe said, putting a finger on her nose. "Lady Clarice would say that you exhibit a deplorable lack of tutoring."

"Lady Clarice was quite right in ascertaining that," Tess confessed. "I'm afraid none of us is very adept in the kind of comportment taught by governesses."

"Then we shall discuss Miss Pythian-Adams at length tomorrow evening, after you've met her," Rafe told her, lowering his voice a trifle. "I assure you that if you find traits which you desperately wish to emulate, I shall hire the appropriate tutors without delay."

"That sounds like a very carefully worded insult. To her or to me, I cannot be sure," Tess observed, turning down the corridor toward her chamber. "I shall be careful, Master Guardian, not to irritate you too much."

He laughed.

Annabel was waiting for her. "He's going to offer for you, isn't he?" she demanded as Tess closed the door.

"Who?"

"The duke, of course."

"No, he isn't," Tess said, pulling off her worn gloves carefully so that she wouldn't rip them.

"Oh pooh," Annabel said, falling onto a chair by the fire. "The two of you looked as cozy as two bugs in a rug last night at supper, and I heard him laughing just now."

"He claims to be uninterested in marriage," Tess observed, "and I must say, I see no such inclinations on his part."

"Thank goodness for the earl," Annabel said, wiggling her toes before the fire. "I had fancied being Her Grace, but I am happy enough with countess."

Tess bit her lip.

"Damnation!" Annabel said, narrowing her eyes. "You've stolen the best suitor in the house, have you?"

"Not willingly," Tess protested.

"You're lucky I hadn't formed a *tendresse* for the man. I must have been born without a romantic bone in my body, which is remarkable good fortune. Just look how seriously Imogen took that dreadful Lady Clarice last evening."

That reminded Tess. "I just told Rafe that we would join Lady Clarice and Miss Pythian-Adams in a trip to some Roman ruins tomorrow."

"Botheration," Annabel exclaimed. "I shall cry a headache. I don't want to be seen in these dreadful clothes."

"I suppose we could decline. After all, if Miss Pythian-Adams is half the paragon that Lady Clarice described, it will be humiliating for Imogen."

Annabel shook her head. "If Miss Pythian-Adams is attending, then so must we."

"Why? I should think it will simply be more difficult for Imogen once she meets this stronghold of ladylike civility."

"Stronghold? You're describing her as a stronghold? Bad phrase," Annabel said.

"Perhaps Draven Maitland, impossible bounder though he is, will be struck with shock at the sight of his bluestocking next to our darling Imogen."

"But I don't want that! The last thing I want is Imogen to marry Maitland."

"*You,* darling, are not the issue here. Imogen wishes to marry him, foolish though her desire may be, and I have not seen any good whatsoever from denying people their heart's desire. Remember what happened to Mrs. Bunbury's daughter?"

"Lucy? Lucy caught a fever and died."

"Pish," Annabel said. "I can't believe I forgot to tell you the truth of it. Lucy had caught a child, not a fever. Mrs. Meggley, in the village, told me. Lucy died in child-birth, and it was all because her mother refused to let her marry the fellow she wanted."

"Oh, poor Lucy," Tess said. "He wasn't a *fellow,* Annabel. Ferdie McDonough was a good match for Lucy, and her mother shouldn't have prevented them. Although," she added, "I don't see how you can blame Lucy's mother for death in childbirth."

Annabel waved her hand impatiently. "It's not precisely the death that I blame her for. But when a woman's as determined as Lucy — or our Imogen, for that matter — one might as well accept it. Now if Maitland truly means to marry this cultivated woman of his, there's nothing more to be done about it. But given that charming little display of temper he put on last night, he doesn't seem all that attached to Miss Pythian-Daisy, or whatever her name is. My guess would be that Lady Clarice put the match together and he accepted for the sake of the Pythian-Daisy estate."

"Were he to back out of the marriage, it would mean a breach-of-promise suit, and you said it was terribly expensive."

"The Maitlands can afford it. Did you see Lady Clarice's gown?"

"I don't want Imogen to marry Maitland," Tess said stubbornly. "He would be a terribly uncomfortable husband. Just witness his attack of temper last night. I would loathe a husband with such a disregard for propriety."

"Ah, but it's only the lucky ones like ourselves who are able to choose a spouse for compatibility," Annabel said, wiggling her toes before the fire. "Just think, Tess, once we're married, we shall never have to wear darned stockings again!"

"I would never know yours are darned," her sister said, squinting at her toes. "You do darn beautifully."

"Yet another skill that I will gladly discard by the wayside," Annabel said. "Along with accounting, gardening, and counting one's pennies. Or ha' pennies, as the case was with Papa."

"I wish you wouldn't be so harsh about him in front of Josephine," Tess said, sitting at the dressing table and beginning to pull pins from her hair. It tumbled to the edge of the stool.

"Well, Josie isn't here," Annabel pointed out. "There's no one here but you, my dear, and I'm not going to start pretending to be in some sort of ecstasy of grief over Papa's death. He never gave a twig for us."

She said it so harshly — and that was so unlike Annabel's normal style — that Tess bit her lip. "I think he loved us," she said, drawing the brush through her hair. "He simply had trouble —"

"He simply loved his horses more," Annabel put in. "But you're right. I'll try to preserve Josie's tender sensibilities."

Tess put down her brush. "I'm sorry," she said. "I'm sorry he made you do the accounting, Annabel."

"I wouldn't have minded," her sister said, staring hard into the fire. "I wouldn't have minded if he had given a thought to *us*, to our futures." Her voice trailed off.

"He did think of our futures," Tess protested.

"Not enough," Annabel said. And that was true. Viscount Brydone had used his daughters to make his life more comfortable and refused to allow them suitors because he swore he would take them all to London someday, so they could marry in style.

"He loved us," Tess said firmly, picking up the brush again.

"The important thing for me," Annabel said, "is to find a man who doesn't know a horse from a donkey. If Mayne has decided to court you, I'm in perfect agreement, since his conversation was a trifle too horsey at dinner last night. I would prefer that my husband is more interested in dancing slippers than horseshoes. So if you would like to marry the earl, Tess, please do it with expediency, so we can all go to London. I imagine he has a palatial residence, don't you think?"

"I suppose you are right."

"And he has exquisite taste," Annabel continued. "Did you see the little fringes on his boots? I'm certain I've never seen anything so elegant at home. Without doubt he will know all the best *modistes* in London."

"I am surprised that you don't make a greater play for his hand yourself," Tess said a trifle irritably. "Since you view him as an archetype of taste."

"While I find Mayne's taste in black velvet irreproachable," Annabel said with honest surprise, "and I also find his legs rather appealing in those tight pantaloons —" She ducked the small cushion that Tess threw at her — "I am quite certain that London is full of men of precisely the same qualifications as the earl. He shows a preference for you, and one must be careful not to make decisions based on unseemly enthusiasm for a man's legs."

"You make it all sound so mundane," Tess said with a sigh, drawing her brush through her hair again.

Her sister was grinning at her. "Not that I intend to ignore the matter when it comes to choosing my own husband, naturally."

"Hush up, you wicked thing!" Tess scolded.

"I must go," Annabel said, jumping to her feet. "I am trying to teach Elsie, my maid, how to braid my hair, and I must say, it's rather a chore. Elsie may have made an excellent nursemaid, but she can't seem to manage hair."

"She must be Gussie's sister, then," Tess said rather gloomily. "I keep waiting until Gussie leaves, and then quickly brushing out my hair and repinning it."

Annabel looked shocked. "I'm never pinning up my own hair again — ever! I don't mind if Elsie has to do it twelve times."

At that moment the aforementioned Gussie herself arrived, so Annabel left. Gussie was a robust young woman who was prepared for nursemaid duties, having watched her mother pop seven small children into the world, but was rather less prepared for the duties of being a lady's maid.

She was making a game try at it though. "Mrs. Beeswick says that I should wash your forehead in camomile," she said cheerfully. Without a second's pause she tipped Tess's head back and sluiced a thoroughly wet cloth on her forehead.

Tess felt cold water trickling down her neck and wondered whether she should say something acerbic. But Gussie had launched into her favorite activity — talking — and Tess felt it would be rather rude to cut her off.

"Being a lady's maid is such a lot of

work," Gussie confided. "It's not merely what I do in your room, miss. It's what I have to do downstairs that's the worst of it. Ironing. Ironing, ironing, ironing!"

"I'm sorry," Tess murmured. The soggy facecloth slopped against her lips as she spoke.

"It's not your fault, Miss. It's the position. And Lord knows, I do understand what an opportunity this is!"

"Wonderful," Tess murmured. There was icy water inching its way down her breastbone. "Wonderful."

Chapter 11

Next morning

Rafe woke with a bitter taste in his mouth, the sensation that his eyelids would not open, and a feeling of sick apprehension. Two minutes later he remembered why that was. Today marked the arrival of Miss Pythian-Adams, the cultivated paragon, and he had agreed to accompany his wards to some benighted hole in the ground thought to be a Roman ruin. If Maitland accompanied his fiancée, there was likely to be yet another dustup between Lady Clarice and her son. It was enough to make a man break his rule of never drinking before the sun was over the yardarm.

He dragged himself out of bed and washed in a foul temper. To this point, he had quite enjoyed having wards, especially Tess. But Imogen was another kettle of fish. To be blunt about it, he didn't like Imogen. She was too passionate for her own good, what with the way she almost visibly shook at the very sight of Maitland. Had the girl no pride? And her adoration was a mystery in itself: the man was a rakehell, for all he spent his blunt on horses rather than hussies. He lived for speed and the race.

Rafe shuddered. One overly passionate young lady and a loose fish like Maitland was a recipe for disaster.

His valet entered his room and held out a frothing drink without a comment. Rafe drained it in one gulp. One of these days he had to stop hitting the brandy with such vigor. Just not today.

Stoically he climbed into an ice-cold tub of water and poured a bucket over his head. When he stopped shaking, and the frothing stopped in his stomach, he felt considerably better.

Try as he might, he couldn't remember Miss Pythian-Adams, although surely he'd met her on some occasion or other. He vaguely thought she might have red hair. Since Peter had died and he became a duke, he'd spent the majority of his time trying to avoid anyone who might be a marriageable female, so it was no wonder he had no memory of the girl.

Naturally, he was not the only person in the house thinking of Miss Pythian-Adams.

"I just don't understand how she managed to catch Draven," Imogen was telling Tess. They had sent Gussie down to the kitchens on an errand, and Imogen was currently occupied in removing all of the hairpins that Gussie had stuck around Tess's head, preparatory to recombing her hair and putting it up again. "Draven is the last man on earth to appreciate literary cultivation. Do you suppose that his mother obliged him to ask for Miss Pythian-Adams's hand?"

"I doubt it," Tess replied.

"Well, why not?" Imogen said, putting down the brush. "Parents do enforce their children's choice of spouse, you know. Do you think — do you think she's more beautiful than I?"

Tess met her little sister's anxious eyes in the mirror. She felt horribly torn. On the one hand, it seemed cruel to encourage Imogen in any fashion. But it was so heartrendingly difficult to squash her hopes. "I doubt that Miss Pythian-Adams is more beautiful than you are, Imogen," she said finally. "But on a practical front, beauty may be the least of Miss Pythian-Adams's traits. She's an heiress, and she has Lady Clarice's approval."

Imogen's eyes flared. "You're saying that

Draven would marry for lucre!"

"I'm saying that we do not know why Maitland asked for Miss Pythian-Adams's hand in marriage," Tess said a bit wearily. "But we do know that the question was asked. It would be best if you could resign yourself to the fact."

"I'm tired of *resigning myself!*" Imogen said, snatching up the brush again. "He should love me, not her!"

There was nothing much to say to this nonsense, so Tess held her tongue.

"If only Papa had been more provident, we might have had a governess, and I would know just as much as *she* does about poetry, and Romans, and sketching, and the rest."

"Of course you would," Tess said.

"I didn't know precisely which fork to use last night," Imogen went on angrily. "And that is Papa's fault too. He should have thought that we would have to compete with — with women of this nature!"

"Papa didn't think that way."

Imogen started pinning up Tess's hair. "When Draven sees the two of us together, he'll turn to me," she said after a moment.

But Tess refused to play along. She had come to the conclusion that their indulgence of Imogen's hopeless adoration had been a mistake. "I very much doubt that."

"I do not," Imogen said, sticking in hairpins so fiercely that Tess felt like a pincushion. "Draven does not love this woman. He could *not* love a bluestocking. So there must be something behind their engagement, and that something is likely to be Lady Clarice."

But an hour later, Imogen was not quite so certain.

Gillian Pythian-Adams was no weedy-looking bluestocking, lanky, pale, and clutching a leather-bound copy of Shakespeare. She was not wearing pince-nez, and she didn't wear her hair raked into a tight bun, the way any self-respecting cultured woman did. Instead copper-colored curls peeked from under her bonnet, and green eyes surveyed the world with aplomb. And even a bit of humor.

Imogen felt the thump of her heart as it tumbled to the bottom of her boots. Any man would be happy to gaze at Miss Pythian-Adams all day long, even if she engaged to read him poetry. Even if it was *historical* poetry.

"How do you do, Miss Imogen?" Miss Pythian-Adams was saying. It should be outlawed for such an educated woman to have a dimple. Let alone be allowed to wear a lilac pelisse that made Imogen faint with envy.

"It's a pleasure to meet you," Imogen replied from between stiff lips. No wonder Draven had never done more than kiss *her* — a stupid, badly dressed Scottish lass with the temerity to worship him. He probably considered kissing her akin to visiting the sick: a charitable action.

"I'm so excited about visiting the ruins," Miss Pythian-Adams said. Even her voice was pleasing: not too low, not too high. "And it is a true pleasure to find that there are four young ladies with whom to be friends in this vicinity."

Imogen met Tess's eyes over Miss Pythian-Adams's shoulder (she was, perhaps, a wee bit short by Essex standards but really, that would be the only negative thing one could say).

"I'm sorry, darling," Tess mouthed.

Imogen smiled in a lopsided kind of way. She was so shocked that she didn't even feel like crying.

"Lady Clarice told us that your sketches have been published in *The Ladies' Magazine*," Tess said, walking about and putting her arm around Imogen's waist. "We were all terribly envious. You must have a wonderful gift for sketching."

"In fact, no," Miss Pythian-Adams said. Then she smiled, a little embarrassed smile. "I gather Lady Clarice neglected to say that my father is on the Board of Directors of the journal in question?"

She was modest as well. Likeable, even. Imogen felt as if her heart was about to break.

"Will Lord Maitland be joining us today?" Tess asked Miss Pythian-Adams.

"I expect not," she replied briskly. "You probably don't realize this, having just met Lord Maitland, but he has such a ruthless obsession with his stables that —"

But at that moment Maitland himself strode into the room and came straight over to them.

Tess watched carefully. Imogen lit up like a Roman candle at his approach (so much for subtlety). Miss Pythian-Adams allowed him to kiss her hand, but displayed no particular sign of exhilaration. Maitland showed no sign of preference for one lady over another; in fact Tess would venture to say that he kissed her own hand with precisely as much enthusiasm as he kissed that of his promised wife.

Finally, they all clambered into carriages and headed off in the direction of the ruins. The Essex sisters ended up in a carriage with their guardian.

The sky was a ravishing pale blue, and it promised to grow quite hot. Tess watched a faint wisp of a cloud evaporate. "I want you to promise to keep your bonnet on," she said to Josie, who had the tendency to throw her bonnet to the winds and toast her face.

Josie looked around at her sisters. "We look like a flock of buzzards!" she said with a gurgle of laughter.

"Only the best sort of buzzards wear bonnets," Rafe said. He had a little silver flagon of something that Tess regarded with some disapproval.

Still, she couldn't help smiling at him. "That was your clue to flatter us, Your Grace, rather than confirm our dreary appearance. May I assume that you are not exactly used to handing out compliments like a Lothario?"

"Don't call me Your Grace," he growled. "And I've never made myself into a noodle for a lady, if that's what you're asking."

"Why not?" Josie asked, with interest. "You're not *so* old yet." There was a hint of doubt in her voice.

"Josie!" Tess admonished, and turned to Rafe. "I do apologize for Josie's brazen question. We are used to talking amongst ourselves in the most impertinent fashion."

"I like it," Rafe said, obviously unperturbed. "I may not be so old yet, Miss Josephine, but I feel old. And thank goodness, to this point I haven't met the woman who could turn me into a jackanapes."

"If you're not turned into a noodle by Annabel or Tess," Josie said with utter conviction, "then I'm afraid you're doomed to remain unmarried."

"I shall resign myself," Rafe said, with obvious cheer.

"You're a grave disappointment to me," Annabel told him.

"First my mother, now you," Rafe said, with a patently counterfeit sigh.

"I suspect that you are an old hand at avoiding the attentions of women," Tess said, watching her guardian smile at Annabel. Just so would a brother smile at his beloved younger sister who was showing the first signs of beauty.

"I do believe that I am considered elusive by London matrons," Rafe agreed amiably. "And I can't say that I have the faintest wish to change that circumstance."

The coach rumbled to a halt. "Here we are," he said, tucking his flagon into his inside coat pocket. "Let us arise and be cultivated." The irony in his voice was as pointed as the north wind.

"For *that,*" Annabel said with a giggle, "I shall demand that Miss Pythian-Adams tell us everything she knows of the Roman Empire!"

The ruins were located in the midst of a pasture that had been cut for hay. Mr. Jessop, the farmer who owned the land, ushered them through the gate himself, pointing into the distance at a grassy mound.

"The ruins lie off that direction," he said. He cast a dubious look at Lady Clarice and Miss Pythian-Adams, both of whom were wearing exquisite little slippers. "The hay is drying nicely, so it won't run to mud. But I don't know as what it will do to your shoes, misses."

Tess's kid boots were old and far from ladylike, made as they were to last, but even so, the hay was terribly prickly on one's ankles. Mr. Jessop strode ahead with Rafe, waving his hands as he talked about his old father who had the land before him and "them holes in the ground" and "them Romans" and "them Londoners." A breeze kept stealing his voice and blowing it across the pasture, so Tess only heard snatches of his diatribe against "them Londoners," which seemed to encompass a historical society that wished to dig his field. " 'Tis *my* field," Mr. Jessop said over and over again, with perfect logic.

Somewhat to Tess's annoyance, Miss Pythian-Adams was steering clear of her fiancé and her future mother-in-law, and had chosen instead to walk at Tess's side. Tess would have liked to have a consolatory talk with Imogen — she had noticed that Miss Pythian-Adams had ankles that weren't as neat as they might have been, and she was anxious to point out that salient fact — but she had no chance. The woman stuck to her like glue.

Finally, they reached the edge of the blanket of drying hay. From here the grass grew an emerald, deep green dotted with Queen Anne's lace. A willow grew at the very edge, its trunk bent sideways in such a way that it threw deep shadows on the grass.

Lady Clarice immediately ordered the footmen to place out the blankets and the nuncheon baskets under the willow. "I shall have to rest," she announced. "In fact, this may be as much of the ruins as I am able to see, given the tenuous nature of my strength. I am simply not used to walking about in the extreme heat. I can have no doubt that the Scots are different from English ladies in this; I am quite certain that you all will be able to tramp about the field to your heart's content. After all, there are so many *more* fields in Scotland, are there not?"

"I believe that England has the larger population of farmers," the Earl of Mayne observed, filling the rather chilly silence that followed Lady Clarice's announcement.

"Ah, but *you* are no farmer!" she cried gaily. "Lord Mayne, I *insist,* I positively *insist* that you stay with me while the others plod about the fields to their hearts' content."

Mayne had just taken Tess's arm, and he let it go with a very flattering show of reluctance.

"What a shame," Miss Pythian-Adams said sympathetically to her future mother-in-law. "But you must, of course, rest." And before Tess quite knew what had happened, Miss Pythian-Adams had grabbed Tess's arm and was dragging her off toward the ruins like a fish on an angler's line.

The rest of the party began straggling after them, but since Miss Pythian-Adams sped through the grass at top speed, she and Tess soon found themselves in the middle of a series of irregular little walls and sunken chambers. Miss Pythian-Adams peered at the tumbling stone walls with appreciative noises. She even took out a small sketchbook from her reticule and noted down something or other. Tess stared into the sky instead. Two starlings were circling through the sunlight, weaving and dancing —

"They're mating," Miss Pythian-Adams said, following her gaze.

Tess blinked. Of course, she knew what *mating* meant, but —

"I do apologize if that disconcerted you," Miss Pythian-Adams says, "but I thought as you were from Scotland, I shouldn't have to obfuscate. I greatly prefer clarity in conversation to social niceties."

"No, indeed," Tess said weakly. There was something in Miss Pythian-Adams's direct gaze that made it clear that she quite liked the idea of being shocking. The starlings wheeled their way off across the pasture, looking half-drunk with the pleasure of flying. Or something.

The heart of the ruins appeared to be nothing more than a few sunken places and what looked like an ancient set of stone steps leading down a little hill. Miss Pythian-Adams's eyes shone with enthusiasm as they clambered over bits of collapsed walls.

Finally, they stumbled on a little pit, all lined with mossy green and rather pretty-looking, to Tess's mind. She and Annabel would have loved to play house there when they were younger.

"An intact chamber," Miss Pythian-Adams gasped, staring down into the little room.

"Could it be a dining room?" Tess said, rather hoping that Miss Pythian-Adams hadn't noticed the fact that Imogen had claimed Maitland's arm in order to clamber over the walls surrounding the ruin.

"I think it is more likely to be a bath," Miss Pythian-Adams replied, beginning to climb down a little rockslide in one corner of the chamber.

"Oh, please," Tess said, "must we?"

But it seemed that they must, so Tess followed her down the bit of tumbled rock. Miss Pythian-Adams's beautiful pale blue gloves were quite dingy from holding on to rocks; Tess's black ones were holding up admirably.

"Yes, it *is* a bath!" Miss Pythian-Adams

said triumphantly, a moment later. "You do know that the Romans piped hot water into their baths, don't you? That must be an aqueduct, to the side."

"Aqueduct?" Tess repeated.

"From Latin, *aquaeductus*," Miss Pythian-Adams said. "Meaning a conduit through which the Romans brought water. A pipe, to us."

"Where did the water come from?" Tess asked, walking over the flagstones that lined the bottom of the chamber to peer into the little hole.

"They heated the pipes in the kitchens, I believe."

"How odd it is to be standing in someone's bathroom," Tess said, looking up. The walls of the chamber were only some five or six feet high, and yet all that could be seen was a patch of deep blue sky, and a few great chestnut leaves drifting down, sailing over the ruins and swooping down into the bathroom. They looked a bit like starlings, mating leaves, one could call them.

"It would be far odder if the Romans were still here," Miss Pythian-Adams said. "After all, given its size, it may well have been a steam room. They used to sit about naked and enjoy each other's company."

Tess looked over at her companion. Miss Pythian-Adams was wearing five or six layers of clothing, including a bonnet to keep the slightest bit of sun from her face, gloves, kid boots . . . She was the picture of a proper English lady, and yet here she was, talking of mating sparrows and naked Romans.

"Are all English ladies like you?" Tess asked.

"Have I shocked you? I do apologize."

"Not at all," Tess said. She felt like sighing. Lord Maitland's betrothed was so very appealing, with her copper-colored curls and intense curiosity. Poor Imogen.

"So is your sister quite desperately in love with Lord Maitland?" Miss Pythian-Adams said, out of the blue.

"I beg your pardon?" Tess was so shocked that she positively gaped at her companion.

"I was merely wondering if Miss Imogen is quite desperately in love with Draven," she repeated.

"That is most improbable," Tess said, with as much dignity as she could gather.

"I am in agreement," Miss Pythian-Adams said, nodding. "And yet it would be premature to judge merely from the nature of Draven's character that *no one* could ever fall in love with him. They do say that there is someone for everyone."

Tess's mouth fell open once more, and she shut it quickly.

"Haven't you heard the same, Miss Essex?"

"I agree that one cannot disregard the possibility," Tess said cautiously. It was shocking to discover that she would quite like Miss Pythian-Adams in normal circumstances although naturally she couldn't do so.

Miss Pythian-Adams glanced up at the oiled blue sky, then walked closer to Tess. "If you will forgive my inquisitiveness, would it be overly optimistic on my part to nurture the hope that your sister might relieve me of my future spouse?"

Tess bit her lip. "Am I to suppose that you . . ."

"I would find it a consummation devoutly to be wished," Miss Pythian-Adams said briskly. "*Hamlet*, Act Four."

"Oh dear," Tess said.

Up close, Miss Pythian-Adams was even more beautiful than Tess had thought. But her eyes were verging on desperate. "You see, Miss Essex, I have done my best to repel my fiancé. I have learned reams of Shakespeare by heart and recited it to

Lord Maitland *ad infinitum:* I insisted that he listen to me recite the whole of Shakespeare's *Henry VIII* —"

"Really?" Tess asked.

"Indeed. And I can only gather that you haven't read that particular play, Miss Essex, or you would express a stronger astonishment. Believe me, I was near to tears with the tedium of it, but yon fiancé of mine simply yawned a few times."

Miss Pythian-Adams looked the very picture of the sweet romantic heroine of any number of gothic novels. Except she didn't speak like one. "Am I to be married to that illiterate and quick-tempered oaf, or is there any chance that your sister would prefer the duty herself?"

"But if you don't wish to marry Lord Maitland," Tess said, carefully sidestepping the issue of Imogen's passionate desire to tie herself to that same illiterate oaf, "why on earth don't you simply break off your engagement? My understanding is that a young lady can end an engagement without reproof."

Miss Pythian-Adams had a crooked little smile. "Not when the future groom's mother holds the mortgage on one's father's estate."

"But I thought you were an heiress!" Tess cried.

"I am. I stand to inherit a bequest from my grandmother upon my marriage, but since the world is designed as it is, *that* inheritance will benefit my husband, not my father. Unfortunately, Lady Clarice has the upper hand."

"Goodness."

"I thought that if I rained culture down on Lord Maitland, he would break off the engagement. My family could claim the mortgage back as a settlement in lieu of a breach-of-marriage contract, and all would be well. But unfortunately even the most ignoble and conceited expressions of culture that I drum up to bore the son appear to enthrall his mother."

"Hello!" a voice called down to them. Mr. Felton was standing at the edge of the room, flanked by their guardian and Lady Clarice herself.

Miss Pythian-Adams gave Tess a meaningful glance. "Watch," she said, hardly moving her lips. Then she threw open her arms. "Welcome, Friends, Romans, Countrymen!"

"Ah," Mr. Felton said dryly. "*Julius Caesar.*"

Lady Clarice turned faintly pink with excitement. "You always know precisely the right thing to say, Miss Pythian-Adams!"

she cried down at them. "I feel more intelligent just listening to you. Shall we come down? Is there anything of interest, of cultural interest, down there in that little pit? A vase, perhaps?"

"I'm afraid not," Miss Pythian-Adams replied, beginning to clamber up the tumbled rock. Mr. Felton immediately descended to help her to a higher elevation. As soon as he deposited Miss Pythian-Adams on the grass, he returned to the room, presumably to give Tess the same help.

Tess suddenly felt as if the little chamber had shrunk. Felton seemed to fill the space entirely, his broad shoulders almost brushing hers as he bent to examine the hole for piped water that Miss Pythian-Adams had discovered.

"I would surmise this is a bath," he remarked.

"We reached the same conclusion," Tess said, wondering if she should clamber back up the rocks. The others had moved away, and she could hear their voices echoing around the ruins. But . . . she stayed.

He was prowling around the small room, poking at protruding rocks with his polished mahogany cane. Tess felt, quite irrationally, as if there wasn't quite enough air to breathe in that small chamber. How in the world had a group of Romans sat around without their clothing, in such a confined space?

Why, if he were unclothed . . .

"Miss Pythian-Adams thinks that this may have been a steam room," she said, as much to push away the foolish images leaping to her mind as anything.

"Indeed," he said noncommittally. "I suppose she may well be right. One might imagine that this stone piece here was designed for a person to lie upon."

They both stared for a moment at a stone ledge along the side of the room, quite covered with mossy green.

Color leaped into Tess's cheeks at the thought. "We must join the others," she said, picking up her skirts, preparatory to scrambling up the rockslide.

Mr. Felton had a faint smile on his face. "I didn't mean to alarm you, Miss Essex."

How she disliked men who always faced the world with a noncommittal expression! One might even prefer Lord Maitland's sulky little pouts to Felton's lack of expression. "I am not alarmed," Tess said, nevertheless backing up. He was such a large man. He was walking toward her, and there was something about that smile . . .

"Because I can only imagine," he said, stopping just before her, "that Scottish lasses react precisely the same as English young ladies to a mere suggestion of the bedchamber."

He clearly intended to fluster her. So apparently behind that sardonic face was the wish to unnerve young women. How charming.

"Oh, not in the least," she snapped. "I adore historical sites. One can just imagine the Romans reclining and —"

"Eating grapes?" he suggested. He was very close to her now. His hair had been blown by the breeze: it didn't lie so strictly along his head but was almost standing up, glowing wheat-colored strands curling in all directions.

"Of course. Eating grapes and writing poetry. All — all those things Romans did." Given their lack of schooling, the only things she knew about Romans was that when they weren't marching around in armor, they ate grapes naked, presumably while listening to all that poetry Annabel loved so much. She certainly wasn't going to mention specific poems. Or naked grape eating. Or —

And the glint in Mr. Felton's eye suggested that he knew just what she was thinking. Tess could feel herself growing a bit pink, but she didn't move.

"Poetry?" he asked. "What Roman poets do you particularly enjoy?"

Was he mocking her? Tess raised her chin. "Catullus is an esteemed poet of the ancient world."

"What a remarkable governess you must have had," Mr. Felton remarked, looking genuinely surprised.

Tess was silent. They'd had, of course, no governess. But at some point she and Annabel had decided that they must read the books in their papa's library before he sold every one. Otherwise, they would be as ignorant as savages if they ever did get to England to have the season Papa was always promising them.

"I would be surprised to find that an educated young woman had read Virgil," Mr. Felton said, "but Catullus!"

In the face of his astonishment, Tess felt compelled to explain. "His name begins with 'C.' Annabel and I formed the idea of reading my father's library; I'm afraid that we did not reach as far as the 'V's."

Mr. Felton seemed mightily amused by this. "So how far did you and Miss Annabel reach in the alphabet?"

Tess frowned at him. "It wasn't only

Annabel and me; all four of us read the works together. And we reached H."

"No Shakespeare?" Felton asked.

Tess nodded. "He fell under 'C' for Collected Works."

Felton laughed. He really was standing uncomfortably close to her. "My favorite poem by Catullus begins like this, although I doubt very much that a proper young lady like yourself has read this particular verse. *You inquire how many kisses of yours would be enough.*"

Tess felt herself growing rosy. His head was bending toward hers with all the brazen shamelessness of a naked Roman. She ought to push him away. To scream, to —

His lips came to hers with a certain stillness, as if he merely wished to taste her, to brush their mouths together. The gesture was almost a chaste one, except he was so close to her, bending near, and Tess could smell a clean smell of the fields and drying hay from his coat and his hair.

Before she knew it, the fingers of her right hand curled into the thick hair at his neck and in a second, something changed in his kiss, something patient became less patient. The lips just brushing over hers slanted to the side; she gasped.

"I doubt that any governess would have let you read that particular poem by Catullus, Miss Essex." There was something amused in his tone. Tess stilled her hand on his hair. He clearly thought that she would be dazzled by the mere touch of his lip. Perhaps knowing that they had never had a governess made him bold. He thought she was naive, because unschooled.

She pulled back, but not abruptly. His eyes were the darkest indigo blue that she had ever seen. She let a faint smile curl on her lips. *"You inquire how many kisses of yours would be enough, and more to satisfy me,"* she said, and was startled to hear a husky catch in her voice. *"As many as the grains of Libyan sand that lie between hot Jupiter's oracle . . . as many . . ."* She paused. The look in his eye had made her forget what she was saying. What came after *hot oracle?*

He didn't look sardonic now, but truly surprised. She had to leave. This was all entirely too intimate and uncomfortable.

"Alas," she said, gathering up her skirts again and turning toward the rockslide. "I have quite forgotten the next line, so we shall have to delay this learned discussion." He was at her shoulder in a moment, helping her over the stones.

"As many as the stars," he said, conversationally, as if they were talking of gardening, or Romans, or any number of polite topics. *"As many as the stars, when the night is still, gazing down on secret human desires."*

"Exactly so," Tess said, coming out onto the wide expanse of green meadow again. She had suddenly remembered that the Earl of Mayne was courting her and that she had decided to encourage his suit. Kissing Mr. Felton was not prudent under those circumstances.

A footman was standing politely at the edge of the ruins. He showed no sign of having peered into the sunken bath, but Tess felt her face heating. "The party awaits you for nuncheon, miss," he said, his gloved hands clasped before him.

Mr. Felton held out his arm, and Tess took it. Now she could see the party gathered under the willow trees at the edge of the ruins, Annabel's bright hair shining in the sun, and Lady Clarice's parasol dipping to the side and threatening to take someone's eyes out.

She had held herself cheap, allowing herself to be kissed like a hurly-burly village girl. Surely young ladies who were raised with governesses had more restraint. It was a rather depressing thought. Mr. Felton must think her a veritable hoyden.

They walked silently.

If the truth be known, Lucius was wrestling with the twin devils of conscience and surprise. Foremost, if he were honest, was a potent sense of shock. What the devil had he done that for? He prided himself on adhering to every gentlemanly precept, other than those dictating an indolent life. Why on earth had he thrown the practices of a lifetime to the wind? Not only had he kissed a young lady, but she was the very same lady whom his friend Mayne had decided to wed. Worse and worse.

Moreover, there were consequences for abandoning decorous conduct. When a gentleman kisses (even if tamely) a young lady in a Roman bathhouse, he is obligated to make an offer of marriage. Everything he had ever known about young ladies implied that one does not kiss that particular genus of mankind without suggesting matrimony in the near aftermath.

True, Miss Essex seemed to have no particular expectations in that direction. She was not peeking at him in anticipation, nor did she even look particularly pleased to accept his arm as they picked their way back over the field.

A thought occurred to him: Mayne would be outraged if Miss Essex accepted his proposal. Unless he gave Mayne a horse from his stables to assuage his feelings. He felt quite sure that Mayne would happily accept the horse over the bride.

So without letting himself think too much about it, but instead summoning up all of his steadfast determination to remember that he was bred a gentleman, Lucius said, "Miss Essex, I should like to request your hand in marriage."

Lucius had only proposed once before; it was accepted with rather embarrassing fervor. This time, however, the young lady walked along without even giving a sign of having heard him.

"Miss Essex," he said more loudly.

She jumped slightly and turned her head. Lucius paused and looked down at her eyes, and then at her mouth, that luscious, deliriously luscious mouth, and thought that perhaps the kiss wasn't such a bad decision on his part. The thought was followed by a shock of surprise. Was he actually thinking such a thing?

"I should like to request your hand in marriage," he said, repeating himself.

No overwhelming pleasure swept into

Miss Essex's face. Instead, she narrowed her eyes at him. "I suppose that your question is a punctilious response to what just happened between us?"

Lucius almost stopped walking. "I find your company enchanting," he said cautiously, looking at her. Their eyes caught and tangled for a moment before she looked away.

"I did not make myself common in order to be enchanting," she answered.

"You did not make yourself common," he said. "The fault was entirely mine. I behaved in an unconscionable fashion."

"I am naturally relieved by your assurance," she said. "All the same, I decline to marry you on such slender grounds." There was a hint of a smile on her face.

Lucius knew he should be feeling relief. It was rather annoying to discover he was deeply curious about *why* she didn't wish to marry him.

"You needn't worry, Mr. Felton. I shan't think twice about that kiss. And since no one saw us, we certainly have no reason to make rash arrangements on the basis of such a triviality."

A triviality? *Triviality?* Lucius would have given it quite another name.

"Much ado about nothing," she said, in

a tone that did not welcome further commentary.

Tess walked a little faster, congratulating herself on her thoroughly careless and — to the best of her ability — sardonic tone. Just so might Mr. Felton reject a similar offer, she was certain of that. Not that ladies ever asked gentlemen to marry them. But if a lady *did* ask Mr. Felton to marry her, he would look at her noncommittally. Sardonically.

"A measure of constraint is likely felt between parties in circumstances such as these," Mr. Felton said, after a long, silent moment.

The picnickers were quite close now. She turned and smiled at him briefly before waving to the group. "Oh, I see no reason for that."

"There you are," Lady Clarice said, rather pettishly, when they finally arrived. "I can't think what was so interesting in that ruin, if one can even call it that. All *I* saw were a few holes in the ground and a great deal of stone that poor Mr. Jessop will have difficulty removing."

The Earl of Mayne leaped to his feet and gave Tess a lavish smile. "My dear Miss Essex," he said, "may I help you to sit down?"

"My goodness, English gentlemen are chivalrous," she said with a quick glance at Mr. Felton. Then she took Mayne's outstretched hand and sank onto a cushion at his side. Mr. Felton had put on his bland expression again and was busying himself next to Annabel, offering to peel an apple for her.

"I found the ruins quite, quite dreary," Lady Clarice announced.

"The ruins were indeed of dubious interest," Felton said.

As if he felt that Tess was watching him under her lashes, he raised his heavy-lidded eyes and drawled, without shifting his expression one iota, "Although there were some areas for which, I am certain, one should feel a romantic and disproportionate enthusiasm."

"Were you referring to the dilapidated stairs or the dilapidated walls?" Annabel inquired.

Felton was still staring at Tess, and she — idiot that she was — didn't seem to be able to look away. "Neither," he said. And then, without blinking an eye, he turned back to Annabel.

Concurrently, Mayne caught Tess's attention and handed her a bit of salmon patty. She had the fleeting thought that it would be rather odd to have a husband whose lashes were longer than her own.

Annabel was laughing at something Mr. Felton was saying in her ear. Tess turned to the Earl of Mayne and gave him a lavish smile.

"You seem to know so much about the polite world," she said to him, pitching her voice so that it would reach Mr. Felton's ear as well. "I would be most grateful for your guidance."

Mr. Felton bent even closer to Annabel, murmuring something to her. Annabel started laughing, and Lady Clarice said, "*Do* share the jest."

"It was only marginally humorous, my lady," Mr. Felton said.

Tess lowered her eyelashes and slowly ate a strawberry. Annabel had discovered long ago that strawberries dyed one's lips a most appealing shade of red. Unfortunately, Mr. Felton didn't even cast a glance at her red lips. Tess ate another, more quickly. Why on earth was she behaving like this? Why did she care if Mr. Felton noticed her lips or not?

Because . . . because he kissed me, she thought. And ate another strawberry, thinking about the kiss. And about marriage. Lady Clarice was making a dead set at poor Rafe, leaning toward him and chattering luridly. But Tess had no worries about Rafe; he was leaning against the willow tree with a lazy expression that suggested he had finished the contents of his flask and was not hearing a whit of Lady Clarice's conversation. She was thinking about Mr. Felton's kiss again when Miss Pythian-Adams's voice caught her ear.

"Surely there can be no one," she was saying, "so petty or apathetic in his outlook that he has no wish to discover under what system of government the Romans succeeded in conquering the greater part of the world."

Lord Maitland was feeding Imogen grape after grape and paying not the slightest attention to his betrothed; Tess had no doubt but that he considered himself both petty and apathetic when it came to Roman history.

Hazy sunlight was stealing through the willow leaves and dappling the picnic delicacies. It picked out the cream of Imogen's complexion and the gleam of her hair. Miss Pythian-Adams was sitting bolt upright as she discoursed on the Romans.

But Imogen seemed to have an instinctive knowledge that the Romans had more on their minds than hunger when they fed each other grapes. Her thank-you's for each grape Maitland gave her were nothing short of enchanting.

Tess sighed. Looking at Imogen made her certain that she was correct to refuse Mr. Felton's punctilious request for marriage. If one could not be glowing with love (as was Imogen), surely one should be comfortable. And if there was one thing she was *not* with Mr. Felton, it was comfortable. He was an annoying, expressionless, sardonic . . . kisser of unwilling women. She peeked at him again and happened to catch his eye.

A hand brought her another strawberry, and she blinked at Mayne. Mayne's glances were not at all like the swift, tight glances that Mr. Felton shot her. Felton looked — then always looked away immediately.

Whereas Mayne . . . Well, Mayne was far more handsome for one thing. His face had the graceful, sweet lines of an aristocrat, with the beauty of an altar boy grown to full adulthood. His eyes danced with merriment and compliments and — all manner of nice things. Tess knew without thought that the two of them would be compatible as a married couple: they would rarely if ever fight; they would be merry and tender to each other. In time genuine affection, if not love, for each other might develop.

He had his head bent now, peeling her an apple. Black curls fell over the rich linen fabric of his neckcloth. At that second he looked up and their eyes met. His had small laugh lines at the corners. It was a good face: a beautiful, strong face. One that would hold up to years of marriage.

It was quite different from Mr. Felton's face. Mr. Felton was harder, leaner, and his eyes held none of Mayne's charming compliments.

And yet he had kissed her.

As he might kiss any young lady who stumbled past, she told herself, accepting the apple from the earl's hands. She knew instinctively that if Felton lost his temper, his tongue would be as sharp as the back of the north wind. He was twenty times more dangerous, more sharp, more —

Obviously, there was no choice at all.

She turned to Mayne and gave him a melting smile. As besotted as any of his smiles had been.

Chapter 12

The next afternoon an extremely interesting event occurred: Mrs. Chace, the village seamstress, delivered a dinner gown for each of them, and brought with her a note from the Earl of Mayne's sister indicating that she would arrive in time to accompany them to the races in Silchester the following day.

Tess was perfectly aware that Lady Griselda was arriving for one reason, and one reason only. Without doubt, Mayne had signaled to his family the intent to marry. His attentions grew more marked from moment to moment. They had played chess the previous evening to the tune of his frivolities, his sweet compliments. While nothing was said, both of them knew without saying a word that he was in earnest. His face positively glowed with admiration. And he said lovely things about her hair, and her eyes, and her — she couldn't even remember what all. He seemed to know a great deal of poetry, as well, and had quoted quite a few poets whose names fell between I and the end of the alphabet, none of whom Tess could bring to mind at the moment, but all of whom she meant to read at some date.

Annabel was delighted. "I would guess that he'll ask you the very moment that Lady Griselda arrives," she said, taking off her gown. Mrs. Chace had only delivered one gown each, although she had promised to deliver riding costumes as soon as possible. "May I try on yours?" And without waiting for a response, she threw Tess's gown over her head.

Tess frowned at her reflection in the mirror. She was pinning up the front of her hair, trying to get it done before Gussie arrived to dress her for their excursion to the Silchester races. Hairdressing aside, Gussie was a lovely, cheerful person who didn't mind one ringing for baths, no matter the time of day.

Tess found hot baths that were available whenever one wanted them — and the water carried by footmen, rather than by oneself! — so enthralling that she had to restrain herself from bathing several times a day.

"Did you hear me?" Annabel said. "Perhaps Mayne will propose tonight, or tomorrow, at the races. You'd better wear

Imogen's bonnet to Silchester; it's the nicest that we have. You must look your best from every angle, just in case he is struck by the desire to make an offer while standing behind you."

"Of course," Tess murmured. "Many is the gentleman who's been overcome by the view of my shoulder blades."

"It's just a shame that Mrs. Chace couldn't deliver the riding costumes," Annabel said. "Look at your gown. I do believe that your bosom has grown larger than mine."

Tess's dinner gown was a silk tissue robe of bishop's blue, worn over a white satin slip, half-mourning, as the *modiste* explained, at its very best. The bodice was round and cut quite low, showing a generous amount of bosom. Tess glanced from Annabel's to her own chest. "I think my gown simply happens to be cut more generously," she said.

Annabel was turning from side to side and examining herself. "Would you mind if we switched garments?" she asked. "Just look what your dress does for my décolletage! And I adore the way it clasps in front. It makes my bosoms look colossal."

"Colossal is a word that applies better to

monumental architecture than one's chest," Tess pointed out. She had the strong suspicion that the earl would offer for her were she wearing sackcloth. And so there was really no reason why she should have a more enticing gown. Then something occurred to her: "Are you hoping to entrance Mr. Felton with your colossal bosom?"

"No," Annabel said absentmindedly. "Oh, how I wish I had *stays!* If I had stays, I could hoist my bosom all the way up here —" She pushed up her bosom until her breasts were in the vicinity of her collarbone.

Tess grinned at her. "We can exhibit you at Bartholomew Fair as the Lady with —" she stopped. "No, that would be quite indelicate."

But Annabel was never one to duck an indelicacy. "The Lady with the Bosom at Her Ears," she said, staring into the mirror. "I do look ridiculous, don't I? Perhaps I don't need stays."

But for some reason Tess didn't like the idea of Annabel exhibiting her bosom while Tess wore a demure gown. "I'm sorry, Annabel, but I wish to wear my gown."

Annabel opened her mouth, but —

"It *is* possible that the earl will ask me to marry him tonight," Tess said. "I simply cannot allow a gentleman to ask for my hand in marriage unless I'm in my very best costume." Never mind the fact that Mr. Felton had asked her just that question, and while she was wearing her dreadful bombazine.

For some reason, she had neglected to tell Annabel about his offer or his kiss.

Annabel sighed and undid the clasp that held the dress tightly under her breasts. "You're right," she agreed. "I shall simply count on you and your new husband to buy me hundreds of gowns, all made of tissue silk, if you please, with bodices low enough to allure the most tired rake."

"A tired rake?" Tess said, grinning at her sister. "Now there's a lovely choice for a husband."

But no one could have a grin more suggestive than her sister's. "Precisely. You never paid enough attention to gossip in the village, Tess. But from everything I learned, one would wish one's husband to be experienced and yet not so energetic that he cannot be pleased at home. A tired rake is precisely the best sort of spouse."

Tess rolled her eyes. "Josie is right. You're contemplating one of those seventy-year-old dukes, aren't you?"

Annabel had put her own gown back on and was rearranging the bodice so that it sat lower on her shoulders. "Oh certainly," she said, with that perfect composure that accompanies an untroubled conscience. "Although it is not yet entirely clear to me which of those rather aged gentlemen is unmarried. I keep meaning to ask Brinkley to point me to a current *Debrett's* so that I can do the necessary research."

But for all Tess wore her new gown, presumably tempting the earl to think of marriage, the only cheerful event of the evening was Lady Clarice's announcement that she would return home in the morning, given the imminent arrival of the Earl of Mayne's sister. The Earl of Mayne himself offered Tess compliments, but not marriage.

Lady Griselda Willoughby reminded Tess of nothing so much as a winsome china shepherdess, bought by her father for her mother during the early years of their marriage. The shepherdess had ringlets, and a simper, and a positive froth of ruffles about her tiny slippers. After Tess's mother died, when Tess was eight years old, she used to tiptoe into her mother's rooms and simply hold things her mother had touched: her brush, her shepherdess, her little prayer book. But within a few months, anything of value began disappearing from the chamber. And one day, when Tess walked in, the shepherdess was missing from the mantelpiece, her bright china smile and blue eyes gone to market in her father's pocket.

Of course, the shepherdess had always been quite silent. Even when Tess had cried, hot tears dripping onto the cool china, the shepherdess just smiled her hard blue-eyed smile. But Lady Griselda talked — and talked. They were having tea in the morning room, a chamber hung in lilac paper that Lady Griselda had declared to be "absolutely mortal for one's complexion. Anyone who saw us would think we all had jaundice." She was reclining on a divan to the side of the room, wearing a gown of amber-colored crape, trimmed with deep flounces of the same color, edged in lace. The amber crape gave her hair delicate bronze tones; her complexion was as creamy as a real milkmaid's; she had the brightest blue eyes that Tess had ever seen. Anyone who looked less like an invalid with jaundice couldn't be imagined. Yet: "Ladies, we shall have to make up our minds never to darken the room again until Rafe bestirs his lazy staff to change the paper," she pronounced.

Josie's eyes widened. "Where shall we eat breakfast?"

Lady Griselda waved her hand in the air. "Breakfast should be taken in one's own chambers. One mustn't allow gentlemen to become too accustomed to seeing you any time of the day that they wish. Darling" — for that was what she called her brother — "Darling, do take Rafe out to some sort of male pursuit, won't you? Find a rabbit and tree it, or something of that nature."

The Earl of Mayne, Tess was happy to note, had a great deal of solid affection for his sister. He leaned over the back of the settee and tweaked one of her curls. "Planning on corrupting poor Miss Essex and her sisters with a great deal of nonsense about what ladies should and shouldn't do, are you?"

"I have a small amount of expertise in that area," Lady Griselda said loftily. "And if I am to bring these ladies into society, I shall naturally give them the benefit of my experience."

"And *I* am sure it will be a most instructive occasion," Rafe put in. He was inclined to laugh at Lady Griselda as well,

Tess noticed. She didn't seem to mind, though, but treated him with the same familiarity as her own brother. "Perhaps we should stay, Mayne, and make certain that we are not maligned in our absence."

"Be off with the two of you," she said roundly. "And no smirking on your part, Your Grace. I'll have you know that as soon as I've married off my own brother, I shall be thinking of you."

"My optimism is unmarred," Rafe said, escaping out the door. "Threaten as you wish, Grissie, your brother's reached a ripe old age without marriage!"

Lady Griselda waited until the door shut behind Mayne before she turned to the sisters. The most important, of course, was Tess. The woman who showed every sign of making her marriage-shy brother actually step up to the altar. She was lovely, even wearing bombazine. Truly lovely.

Griselda felt a smile curl on her lips. Things couldn't be better. "Now," she said, "we can talk." She sat up. Griselda made it a point to sit up straight as rarely as possible, since her figure showed to its best advantage on a slight incline, but that particular rule — like so many others in life — only had pertinence when there were gentlemen in the room.

"We are most grateful that you agreed to chaperone us," Tess ventured, eyeing Lady Griselda rather nervously. Mayne's sister was quite intimidating, if the truth be known. Tess could tell that Annabel was memorizing every single aspect of Griselda's appearance, from the tiny ribbons on her slippers to the matching ribbons adorning her ringlets.

"It is my pleasure," Griselda replied. "In all truth." Then she smiled at Tess, and it was as if that china shepherdess came to vivid life. "I had almost lost hope that my darling brother would marry, and now I have hopes in that direction."

Tess could feel her cheeks warming and would have protested that Mayne had said nothing to her, but Annabel intervened.

"We are naturally delighted to think that Tess may have attracted the attention of the earl," she said.

"Annabel!" Tess protested.

"I much prefer plain speaking," Griselda said. "In fact, in order for me to launch the four of you onto the marriage market, we shall have to be ruthlessly clear about certain facts among us. Four husbands are not easy to acquire in one fell swoop, even if we include my brother amongst the four. Although, *you* may be a little young, my dear." She turned to Josie. "Do forgive me for not knowing your age. Are you out of the schoolroom?"

"No," Josie said quickly. "I'm not. Our guardian has hired a governess, who should arrive tomorrow morning."

Tess opened her mouth, and then thought twice of it. If Josie wasn't ready to be launched onto the season, then who was she to insist that her little sister do so? She was only fifteen, after all.

"Good," Griselda said briskly. "Because I don't mind telling you, dearest, that with your figure, the gentlemen are going to line up in droves pawing at the door. 'Twould be best for your sisters if we fire them off on the market without *your* competition."

Josie blinked incredulously. "I'm *fat*," she finally said.

"No, you are not," Griselda stated with utmost confidence. "Believe me, gentlemen *see* slim and *think* scrawny. Scrawny is most unattractive. Thank goodness, that is not a fault that we share!" She gracefully reclined back against the settee. "Tell me, Juliet — is it Juliet?"

"Josephine, actually, but I am called Josie within the family."

"We are family now," Griselda said with a twinkle. "Now, Josie dearest, would you call me *fat* by any stretch of the imagination?"

"No, certainly not," Josie gasped. Griselda's body had the sultry curves of a Renaissance gentlewoman, those luscious curves that used to be nursed and enhanced by Renaissance clothing, designed to swoon to a narrow waist, and then blossom (with the help of starched petticoats) to rounded hips. Of course, these days clothing was designed to hang on a slim form as if a woman had no more curves than a tree.

"I suppose one could be foolish enough to call me plump," Griselda said, looking still only at Josie. "But I assure you that no gentleman in the world would agree with such a brainless assessment." There was a sultry look in her eyes that showed she understood precisely how potent curves could be and that she wouldn't trade one of her lush curves for a moment.

Tess truly liked Griselda now.

Griselda gave a mesmerized Josie one final smile and straightened again. "So," she said briskly, "Josie would like to wait for a year before entering the season. Who's next in age after Josie? I am guessing that you are, Miss Imogen. How old are you, if you don't mind my asking?"

"Please, you must call me Imogen as well."

"As long as you all address me as Griselda," she said unperturbed. "*Not* Grissie, if you please. My brother addresses me by that paltry diminutive, and it always makes me feel like a frizzled curl."

"I am twenty," Imogen said, "and I have no wish to go on the season either."

Griselda raised one eyebrow. "Now *that* might pose a problem, my dear. You are not precisely a spring chicken, you know."

But Imogen was unoffended. "Since I don't intend to marry, I would consider entering the season with the pretense of being eligible for marriage a falsehood."

"And why, pray, do you not intend to marry?"

Imogen raised her chin. "I have given my heart away."

"Ah," Griselda said. "You lucky child. I seem to be quite unable to do that myself, although I regularly try to encourage the practice. In the end, you know, they're just *men,* aren't they?"

Tess choked, and Annabel giggled outright, but Imogen's chin just went higher. "It was no hardship to give my heart to Draven. I love him!"

"And does this Draven return your feelings?" Griselda inquired.

"Lord Maitland is promised in marriage," Tess put in, trying to head off the question of his feelings for Imogen.

"Maitland? Maitland?" Griselda said. "Do you mean Draven Maitland?"

Imogen nodded.

Griselda eyed her and clearly almost said something, but rethought it. "A predicament," she said at last. "I do adore a social problem. Something to sink my teeth into. Now the problem here is twofold."

Imogen waited, eyes wide.

Griselda said, "You do remember that I advocated utter honesty among us, darling? Because otherwise how am I to launch you on the season and chaperone you, etc., etc.?"

Imogen nodded. She was sitting bolt upright on the sofa, looking as if she were about to face the Inquisition.

"The truth of the matter is that Draven Maitland is, by all accounts, something of a hellion. Unlikely to make a good husband, due to an addiction to the track and —" Griselda coughed delicately — "although this may well be odious gossip and not true, slightly less intelligent than what one might hope in a husband. The former characteristic is naturally more difficult. A lack of intelligence in a man is not always a fault, after all. But am I incorrect in thinking that he spends a good portion of his day at the racetrack?"

"No," Imogen said reluctantly.

"That speaks for itself, doesn't it?" Griselda said. "My, how boring I find all that talk of fetlocks and furlongs and all the rest of it. Mind you," she said to Tess, "my brother can talk up quite a dust storm when he wishes, and all over that stable of his."

"I don't mind talk of horses," Tess replied, somewhat untruthfully. "My father was just the same."

"Your father," Griselda said, and stopped again. "Well, sometime you're going to have to explain him to me. You do know that your dowries are horseflesh, do you not?"

Tess nodded.

Imogen said, "The fact that you consider Draven to be an objectionable spouse due to his — his racing and his — well, I think he's remarkably intelligent — that is beside the point because he is betrothed!"

"Yes," Griselda said thoughtfully. "So I've heard." She turned to Annabel. "Have you a man hiding in the wings as well?"

"Absolutely not," said Annabel with a huge grin. She had clearly recognized a kindred spirit. "I am open to suggestion, although I have decided that I should like a title."

"This is the very first time I have chaperoned anyone onto the market, darling, but I might as well confess that I would take it extremely badly if one of you were to marry a plain *mister.*" Griselda and Annabel exchanged looks of perfect understanding.

"Now," she said, turning to Tess, "I don't want you to think that merely because my brother is utterly enchanted with you that I am not your advocate if you wish to refuse him. I am the first to admit that Mayne is not everyone's blue-eyed boy. In fact, ever since he was jilted last spring —"

She stopped abruptly, looking as if she'd swallowed a spider.

That probably happened quite often to Griselda, Tess thought. Her tongue rattled on ahead of her mind. "Jilted?" she asked. "Was the earl betrothed, then?"

Griselda cast a glance at Josie. "Ah, no. And the past hardly signifies, given that he's on the point of declaring himself to you, darling."

"Of course," Tess murmured. She couldn't decide whether it made Mayne more attractive or less, to think of another woman rejecting him. A married woman, it appeared, from Griselda's discomfiture. Probably less attractive.

"Now the question is," Griselda said, "what about Felton? I mean, here he is in the house. One couldn't pray for a better opportunity — and believe me, there are ladies all over England praying for just that opportunity."

Annabel said, "Opportunity?"

"My darling, surely you have been told who Felton is?"

They all blinked at her.

"You haven't? Oh my. He's better than titled." Griselda turned to Annabel. "Over two thousand pounds a year in rents, and that's only the land. There are those who say that he owns the greater part of Bond Street, which is to say nothing of his holdings in stocks. He plays the market."

"Oh," Annabel said, light dawning in her eyes.

"Precisely." Griselda nodded. "Here is Felton, providentially to hand. He may be a mere gentleman, but he has the most exquisite manners of anyone under a duke — and believe me, dears, his manners are *far* more polished than our royal dukes. It would make me extremely happy to see both you and Tess well away before we dealt with the little problem of Imogen and Lord Maitland."

"There's no way to *deal* with my feelings for Draven," Imogen said half-angrily. She was the only sister who seemed untouched by Griselda's charm. "I feel the way I feel, and I will not marry anyone other than Draven. And since he doesn't wish to marry me, I shall remain unmarried."

Griselda cast her a cool look that made Imogen's back stiffen even more. "In that case, our only request would be that you not stand in the way of your sisters."

"I can assure you that I would never stand in their way!" Imogen said rather wildly.

"Excellent. I would ask you to reconsider your notion of declining a season. If you are less than a success, then there will be no further questions should you eschew the season next year. But if you simply don't attend, everyone will be curious."

Imogen opened her mouth, but Griselda held up a magisterial hand.

"When the *ton* is curious, their imaginations grow quite fertile. As soon as they discover the Essex sisters are marriageable young women, they would wonder mightily at the absence of one of you. Wonder leads to speculation, and before you know it, you'll be known as the sister with one leg. Or an attribute even less attractive."

Imogen seemed struck by this.

Griselda turned back to Annabel. "Now, as to you, I think we are in agreement as to Mr. Felton's superb qualifications for matrimony?"

Annabel's mouth curved. "Absolutely."

"Felton is rather extraordinary," Griselda said meditatively. "There are those who accuse him of all sorts of hard-hearted dealings in business. Certainly he has never maintained a gentlemanly distance from the markets, a fact that his mother has never been able to forgive him for."

"What do you mean?" Tess asked.

Griselda shrugged. "One hears rumors. His mother is very sensitive to matters of consequence, because she married below herself; *she* is the daughter of an earl, but *he* is merely a baron's third son, or some such. I suppose she'd prefer her son was not so flamboyantly successful at commerce." Her mouth curved. "There's not a woman in London who agrees with her."

"They're estranged because he plays the markets?" Annabel said. "Are his parents so wealthy, then?"

"Oh, they're well enough off, with a large estate in the country," Griselda said. "I think the real crux of the disharmony must be Felton's financial dealings, but I never heard the right of it. I did hear a rumor that he declines to share his ill-gotten gains with his family, so that might be it."

She looked directly at Annabel. "None of that matters a pin. A man who won't speak to his mother, after all, is a man who comes without a mother-in-law, and you may take *that* from me, m'dear: 'tis a marvelous piece of luck."

To Tess, it sounded quite sad, but when she opened her mouth to ask another question, Griselda cut her off. "Why, they practically live next door and never speak. It's quite amusing, in its own way. But enough of that lamentable family."

"I think we are fairly well set," Annabel said. "Tess shall quite possibly marry your brother Mayne. I shall quite possibly marry Mr. Felton, if he is in the least amenable. I shall make a concerted effort to inform him of my intentions, beginning this very afternoon at the races."

Griselda looked at her thoughtfully. "If you don't mind my saying so, darling, I shall look forward to it. One is never too old to learn from a master."

"A high compliment indeed," Annabel said, grinning at her. "Although quite unwarranted, I assure you."

"Lord Maitland and his mother are joining us for the races," Imogen broke in with her usual lack of attention to the subject of conversation. "Apparently Miss Pythian-Adams will follow in a carriage, as she doesn't ride." Her lips curled.

"Neither do I," said Griselda, unperturbed by Imogen's scornful eyes. "I have always found bouncing around on the tail of a horse enveloped in a cloud of dust more than tedious. Plus, horses invariably have yellow teeth. I loathe yellow teeth. My father-in-law had them, and I lived in fear that poor, poor Willoughby's teeth would yellow before my very eyes. Perhaps it was fortunate that he died before it came to that."

"Was your husband named Willoughby?" Tess asked, with some fascination.

Griselda nodded. "It's been ten years since he died. Naturally, I miss him more every day. But enough of that unsavory subject. I shall enact my chaperonage to the best of my ability, meaning that I will attempt to leave you unchaperoned on every possible occasion and let you both effect the business without fuss. And I shall arrange for waltzing. There is nothing like the marked impropriety of clasping a lady to his breast to encourage a reluctant male into the path of virtue. By which I mean marriage, of course," she added, probably because Tess, for one, was likely looking bewildered.

She turned a sharp eye on Imogen. "The *only* way to extract a man from an undesirable engagement is to play a very chilly game indeed. Do you understand me?"

Imogen nodded.

Griselda rose to her feet. "I am quite looking forward to the next fortnight or so. I'm not sure which will be the more delightful: to watch my brother court a lovely young woman or see the elusive Mr. Felton ensnared whilst I am there and able to make a full report to all the dowagers in London who have tried to match him to their daughters."

She paused in thought with her fingers to her lips, presenting a magnificent picture of elegant womanhood from the blushing rose on her bonnet to the silken toes of her slippers.

"Mr. Felton," she decided, turning toward the door. "One's family must always take second place, alas, to an *on-dit* such as this. Luckily, I brought a great quantity of stationery with me."

Annabel took Tess's arm as they left the room, and whispered, "I hope you know what a responsibility you have escaped by allowing yourself to be courted by Mayne. *I* am apparently going to launch a courtship in which a simple kiss is likely to be broadcast to all of London."

"Mr. Felton is not the sort of gentleman who will kiss you without asking for one's hand in marriage," Tess said.

"Well, there's no need to frown over it," Annabel said, starting up the stairs. Lady Griselda was already whisking around the corner toward her chamber. "A gentlemanly attitude, of course, will make my task all the easier. I have always thought that men hidebound by propriety were extremely easy to lead by the nose."

Tess found that her frown was deepening and that she was apparently developing a headache.

Chapter 13

The Courtyard
Holbrook Court

Being an only child, and that of parents who saw no reason to encounter their son and heir more than a few times a year, Lucius had never had to accustom himself to waiting for a familial group to assemble. Having remained unmarried, he was also unfamiliar with the length of time that it apparently took young ladies to prepare themselves for something as harrowing as a brief riding excursion to the village of Silchester.

Yet the tedium and the wait was something he would have expected. These were the very reasons that he had long eschewed family groups, and the reasons that he had adroitly avoided anything that resembled a house party.

No, what was shocking him to the marrow of his bones had nothing to do with time. Ladies, as anyone in their right mind knew, rode plodding mounts, suitable for those of a gender plagued by delicate nerves and even more delicate limbs. Lucius doubted very much that his own mother had ever mounted a horse, but if she had, the horse would have needed a back as wide as a backgammon board, and a constitution mild enough to ignore a full-blown fit of hysteria taking place on his back.

Not so the Essex sisters, at least the three Essex sisters who were riding, Josie having decided to remain at home with her new governess.

To all appearances, these particular ladies rode polished Thoroughbreds that spent their free time irritably flattening their ears at each other, when they weren't throwing their heads into the air and bucking at the clouds. Three exquisite, gleaming horses awaited the elder Essexes, each of which seemed to think that stamping would make their mistresses appear with more speed. The scene was all the more remarkable because Rafe's courtyard was paved in large rounded stones that caught the horses' shoes and sent showers of sparks into the air.

Miss Imogen was the first to appear from the house. "We are extremely good horsewomen," she said, catching Lucius's dubious gaze as she tucked a short crop into the waist of her riding costume. "My Posy was considered a likely shot at the Derby until she suffered a severe strain two years ago. I've been riding her ever since she recovered."

Her Posy was skittering sideways as if she were being bitten by midges and looked nervous enough to leap the huge gate around the courtyard. "She seems to have an inappropriately flowery name," Lucius said, moving to the side to avoid being struck by Posy's enormous, muscled haunches.

"I gave her the name because she's a *poseur*," Imogen said, pulling on well-worn riding gloves. "Posy is a faker, a fraud. She likes to pretend to racehorse status, but in fact she's a lovely mount. And quite polite, although, as I said, she pretends to be fiercely difficult."

"A beautiful horse," Rafe said, appearing at Lucius's shoulder. "I saw her run in the Ascot, the year before she was lamed. Lovely mount."

Lucius frowned; Rafe was hardly showing a proper guardian's concern for the safety of his wards.

Annabel had walked into the courtyard and was greeting a gelding whose ears were flat to his head. She looked up and smiled at Lucius. "This is Sweetpea," she said. "He's a bit cross this morning; I think he might be homesick." Sweetpea bared his teeth and shook himself all over, like a steed preparing to enter a battle.

"My mount is nothing to Tess's," Imogen was telling Rafe. "Well, here she comes; she can tell you herself."

Lucius turned.

Miss Essex was walking through a patch of sunshine in the courtyard, looking slender, fragile, and suited for only the sweetest mount in the stables.

"Tess is the bravest of us all," Imogen was saying. "She rides Midnight Blossom, out of Belworthy, you know."

"Midnight Blossom," Lucius said sharply. "The gelding who threw a man at the Newmarket three years ago?"

"The same," Imogen said. "Do you think that the Maitlands will arrive soon? I'm afraid that Posy is a wee bit restless."

That was an understatement; Posy was like a fiend in a horse's body, prancing and stamping. Lucius reached out a hand, and Posy calmed.

"She likes you," Imogen said, with some surprise.

"Horses do," Lucius said. He was

watching as a groomsman threw Tess up onto the back of a monstrously large horse, a horse the color of midnight. Unlike Posy, Midnight Blossom didn't bother with prancing or fidgets. All he did was arch his neck once, blowing his nostrils as if sighing for the moment when he would run free. Midnight Blossom was no *poseur,* pretending to be a racehorse. He was built for speed.

Yet Tess seemed unmoved by the fact she was perched precariously, sidesaddle, on the back of such an animal.

"You shouldn't allow your ward to ride on that horse!" Lucius said to Rafe. "Midnight Blossom threw a man a few years ago."

Imogen cocked an eyebrow at him. "Are you worried about Tess, Mr. Felton? You shouldn't be. She's the best of us. Papa said she has a bone-deep understanding of horses."

"I would assume that my wards have more than enough ability to handle their cattle," Rafe observed. "They are grown women, and none of them seems unused to her mount."

"A guardian should take a more active role than that," Lucius snarled. Midnight Blossom had lapsed into a stand now, and the only motion he made was the flicking back and forth of his ears as Tess spoke to him, a much-darned glove patting his muscled neck.

In a silent storm of fury, Lucius went to his own horse and swung up onto his great polished back. At least he could keep pace with Miss Essex when her horse ran away from her.

At that moment Draven Maitland came through the great rounded gates of Holbrook Court at a near gallop and stopped his horse by pulling it straight into the air. Lucius had just reached Tess's side and was allowing their two horses to exchange friendly puffs of air.

"That foolish boy!" she said, in a low voice.

Lucius looked over his shoulder. Maitland had flung himself off his horse and was standing at Posy's head, making a great show of admiring Imogen's horse.

"His foolishness lies in reckless riding?" Lucius asked. "Could one not accuse you of calling the kettle black?"

"I suppose you think that Midnight is too much for me."

"Probably for me as well," Lucius replied calmly.

"I doubt it. Your mount is no tame

youngster, is he?" She reached over and scratched Lucius's horse on the neck.

"Pantaloon," Lucius said, "out of Hautboy."

"He's a beauty."

Pantaloon stilled his massive head and snorted with pleasure as she scratched him behind the ear.

There was a clatter as the rest of the Maitland party entered the courtyard. Lady Clarice was riding a velvety little mare, who looked capable of going a mile or two with pleasure, and then would drag her hocks all the way home. Not that it mattered, as Lady Clarice was currently explaining that her carriage would apparently follow them every step of the way, in case the ladies tired.

"For one *does!*" she shrilled. "And exhaustion simply does not enhance one's complexion. Miss Pythian-Adams is already in the carriage. She doesn't care for the sensation of horseflesh beneath her."

Maitland walked over to Tess, his eyes on her horse. One could fault the man for many things, but he certainly knew the racetrack inside out. "Haven't seen Midnight Blossom in a year or so," he said, grinning. "I almost won him from your father in a bet, you know. That was just after

Midnight won the trial at Banstead Downs and before he had to be retired. I could have taken him to the Ascot."

Lucius watched as Miss Essex's cheeks turned a little pink. "I am very glad that you did not win that particular wager," she said.

"Oh, I did win," Maitland said genially. "Essex thought that roosters always crowed atop a fence post. That wager was easy enough to win."

Lucius bit back a smile as Miss Essex looked down at Maitland. Maitland was so utterly unaware of the expression in her eye and, in fact, had taken to checking Midnight Blossom's teeth as if he thought the animal was for sale. "Let me guess," she said in colorless voice, "you trained a rooster to crow from a dung heap, and then demonstrated its skill to my father."

"Better than that," Maitland said, jumping back as Midnight Blossom laid back his ears. "I cut the tendon in the bird's heels. Once he couldn't get up to a fence post, the animal crowed wherever he happened to be. But I didn't accept the horse, of course. No, no. Your father was a man who took a wager seriously; I would never take Midnight Blossom from him on a piece of cajolery, much though I love the joke of it."

Miss Essex had just finished soothing Midnight Blossom. Her hand stilled in stroking, and then she said, very evenly, "I'm certain that my father was grateful for your forbearance."

"Must have been," Maitland said cheerfully. "Now, if this fellow would just let me take a peek at his molars —"

But Midnight Blossom had not taken kindly to Maitland, nor to his prying ministrations to his jaws. The next moment Tess was fully occupied in controlling her mount as Midnight Blossom pawed the ground, and then reared straight into the air.

"Be still, you foolish beast!" she told him, leaning forward over his neck. Her voice was amused rather than angry, and there wasn't even a second in which she appeared to have lost her balance.

Lucius had started up, onto his stirrups, ready to pull Tess's bridle down — but she didn't need any help. Those arms were as slender as a reed, and yet the great Thoroughbred quieted at her touch and settled, contenting himself with snorting at Maitland's back and rolling his eyes as if he were having carnivorous thoughts.

Lady Clarice was leading her mare around the courtyard, greeting each member of the party in her high, rather irritable voice as she jerked on the animal's bridle in a manner that was painful to see.

"My *dear* Miss Essex," she called, "I fear you are not quite the horsewoman to handle this . . . *animal.* Aren't you concerned for your ward's health, Duke? I do believe that the horse should be barred civil company. Do you see the way he's looking at my son? One would almost think that he . . ."

Her voice trailed off. Clearly the idea that someone might wish to chomp her son's rear end was inconceivable.

"Your wards are in danger from these mounts!" she said sharply to Rafe, having now got the measure of all three horses.

Never mind the fact that Lucius had thought the same thing himself. "Miss Essex has her mount under perfect control," he noted.

Rafe ignored Lady Clarice, throwing himself onto his own horse. "Let's go!" he shouted. "Is everyone mounted, *finally?*"

Lucius quelled a grin. Of course, Rafe was as unused to family groups as he was.

"Not quite," came a cool voice from the door. Mayne paused in the doorway, pulling on his gloves. He was wearing tight-fitting breeches tucked into riding boots and a coat of superfine broad cloth in Spanish blue. Lucius blinked; he was unused to seeing Mayne rigged out in full regalia. Generally, when the three of them were together, they all wore leather breeches and a drab coat. But Mayne's jacket — which Lucius had to admit made him look princelike — was a marvel of exquisite tailoring and cut-steel buttons, and his breeches fit without a wrinkle.

Mayne glanced around the group, now beginning to walk their mounts from the courtyard, and then walked straight toward Tess.

Lucius's mouth twisted a bit. He'd managed to forget Mayne's marital plans. Again.

"Midnight Blossom," Mayne said, and his voice had all the true pleasure of a horse lover. "Miss Essex, you have just risen in my estimation to the unsurpassed equestrienne of your generation!"

Tess was smiling at him, and the sun was turning her brandy-colored hair into a thousand strains of taffy, gold threads twining into russet. With a touch of his finger, Lucius sent his mount to walking from the courtyard.

Unless he was quite mistaken, Mayne had just found a touch of utterly genuine emotion to bring to all his courtship flummery. That note of heady respect in his voice rang true.

They would make a good match, Lucius thought. Mayne was an excellent man, for all he had slept with half the married women of London. That would change once he was married. No one who had Tess in his bed would feel the need to seek out the tawdry pleasures of an adulterous affair.

How could Mayne not fall in love with Tess, with her steadfast gaze and her curious questions, with her superb riding ability and her natural seat on a horse, with her exquisite self? And when Mayne loved — well, he would love with a passion that was bone-deep. Lucius knew that from watching him reel and recover from the one woman he *had* loved during his life, Lady Godwin.

Of course, the countess had never loved Mayne. But she had taught him something about the poverty and shallowness of all those extramarital affairs he had engaged in.

To Lucius's way of thinking, the countess's rejection had made his friend ready to truly fall in love. And Tess would love him in return. Tess, with her passionate mouth and tender gaze — she would fall in love with her husband. It would take time, perhaps months, even a year, but that marriage —

He wrenched his mind away. What concern was it of his?

Pantaloon pranced delicately out of the great stone archway that led into the courtyard of Holbrook Court. After Lucius came Tess and Mayne, laughing over the clipping sound of their horses' hooves.

She was Mayne's.

Chapter 14

Tess wasn't quite certain how she found herself wandering down a long row of stables at the Queen's Arrow Inn with Mr. Felton, and Mr. Felton alone. Obviously, she should be accompanied by the Earl of Mayne, who had spent all afternoon paying nothing less than lavish attention to her. Mr. Felton should be walking with Annabel, who was paying precisely the same attention to him.

But somehow in the crooked rows of stables she found herself next to Mr. Felton, and they turned a corner, or perhaps the others did. And now they were each walking without their suitors. Rather absurdly, Tess had the giddy feeling of a child fleeing from the schoolroom.

The stables were long and smelled of warm alfalfa once it starts to brew alcohol, deep in its musty green stalks. It was a smell Tess loved and loathed: it reminded her of home and Papa; and at the same time, it reminded her of all that had taken

Papa away from them, years before he left them in truth.

They paused before a stall. "Lord Finster's Ramaby," Felton told her. "I didn't know he thought to run him in the local races. I'm afraid he'll have the best of my horses with ease."

"Not this time," Tess said, scratching the bay under the nose. "Ramaby's not feeling like winning, are you, love?"

Lucius chuckled, watching the way Ramaby's ears perked back and forth, trying to catch every liquid syllable of her voice. "Are you some sort of Scottish witch, then?" he asked. "Telling Ramaby that he doesn't feel like winning and casting a spell on the poor horse?"

"Oh no," Tess said, beginning to scratch behind Ramaby's right ear. "But when you've grown up in a stable, as I have, it's hard not to see how a horse feels. And Ramaby doesn't feel like winning, not at the moment." She gave him a final pat and moved away.

They walked down the straw-strewn aisles, peering into the stalls. Lucius was quite aware that he was walking slowly. He didn't want to reach the great doors at the end, where the light spilled in, and the crowds awaited. Where he would, of course, relinquish Miss Essex to Mayne's ardent wooing.

"Can you tell if a horse is hungry?" he asked her.

"Sometimes," Tess said. "But I'm not a mind reader."

"But it seems that you *are*."

"Oh no. There's no reading minds about it. Horses are affectionate creatures, after all, but just creatures. They're not like humans. They don't betray, and they don't hide their motives."

"They also don't speak English," Lucius pointed out.

She stopped abruptly before another stall, startled by her reaction to his glance. Hadn't she thought that his expression was impossible to read? "This horse won't win either," she stated.

"I could have told you that," he said. "She's in foal."

"Oh," Tess said, rather embarrassed. "I didn't see that."

"Well, what did you see?" he asked, tucking her arm closer to his body as they stood there, staring at the glossy brown mare.

"She's sleepy," Tess said. "See how her eyes are drooping?"

And sure enough, once Tess's little hand

started scratching behind her ears, the mare huffed out a great sigh and closed her eyes altogether.

"Well, that must be a remarkably useful talent," he said, after a moment of silence.

"There's no talent to it," Tess said uncomfortably. "Shall we rejoin the others?"

"By all means, Miss Essex." A moment later they were back in the chilly air.

The rough seats set up around the circle track were glowing in the last streams of slanting afternoon sunshine. There was a smoky tang of burning sausages in the air — from a stand selling the same — and the familiar burr of a hundred male voices discussing the haunches and hocks of a horse, or two horses, or the whole bunch of them at once.

"Here come my horses," Lucius said suddenly.

Two horses were led by, heavily blanketed, their delicate necks arching. He didn't ask. And Tess said nothing.

"I once told my father that I was quite certain that a horse called Highbrow would win the next race he was put into," she said, without looking at him. "My father put all the money he had saved for our dowries on that race. Because I had been correct before."

There was a moment's silence, and then Lucius said, "And if I remember correctly, this would be the same Newmarket in which a horse named Petunia galloped her way to the finish line?"

"Highbrow never finished," Tess said abstractly, watching Lucius's horses.

"He stumbled and broke a leg," he said, remembering now. "He had to be shot."

"And that is why, Mr. Felton, I shall not even venture an opinion about your horses. Because it is all poppycock, frankly. Anything can happen in a race."

"Humor me," he said.

She looked up at him. His face was utterly arresting, utterly silent, contained. He looked like a person with no need for human companionship, someone whose serenity was more than skin-deep. "We must find the others," she said, letting a trace of irritation enter her voice. After all, Mayne was courting her. Perhaps he had planned to propose to her at this very moment, and here she was, gallivanting about and making imprudent statements to Mr. Felton.

"Miss Essex," he said, and his voice had a deep steadiness that made her nerves mount even higher.

"I'd like to return to the box," she said.

"My sisters must be wondering where I am." But she had a sense of fair play, after all. "Very well. I'm not at all sure how your bay is feeling. But look at the way that one —"

"Royal Oak," he said.

"How Royal Oak is walking. He's too hot; he's not comfortable; and I think he may be hungry. Has your groom been sweating him?"

"He tells me it's necessary to keep the horse's flesh off," Lucius said with a frown.

"I find it barbaric. Both purging and sweating. If I know anything about horses, Mr. Felton, it is that such methods make them feel ill." She began walking toward the box where their party presumably waited.

But he stopped her with a light touch to her arm. "I was under the impression that your father was a great proponent of purging, Miss Essex. I heard him argue the case vehemently at the Derby two years ago."

"My father did advocate such methods," she said after a moment. "I did not agree with him."

Mr. Felton's gaze was so vivid that she almost closed her eyes to keep him out.

They entered the box to find only

Annabel and Mayne, who seemed to be on terms of the easiest companionship.

"They've all trotted off to the refreshment hall," Annabel explained. "Lady Clarice encountered one of her very best friends, Mrs. Homily, who informed her that they are serving truly delectable Yorkshire ham in the hall."

"Everyone?" Lucius asked, raising an eyebrow.

"Except for Lord Maitland, who, I believe, is in the stables," Annabel said, smiling at Felton in a roguish manner. "Won't you both join us, unless you too are eager for ham?"

From the moment Tess sat down beside the Earl of Mayne, his black eyes were sparkling with secret messages. He was truly interested in her ability to ride, she realized. He found her ability to control a racehorse intoxicating.

His courtship had taken on another note, a deeper, surer note. He wasn't talking flummery, but kept telling her casual little details about his stables and his household. He was speaking less as a man experienced in the fine art of dalliance and more as a man genuinely interested in his companion.

He was five hundred times more attractive for his candor. That, combined with his gypsy-eyed beauty, made him a formidable wooer indeed. Yet Tess couldn't help listening to Annabel chatter to Mr. Felton. Annabel, of course, was a formidable wooer as well. In fact, she should probably just start thinking of Mr. Felton as a brother-in-law from this moment forward.

"My mother had a restless soul," Mayne said. "She rode like the wind, even sidesaddle. In England, young ladies only ride sidesaddle, Miss Essex. But I know that in Ireland women sometimes ride astride. Forgive my ignorance on the subject of Scottish customs, but have you ever ridden astride?"

"Of course not!" Tess said tartly. She and her sisters hadn't ridden so for well over a year, and to reveal those occasions required an excess of candor.

Mr. Felton turned suddenly and looked at her. He had beautiful eyes: like those of a curiously intelligent wolf. She blinked, wondering how he knew she, Annabel, and Imogen used to fling themselves on horses and ride astride — but only on their father's land, where they couldn't be seen. There was a faint smile in his eyes that called her bluff.

He said nothing, turning back to the track without a comment. She was acutely aware of his broad shoulder. While Mayne's shoulder occasionally brushed hers as he handed her a program, or pointed to a certain horse, Mr. Felton didn't touch her at all.

"The downs behind my estate in Yorkshire are exquisite," Mayne said. "Many times I have ridden there for an hour without seeing a cottage. One feels as if it is Arcadia, a golden place without worldly occupations." He lifted her hand to his lips, his eyes holding hers. "I should very much like to introduce it to you, Miss Essex. I warrant its beauty will make you forget the moors of Scotland."

The mute invitation in his eyes was unmistakable. "There is a lovely little apple orchard behind the racetrack that has some resemblance to my own orchard, Miss Essex. May I entice you into a short walk in that direction?"

Tess felt as if some sort of paralysis had seized her mind. Did she wish to accept his proposal? Annabel looked around Felton's shoulder; she had a gleam in her eye that confirmed Tess's sense. Mayne was going to offer for her in that orchard. And she should accept. After all, no one else had made a *serious* proposal, and her sisters must be brought out.

"Actually," Mr. Felton interrupted, "I was about to beg Miss Essex to allow me the pleasure of escorting her to the track." He was on his feet again and holding out his hand. "I would like to introduce her to a horse if she has no objection."

"Miss Essex need not put you to the trouble of introducing her to animals," Mayne said with a pointed glance at his friend. "I have already asked her to walk with me."

"*Do* stay here with us," Annabel said to Mr. Felton, her voice a stream of honey.

Tess felt a pulse of exasperation. Didn't their suitors understand that Mr. Felton showed little interest in her as a woman? If they didn't see it, she did. Mayne had ignored all four of the races that had just occurred, but Felton's eyes hardly moved from the track, no matter how handsomely Annabel cajoled him. Felton was quite like her father in that. It was a chilling thought.

As she might have expected, Felton gave his friend a genial smile that made it clear he was in no way poaching on Mayne's territory. "I'll return Miss Essex safe and sound in a mere two minutes. I am considering adding a horse to my stables, and

Miss Essex is a remarkable judge of horseflesh."

Mayne cocked an eyebrow but obviously recognized that the businesslike tone of his friend's voice posed no threat to his courtship. From Tess's point of view, the only thing that differed between Felton's obsession for horses and her father's was that Felton showed some signs of valuing her opinion.

Actually, it would be best if Mayne learned that a wife was not one to be herded hither and yon at his command. "I will return in a mere moment," she said, rising and taking Mr. Felton's arm. She was rewarded with a smile that transformed a face that tended toward bleakness.

Mayne had smiled at her fifteen hundred times in the past hour. Each smile was a caress, an endearment, a signal of his intentions, of his status as her future husband, in truth. Yet Felton's smile left her shaken.

But he has no intention of wooing me, Tess reminded herself. As if to prove her point, he walked directly to the track. "What do you think of that horse?"

It was a gray with dappled spots. As they watched, it took a few big, happy strides before the groom on its back pulled him up short so the horse twitched all over, shook just a bit, causing the groom's knee to pull loose. Tess laughed.

"I thought so too," he said with satisfaction.

She looked up at him. "I haven't said a word."

"*You* read the horse's face. *I* looked at yours."

There was a stinging moment when their eyes met before she turned away. "I should —"

The gray pranced off, to win, she was quite certain of that.

They returned to the box directly. Mr. Felton didn't take her arm, or smile at her again, or make any sign in the least that — that —

"May I take you to the orchards?" Mayne asked as soon as they returned, his voice purring with intention.

Tess looked instinctively at Mr. Felton. For once, he didn't have his opera glasses trained on the track. Instead, he was looking at the two of them, and she knew that he was quite aware of the earl's intentions — and he had no plan whatsoever to counter them.

Instead, he turned away and sat down

next to Annabel, who greeted him with a piece of artful flummery and a chuckle. It seemed to Tess that he turned to her sister with pleasure.

Tess stood up and placed her fingers delicately on the earl's arm. She could feel the weave under her fingers, a wool so delicate and expensive it felt like satin. "I would be most pleased to walk with you," she told him, looking through her eyelashes.

She did not look back at Mr. Felton.

They walked a short distance to an apple tree and paused. It was quite as if she were in a play, really.

Mayne picked her an apple; she graciously accepted. He kissed her hand; she looked into his face. He asked her the question; she assented (quietly dropping the apple). He begged permission, and then brushed a kiss on her cheek. She smiled at him, and he kissed her again, this time on the mouth. It was very pleasant.

She tucked her hand back under his arm, and they walked back, future man and wife.

Or rather, earl and future countess.

Chapter 15

They were all curled on Tess's bed, each with her own bedpost to lean upon, Tess and Josie at the head, Imogen and Annabel at the foot. Josie had a book with her, of course, which she was reading by the candle set on Tess's bedside table.

"I just can't quite believe it," Imogen was saying, staring at Tess as if she had suddenly grown horns. "You're going to be married, Tess. Do you remember how we used to fear that no one would marry us? Here we've been in England less than a week, and you're already affianced to an earl. You should feel quite triumphant."

Tess found herself curiously uncertain when it came to thinking of herself as a married woman; she kept forgetting that the proposal had happened altogether. Definitely she didn't feel triumphant.

"Our worries were connected to Papa's inability to take us to London," Annabel pointed out. "I don't think any of us doubted our marriageability."

"My new governess, Miss Flecknoe, would say that was an utterly improper comment," Josie commented, raising her eyes from her book. "I can say that without hesitation because Miss Flecknoe finds any realistic assessment of relations between men and women improper."

"I have something to say," Imogen said. Her cheeks were flushed rose, and she was hugging her knees.

They all looked over at her, even Josie.

"Draven kissed me. He *kissed* me."

"Are you referring to the falling-out-of-the-apple-tree story, or did you accost the man again?" Josie asked.

Imogen was clearly too happy to bother chastising her little sister. "He kissed me at the races. Out of the blue. I think he's beginning to love me!"

"You show a touching confidence in kisses," Josie said acidly, returning to her book. "Miss Flecknoe wouldn't agree with you. She says that when gentlemen are agreeable they are invariably hiding ulterior motives. Although," she added reflectively, "I'm not at all convinced that Miss Flecknoe has a clear understanding of the motives in question."

"But Imogen, Lord Maitland is promised to Miss Pythian-Adams," Tess said gently.

"You can say what you wish," Imogen said, with a toss of her head. "I asked him to accompany me to the track so that I could watch the horses more closely, and he did —"

"I knew you were behind it somehow," Josie put it.

"The reason we were together is irrelevant," Imogen snapped.

"Don't tell us that your motives were not highly improper," Josie taunted. "Why didn't you go to the stables? You could have tumbled off a hayrack into his arms."

"Josie," Tess remarked, "your tone is rather distasteful."

"We were walking toward the finish line," Imogen said, "and Draven was saying such intelligent things about the horses we passed . . . you can't imagine. I think he knows everything there is about horses. And then he decided to put fifty pounds on a filly in that very race. The bookmaker took his money, and it seemed only a moment later — he'd *won!* And then he kissed me, because he said I was good luck."

Tess bit her lip, trying to think what to say, but Annabel waded in. "Draven Maitland is the very image of Papa, Imogen. Are you quite certain that you would wish to spend the rest of your life talking about fillies and watching your husband throw all the money in the house at the track?"

"He's not in the least like Papa," Imogen said, hugging her knees.

"Actually, I believe Imogen has a point," Josie said. "Father would not have wandered about the track kissing other women after he was promised to mother. He was a man of honor."

"So is Draven! He was simply overcome by emotion," Imogen protested. "He is utterly different from Papa because Draven actually knows what he's doing when he bets. He has a system, you see, and he understands horses in a way that Papa never did."

Tess leaned her head back against the bedpost and stared up at the deep blue canopy above their head. She wondered whether their mother had felt the same about her husband. Imogen's eyes glowed with pride and adoration when she talked of Draven's *system* and his knowledge of horses.

Even Josie seemed momentarily defeated. "Well, just don't forget about Miss Flecknoe's notion of propriety in your further pursuit," she said, but her voice lacked sharpness.

"I gather you *do* intend to pursue Lord Maitland, regardless of Miss Pythian-Adams?" Annabel said, frowning at Imogen.

She raised her chin. "We are meant to be together."

"In that case," Tess said, "you might want to stop being quite so apparent. Don't stare at the poor man so much. I'm sure you make him uncomfortable."

"Stare at someone else," Annabel agreed. "Make eyes at Rafe or Mr. Felton, if you have to. Jealousy can be a powerful motivator in a man. And Josie, please do *not* inform Miss Flecknoe of the particulars of this conversation."

"I will try not to regard Draven more than — than once in a great while," Imogen said. Her tone indicated a certain doubt in her own abilities, but Tess decided to let it pass.

"Tess is marrying the earl," Annabel said briskly. "Imogen is pursuing Lord Maitland, and Josie is happy in the schoolroom."

"Happy is overstating the case," Josie corrected her. "No one could be precisely *happy* with Miss Flecknoe hounding one from morning to night. She's dreadfully fearful about the horrid habits I have developed, because of growing up without a governess."

"Such as what?" Tess asked, with some interest.

"Reading," Josie said with a sniff. "She thinks reading is an anathema. If Miss Flecknoe had any idea that Imogen was accepting kisses from Lord Maitland, she would likely have to do a ritual exorcism."

"Well, one of us must needs grow into a proper and decorous young lady," Annabel said, "and it's too late for the rest of us, so you had better do it. Just to prove my unseemly nature, I might as well tell you that I've been doing little else than think about what Lady Griselda said of Mr. Felton — to be specific, of his fortune — and it's my belief that I am making progress in his esteem."

"You needn't marry Mr. Felton," Tess said. "I'm quite certain that Mayne will sponsor you onto the season, if you don't wish to stay with Rafe and Lady Griselda, who also seem eager to chaperone you."

"Yes, but Mr. Felton is *here*," Annabel said. "What if I find that Lady Griselda is right, and Mr. Felton is the best catch in London, and I've wasted my time?"

"Mr. Felton has no title," Tess pointed out, "and you have been saying for years that a title was of vital importance to you."

"I shouldn't have been so finicky. The truth is that money is the only really important currency in the world."

"I think you should wait for the season," Tess said. "There's no need for such a sacrifice."

"What sacrifice?" Annabel said with an easy shrug. "I am not the sort of woman to find myself hopelessly attracted to a slender, artistic young man, and Mr. Felton has a —"

"Miss Flecknoe would not approve of whatever you are about to say," Josie observed, raising her eyes from her book again.

"Pray, don't repeat it to her," Annabel said. "I was merely going to point out that while I would find it difficult to admire a willowy husband, Mr. Felton's physique is muscular rather than otherwise; his figure is admirable, and he has not lost his hair. And I rather like the tawny-haired look of him. It would be like having a pet lion around the house."

"That's an absurd comment," Josie said. "Mr. Felton in no way resembles one of the great cats. Not that you would know, since none of us has ever seen anything other than a drawing, but he —" She paused. "Well, perhaps a panther. I believe they have that sleek and dangerous look."

Tess bit her lip.

"Unless," Annabel said gently, looking straight at Tess, "you have any particular objection, Tess?"

"Why should she?" Imogen wanted to know.

"Because there is always the chance that Mr. Felton has taken Tess's fancy," Annabel told her. "I thought I saw —"

"You saw nothing," Tess said hastily. "I have no feeling one way or the other for Mr. Felton. Of course, you should marry him."

"Because if Mr. Felton had kissed *you* —" Annabel said.

"It's a good thing Miss Flecknoe isn't here," Josie said. "This whole conversation would be an unpleasant revelation."

"It's just as we said to Imogen," Tess said, looking straight back at Annabel. "Kisses do not indicate a man's inclination to marry. And *if* Mr. Felton had made such an improper gesture toward me —" She raised her hand in Josie's direction. "I said *if*, Josie, so there is no need to make a sarcastic comment, *if* Mr. Felton had offered me a kiss, it matters little, because the Earl of Mayne made his intentions quite clear, did he not?"

Annabel nodded. "I noticed that the earl all but told Felton directly that he was going to propose."

"And Mr. Felton did nothing to stop him," Tess said, dismissing the rather hollow sound in her voice.

"What a disappointment," Annabel said. "No wonder the man has managed to remain single, with that enormous fortune acting as a beacon to every unmarried woman in the British Isles. I expect he will never marry."

Tess did not feel herself able to prophesy on that subject. In fact, even thinking of that subject made her feel queasy.

"If Mr. Felton kissed Tess, and did not offer for her," Annabel continued, giving her sister a sharp glance, "then I shall have nothing to do with him."

Tess rested her chin on her knees and tried not to think about why Annabel's pronouncement made her feel so relieved. After all, *she* herself was promised to an entirely appropriate earl, who — who was entirely appropriate.

"Well, *I* think that Mayne is far more handsome than Mr. Felton," Josie said, putting her book aside.

"I agree," Annabel said promptly.

It was a moment before Tess realized

that they were all looking at her expectantly.

"Oh, so do I!" she said, feeling queerly late on all counts.

Chapter 16

Tess walked down the stairs, her fingers trailing on the polished mahogany of the stair rail. She was wearing Annabel's dark ruby dress, rather than her own blue dress with the more risqué bosom; Annabel would be exposing an exuberant amount of décolletage this evening. Tess obviously had no need for sartorial prodding, since Mayne sprang the question while she was wearing her old riding habit. Clearly, an extra inch of exposed bosom made no difference to him.

When she entered the sitting room, it was to find that Annabel had not yet made her appearance. Neither, for that matter, had anyone else, other than Mr. Felton, who was precisely the person that Tess least wished to see.

He was wearing an exquisite coat of dark, dark green, so dusky it was nearly black. It made Tess wonder how on earth Annabel had missed that air he had: one of command, one that said: I might own the very air you breathe. Really, for someone as driven to marry well as Annabel, she was remarkably unobservant.

"I understand that congratulations are in order," he said, with a deep bow.

But Tess saw no reason for prevarication. "You knew that," she said, giving him a direct look. He could not pretend that he had not known his friend's intentions and, even more, that he had not stepped aside in the most obvious way, at the racecourse.

"You're quite right, of course," Mr. Felton agreed. "I am happy for you and Mayne."

"I suppose relief does make one feel happy," Tess said, wandering over to examine a large walnut cabinet against the wall. It was old, with bow-fronted glass doors, and crammed with what appeared to be ancient silver boxes.

He appeared at her shoulder as she peered through the dappled glass.

"Goodness, you walk quietly!" she said, a little pettishly, looking up at him.

There was something in his eyes. "You turned down my proposal," he said to her. "I assure you that I feel no relief."

"Oh, for goodness' sake," Tess said. "You mustn't pretend that you really meant to ask me to marry you. Imogen is the only one of us who can defend a claim to be experiencing anguish."

"True, I do not feel anguish."

She was learning to read him, even though he was as expressionless as a puppet. He was amused. Tess pulled open a door of the cabinet with rather more force than was called for. "How lovely," she said flatly, pulling out a box for the sake of having something to do.

"My emotions, or the box?"

"The box."

"A marriage box," he told her. "Around a hundred years old, from the looks of it."

"Marriage box?" she repeated stupidly, staring down at the box in her hand. It wasn't much larger than the palm of her hand, engraved with little scenes on all sides. The cover showed a man's hand holding a woman's.

"An old custom," Felton said, pulling off the cover. The box was lined in tired red velvet. "The groom would fill the box with gold coins, I believe, and give it to his bride. You see here" — he pointed to the top — "they hold hands. And here" — he pointed to one side — "they are presumably courting, since he stands below her window. Perhaps he sings to her."

Tess was excruciatingly aware of Mr. Felton's body, just inches from hers. His hair had fallen forward from its normally sleeked-back position and swung on his brow. His hand was much browner than hers, and fully three times as large. As large as his shoulders. And he smelled — oh — wonderful. Not perfumed, just —

"Here," Mr. Felton said, "we probably have a scene from early married life. You see, they are seated at the breakfast table."

"Ah," Tess said, barely paying attention. The box sat in his hand now, the silver glowing against his honeyed skin.

"Surely a fraught occasion," he said, and she caught the thread of amusement in his voice again.

"Why so?"

"One's first breakfast." Their eyes met. "After all, one is so used to eating quite separately. And suddenly, one is faced with a spouse across the table."

"I am not accustomed to eating in a solitary fashion," Tess put in, not quite certain where this conversation was leading. It appeared to have a *double entendre* to it somehow, although she wasn't sure what the second meaning could be. "My sisters are lively breakfast companions."

"A first wedding breakfast is probably quite silent," he said, and there was that strain of wicked laughter in his voice again.

"Fatigued, as they are." He bent his head, pretending to look closer. "Is it my fancy, or is she leaning back against her chair in a posture that could be interpreted as utter . . . exhaustion?"

That was mischief on his face. Tess knew it, even though another person likely would have found his face noncommittal. "I expect you're right," she said, with just the right air of calm. "A tiring day, one's wedding."

"Here —" he said, turning the silver box, "one has a scene approved from ancient times. An allegorical reference."

Tess blinked at it. From what she could see, it depicted a field of rabbits.

"A fertility talisman," his voice said, deep and certainly amused. "Rabbits are so very prolific."

"Poor woman," Tess said tartly, putting the little top back onto the box. "Rabbits!"

"But you do wish to have children, don't you, Miss Essex?" He was putting the box back into the cabinet and not looking at her.

"Why did you kiss me in that Roman bath?" she asked impulsively.

His hand froze, and then he withdrew it and closed the cabinet. He countered with his own question: "Are all Scotswomen like yourself, Miss Essex?"

"Naturally," she said, raising one eyebrow, just in Lady Griselda's manner.

"I wished to kiss you," he said. His eyes were a fierce blue. "I simply wished to, Miss Essex. Naturally, I know that a gentlemen never bows to such an impulse, but —"

Tess held her breath, not thinking, not breathing, not moving.

His hands curled around her shoulders. His head bent, and his mouth pressed against hers. It was frustrating. She had always, rather dimly, thought of horses and men in the same way. She knew in a moment when her father was irritated, or exhausted, or fairly choking with choler, before he even spoke. It was all written on his face. But Mr. Felton's tight grip over his expression was aggravating. Exasperating, even.

But his mouth spoke to her. She could taste something simmering under his kiss. Desire? She knew little of that famed emotion. But his kiss scorched. It talked of — something.

Tess was feeling a little dazed, a little dizzy. Very curious. So she opened her mouth to ask any number of things. Why are you kissing me? Another good question: why are you kissing your friend's betrothed? A third: why did you let me go? But she was casting about for a less plaintive way to formulate that question . . .

She opened her mouth to try, but he was there. Kissing Felton was like talking to someone who showed more expression on his face, Tess thought dimly. She could taste everything he was thinking: hunger, desire, a fierceness that made her shake, made her knees feel weak, made her yearning and bold all at once.

"Tess," he said, his voice dark as midnight. She didn't answer. He growled it: *"Tess."*

She broke away from his mouth and looked up at him. Her mouth was stung to a lush red, her eyes rather dazed — and yet, there was no timid virgin's fear in her eyes.

"Yes?" she gasped.

And Lucius couldn't think what he wanted to ask her. Of course, he had to say that they could not kiss. That he was a man of honor, and she a gently born lady, and yet he was nothing more than a loathsome snake to kiss his friend's betrothed.

But the words all died in his throat, because there was something in her eyes, a sultry question.

"I cannot offer you enough," he said to her, forcing his body to stay still and not gather her into his arms again. "I once asked a lady to marry me, but I recognized the truth to it before we wed. I haven't the heart for marriage."

"The heart? Are you in love, then?"

Her face had wiped clear of those traces of sultry pleasure and turned to polite inquiry, as if she were questioning the reasons behind his attachment to carrots, rather than cabbage.

"I never have felt that emotion. I do not seem to feel as deeply as many men." There was no kinder way to put it. "Someone like yourself, Tess, you deserve a man who will love you with passion of soul as well as of body."

The fire in her eyes was banked now. They were slightly narrowed, thinking. He felt an awful longing to give in and marry her. To tell her that he would take her away from Mayne and keep her for himself, and the devil with what she expected, or deserved in the way of emotion.

"Don't give it a thought," she told him with an airy wave. "I did not say that I wished to marry you. In fact, as I recall, I already refused your request." Her voice was light, a trifle amused.

Lucius's back stiffened. He had actually spoken aloud his deepest fear, that he had only shallow emotions at his command, and she laughed at him?

She did. That luscious red mouth curved upward even as he watched her face.

"Do you always assume that young ladies are so ardent to marry you, sir?"

She had a dimple in her right cheek. Lucius felt a feverish wave of rage. He should kiss that supercilious laughter from her face. "It was, perhaps, a natural error on my part," he said with a savage edge. "I am not used to young ladies who kiss with such enthusiasm as you do. But England is, of course, a hidebound culture in comparison to our neighbors to the north."

Tess's heart was beating so quickly that she could scarcely breathe; it was taking all the control she could command to keep her face as expressionless as his. "I fear that it is true that Scottish ladies are unlikely to beg you to marry them, sir." She patted his arm. "Luckily, from what you say, there are Englishwomen who will take on the task." The slight tone of disbelief in her voice was exquisitely pitched to indicate utter unbelievability.

"I see," Lucius said, bowing. "I have been inexcusably rude. I apologize."

"I do think that Mayne may be rather less than pleased with your affability toward his affianced wife," Tess observed. Her heart was slowing, and she was beginning to feel chilly.

He bowed again. "I will offer him my apologies."

Tess looked at him and felt another surge of rage. How *dare* he kiss her, and then announce that he wasn't fit for marriage? And all the time he was doing nothing more than making her unfit for her very appropriate marriage to the earl? How dare he? "Please don't bother with apologies," she said airily, drifting away from him. "I consider this nothing more than a — a taradiddle. There's naught important about it." When she was beside herself, just a hint of Scottish rhythm slipped in her voice, for all their father had coached that accent away.

And when he spoke, his voice had deepened to a dangerous purr. "Whether I inform my friend that his wife is a light-heeled wench . . . now there's a moral question, wouldn't you say?"

Tess turned in a swirl of her skirts. She had caught sight of herself in a great gold-leafed mirror to the side of the room. Her color was high, her eyes were glittering, and her bosom looked magnificent. "You must please yourself, sir."

"Please myself?" He was beside her again, staring down at her. "Please myself, Tess?"

"Yes," she said, suddenly seeing a double meaning there.

She knew, and he knew, what was about to happen.

"I *shall* please myself, then," he said.

"Yes," she whispered.

He pulled her slowly up against his chest and pressed his mouth over hers. For a moment Tess was too startled by the aching heat in her body, her instant response to his touch, to notice more than that. But then she found that this time he tasted of anger and frustration. Of desire too, of course.

But the frustration — yes. And hurt too. She'd hurt him. He was punishing her mouth for it now, as if he knew that his kisses were likely to make her deranged, a fit punishment . . . for what?

"I didn't mean to hurt your feelings," she said into his lips. It was as if the words formed in his mouth rather than hers. Somehow her hands had found their way to his chest, and she could feel his heart beating under her palm.

Of course she couldn't read anything in his face. "There is no question of that," he said.

But Tess had discovered something very important about kisses — about kissing Lucius Felton, anyway. Kisses were like horse's faces: they didn't lie. She knew it with the same instinct that told her that the weakness in the back of her knees, and the ragged way her breath felt in her chest signaled trouble. "I apologize for dismissing your reasons for remaining a bachelor," she said, backing away.

He bowed but said nothing. The gleam of frustrated longing was gone from his eyes. There was nothing to be read in his face but a kind of well-bred indifference.

The door opened, and Lady Griselda rushed into the room in a babble of words. "Tess, darling!" she cried. "You will be wretched at my news, but my brother has hied off to London on an errand. He will do his very best to return in time for dancing this evening."

"Dancing?" Tess asked, feeling not in the least wretched at the news of her betrothed's departure.

"Merely an informal affair amongst ourselves," Lady Griselda said, "ourselves and the Maitlands, of course. I asked Brinkley to find us a trio or some such, and the estimable man has done just that." Sure enough, footmen had followed her and were beginning to clear a dancing floor toward the end of the long sitting room.

Tess suddenly remembered Griselda's plan to arrange waltzing, and thereby encourage a proposal from Mr. Felton. The relief she felt on remembering Annabel's decision *not* to woo Mr. Felton was quite out of proportion.

He had moved away from them and was staring out the window at the dark courtyard. She could see his face reflected in the dark glass: a lucid, austere face. The face of a man who valued restraint and breeding.

That was no angel, as she'd thought on first seeing him.

Chapter 17

A moment later, the room was crowded. Lady Clarice and Miss Pythian-Adams entered, cooing over Miss Pythian-Adams's reticule; Imogen followed with her hand on Rafe's arm. She appeared to be regarding him with a doting expression, perhaps in an effort to force Lord Maitland into jealousy as Annabel had suggested. Rafe looked rather desperate. He probably needed a drink. Imogen could be overwhelming, as Tess knew well.

"I have arranged for a lovely surprise!" Lady Griselda was telling Lady Clarice with great enthusiasm. "A small orchestra. After all, dancing is the food of the gods, as Shakespeare said." She stopped for a moment. "Or is music the food of the gods? I always forget."

Lady Clarice put an arm on Miss Pythian-Adams's arm. "My dear, if you would be so kind?"

"If music be the food of love, play on," Miss Pythian-Adams said obediently. "*Twelfth Night.*"

"What an accomplished young woman you are," Lady Griselda said, as Lady Clarice beamed like a proud mother.

Miss Pythian-Adams simpered at her, and said, "*Give me excess of it, that, surfeiting, the appetite may sicken, and so die.* Still *Twelfth Night.*" In diametrical opposite to her behavior of a few days ago, she was clinging to her betrothed's arm. "You, sir, would make a wonderful Duke Orsino," she told Maitland. "When we are married, it will be my first action to stage the entire play with yourself in the leading role!"

"Memorizing isn't my forte," Maitland stated. Tess had no doubt but that he was absolutely correct.

"Ah, but memorization is so *easy!*" Miss Pythian-Adams cried. "Why, I know all of Duke Orsino's speeches." She let go of his arm and struck a declamatory pose. "*That strain again! It had a dying fall. Ooooooo, it came o'er my ear like the sweet sound, that breathes upon a bank of violets, stealing and giving odor.*"

Tess watched for another moment before she realized what was happening. Miss Pythian-Adams had obviously decided to use heavy artillery on her betrothed, a fine effort to make him cry off owing to an excess of poetry.

"I shall recite your speeches to you each afternoon, nay, evening as well. Within a month or so, you'll come to breathe Shakespeare like the very air!" she promised him.

To Tess's mind there was a very palpable air of dislike about the way Maitland looked down at his future wife, but at that moment there was a twang of tuning instruments from the far end of the room.

"We couldn't possibly dance before supper," Lady Clarice stated, waving a fan before her face.

"Of course we can!" Lady Griselda said gaily. "You mustn't start *feeling* old, Lady Clarice darling. Before you know it, you'd *be* old!"

Lady Clarice bared her teeth in what might have passed for a smile amongst a family of jackals.

Rafe came over to Tess clutching a glass of brandy. "Why is your sister Imogen acting in this fashion?" he hissed at her.

"Why, what do you refer to?" Tess asked, widening her eyes.

"You know precisely what I'm talking about," he said. On the side of the room Imogen began waving her hand, and saying, "Rafe! Oooooh, Rafe!"

"I see nothing amiss with my sister's deportment," Tess observed, resisting a strong impulse to laugh.

Rafe cast a haunted look over his shoulder. "Call her off, Tess."

"I can't," Tess said, casting prudence to the winds. He was their guardian, after all. He must do his part in protecting Imogen from Maitland.

"Why not?" Rafe snapped, draining his glass.

"I wish her to avoid Maitland," Tess said in a low voice.

"Does that mean she has to haunt me? I feel as if I'm a nice stuffed duck, and she's about to take out a fork."

"Think of it as part of your guardian duties," Tess advised. And, when Rafe opened his mouth to argue, she said, "She must save face in front of Maitland, Rafe!"

He stopped, mouth open. "Ah."

"Lady Clarice is not happy with my sister's feelings toward her son," Tess said, in a voice so low even she could hardly hear it.

"Ah."

Rafe was not the slowest gentleman whom she had ever met, but he was definitely vying for a place amongst the imperceptive. He made a kind of snorting sound and took himself off, she hoped in Imogen's direction.

There weren't enough gentlemen for all to engage in dancing, so Tess found herself watching first a Rufty Tufty for two couples, and then a waltz. Annabel's bosom was about to fall from the fragile constraint of Tess's dress. And for all Annabel had announced a disinclination to marry Mr. Felton, she was smiling up at him in a way that suggested she might change her mind.

"We shall dance again after supper," Lady Griselda called to Tess, "and you shall join us, darling. By then, my brother may have returned from London!" She gave her such a meaningful smile that Tess suddenly understood why Mayne was absent.

He had gone to London to fetch a ring. Probably a ring from his family. A symbol of their future marriage, of his possession, of their — affection for each other.

The music played on, but Tess walked around the edge of the room and slipped out the door.

She walked down the corridor, wishing nothing more than to return to their simple life in Scotland where there wasn't any silk to turn her favorite sister into a shimmering siren capable of drawing the attention of any man for miles around, let alone Mr. Felton from London. Back to her father's house, where there weren't any polished marble or polished rosewood or polished smiles. Tears pricked her eyes. There was a sudden swell of music as the door to the sitting room behind her opened.

Tess turned sharply, opened a door to her right, and slipped in. It was a small room that must have been used as a music room at some point. There was a harp standing in the corner and a large chair with a bass viol leaning against it. A tiny harpsichord was jammed against one wall. The far end of the room was a recessed window, framed in drapes of scarlet velvet.

Tess walked over to the window seat tucked into the alcove and looked down. The stones in the courtyard were polished with rain, making them look sleek and hazy in the twilight. She swallowed hard. What had she to cry about? She was about to marry a man who professed fascination with her face and admiration for her character. And that — she reminded herself — was more than enough as a foundation for marriage. Never mind the fact that sometimes all his flowery compliments made Mayne sound like an empty-headed *fool* —

Could she have even thought of that word in terms of her future husband?

Tess shook her head. She had to remember how lucky she was. Her sisters were quite likely to make brilliant marriages; if Annabel married the richest man in all England, no one could be more happy than she. Right?

There was a sudden noise at the door, and Tess was horrified to find that tears were snaking down her cheeks. She pulled the velvet curtains closed, sheltering her window seat from the room, hoping that the intruder would simply peek into the room and leave.

The door opened and then closed again. Footsteps walked across the room. The note from one plucked harp string trembled on the air. She swallowed and scrubbed away another tear. The room was papered in exuberant apple trees. She tried to breathe silently, leaned her head against the paper orchard and told herself that she would be perfectly happy to stay here all evening. It was irritating to watch Annabel seduce Mr. Felton. Irritating, that's all.

Then the curtain was plucked aside and she jumped to her feet.

Of course, she knew who it was. She'd known from the moment he entered the room, even if she was pretending to herself that she didn't know.

His eyes were very dark, looking down into hers. "Hello."

Tess said nothing.

"I appear to be following you wherever you go."

Tess suddenly felt as if her whole body were alive, the blood thrumming through her body with reckless haste, making her head feel slightly dizzy. She still said nothing, watching the way that his eyes crinkled slightly at the corners.

"I suppose you think that I'll kiss you again," he said.

Speak, Tess thought to herself. "You have shown a marked propensity for that particular activity, Mr. Felton," she observed.

"True," he muttered. He didn't look quite so impervious now, so expressionless. There was something puzzled in his eyes.

He moved toward her, silently, like a cat. Tess pressed back against the wall and concentrated on breathing. His mouth — his body — was very close to hers. But she refused to look away.

"I won't kiss you again, Tess," he said to her. "You belong to someone else. I wouldn't want it to become a habit."

Disappointment coursed to the tips of her fingertips. "Habits can be disagreeable," she agreed, dropping her eyes.

"After all, you *have* agreed to marry another," he prompted, watching her sooty lashes against her cheek.

There was a sudden noise at the door. He moved even closer to her, until the velvet curtain at his shoulder swung free, and they were both hidden in the curtained alcove. Obviously, protection of Tess's reputation demanded that he stand so close to her that no one knew they were unchaperoned.

A woman began speaking in rushed, emphatic tones on the other side of the curtain.

The room was as busy as the Royal Exchange: not that Lucius cared. It was quite dusky as the sky darkened through the window, but he could see the cream of Tess's cheek, curving down to her small chin. The shadow of her eyelashes. The way she seemed to disappear into stillness, holding herself quiet with the concentration of a cat.

He bent over her deliberately and put his mouth to her ear. "Of course," he said, under the babble of the voice behind him, "*you* could kiss *me*."

Tess's mouth curved into a reluctant smile. She was beginning to listen to the conversation taking place outside the curtain.

A man — not any man, but Draven Maitland — was talking now. "Do you mind telling me precisely why you dragged me into this room, Miss Pythian-Adams? My mother wouldn't approve."

"I must speak to you. As I just explained to you, Lord Maitland."

There was a heavy sigh.

"I am proposing," Miss Pythian-Adams said painstakingly, "that you inform your mama that we are not suited."

"But I don't think we are unsuited," Maitland said, sounding profoundly uninterested. "I'm sure we'll rub along fine together. You have your — your Shakespeare and the like, and I have my pursuits. There's no doubt I would prefer a little less poetry, especially during meals. It puts me off my beef, but I don't mind it in other places."

"We will not be happy together. *I* shall not be happy."

There was a silence while Maitland digested her statement. "If you feel that way, you'd better call it off," he said, without a shadow of remorse in his voice.

"I can't," she snapped. "You know as well as I do that your mother is holding the papers to my father's estate."

"As far as that goes, my mother has made it quite clear that she'll cut off the funding to my stables if I throw you over. So I'm afraid, m'dear, that we're destined for the altar."

"But Lord Maitland —"

"There's no point in further discussing it," he said, interrupting her without ceremony. "I've no particular aversion to marrying you — told my mama so when she picked you out. And you agreed to do the pretty as well. So we might as well go through with it, because things will be unpleasant if we don't."

"Haven't you any sensibility?" she gasped.

"None," he said without hesitation.

"You would be a great deal happier with Imogen Essex. She shares your interest in horses. And more importantly — she *loves* you!"

"I've noticed that." A thread of pride crept into Maitland's tone. "But she'll have to find someone else."

"Won't you mind dreadfully?"

Another silence, then: "Not particularly." Tess wished Imogen were in the room. There was something profoundly convincing about Lord Maitland's answer. He truly wouldn't mind if Imogen married another man.

"Miss Imogen has a horse for a dowry," Miss Pythian-Adams noted, trying another avenue. "I gather the animal in question is quite famous. I'm sure he would be a notable addition to your stables."

"Enough," Lord Maitland said. "My mama has her heart set on my marrying you. And while Imogen is beautiful enough, she'd make an uncomfortable wife. I can only take that sort of emotion in very short doses. I expect you and I will suit each other well enough. Imogen would expect an entirely different level of devotion on my part."

Lucius's fingers touched Tess's lips just as she was about to explode from the recessed window.

But Miss Pythian-Adams had not given up. "I'm amazed you aren't ashamed to be so tied to your mother's apron strings," she said, her voice generously lashing on scorn. "And what pleasure *I* have to look forward to in my married life! Why, I always meant to marry a milksop man, driven hither and thither by his mama's hold on the purse strings. I assure you, it has long been my *deepest* desire!"

"Well, if you ain't a tallow-faced witch," Maitland observed, sounding (for the first time) a bit nettled.

"Precisely," Miss Pythian-Adams returned coldly. "I expect it will do my temper no end of good to be married to a man as shallow and easily driven as yourself. After all, the cure for any shrew is to be given her way at all times. Once I control the household, you shall have to curb your gambling. I am quite certain that your mother will give me control of the household funds. She is *so* fond of me."

Although Miss Pythian-Adams paused, Maitland said nothing.

"Your poor, dear mother," she continued, "What a remarkable situation it is, to find a dowager so entirely in control of the estate. Yet one can hardly disagree with your father's judgment in that regard. And your mother undoubtedly agrees: she seems to have a particularly unambiguous doubt in your ability to keep two guineas in the same pocket without putting one out on a bet."

"You're hiding your real character under all that cultural twaddle. You've tricked my mother!" Maitland sounded utterly stunned. Mr. Felton's eyes were gleaming with laughter.

"You've — you've tricked *me!*" Maitland gulped.

"Since I have the choice of being shrewish versus cultured, would you like to bet on which of my characteristics rule once we are married?" There was the sound of a door being pulled open and a rapid exit.

Lucius's mouth was at Tess's ear. "Do you think they both left?" he breathed.

His hand was on her back. It felt warm, even through her gown, almost scorching. It was most distracting to feel a shuddering wish that he would pull her even closer.

"Hush!" Sure enough, a moment later they heard the scrape of a boot, and then the protesting squeal of a harp string being snapped, leaving a screeching little echo in the air. The door opened again, and then slammed shut.

Lucius's hand dropped from her back. "The auspices for that particular match are not altogether blissful," he said. He had made no attempt to move away from her, or to open the velvet curtain. "Miss Pythian-Adams appears to believe that Lord Maitland never progressed intellectually after age eleven."

"One would be foolish not to agree with her," Tess said. "If only I were certain that

Maitland wouldn't turn to my little sister in despair, I would celebrate her effort to break free."

"Dear me," Lucius said. "An unexpectedly bloodthirsty vein emerges in the placid Miss Essex."

"I am not placid," Tess protested.

"Oh yes, you are," he said, sounding amused. "Always watching and thinking about others, aren't you. Observing."

"That cannot be construed as a complimentary description of my behavior," Tess said.

"No, no." His finger ran slowly down her cheek. "I merely noted that you are, by nature, an observer. Watching it all go by rather than rushing into the fray yourself."

Tess frowned. "You seem to be offering me an oblique insult," she observed, reaching toward the curtain. "I shall certainly —"

But his hand stopped hers before she could pull back the velvet. And suddenly he had both her hands, pulling her palms to his mouth.

Instantly her heart began to thunder again. "Am I wrong then?" he asked, watching her intently.

"Of course you are," Tess said. But she had lost track of the argument.

"Do you not simply accept what happens to you: my kisses, Mayne's proposal of marriage . . ."

"And what else can I do?" Tess said, staring up at him. She didn't even try to take her hands away. "You kiss me for some sort of diversion that I don't quite understand. But you show no real wish to marry me. The Earl of Mayne does wish to marry me —"

"Also due to some desire that you don't quite understand?" Lucius murmured, kissing each palm in turn.

"Perhaps," she managed. "As the eldest, it is my duty to marry so that my sisters can have their seasons. I see my actions as arising not from lethargy, but from common sense. *You* seem to be suggesting actions that would arise from a disproportionate romanticism. That, sir, is not in my nature." And this time, when she pulled away her hands, he let them go. They tingled from his kisses. She left the alcove and skirted the harp, its broken string trailing to the ground.

She could feel his gaze burning into her back, so she turned, on the very edge of opening the door. "I don't know what sort of actions you expect from me!" she said with exasperation. "Are you implying that

I should have run wailing to Rafe because you have occasionally kissed me in a hurly-burly fashion? I am not a child, sir! Or are you thinking that I should have accepted your oh-so-reluctant proposal of marriage? Would that somehow count as less lethargic than accepting the earl?"

"Only if you wanted to marry me," he said.

She ignored that question. "Your proposal was reluctantly given."

"So that is the criterion for your acceptance: genuine enthusiasm? You accept my kisses because I am genuinely enthusiastic about giving them? And you accept Mayne's hand in marriage because —" He paused.

She nodded and turned to go. "Precisely. He genuinely wishes to marry me. Perhaps you overestimate how much command a lady has over her future, Mr. Felton. As I see it, the best I can do is observe who is authentic in his attentions, and choose that man."

She left Lucius staring at the door, a faint smile playing around his mouth.

For all Tess spent her life observing, she was being damned unobservant at the moment.

Chapter 18

If there was one thing in the world that Imogen loved better than Draven Maitland, it was her own horse, Posy. For a time, Posy had been Papa's favorite. Her ears had perked back and forth as she listened to the stream of affection coming from his lips, telling her that she had beautiful legs and the withers of a winner. But Papa quickly grew disillusioned with Posy. She liked to canter, not gallop, especially during races. In short, she was lazy.

"She doesn't want it," Papa had said in disgust one day. And after that he walked past Posy's stall with just an absentminded pat on the nose, never noticing the way her dark glossy eyes grew sad to see him whisper and chuckle to Balladino, whom he had begun grooming to make their fortunes.

Imogen waited until Balladino won his first race (that was before the poor horse collided head-on with another horse during training and strained a fetlock). When

Papa was in the glow of the winner's circle, she asked if she might have Posy for her very own, and because the dibs were in tune that particular day, he said yes. It took only a few weeks for Posy to start whickering for Imogen, rather than for her father. Imogen never visited the stables without bringing her a treat and staying to rub her nose.

Thoroughbreds could be mean. Imogen had seen her papa's prize horse, Patchem, watching, watching, watching. He knew she was afraid of him. He would wait until she wasn't expecting it and chomp on her hair, or catch her coat in his yellow teeth. Posy would never think of such a thing. She had a whiskery nose, and she loved to put her chin on Imogen's shoulder and huff into her hair and snuffle a bit while Imogen leaned against her and smelled her horsy smell.

In short, Imogen loved Posy, and if she couldn't have the man who made her knees weak and her head swirl . . . at least she had Posy.

"Oh, Posy," she whispered into the horse's mane. Posy whickered softly and slobbered a bit on Imogen's arm.

"Would you like a saddle on her, miss?" The stable master, who'd introduced himself as Ridley, was standing at the door to the stall. He was a tall, overly thin man missing a quantity of teeth. Oddly enough, his lack of teeth only made his smile more cheerful.

"Yes, I would, thank you, Ridley."

Ridley led Posy into the yard and nimbly threw a saddle over her. "I'll have a groom saddled in a moment, miss."

"Groom?" Imogen asked.

Ridley nodded, tightening Posy's cinch.

"Must I?" Imogen asked. "I'm quite used to taking Posy out on my own."

Ridley thought about it for a moment. "It won't do in London, of course," he said to her. "A young lady mustn't be seen alone. But perhaps if you were to stay on His Grace's land, you're unlikely to meet another. But I'd feel more comfortable sending a groom out with you, or perhaps your maid?"

"I don't want a groom or my maid," Imogen said firmly. There had been an early frost the night before, and the cobblestones had glittered beneath her boots as she walked to the stables. The early-morning air was chilly and promised to take away the aching misery of watching Lady Clarice blather on about Miss Pythian-Adams while Draven passively accepted his future marriage. "I'll go alone," she said again.

Ridley nodded with obvious reluctance. "His Grace's land goes as far as the eye can see to the south, and to that ridge of trees to the west. Past there is Maitland land," he said. "Don't go north, because the Woolly River can be treacherous if you don't know precisely where it's cutting through. We've had men tumble right down her banks. If you'll just tell me your direction, miss, I can send someone after you if you don't return."

Imogen looked at him and saw the firm set of his jaw. "I'll — I'll go west," she said with a deep breath. Of course, west was the direction of her heart. West was Draven. West was — "I'll go west, and I should be back in an hour. Posy has a mind of her own, and she doesn't like cold weather very much."

"You'll be chilled yourself if you're out much longer than that," Ridley said, tossing her up on Posy.

Her horse shook her head and pawed the ground. Imogen smiled down at Ridley. "Posy is not the sort to make a run for the river, Ridley."

"I'd still feel more comfortable if you had an escort," Ridley said, giving Posy a bit of carrot. “Don’t go too far now, miss.”

They clopped out the gate and turned into a field. This field, and probably another, and then it would be Draven’s land, Imogen thought. Posy was picking her way through cow parsnip crystallized into fantastic curls by ice. The morning sky was chilly blue, not the gray that promised snow, but a high, arching sky that would turn warm by noon.

Of course she could live without Draven. Of course she could. It was only that he was so very — so very —

She couldn’t finish the thought. He was so very *everything:* so beautiful that her heart hurt to look at him, and her head felt dizzy. So entrancing to hear speak, that she could listen to him talk of races and bets and things that, coming from her father’s mouth, bored her to tears.

Posy was wandering through the field. Imogen made up her mind not to allow a single tear to fall because it would probably freeze on the spot. She could feel her nose growing red.

“Let’s go a little faster, Posy,” she urged, and clapped her foot against the mare’s belly.

Posy snorted and sped up slightly. They began trotting along through the field, and then Posy stretched into a canter, clomping through a stubble field of barley stalks caught with silver ribbons of dew.

The world was silent but for the sound of Posy's hooves. She probably should turn back, but instead . . . Imogen guided Posy through a barrier of thin white birch, onto Draven's land. Her heart was beating so quickly that she could hear its thumps in her ears. Posy shook her halter. Clearly, *she* thought they'd been outside long enough.

"Just one second, Posy," Imogen said, patting her neck. Posy pawed the ground and shook her halter again. She was sweaty after their brief run, and Imogen knew she had to bring the mare back to the stables before she grew chilled. Besides, there was nothing to be seen. No Draven, just a huge stone house that sat squarely in the chilly sunshine, looking ancient, and monied, and all the things that made her an ineligible bride for Draven.

Imogen sighed. She and Posy walked closer, to the very edge of the gardens stretching before the house. The heroine of a book that she and Tess read last summer had walked across the fields toward a neighbor's manor, shivering the whole way, and then managed to take ill. That girl was smart enough to come down with an influenza that led to her and her sister staying in the manor for a number of weeks, even though they were poor and quite ineligible to marry the gentlemen who lived there. Imogen sniffed tentatively, but she had shockingly good health and showed no sign of growing ill. Besides, were she ill, she had a feeling that Draven's mama would simply toss her into the carriage and send her back to Rafe's house.

Posy pawed the ground again and even reared up a bit, expressing extreme displeasure.

"Stop that," Imogen said to her. "Ridley would be shocked by your behavior!"

Posy reared again and the world tilted backward as Imogen automatically adjusted her leg even more firmly in her saddle.

Suddenly an idea darted into her head. A twisted ankle. If only she fell from Posy, she would be certain to injure *something*, Posy being such a tall horse. Actually, she wouldn't even really have to injure anything.

Blinking, she looked down at the ground. Tess wouldn't approve. Tess would think she was cracked for even having such a thought. But then Draven's face crept into her mind, the way he'd looked at her so tenderly last night. If only she had more time with him. She was certain she could win his heart even though Miss Pythian-Adams was irritatingly beautiful.

And before the thought even left her mind, she relaxed the reins and Posy took immediate advantage, rearing high in the air and pawing just like a foolish Thoroughbred. Imogen automatically shortened the reins. And just as suddenly, she let go of them. A second later she was flying through the crisp air, the birch trees a dizzying whirl of black branches before her eyes.

And slamming into the hard ground, before she even had time to remember that she meant to stop being so reckless.

Within a second of hitting the ground, she knew that she wouldn't have to pretend to have an injury. Her right ankle was throbbing as if someone had poured boiling water on it. Posy turned around and looked at her, and she whispered in a rough voice, "Go! Go to the house!"

Posy ambled over to her curiously, but Imogen was too busy cursing her own stupidity and remembering how much she didn't like pain, to say anything other than, "Go there, go there, Posy!"

Posy turned a head and looked at the great stone house. Finally, she loped off in that direction. Imogen could only hope that she didn't head back to Scotland.

It hurt. It really hurt. If her father were there, he would say, "Bite your lip, darrrling." He always called her darling. Well, he called all the horses and all his daughters *darling*. But even so . . .

Imogen let tears slide down her face. Papa never stopped her from loving Draven. He only said to her, once, "He's not a likely sort to marry a Scottish lass, darling."

And she had said to him, "He *has* to marry me, Papa, he has to. He's my true love."

But even by the time she'd finished those two sentences, she could tell that Papa had started thinking of something else, likely something in the stables. "Right you are, then, darling," he had said, and given her an absentminded hug.

"Don't you agree with me, Papa?" she had asked anxiously.

"Of course," he had said. And even though she knew that he was thinking of liniment, or apple-mash, or something to do with a horse rather than a daughter, she took it as approval.

In fact, her father's agreement was paramount to a parental blessing, as Imogen thought about it now. She braced herself on her hands and tried to ignore the pain blossoming in her knee. What happened to the simple, elegant sprained ankle she had pictured?

But now she could see a little stirring at the front of the house. She squinted in that direction. She was starting to feel ashamed. She was too reckless. *High-spirited,* Papa had called it. But she couldn't pretend to herself that high-spirited was a compliment, not when her leg was throbbing in such a fashion. Stupid was more like it.

A boy in livery ran across the gardens toward her. She waved at him, rather feebly, and he turned around directly and ran back to the house. Imogen sighed. If she didn't learn her lesson from this dimwitted foolishness, she might as well give up a claim to maturity.

Chapter 19

Draven carried her in the front door, past a gaggle of servants. "My mother is in the sitting room," he told her.

Imogen laid her head against his shoulder. He was almost carrying her just with one arm; that was how strong he was. His coat was made of the softest wool she had ever felt in her life. She felt an overwhelming urge to memorize the moment — the way he kept looking down at her, the strength of his arms around her, even the way her leg sent bolts of pain up her knee.

"Miss Imogen has suffered an accident and hurt her ankle," Draven was saying to his mother.

"Her ankle?" Lady Clarice said, in a high, wondering voice. "How did such a thing happen?"

"I fell from my horse," Imogen said. "I simply . . . fell from my horse." She was starting to wonder whether she wasn't more affected by the accident than she thought. She had the oddest sensation in her head. But she *never* fainted. Never.

"Goodness sakes," Lady Clarice said. "We must return her to Holbrook Court immediately so that she can be seen by a doctor. Have you called for the carriage, dear? And perhaps you should send a footman ahead to inform the duke of his ward's unfortunate mishap."

There was a distinct iciness in her voice. Imogen listened to the strong beating of Draven's heart. She didn't even care if she were sent home directly, like an errant kitchen maid. Draven had carried her in his arms. It was enough.

"We can't do that," Draven snapped. "I've told Hilton to summon Dr. Wells and have her seen immediately. We have no way of ascertaining whether she should be moved."

"Pshaw! A silly little fall like that!" Lady Clarice said, and there was a definite edge to her voice now. "I am persuaded that Miss Imogen would never wish to dis-accommodate us, dearest. Miss Pythian-Adams and I intend to leave for London tomorrow! You are due to leave with me, if you remember. You can hardly send your betrothed to London without you."

"Mother, naturally you may do as you

wish," Draven said, his tone far stronger than Imogen had ever heard him address his mother. "But Miss Imogen cannot be moved until she has seen a doctor. Why, if she's seriously injured her ankle, she may not be able to ride again."

"Quite likely she won't ride again!" Lady Clarice said. "She's been tossed to the ground. What lady would return to a horse after an event of that nature?"

"A lady who cared for more than the sound of her own voice," Draven snapped. "Miss Imogen is not the kind of woman to be frightened by a mere spill."

"I'm fine," Imogen managed, gathering her woolly wits. Really, what *was* the matter with her? She felt unaccountably dizzy. She was ceasing to enjoy being in Draven's arms as the world felt more and more unsteady. "I should like to stand up, please, Lord Maitland."

"Yes, do put her down," Lady Clarice said crossly. "This is all quite, quite provoking. *Not* that it's your fault," she said to Imogen, with obvious insincerity.

Draven carefully put Imogen on her feet. Imogen smiled at Lady Clarice, and began to bend her knee automatically to drop into a curtsy.

Fire rushed down her knee. The world

turned black, and gray spots swam before her eyes.

Then Miss Imogen Essex, for the first time in her life, fainted dead away.

Alas, she didn't faint gracefully into Draven's waiting arms, as she had pictured in the field.

Neither did she faint rather more usefully into the sofa to her left.

Instead, she pitched forward into Lady Clarice, who promptly shrieked and (by all reports) plunged to the ground like a tree felled by lightning.

Chapter 20

Imogen knew nothing of Lady Clarice's ignominious fall, nor of the hysterics prompted by that untoward event. Nor did she know of the doctor who arrived, prodded her knee, and shook his head. Nor of the notes Lady Clarice reluctantly sent off to London and the brief conversation between Draven and his betrothed. She didn't wake up when Tess bent over her bed and called to her, nor yet when Annabel pinched her toe, hard. She had no idea that Josie stood at the bottom of the bed, burst into tears, and howled that Imogen looked just like Papa and, therefore, she was sure to die.

In fact, Imogen missed a whole procession of people at her bedside. "It's my fault," her guardian said, looking down at her. Imogen was startlingly beautiful, lying against the white sheets. Yet even Rafe, who hadn't known her very long, was shocked by how different she appeared without the spark of passionate life that shone in her eyes.

"Nonsense," Tess said from the other side of the bed. "What the devil have you to do with it?"

"I should have informed her that in England young ladies do not ride without a groom," Rafe said miserably.

"And what difference would that have made, pray? Imogen has always ridden like the wind. She's like our father in that. A groom could not have stopped that wretched Posy from dropping my sister in a ditch. I've no question but that Imogen was probably riding her too hard. If you wish to make yourself useful, try to sweeten Lady Clarice. I'm afraid she's sadly out of frame."

"I shall do my best," Rafe promised. "I am sending my man to London to fetch a specialist, then I'll return to Lady Clarice."

He stood for a moment longer, thinking about what trouble this particular ward of his was and feeling a flash of guilt at the very thought. He circled the bed and took Tess's hands. "Imogen will be all right," he said. "The doctor found no sign of a head injury. She will wake up. I am sorry, Tess. This must bring memories of your father's death."

Tess's mouth wobbled. Her chest felt so

constricted by fear and anger that she couldn't even answer.

He squeezed her hand, then left.

Tess had arrived at the house quite certain that she would find Imogen instituting a prank, playing the injured heroine so that she could make a stay in Maitland's house. That was just the sort of high-spirited trick that Imogen would concoct. But here her sister was, looking so white and unmoving that Tess felt as if she were standing at her father's side again.

Josie was standing at the bottom of the bed, tears pouring down her face. "It's just like Papa," she sobbed, saying aloud just what Tess was thinking. "She'll die now, just the way he did. He never woke up" — she struggled for breath — "we never could wake him up that last time."

"She won't die!" Tess said bracingly. She thought frantically of everything they had used to attempt to wake their father: the talk of the stables, the hot apple-mash . . . There was only one thing she could think of that might rouse Imogen, even though it was the last thing she wanted. One more glance at her sister's closed eyes and white face, and she flung open the door.

"Lord Maitland!" she called, running down the stairs.

He was sitting in the ornate, gold-hung drawing room with his mother, looking altogether too relaxed.

"Lord Maitland," Tess said, catching her breath. "If you would be so kind as to help me with something for a moment."

"Oh, *must* he?" Lady Clarice said with a petulant twist of her mouth. "We've only just got comfortable, Miss Essex. This is all terribly wearing on my nerves, I assure you." She raised a scrap of handkerchief to her brow.

"Just for the merest second, Lady Clarice," Tess said, curling her lips in what she hoped was a smile.

Draven Maitland had, of course, risen to his feet when she entered the room, and now he walked after her up the stairs and down the corridor with all the enthusiasm of a child being sent to school. He hesitated outside the bedchamber given to Imogen. "This isn't exactly proper, is it?" he asked. "Shouldn't I call my mother to act as a chaperone? I'm afraid that it will not be seen as —"

"Oh, do go in," Tess said crossly, pushing him over the threshold. "You needn't stand on ceremony with us. You certainly have shared many a meal with us in the past."

"But that was in *Scotland,*" he said painstakingly.

"I don't see a difference."

"My mother would," Draven said, and then, as if the very mention of his mother was a magic wand, he walked over the threshold.

Josie realized that a man had entered the bedchamber and ran out, giving Tess a furious look. Her face was all blubbered with tears.

Imogen was lying against the pillows, looking so white that Tess's heart thumped in her chest. "Wake her!" she charged Maitland.

He fell back a pace and blinked at Tess. "Resurrection isn't my strong suit."

Tess narrowed her eyes and moved toward him. "She doesn't need resurrecting. She needs you to wake her up. Kiss her."

"Kiss her?" His eyebrow shot up. "While I'm always happy to help a lady, I fail to see how —"

"Just do it," Tess said fiercely. Lord knows it was the very last thing she wanted that irresponsible, care-for-nothing boy to be doing . . . and yet Imogen had to wake up. She had to.

"As you wish." He bent down over the bed, as Tess watched. Maitland had a sleekness about him that she couldn't like, but that seemed to turn Imogen turn to water. Still, Tess had to admit he was handsome, with his cleft chin and generous mouth.

"Imogen," he said. "Wake up."

She didn't move. He looked up at Tess.

"There's no one but the two of us here," she snapped. "Consider yourself uncompromised. Of course, your mother *would* hugely dislike what you are doing now, even if it is for the very best reasons."

"Believe it or not, that wasn't first on my mind," he said. Then he put his hands on either side of the pillow and pitched his voice very low. "Imogen, I want you to wake up now. Wake up!"

Tess's sister looked exactly like Sleeping Beauty in the fairy tale, her hair curling around her face, long eyelashes lying against her cheeks.

His mouth curled again into a smile. "Ah, but you're beautiful, lass." He touched her face. "Wake up, now."

Tess could see the attraction, oh yes, she could. Those big hands that held a horse so easily, that keen way he looked at her sister. There was something so possessed about Draven Maitland, as if he'd always gotten what he wanted and always would.

It was strangely attractive. It was just too bad that the obverse of all that possession was a reckless temperament and a spoiled character.

"Imogen," he said, and his mouth touched hers. Tess closed her eyes. It didn't seem right to watch. "Imogen," she heard him say again, low and commanding.

Tess opened her eyes again. Maitland was looking down at her sister, and there was something in his face that made her feel suddenly uneasy. He put his hands on her face, and he didn't look lazy anymore. "Imogen," he said, "I want you to wake up."

Imogen stirred.

"I want you to wake up," he said deliberately, "and if you don't, I shan't marry you."

Tess gasped.

He was kissing her sister again, but this time it wasn't a gentle buss on the lips. "I shan't marry you," he growled. Tess took a panicked breath and looked away for a moment. It didn't seem right to watch and yet —

And when Tess looked back, well, Imogen was awake.

Of course.

Chapter 21

Holbrook Court

Early afternoon

Faced by a woman whose very flounces were dancing with fury, Rafe tried to find a germ of fact in a flood of words that appeared so quickly they seemed to eat the very air around them. "What do you mean, Lady Clarice?"

"Precisely what I said," she spat. "That ward of yours has made a direct set at my son. And don't think I won't see her ruined, Holbrook, because I will. Ruined! You have to send her back to Scotland this moment, and perhaps — perhaps! — I will forget her temerity."

Rafe took a deep breath. "What exactly has Miss Essex done?"

"Not the eldest one, the injured one!" Clarice shrieked at him.

"Well, what has Miss Imogen done?"

"She's — she's — You'll have to see for yourself," Clarice snapped. "I only hope that Miss Pythian-Adams can forgive my son for his notable stupidity. I consider this entirely your fault, Holbrook, and so I called to tell you. Entirely your fault! You have acted disgracefully as a guardian. Which is no more than anyone could have foretold."

"But —"

She turned around on the point of leaving the room. "The doctor says she's not to be moved today. But you'll send your carriage for her first thing in the morning. If you do not, I shall send her home in one of mine, and never mind how it looks to the servants!"

Rafe blinked as she left the room in a breeze of French scent and waggling fox tails. "Brinkley," he called.

"Yes, Your Grace?"

Brinkley looked as composed as ever. As if he knew nothing, thought nothing, and was far above gossip. But Rafe wasn't stupid. "What the hell is Lady Clarice talking about?"

Brinkley pressed his lips together but Rafe could see the faintest glimmer of enjoyment there. "It appears that Miss Imogen has won Lord Maitland's heart."

"Won his heart?" Rafe repeated.

"According to my information, he has

vowed to marry Miss Imogen," Brinkley said. "He informed his mother over breakfast this morning."

"Marry!" Rafe said, astounded. "He can't marry Imogen. He's promised to Miss Pythian-Adams. Was she at the breakfast table as well?"

"She was not, to the best of my knowledge," Brinkley remarked. "Will there be anything further, Your Grace?"

"No," Rafe said. He felt as if a headache was coming on already. And he'd made up his mind not to drink until the sun was over the yard-arm. Perhaps there would be an eclipse today.

Lucius strolled in the room. Typically, he showed no reaction other than a lifted eyebrow at Rafe's news.

"What does a guardian do in this situation?" Rafe asked him. "I suppose I could ban their marriage. Or could I? I can't quite remember whether Imogen is of age, but I do think that I have the right to approve all marriages no matter her age. Lord, but that girl is a pest." There was a heartfelt ring to his voice. "Lady Clarice is in a rage. I suppose I'll have to go over there."

"A guardian's role," Lucius said, a mocking devil in his eye. "Do the pretty, make it all right, smooth things over. Perhaps you should offer yourself to Lady Clarice as a sacrifice."

Rafe fixed him with a chilling glare. "I shall smooth things over. If possible."

"When will Miss Essex and her sister return to the house?" Lucius asked. He had turned away and was rifling through a stack of books on the table.

"Tomorrow. I'll go over there tomorrow morning and bring them all back," Rafe said. "Then we'll let things quiet."

"*Things* meaning Lady Clarice?"

"Precisely."

Lucius snorted. "Good luck."

"I'll rise early," Rafe said, thinking that was sacrifice enough. "Get over there by noon."

As it happened, noon was not early enough.

He walked into utter Bedlam. For a moment Rafe couldn't even take it all in; his head was pounding from the glare of the sun. Who would have thought it was so bright at this hour? No wonder he made it a point never to rise before midday.

Lady Clarice was stretched out on a settee, looking utterly deranged, her ringlets tousled and pasted to her neck. She was alternately shrieking and sobbing; Rafe had even heard her from the corridor. She reared up her head when the butler opened the door, stared at him for a moment, and then cried, "You're too late! Oh, my child, my child!"

Rafe strolled into the room even though every cell in his body advised him to walk straight out the door. "Lady Clarice," he said, "where —"

"That loathsome, wretched girl," she said, sitting bolt upright now and staring at him for all the world like Medusa. "I knew from the moment I saw her that she was nothing more than a — a trollop!"

"Hush, madam," came a soothing voice, and Rafe noticed for the first time that Miss Pythian-Adams was seated at the head of the settee.

"A trollop!" Lady Clarice hissed. "And now — and now — I shall never live down the disgrace of it, the utter disgrace of it! I am ruined, utterly ruined. My life is *ruined!*" Her voice rose to a whistling shriek.

Rafe turned around. Lady Clarice's butler had an expression that suggested he had found a week-old fish in his bedclothes. "Bring me a brandy," Rafe told him.

"That's right!" Lady Clarice snapped,

flopping back onto the settee. "Drink yourself into a stupor at this moment of all moments, when —" Her voice broke, and she started sobbing again. Rafe could only make out incoherent phrases here and there, about *scandal* and *son*. He looked to Miss Pythian-Adams, but she was dabbing Lady Clarice's forehead with a scented cloth.

He backed out of the room and caught the butler as he was bringing the brandy. Rafe grabbed the glass and let a lovely river of fire tip down his throat. Behind him there was another howling wail. He moved away from the door in case the condition was contagious.

"May I escort you to the sitting room, where Miss Essex awaits you?" the butler intoned. He was obviously one of those servants who took his owners' reputations as his own. He looked as wracked as Lady Clarice.

Even the brandy couldn't soften Tess's news.

"What do you mean, they've eloped?" Rafe thundered, sounding for all the world like a male version of Lady Clarice.

"They're gone!" she said, one tear after another chasing itself down her face. "I went to call Imogen, to ready her for returning to Holbrook Court, and all I found was a note." She held it out, crumpled and tear-stained. "She didn't even tell me —" Her voice broke off on a sob.

Rafe smoothed out the note and read it.

Dear Tess, Annabel & Josie,

My darling Draven has offered an elopement, and naturally I shall accept his offer. You know how very much he means — has always meant — to me. Please, do forgive me for the scandal; I am persuaded that it will pass quickly.

With all love, your sister,
Imogen (Lady Maitland)

"She's persuaded the scandal will pass quickly?" he said, stunned. "What kind of idiotic idea is that? Doesn't she have any idea of the impact of a Scottish wedding?"

"No," Tess said, wiping away tears. "I'm afraid none of us did. Lady Clarice has told me, though . . ."

"Damnation. How much of a head start do they have?"

"Quite a lot," Tess said. "Apparently they left just after the morning meal. Lord Draven had given his mother a shock yesterday by announcing that he planned to marry Imogen, but I believe Lady Clarice had hoped she would be able to persuade him otherwise. At least, she tried to dissuade him throughout most of our evening meal last night. Of course, Imogen wasn't there but it was still quite — quite embarrassing."

"That likely drove Maitland to the elopement," Rafe said grimly.

"I would prefer to think that he is in love with my sister," Tess said, trying desperately to erase the memory of Maitland's disparaging comments in the music room.

Rafe handed her a handkerchief. "Perhaps you're right."

Tess sniffed and reversed herself. "I know he's not desperately in love with Imogen. So does she, for that matter. But *she* is quite desperately in love with him. And perhaps that will be enough to make a happy marriage. Do you think so?"

Rafe hesitated. "One must assume it can be, given the number of couples I know who are in that very situation." He ran a hand through his hair. "Dammit, I feel like the worst sort of guardian! I should have turned your father down. Here we are, not even a week into my guardianship, and one of his daughters has already ruined her reputation. And with an empty-headed high player like Maitland! Your father's probably cursing me at this moment."

Tess smiled at him wanly. "Papa was never able to stop Imogen's adoration for Lord Maitland, for all he told her that the man was a horse-mad fool who would never hold on to a penny. The truth is that Papa was quite similar to Lord Maitland."

"I should have locked her up," Rafe muttered. "From now on, none of you are to leave the house without being accompanied by a groom and a maid. No, a groom and *two* maids!"

The door burst open. "I am accompanied by my son's betrothed wife. *Betrothed!*" Lady Clarice said shrilly. "I consider it appropriate that *you* explain to her precisely how it happened that your ward has enticed my son into this improvident and scandalous match."

Miss Pythian-Adams followed Lady Clarice into the room, looking the very picture of charming contentment.

Rafe slammed his glass onto the sideboard so sharply that brandy sloshed onto the rosewood surface. "And how in the devil's name was I to stop your dissolute son from stealing away my underage ward, madam? I consider Maitland entirely at fault. He has seduced an innocent maiden, stolen her fancies with clever words, and destroyed her reputation by this wild and improvident act! If anyone deserves an apology, it is Miss Essex, whose infant sister was stolen by your depraved offspring!"

Lady Clarice fell back in the face of Rafe's howling voice, but quickly rallied. "The woman is nothing more than a grasping chit who stole my son. Nothing to her name but a horse. A horse! As if Draven hadn't more than enough horses. I'm sure that I've never denied him a *horse*."

Tess retreated toward the back of the room. How could Imogen have done this to all of them? But she knew the answer as well as she knew the question. Imogen had eloped because, even if Draven Maitland did not love Imogen the way Romeo loved Juliet, Imogen herself was every bit as passionate as the Shakespearean heroine. More, perhaps. She had simply reached out and taken what she wanted. She was no passive observer. Although, Tess reminded herself, naturally Imogen will be a great deal happier and longer-lived than Juliet.

"That *hussy*," Lady Clarice shrieked, "has broken not only my heart but that of his fiancée as well. No thought for others, none! Miss Pythian-Adams is utterly distraught, as well she might be! The heartache of having one's future husband stolen by a loose girl who —"

"That's enough!" Rafe bellowed.

Miss Pythian-Adams was displaying her heartache by smiling like someone freed from the hangman's noose. She drifted over to Tess and, under cover of Rafe's prolonged diatribe on Maitland's undesirable qualities, said, "I feel an urge to apologize to you, although I assure you I had nothing to do with this affair. I do hope your sister's reputation does not suffer unduly."

"It's quite all right," Tess said wearily. Rafe had found a brandy decanter on the sideboard. "Rafe," she said, taking advantage of Lady Clarice's pause for dramatic sobs, "are you quite certain that you couldn't overtake Lord Maitland on the road?" She swallowed hard. "It's just — I don't believe that Imogen knows what — she's really quite young." Tears choked her throat. "She just doesn't know what Maitland is like."

"He's not a monster," Miss Pythian-Adams said sympathetically. "I admit that I am quite pleased to be free of the attachment, but I believe your sister has a genuine attachment to Lord Maitland."

"Please, Rafe," Tess said, ignoring Miss Pythian-Adams. "Couldn't you try to stop her?"

"It's no use," Rafe said wearily. "Maitland drives like the very devil, even when he's on a simple excursion. The very idea that he might be chased will delight him and make him go even faster. His horses are the best. There's no chance, not with a five-hour start on his part." He tossed back the drink in his hand.

"You could *try*," Tess insisted.

"Frankly, at this point I'm not sure we want to catch her," he said. "Her reputation is ruined. Better married in disgrace than merely disgraced."

Tess swallowed, then curtsied to Miss Pythian-Adams and Lady Clarice, who was now sobbing into her handkerchief and ignoring the company utterly. "If you will forgive me, I must return to Holbrook Court and inform my sisters of Imogen's . . . marital status."

"I shall return to London this afternoon," Miss Pythian-Adams answered. "I know we do not part under auspicious circumstances, Miss Essex, but I would feel great pleasure to meet you again in London."

Tess murmured something and escaped. The moment she reached the corridor, tears began to pour down her face. Her sweet, silly little sister. All those years Imogen spent tracing the title *Lady Maitland* came to this.

I should have tried harder to convince her that Maitland was a stupid, blockhead of a man, she thought with anguish. I should have known that she would take any opportunity to marry Maitland, even if it meant ruining herself. If I had told her — if we had all told her — over and over that she had no chance of marrying Lord Maitland, this wouldn't have happened.

She began to run down the stairs, only to be brought up short by Lucius Felton's voice.

He was standing in the entryway and had clearly just arrived, as he was in a greatcoat. "Miss Essex," he said, and took a few quick steps up to her.

"I can't —" she said in a trembling voice. Then he was next to her and had taken out a large white handkerchief.

"Hush," he said, wiping her cheeks. "I just heard what has happened. I'm going to go after them, as far as the post road. It's worth the effort, just in case something happened to Maitland's cattle and he's had to hire some broken-down job horses crossing the border." His jaw set; he looked more than a match for Draven Maitland.

"I'll come with you!" she said, clutching his arm.

"No." His voice was uncompromising. "I'm certain you wouldn't wish to be as compromised as your sister now is, Tess."

She bit her lip. "Of course not."

"Unless —" he said, and stopped.

She blinked at him, but he said nothing. So she said, "I must return home and tell Annabel and Josie. They will be distraught."

He bowed. "I shall do my best to bring your little sister back to you."

"Oh —" But everything she could say was inadequate. "Good luck," she finally whispered.

He smiled at her, a lopsided smile, and was gone.

Chapter 22

The next morning

"If you don't find the notion too distressing," Mayne said, raising Tess's hands to his lips in a brief caress, "I suggest that we marry without delay."

Tess felt all the exhaustion of a sleepless night and all the confusion of their miserable situation. She certainly didn't feel like undertaking a marriage.

He took one swift look at her and obviously guessed what she was about to say. "If we were married, I could whisk your sisters up to London and separate them entirely from the unhappy circumstances of your sister's elopement," he continued. "I wouldn't wish Annabel's prospects on the marriage market to be at all dimmed by Imogen's behavior."

Lady Griselda gave her a sympathetic smile from the opposite divan. "I know that marriage must be the very last thing on your mind," she said.

"Yes, it is," Tess said gratefully.

But Griselda proved herself a traitor by saying, "I would never push such a thing upon you, Tess darling, but truly we must move quickly to protect Annabel's reputation. *Nothing* can be more fatal than if the *ton* gained the impression that you were four Scottish hoydens. I'm afraid that there is a lamentable misunderstanding about the morals of women from northern climates."

Tess frowned. She saw no reason to kowtow to the prejudices of Londoners. But Griselda wasn't finished.

"I am going to speak quite, quite freely," Griselda said, with all the gentle force of an advancing army. "Annabel is lovely. Truly lovely. She can marry whom she pleases. But she does not present herself as a young lady of utmost *propriety,* if I may be frank."

Tess nodded, wondering what on earth this had to do with marriage to Griselda's brother.

"It would be fatal," Griselda said, "if those in London were to decide that Annabel was cut from the same cloth as her sister Imogen. And if it gets about that you were all here, under Rafe's dubious chaperonage for more than a day or so,

Annabel's reputation will be ruined. I am also worried that Lady Clarice's wrath will lead her to say imprudent things of the family."

Tess stared at her. On Griselda's face was the force of utter conviction.

She rose from her seat, saying, "Annabel's chances of an excellent marriage will be ruined, and I promise you that with all my years in London behind me. Oh, she will marry. But her suitors will not be of a caliber of man whom I would wish for her. But I shall leave the two of you to decide this business between you. Whatever you decide, Tess, I shall do my very best to protect the three of you from the high sticklers." And with that she left the room with a waggle of her fingers and a last encouraging smile for her brother.

"Rafe is doing his best as a guardian," Mayne said. He was still holding Tess's hand. "But he doesn't go into society much."

Tess knew that. Her darling guardian drank too much and cared too little to cut a figure in society.

"He won't be a help to Annabel and Josie," Mayne said quietly. "But I can be such a help, Tess, if you wish. Should you appear in two or three days as the

Countess of Mayne, the *ton* will follow your lead without hesitation. Grissie thinks it would be much better if it appeared that we were already married by the time your sister eloped."

Tess took a deep breath. "You are not marrying me for love, Lord Mayne. Nor — as far as I see — due to any overwhelming feeling of a less . . . less proper nature." She could feel color rising into her cheeks.

"Now that's not true," Mayne said. There was a hint of wicked laughter in his eyes, and his fingers tightened on hers. "I feel quite improperly toward you."

Goodness, but he was attractive when he wasn't hedging, when he was being honest. "Are you not disturbed by the fact that we do not feel warmer emotions for each other?" she asked him.

"I would be disturbed if we *did.* In my estimation, marriages based on anything other than mutual respect and a genuine affection for each other are often disastrous. I do not wish for a tempestuous marriage, although I am quite certain that there will be sufficient warmth between us."

"And in your estimation, tempests must accompany love," she said, raising an eyebrow.

"Only the foolish, romantic sort of love," he answered. "I think it would be no hardship at all to care for you deeply, Tess. And I most gravely hope that we will both feel that emotion for the other. But I would never marry when I was under the grip of the sort of fever that passes for romantic love. Never."

Tess could see that he meant it. "Why are you so cynical?" she asked.

He shrugged. "To be utterly frank, I have slept with many wives who entered their marriages in a burst of rosy enthusiasm. I made up my mind years ago that when I chose to marry, it would not be due to a heady emotion that fades in days or weeks. I would like to have children, and have those children raised by parents who were not engaged in constant battles."

"Your parents?" she asked.

"A warring duo," he acknowledged, with a twist of his lips.

Tess was silent. "I know very little about constructing good marriages," she said. "My mother died many years ago, and my father never showed the slightest interest in taking another spouse."

"We can find our way together," Mayne said. "If you are amenable, my uncle, the bishop, could arrive this evening. I sent off a message at first dawn."

"So soon?" Tess asked faintly.

His fingers tightened on hers again. "I loathe the idea that I am rushing you into this occasion. But if you still wish to marry me, I think we could help your sisters in the best possible fashion by marrying with expediency. If you don't wish to marry me, the situation is quite different."

The question in his eyes startled Tess.

"Mr. Felton has not returned," she said, grasping at straws. "What if he brings Imogen back with him? What if he managed to stop the elopement altogether?"

"The news will leak out. Elopements are like murders; they refuse to stay buried. Imogen is ruined, no matter whether Lucius somehow manages to wrench her away from Maitland or not. 'Twould be better for her now if Lucius didn't manage to catch her."

"How can you say that!" Tess cried. "Maitland is a fool!"

"He's not quite so bad as that," Mayne said. "Is it worse for her never to marry, and be bundled away in the country, or marry the man she loves?"

Tess said nothing, and he followed up his advantage. "For she does love him, does she not? I saw her looking at him, and a clearer case of calf-love I never saw."

"I cannot like it," Tess said, wringing her hands.

"The important thing is that we make it possible for your other sisters to marry men who do not share Maitland's uncertain qualities."

"Yes, I see."

"Good," Mayne said promptly. "Then we shall be married first thing in the morning. My uncle has many responsibilities and will make only a short stay with us."

"Tomorrow morning? And if — if Mr. Felton has not returned with —"

"As I said, that is irrelevant," Mayne said with a hint of impatience.

"Yes, of course," Tess said.

"You will make me the happiest of men." He leaned toward her and brushed his mouth against hers. As kisses go, it was light, almost nonchalant.

Quite pleasant.

Chapter 23

Later that evening

"I'll tell you what pleasure is," the Bishop of Rochester said jovially. "Pleasure is seeing this rapscallion nephew of mine nicely espoused, and to a lovely woman like yourself, m'dear! This is a true pleasure."

Tess tried to smile at him, but she was feeling queasy, and smiles seemed to die in her cheeks before she moved her lips. When Mayne spoke to her in that forthright manner as he had used when proposing, she felt she could marry him, and even without hesitation. But when he was full of flummery and manners, as he had been all afternoon, she felt increasing waves of panic. He was always putting her hand to his lips or whispering compliments to her confidentially. It was wearing merely to watch him. How could she live with such a man for years?

Annabel had a gossip sheet that Lady Griselda had received that morning, and was asking Mayne about names that appeared in its columns.

"And Lady C —" she asked, giggling.

"Now how would I know that? Lady Colterer, perhaps. Or Lady Cristleham."

"Whoever she is," Annabel gurgled, "she has been foolish enough to run away with a Frenchman."

"Ah, well," Mayne said with satisfaction, "*that* must be Lady Cristleham. Daughter of a duke, married to a baron, and been going to the dogs ever since her debut."

"Never say so!" Annabel said, fascinated. "Do you know simply *everyone*, Lord Mayne? What of this Portuguese nobleman?"

Lucius strode into the room. Tess turned toward him with a little cry — but he shook his head. Mayne gave her a sympathetic look, and then turned back to the gossip sheet.

"I managed to catch them," Lucius was telling Rafe.

Up close, she could see that he was far from his composed, elegant self. There was dust in the creases of his cloak. He looked utterly exhausted, as if he'd driven all night without pause.

"You must forgive me for entering the room in all my dirt," he said, and his voice was hoarse.

"You caught them?" Annabel repeat[illegible]

"You must have ridden like the ve[illegible] wind," Rafe said. "How the devil did you do it?"

"I went cross-country part of the way," Lucius said. "I thought I'd know what he would do, you see. Maitland is fast, but he's predictable."

"But when you caught them, what happened?" Tess cried.

"She refused to come," he said heavily. "And —" He looked about and then spoke in a low voice. "I'm afraid it was too late, Tess. I couldn't separate them."

Tess felt as if she could howl with the grief of it. "Of course," she said numbly.

"Is she married now?" Annabel asked. And at Rafe's nod, she walked back to the other side of the room without another word.

"I'm forever in your debt for this," Rafe said to Lucius.

"And I," Tess said, trying to make the bleak look go from his eyes, even though she knew the same look was on her face.

"Don't be." His voice was hard. "I failed."

"I'm sorry," Tess said miserably. "I'm so sorry."

"No reason to be." He looked about.

"You're all looking remarkably festive. I'll just retire —"

Rafe gave him a narrow-eyed look. "Yes, but you must return briskly, Lucius. We're having something of a celebration, as Tess is to marry Mayne tomorrow morning by special license. You see" — he nodded toward the bishop — "Mayne has summoned his uncle for that very purpose."

"Ah," Lucius said, not even glancing at Tess. "In that case, I shall make my congratulations to Mayne before I retire."

Tess felt her smile tremble so she moved away, back toward her sister and future husband. Lucius and Rafe followed her to the group.

Annabel was poring over the gossip sheet again, reading bits aloud for Lady Griselda's and Mayne's commentary.

> A certain brisk widow, who has had three husbands come to untimely ends, is desirous of a fourth. We know this due to her larding her conversation with giddy descriptions of fellows she knows only by sight. We would like to warn her that to banter about matrimony is not to engage in it, and further to warn any gentleman who finds himself the subject of her conversation to beware.

"Oh, that is *so* unkind," Annabel cried. "Who is the poor lady?"

"My own dear sister," Mayne said.

Lady Griselda rapped him on the head with her fan. "Nonsense, you impudent dog. I've had but one husband and no stomach for another, so that description's right out. I would guess that *brisk widow* likely refers to Mrs. Brisquet, wouldn't you say?"

"Of course," Mayne said, grinning. "Quite a number of the persons are disguised by puns, as you see, Miss Annabel."

"I can't wait until I know every single person referred to," Annabel said with a sigh, looking back at the newspaper. "Who could possibly be called an operatic countess? She seems a lucky woman."

A second later, Mayne had taken the gossip sheet from her hands and was looking down at it, his face suddenly stonelike, as if he'd been struck.

"Lord Mayne," Annabel said, rather uncertainly. "Are you quite all right?"

"Never more so," he said, handing her back the sheet. "But I should —" He bowed extravagantly. Then he turned on his heel and left.

They all stood blinking after him.

The edge of Lucius's mouth curled into a smile. "If you will all excuse me," he said with a bow. "I must retire. As you can see, my clothing is rather the worse for my travels."

"Was it something I said?" Annabel said to Rafe. But he was picking up the gossip sheet, Tess and Lady Griselda at his shoulder.

> A certain operatic countess is reportedly expecting a happy event in the new year. She and her husband have made themselves notorious in the past months due to their reluctance to spend any time away from each other's sides.

"Ah," Lady Griselda said, putting the paper gently back on the side table. "Poor Garret."

Rafe didn't say a word, just headed out of the chamber after Mayne.

"Who is this operatic countess?" Annabel asked. "And why did the news affect the earl so deeply?"

"I don't think that's our concern," Tess said, drawing her sister away toward the window.

"Really!" Annabel said crossly. "He's to be *your* husband, Tess. Don't you wish to know who this woman is? Mayne looked as if he'd been struck by lightning."

"No," Tess said, realizing that it was quite true. "No, I am not interested in who the lady in question is."

"I think you are very strange. Very! If he were *my* bridegroom —"

But Tess was looking out the window at the courtyard. "Unless I'm much mistaken," she murmured, "my bridegroom has just left the house."

Annabel gasped. "Where can he be going?"

Even as they watched, Mayne shook off Rafe's hand. But Rafe swung him around and was talking fiercely.

"Rafe will take care of it," Annabel said. "Mayne can't leave! Why, he's due to marry you first thing in the morning."

"Yes," Tess said, watching closely. Mayne had turned and was now walking back into the house, his face tight and dark as a thundercloud.

"Oh, good," Annabel said. "Now it's all taken care of. You'll have to watch for a musical countess, but it sounds as if *she* is quite uninterested in Mayne, no matter what his feelings may be."

"You're being remarkably vulgar," Tess said sharply.

Rafe had followed Mayne back into the house, and there was nothing more to be seen from the window.

Chapter 24

Not having slept the previous night, Lucius took a bath and lay down for a brief repose — only to wake in thick darkness. Apparently he'd slept through supper and into the night. The tangles of some half-forgotten dream clung in his mind: Tess had been dancing and laughing, but then she dropped her fan, and the fan turned into a rabbit, a rather sweet brown rabbit that he wanted to give to her, but when he ran after the rabbit . . . Lucius stared into the darkness for a moment, and then swung his legs off the bed with a curse.

If Mayne wasn't more careful, Tess would catch wind of his ridiculous infatuation with Lady Godwin.

He lit a candle, only to find that it wasn't so late at night. Mayne was likely to be awake. Lucius dismissed the fleeting thought that he would be carousing, celebrating his last night of bachelorhood. Even when they were boys together at Eton, Mayne was never coarse: wild to a fault, violent in his passions, desperate in his affections: never coarse.

Lucius dressed and then walked down the long hall, checking the sitting room, the music room, the breakfast room. It was in the library, that sanctuary of male pursuits, that he found Mayne.

He was sitting in his favorite seat before the fireplace. The fire had burned to mere embers. He was sitting as if frozen, long legs stretched out, a glass in one hand, and a decanter on the floor close by the other. His shirt was pulled from his trousers, his eyes were half-closed, and his face was set in rigid lines.

"Where's Rafe?" Lucius asked.

"I drank him into his bed," Mayne said, not even turning his head. "That's not easy, with a four-bottle man like Rafe, but I've done it."

"Don't tell me you've fallen into a megrim on the very eve of your wedding?" Lucius said, still from the doorway, a surge of rage that he didn't understand lending his voice a harsh undertone.

Mayne raised his eyes and took a moment to focus on him, and then tossed back the rest of his glass. "She might have fallen in love with you, you know," he said conversationally.

Lucius's heart thumped in his chest. He walked forward and casually nudged the decanter in passing.

It almost turned over, but Mayne's hand shot out and caught the neck, just in time. "Watch my claret," he said, sloshing a quantity into his glass.

"I see no reason why she should fall in love with *me* as opposed to *you*," Lucius said.

"You're a gentleman," Mayne said, rolling his head backward and staring at the ceiling. "She's a lady, for all she cut off her hair and started wearing clothing that would have made a high-flyer proud."

Lucius blinked. Apparently he'd mistaken the lady at issue. Mayne was talking about Lady Godwin, the woman he'd fallen in love with last spring, whereas he himself was thinking . . . of another woman.

"Helene might have loved you," Mayne continued, his voice rough and unsteady. "Might have loved you enough to stay away from that muckworm of a husband of hers. I've figured it out. Helene needed an antidote to him — to all his opera singers and the Russian dancers on the dining room table. So she turned to me, but I wasn't good enough either. But if I had been *you,* all that *politesse,* pretty manners, old-fashioned virtues . . ." His voice trailed off.

"Lady Godwin, by all accounts, is in love with her husband," Lucius said uncompromisingly, sitting down opposite Mayne. "No pretty manners could have changed that."

"Nonsense," Mayne said. "I wouldn't have gone near her if she were happy with her husband. She and Godwin hadn't lived together for ten years."

Lucius didn't say anything. Mayne knew as well as he did that whatever had been the case previously, Helene, Lady Godwin, fairly glowed when the earl entered a room these days. And Godwin might have had an opera singer or two around the house a while ago, but he had eyes for no one but his wife now.

"Well, aren't you going to say something?" Mayne said belligerently, glaring at Lucius.

"You're foxed. I would suggest you retire. If you remember, you are embarking on married life tomorrow morning after breakfast."

Mayne didn't take that very well. He narrowed his eyes and his speech grew even thicker. "You're turning into a pretentious little prig, do you know that? You were never exactly easy in your manner, but now your prudery is close to sinful."

"Since you're cast-away, I'll ignore that," Lucius said calmly.

"Above correction, are you?"

"No. But above fighting with a man who's drunk as a wheelbarrow."

"I'm not drunk," Mayne said, returning his glowering eyes to the fireplace. "I wish I were drunk."

Lucius refrained from comment.

"I've no doubt *you* think I'm jug-bitten," Mayne said with a heavy sneer. "A gentleman of your caliber finds himself on the go from a glass of milk."

Lucius got up and walked to the door, but Mayne was out of his chair in a violent surge of unsteady limbs.

"You didn't used to be like this," he said, jerking Lucius back by the arm. "I remember you casting up your accounts into the Thames — or are you too abstemious to acknowledge such a thing?"

Lucius turned to face him, pulling away his arm so swiftly that Mayne swayed and almost disbalanced. "I was seventeen."

"Stubble it," Mayne snapped. "The only thing that's changed between us is that your blasted mother decided you were smelling of the merchant classes. And since then you've been a regular Holy Willy."

Lucius froze. "I would greatly prefer that you didn't comment on my mother." His voice had the smooth threat of a pope chastising a junior devil.

But Mayne was too far intoxicated to have an ear for innuendo. "We've handled the subject of your family with kid gloves for years. The hell with it. She may be the daughter of an earl, but she's a right b—" He caught himself, just in time.

Lucius just waited. He was leaning against the door, arms folded over his chest.

But Mayne had seemingly realized that he was on the verge of causing a breach from which there could be no recovery and was sorting through his rather bleary brain, trying to find a way to rectify the situation.

"Yes?" Lucius asked, his tone excruciatingly polite and just as icy. "Surely there is more that you would like to get off your chest?"

Mayne had apparently decided that he might as well be hanged for a sheep as a lamp. "I don't really give a damn about your parents. I've always thought your mother was a mean-spirited woman who never got over the shock of her own marriage. Now you — you're turning into the type of self-righteous prig whom no one really likes, even if they pretend that they do."

Lucius felt the blow to his chest as if it were physical. Mayne turned and dropped into his chair again.

"Your father is a small-minded wart on the ass of — of — of the *ton*," he added, with rather less clarity than could be desired.

Lucius turned, but Mayne's bleary voice from the depths of the chair stopped him. "You'd better drop all that stiff-rumped nonsense before it's too late, before you turn into an even bigger wart yourself."

Lucius stood for a long moment, his jaw clenched, thinking longingly about smashing Mayne's nose into the back of his throat.

But when he strode over to see if Mayne wanted to add a final insult that would tip the whole conversation over into violence, he heard a snore.

Mayne had spilled the rest of the glass of claret on the white linen of his shirt. His hair was tumbling over his forehead. He looked drunk — drunk and miserable.

Lucius stood for a moment, eyes narrowed, staring down at his friend. He stopped in the hall and told a footman that the earl was in need of assistance.

Then he went up to his own chamber and thought. About warts, drunks, and marriage.

Chapter 25

The next morning came all too soon. Tess woke up and stared at the canopy over her bed. She thought about running out to the stables and calling for her horse, but where would she go? What would she do?

Marrying Mayne made sense. She would be able to save Annabel's and Josie's future marriages. She would be married to a man of substance and worth. She and Mayne would have a civil, friendly, courteous relationship.

She got up, shivering a little in the chilly air. Her maid, Gussie, ushered in cans of hot water and a tin bath.

At some point the door popped open. "You simply cannot marry my dearest brother wearing *black,*" Lady Griselda Willoughby said. "So I've brought you one of my gowns. It's half-mourning and really, quite quite gorgeous."

Tess looked up, surprised. "Oh, I couldn't!"

"Of course you can," Lady Griselda said.

"I can't abide the idea that my brother would marry a crow. I'm sure it's bad luck." She thought about saying that the marriage needed every ounce of available luck to succeed and swallowed her words. Instead she bustled about the room. The important thing was that Garret had finally decided *to* marry. His bout of nerves the previous afternoon was irrelevant and nothing that his bride needed to know about.

She stole a look at Tess. The girl was truly lovely, especially with all that brandy-colored hair tumbling down her back. For a moment Griselda felt envious, then dismissed the emotion. To be envious would imply that she, Griselda, wished to marry, and she didn't. She had quite enough of the married state when poor, dear Willoughby was alive, thank you very much.

Her maid was throwing the gown over Tess's head.

"I don't know," she said, looking down at her low neckline. "Are you certain it's proper?"

"Of course it's proper," Griselda said bracingly. "It's half-mourning, and I wore it only once, for Lady Granville's champagne breakfast. That was when we were all mourning for Sir William Ponsby, one of the heroes of Waterloo, you know — or perhaps you don't, since you were in Scotland."

"We did know of Waterloo," Tess said, turning before the glass. The dress was designed in the very height of fashion: low in the bosom, with tiny sleeves that draped from her shoulders. Seed pearls clustered around the bodice and caught the light. "I don't feel comfortable," Tess confessed. "It seems odd to show quite so much of my bosom during my wedding."

Griselda waved at Tess's maid, and the girl slipped out of the room. Then she sat down on the bed, and said, "Dearest, I'm going to be absolutely frank with you."

"Yes?" Tess asked.

"My brother is used to making love with the most exquisite women in the *ton*. He's had them all, at least all those that are married and available." She raised her hand. "You equal any of them in beauty and surpass most. The problem is — as I see it — that Garret has never been able to form an attachment to one particular woman."

"Yet he's never been married," Tess said, making certain that she understood the subject of conversation.

"Of course not! And you're right: that *is*

the important point. The fact that his affairs have lasted only a few days needn't affect your marriage at all!" Griselda said, beaming at her as if she were a particularly apt student of the marital state.

"Are you implying," Tess said rather faintly, "that he — that his affairs —"

"Never lasted long," Griselda said, nodding. "To this point, I do believe that the longest period he's spent with a single woman has been a matter of a week or two."

"The musical countess?" Tess asked.

"Less," Griselda said promptly. "To the best of my knowledge, they had no affair whatsoever. She may have toyed with the idea for a day or so."

"Goodness," Tess murmured.

"But it will all be different now that he's married!" Griselda said, opening the door.

They made their way down the polished mahogany stairs. Brinkley was standing in the hallway. He gave a deep bow on seeing them and swept open the door to the sitting room.

The first person Tess saw was Lucius Felton. He turned about when she entered, and for a moment it was if she froze in the doorway, caught by his black eyes. Then Griselda peered over her shoulder, giving a shrill laugh, and said, "Your bridegroom will be here in a matter of seconds."

Tess moved into the room and found herself curtsying before the bishop. He was very jovial, and kept pinching her cheek and telling her that his nephew was a lucky fellow indeed.

Tess smiled faintly and tried not to think. Annabel swept into the room, making a grand entrance.

"You are annoyingly lovely," Tess heard Lady Griselda telling Annabel. They were laughing together.

Lucius was leaving the room, not that Tess was watching him in particular. It was just that he was so — well, somehow, to Tess, his quiet possession was just what she thought a duke ought to be. Or an earl, for that matter.

Not that it mattered.

She heard steps coming down the stairs outside; surely that was Garret.

"That'll be your husband," the bishop said in his deep voice. "Good! I'd like to get this ceremony on the way and make our way to breakfast. It's a pagan thing, running a marriage before a man has even had his porridge." He laughed, and his belly shook gaily.

The door behind Tess didn't open.

"I'll tell them to hurry up," Griselda said, rushing out into the hall. Tess tried to take a deep breath, but she felt as if Griselda's dress was too tight to allow her to take in air properly.

"Isn't this exciting?" Annabel said, slipping her hand under Tess's arm. "I just wish that Imogen were here. I still can't believe —"

The door opened, and Tess turned around so sharply that Annabel's arm fell away from her.

It was Rafe.

"Tess," he said. "May I speak to you for a moment?"

An odd moment of silence fell over the group.

"I'll come with you," Annabel said sharply.

"No," Tess said, moving toward Rafe. Suddenly she could breathe again. There was no one in the entrance, not Lucius, Griselda, or the Earl of Mayne.

Rafe led her into the library. "I loathe having to tell you such unpleasant news," he said, looking, indeed, quite unhappy.

"Imogen?" Tess cried.

"No." A wash of relief swept up her spine. "Then?"

Rafe swept his hand through his hair.

"Your bloody bridegroom's fled."

"Fled?" She caught back a sudden smile. "That's not a very complimentary way of phrasing it, Rafe." She walked over and sat down in a large chair. For the first time in the last four days, she felt calm. As if her scalp were relaxing.

Rafe sat down opposite her. His eyes crinkled at the corners with worry. "If he were here, I would beat the stuffing out of him," he said, running a hand through his hair again. "If I'd had any idea he would pull a stunt like this, I never would have introduced you to him. No less would I have promoted a match between the two of you!"

Tess smiled at him. "It's *all right,* Rafe," she said. "I don't mind." And she let her smile grow, just to show him.

But he wasn't looking at her. "What a fool I was," he said. "Mayne hasn't been himself since this past spring. I knew it, and I ignored it. I'm not used to the responsibility of being a guardian. There can't be a worse guardian in all Christendom than I!"

He looked so unhappy that Tess almost laughed. "You are *not* a failure!" she said cheerfully.

He shook his head. "You don't understand, Tess."

"Yes I do. The Earl of Mayne has taken himself away and left me at the altar, so to speak."

"Precisely."

"But we weren't really suited," Tess noted.

"That's irrelevant," Rafe said. "The important fact is that the jackass has up and *jilted* you. Jilted you! I wouldn't have thought it possible!"

"No one will know."

"Everyone will know. The *ton* lives for this sort of gossip. Believe me. They'll know."

"Ah," Tess said, not caring much.

"There is one solution." Rafe paused. "It's an odd one, and likely to cause as much scandal in its own way."

"I don't wish you to go after Mayne," Tess said, alarmed.

"Never. No, no. It's — well." Rafe got up. "I think I'll let someone else explain this particular possibility. But if you decide not to do it, my dear, I would be most happy to bring you out myself." He walked over and touched her on the shoulder. "I'm sure you realized how little family I have. I am quite aware of my manifold failures as a guardian, but I am still glad to have you as my ward."

Tess smiled up at him. "I'm so glad that Papa chose you, Rafe."

He walked to the door and opened it. "One minute, then."

When the door closed, Tess leaned her head back against her chair. She waited to feel tragic. The only thing she felt was stunned and rather pleased.

Of course, when the door opened, it was Lucius. She looked up at him. It was the oddest feeling: life had taken another sharp turn, as it had when her father died.

Lucius walked over, and then reached out a hand and brought her to her feet. His eyes didn't even drift to her bosom, but suddenly her dress felt not tawdry, but dangerous, sensuous, and powerful.

"Miss Essex," he said, "I have come to ask for your hand in marriage."

"Why do you wish to marry me?" she asked, watching his face.

He flinched slightly. "You find yourself in an unenviable position," he said, "due to my closest friend's behavior. I am constrained, as an honorable man, to —"

"Is it because you wish to race Something Wanton in the Silchester cup?" she asked.

He looked surprised, and a drop of relief went down her spine.

"No," he said.

"Doesn't it seem rather a sacrifice, to marry only in order to ameliorate your friend's ill deeds? You are not, after all, the earl's brother."

"No."

She waited, but he wasn't going to say anything else. Of course she would refuse him. She was no piece of firewood, to be delivered from hand to hand. She opened her mouth to give him a set-down, and a sharp one too.

However, she had made up her mind not to drift along like a leaf caught in a river eddy. She wasn't merely an observer to her own life. The thought jumbled together with Imogen's triumphant little note, and:

"All right."

His eyes were on hers: blazing with a fallen-angel quality. "Why?"

She raised her hands to her mouth but her fingers were unsteady. So she shrugged instead. "I must needs marry." She managed that fairly well. Her voice sounded light, almost uninterested, truly sophisticated. "You have no title, Mr. Felton, but . . ." Her voice trailed away.

"But I have the — the substance that you desire, is that it?"

"Something of that." She had to get away.

"But —"

She turned back to him sharply. This was all too humiliating. "I shall be a comfortable spouse, sir. I promise you that."

His hand fell from her arm. "I shall endeavor to be the same to you, Tess."

"Thank you." She said it coolly but with desperation. She had to leave now.

"Don't you think that we should discuss our forthcoming marriage?"

Tess pressed her hands together tightly and said, "I don't know much about marriage."

He smiled slightly. "I shouldn't expect you to have that particular knowledge."

"Well, you know very little about me," Tess said with a slight edge.

He tipped up her chin. She felt herself grow pink. "I know a few things." His voice was velvet dark.

She opened her mouth, but he was still talking. "Have you shared an intimate breakfast, a supper *a deux*, a . . . bedtime chocolate?"

Tess desperately tried to think of something to say that would be sophisticated, urbane, funny — the sort of thing Annabel would say without thinking twice. "Why did you ask me that question?" she asked instead, looking straight into his eyes and ignoring the laughter there. "Do you really want to know what I think of marriage?"

The laughter disappeared, as if extinguished. "With good fortune, we'll be married a very long time."

That was something of an answer, Tess supposed. "I have seen marriages in which the couple never speak. They just walk past each other. Mrs. Stewart, whose land ran next to ours in Scotland, talked of her husband in the third person only, even when he was standing next to her: '*He* doesn't care for asparagus,' she would say, with Mr. Stewart just at her shoulder. '*He* will only eat cottage pie, and that only on a second Tuesday.' "

The edge of Lucius's mouth curled, and Tess realized with a horrible shock how much she wanted him to be amused by her. Because otherwise — she mentally shook her head.

"I hope we shan't have a silent marriage," he said, taking her hand. "I feel that if we have clear expectations of each other, we are far more likely to have a happy marriage. And I would very much like you to be happy with me, Tess."

Tess noticed that he didn't say anything about being happy with *her,* but she wasn't sure what to make of it.

"What are your expectations?" she

asked. And then colored. Could this have something to do with bedroom matters? "I — I —"

There was that smile in his eyes again. "Simple things." He was rubbing a thumb over her palm. "If we understand each other, I would hope that we don't find ourselves in a chilly relationship."

"What is there to understand?" Tess said, looking at him.

"I have an uneasy feeling that you know me so well already, just by watching me, that I can tell you nothing."

"No!" she said.

"If I were a horse, would I win the race?" he asked, looking at her intently.

For a second she tried to look at him as a Thoroughbred. He would be a hugely muscled one, ready to kick a rival, edgy, faster than anyone else . . . a winner.

"You would win," she said with utter positiveness. "I expect you always win, don't you?"

"Often." He was looking down at her hand again. "The problem with winning is that I win because I don't care very much."

"About winning?"

His right shoulder moved: almost a shrug, not quite. "Precisely. I never allow myself to care very deeply for any particular exchange of goods. I learned years ago that the key to winning is to feel no emotion at losing."

"Goodness," Tess said faintly.

"I am telling you this, Tess, because I want to be absolutely honest with you. I am not suited for marriage, in truth. I like you enormously. But I do not seem — by nature — to have a capacity for deep feeling."

"I am not —" But she couldn't find the words. "I shall make no demands," she said.

He smiled, and there was a laughing devil in his eyes. "I shall make demands," he said, scooping up her hands and bringing them to his mouth. "I *shall* make demands, Tess."

She was a virgin. She'd never been married, as he pointed out. But she recognized the naked longing in his voice as surely as any minister would point to a cloven hoof in his own parlor. She could feel a blush that started in her chest and turned her cheeks pink.

He didn't wait for an answer. His kiss was swift and savage, a kiss that demanded everything she had to give. And like all of Lucius's kisses, it told her much: there was a proprietorial claim there that made her head spin and her knees tremble, so that she leaned toward him, her fingers pulling his head closer to her.

He was the one who pulled back. He was breathing hard. "Are you certain that you will make no demands of me, Tess?" he whispered to her, his voice deeper than she'd ever heard it before.

It was a new Tess he was looking at. A Tess who was clearly not going to be merely a proper, modest wife.

Even as he watched, her lips curled into a smile that would grace a courtesan. She reached out a hand and put one unsteady finger on his lips. "I might make a few demands of my own," she said.

Lucius's heart sang at the note in her voice, at the pure desire in her eyes.

"Thank God Mayne was kind enough to provide a bishop so that we could marry immediately," he said rather hoarsely.

"Indeed," she said.

So he kissed her again.

Chapter 26

The rest of the morning passed in something of a dream. Griselda, poor Griselda, appeared in tears, announcing her intention to leave immediately. She was dissuaded by Rafe, who pointed out that the girls still needed chaperoning.

"I simply can't believe that my own brother would do such a despicable thing," she wailed, wringing her hands. "He's never done —" But then she seemed to remember some other egregious action of Mayne's and closed her mouth. "You're better off without him," she told Tess. "Though he's my brother, and I love him, I tell you this — he's not behaved like himself for some time now. I thought you were the cure, my dear, but . . ."

"He must find his own cure," Tess said gently. Excitement was pumping through her body, making her feel light-headed, almost dizzy, as if her ears were roaring, as if the blood was rushing about her body twice as fast as was normal. Every few moments she would look up and catch Lucius's eye, and heat would wash over her body.

Annabel was grinning like a simpleton and kept drifting by and whispering in her ear, "I knew it; I simply knew it; oh, I am so intelligent!"

The bishop, horrified by his nephew's behavior, agreed to marry them by special license, promptly scratching out Mayne's name and writing in Lucius Felton.

"Good man!" he kept saying, making as if to slap Lucius on the back and then faltering. Lucius was not the sort of man one slaps on the back. "My nephew is a blackguard, leaving this lovely lady in the dust, but he has excellent friends. He doesn't deserve them."

"Yes," Lucius said noncommittally.

Finally, the bishop opened his book and began rushing through the opening of the service. Clearly he felt that any romantic flourishes should be dropped from this particular ceremony; Tess felt as if the words rushed by her ears like water, he was speaking so fast. "Will-you-take-this-woman," he gabbled, and then there was a pause.

Lucius's voice, dark and clear, said, "I will."

The bishop turned to Tess. "Will-you-take . . ." and she couldn't even understand the rest, even though she tried desperately to listen closely to Lucius's full name. The bishop paused and looked at her, and she felt herself opening her mouth, without conscious volition. "I will."

"Good!" the bishop said heartily, and then returned to the Bible, clearly relieved to find his nephew's reputation saved.

Tess bit her lip, feeling rather miserably like a piece of meat Cook had decided to stew as it was on the verge of rotting. Suddenly she felt large hands take hers, and she looked up to find Lucius looking down at her.

And where others might have seen an unexpressionless face, she saw laughter in his eyes, and a reassuring hint of affection, and a twinkle that suggested they would laugh together later at their gabbled wedding ceremony.

The bishop calmed down as he turned to the next section of the ceremony: "I, Lucius John Percival Felton, take thee, Teresa Elizabeth Essex, to my wedded wife, to have and to hold from this day forward . . ."

This time Tess heard his name clearly.

She raised an eyebrow at him. *Percival?*

"For better for worse," Lucius said steadily, still holding her hands in his and looking down at her, "for richer for poorer . . ."

Not that money was a problem for him, for them, Tess thought. Perhaps it would be easier for them if there weren't so much money. But she dismissed the idea as ridiculous.

"In sickness and in health," Lucius continued, "to love and to cherish, till death us do part, according to God's holy ordinance; and thereto I plight thee my troth."

She met Lucius's eyes. 'Twas was a grave thing they were doing. She had a sudden flash of blinding joy that she was plighting her troth to Lucius and not to Mayne.

"I, Teresa Elizabeth Essex, take thee, Lucius John Percival Felton, to my wedded husband," she said, hanging on to his hands, "to have and to hold from this day forward, for better for worse, for richer for poorer, in sickness and in health, to love, cherish, and to obey . . ."

Then before she had time to think again, he brushed a chaste kiss on her cheek, took her arm, and they turned about. Annabel was crying, and Josie was grinning. Rafe was instructing Brinkley to pop the corks on as many bottles of champagne as he could find in the cellar.

"A short repast," he shouted, waving a glass and grinning, "then we shall see the wedding couple off to their own abode."

Tess blinked and looked at Lucius.

"I have a house just an hour or so down the road," he said to her. "I thought we might have a brief time to ourselves."

"Shouldn't we go immediately to London?" Tess asked confusedly, thinking of the need to whisk Annabel away from Rafe's house.

But he merely said, "Your sisters will be fine. Lady Griselda has agreed to stay as chaperone."

Tess frowned, but:

"Trust me, Tess?"

She met his eyes. "Yes." And that was that.

Just one moment stood out clearly in the next few hours: when she sat in front of her dressing table preparing to leave, with Annabel and Josie sitting on the bed behind her. Josie was crying a little because, as she said, "Imogen would love to be here. And now we'll never all be sisters together again. It won't be the same."

"It will be better," Annabel said. "Tess, you are married to the richest man in England! Our sister will be the richest woman in England."

Josie interjected. "By all accounts, William Beckford of Fonthill Abbey is the most wealthy man in England."

Tess wrinkled her nose at them. "And what would Miss Flecknoe say of this vulgar conversation?"

"Do you suppose that your husband owns a *castle?*" Josie asked. "It's possible that you will be the Lady of the Castle. Oh, my, Tess, how lucky you are!"

"A castle," Tess repeated.

"I'm certain that he will have some such structure," Annabel put in. "All the heroes in novels have castles. Who better to be in a castle than the richest man in England?"

"Kings belong in castles," Tess said firmly, pushing one last hairpin into place, "not plain folk such as we."

Josie hooted. "Plain folk! You're dreaming, Tess!"

Annabel met Tess's eyes in the mirror. "Josie, I would like a moment or two alone with Tess, if you please."

Josie narrowed her eyes. "If you're going to talk of mating, I am fully aware of the particulars."

"I shouldn't advise Miss Flecknoe of

that fact," Annabel said, pushing her out the door.

"I too am acquainted with the matter," Tess remarked, noticing that her hands were trembling slightly. "And we discussed the subject last night, Annabel."

"It has always seemed to me that being acquainted with the fundamentals of such domestic activity and actually engaging in it oneself are *not* the same thing," Annabel said firmly. "Are you frightened?"

Tess thought about it for a moment. "A bit. I hope I can acquit myself properly, whatever that means under the circumstances."

"It seems a thoroughly tasteless business." Annabel sighed. "From what I've learned, Tess, the important thing is to endure it in a smiling fashion. Mrs. Howland, in the village, told me that there's nothing a man dislikes more than being refused one's company."

Tess thought about Mrs. Howland's generosity.

"But let's not be needlessly disheartened," Annabel continued. "There must be *something* appealing about it, or there wouldn't be so many children in the world."

"Do try to hide your rather less than maternal nature when you're in London, won't you?" Tess said, amused.

"I doubt that many men choose a spouse on the grounds of maternal longings," Annabel said. "And if the gentleman I choose shows that propensity, I am certain I can prevaricate on the subject long enough to catch his attention."

Annabel was always certain that she could do whatever was called for: pretend to maternal virtues, capture the heart of all and sundry, endure any number of intimate unpleasantries in a smiling fashion . . .

"I wish I had your confidence," Tess said, standing up and giving her reflection one last glance. There was no excuse for not returning to the drawing room, where her husband was waiting. Lucius's carriage was waiting; her new marriage was waiting, like a set of clothing that she had not yet put on.

"I shall doubtless be trembling like a cornered hare when it is actually my turn to take to the marital bed," Annabel said lightly. "But at least I shall have the benefit of your advice. Thank goodness, we have never been reluctant to discuss anything at length. I shall want to know even the smallest details when I see you next week."

Tess turned and gave her a fierce hug in

farewell. But inside, she was thinking that Annabel didn't yet understand. Tess could not imagine pouring a description of whatever was to come between herself and Lucius into her sister's ears.

Truly, as Josie had said, things would never be the same.

Chapter 27

It turned out that Lucius owned the most elegant carriage that Tess had ever seen, let alone ridden in. It was painted a dark glossy green and drawn by exquisite matched grays.

Tess kissed Annabel, ignoring the twinkle in her eye, and kissed Josie, promising to see her very soon and write every day. She sat down on the velvet seats, and looked at the small gilded lamps, at the cloth of gold fringe —

"Do you find it overlavish?" her husband asked.

Her husband!

Tess couldn't even think what to say. There was only one thought in her mind, and sure she was a wicked doxy to have such a thought at all. She felt almost dizzy with it. Fearful and yet —

How did one deal with the embarrassment? With the humiliation of it all? Would Gussie put her in a nightgown and leave her in bed? Would Mr. Felton undress her? She devoutly hoped that wasn't the case. For one thing, she had no corset. She did have a lovely chemise, thanks to Lady Griselda, but what if it were damaged? Annabel had been so certain that the prelude to mating was a gentleman ripping off his wife's clothing.

Nothing Tess said could dissuade her. "They rip the clothing off their wife's body," she had said the previous night, with distinct relish.

"That is simply unlikely," Tess had said. "Look at the smithy and his wife, for example. Mr. Helgarson has six children. Obviously he and his wife have . . ." Her voice trailed off.

"Don't be so missish!" Annabel had said. "You're a married woman now. I bet Mr. Helgarson loves the bedsheet dance!"

"Well, if *I'm* almost a married woman, what's your excuse? Where do *you* learn these vulgar terms!" Tess had scolded.

"From the maids. Anyway, husbands of twenty years duration may not engage in clothing-ripping, but I am absolutely certain that newlyweds do. Absolutely certain. The man can't wait, you know. He's — he's like a stallion in the springtime." The girls had never been allowed to see a mating, of course, but no one could be around a stable without understanding a stallion's main reason for living.

"Why," Annabel had added, "if your husband doesn't rip off your clothing, it would be a sign of a virtual lack of interest in the act, don't you think? As if you'd already been married for years. In fact, Felton will probably tear your clothes off right there in the carriage!"

Now Tess looked at the little spark in her husband's eyes and had no doubt that if ripping clothing was a prelude that indicated interest, Lucius was likely to start ripping.

She had never felt stupider in her life. How does one say: please do not destroy my clothing until I have more? Was there some way that she could delay the inevitable? Fall sick? Plead her monthly? But then what would happen when her monthly did arrive? Oh, why had Mama died, and left her without advice? Tess bit her lip hard. Soon it would all be over, and she could just accustom herself to married life.

"My house in these parts is not far past the ruins we visited the other day," Lucius said. He was still watching her.

Tess summoned up a smile. "How lovely," she murmured.

"I thought we might stop for a picnic. Rafe's cook packed us a hamper."

"Oh," Tess said flatly. It seemed her new husband wasn't nearly as eager as she had thought to — she wrenched her mind away. It almost felt as if *she* — no! "That would be wonderful! I adore the ruins!"

Lucius swallowed a grin. It seemed his new bride had a thing or two on her mind. But he meant to begin as he would go on. He had a busy life. He traveled frequently and alone. He and Tess had to establish a comfortable married life now: one that promised pleasant company during those days when they happened to be together and pleasant recreation at night, if he happened to be in the same house as she, and they were both amenable.

He had thought about it a great deal, and as long as he never played the *part* of a passionate husband, he would protect her from falling into the illusion that he *was* one. In other words, that he would protect her from the illusion that he was — or would ever be — in love with her. A normal groom wouldn't even consider stopping in a field for a picnic. But they weren't that sort of couple. They were a less intimate couple. He didn't want that sort of intimacy: it suggested too many hidden promises that he would fail to keep. Being that kind of couple would break Tess's heart.

If there was one thing that Lucius was quite sure about, it was that he couldn't bear to see disappointment in Tess's eyes. If she were well aware of his limitations, she would never be disillusioned.

"I'm hungry," he remarked. "And since it's an hour to my house, I'm sure we would be quite uncomfortable if we ignore our appetites."

Her eyes widened again, but she nodded. Obviously, she thought that those just wed didn't feel hunger.

The only problem with Lucius's scheme was that it was damned hard to keep his hands off her. Tess was sitting opposite him, her slender body swaying with the motion of the coach, and all he could think about was pulling her into his arms like the most miserable kind of rascal. He was thinking perfectly rational thoughts about their future, and yet some part of his mind engaged in frenzied thoughts of an entirely different tenor.

What's more, that part of his mind was making an attempt to control his body, too. Lucius casually pulled the fold of his greatcoat over his lap. There was nothing wrong with thinking about what he *wanted* to do. In fact, what he *would* do once they were in their dark bedroom, and the proper amount of time had passed after dinner so that she understood that marital proceedings had a small part in his life, a circumscribed, pleasurable — of course, he would make it pleasurable —

For a moment his rational mind slipped its control, and his head reeled with an image of Tess in a glow of candlelight . . . he would stand before her, kiss her — no. Rub a thumb over the peak of her breast. She would tremble in his arms; he would drink from her sweet mouth, that wicked mouth, drink deep —

No.

His loins were raging, and his control was slipping. He leaned back against the seat and closed his eyes.

"I do believe that I'll take a brief nap," he said to her. His voice was rusty with desire, but surely she would never recognize the note. He looked at her through his eyelashes. Tess looked disconcerted. Good. It was working. She was coming to understand that he wasn't a man of strong emotion.

Of course, he did have one strong emotion. At the moment he was a raging mass of animal lust, every muscle tensed to stop himself from leaping across the seat, kissing her, begging her to forget his stupidity, showing her every way that he could that he was possessed — nay, dying for the touch of her lip. For the touch of her finger . . .

In his imagination, Tess's small hand touched his lips, as she had the other night, and his skin stung with the fire of it, with just the thought of it. Her fingers . . . perhaps touching his neck. Even — mentally, he consigned his neckcloth to perdition. He was almost shuddering

God! That was the carriage shuddering to a halt.

He opened his eyes and pretended that a nap of some forty-five seconds was an utterly refreshing and normal occupation for him.

His footman pulled open the door. Lucius handed out Tess, as perfectly attired and bonneted as she had been when she entered the carriage, and stepped out himself. He avoided meeting the footman's eyes.

Footmen, of course, were free to kiss their brides at any time of day and in any situation. The man probably thought that his master wasn't up to the task, a stone lighter than one could wish.

Another footman was standing to the side, holding what appeared to be several blankets. Dammit, Rafe must have ordered those. And since Rafe didn't have a romantic bone in his body, Lucius could just imagine what he thought this picnic was all about.

A flare of disgust tasted bitter in his mouth. Could Rafe honestly think that he would deflower his new bride in a field where all and sundry, including a spare cow or two, might wander by?

Not he.

Lucius offered an arm to Tess. She smiled at him sweetly.

"Isn't it a beautiful day?"

Lucius looked around rather blindly and nodded. Emerald green grass was appearing where Mr. Jessop had shorn his hay. The willow was beginning to shed yellow leaves onto the grass. It was all rather picturesque.

"Mr. Felton," Tess said.

"Lucius," he interrupted.

She looked up at him. Her face was an enchanting oval. He wrenched his mind away again.

"My name is Lucius," he said, the strain shading his voice with a rather cool tone.

She colored and looked embarrassed. "I'm sorry. I didn't realize — that is, my parents addressed each other formally."

"Probably not when they were alone together," he suggested.

She thought about that for a moment, while he considered the fact that his mother undoubtedly addressed her husband as *Mr. Felton* in every situation, including the most intimate. "I *never* wish to be addressed formally by you," he added.

"Of course," she said. "Lucius."

It sounded wonderful on her lips. The footman spread the blankets under the willow and put the basket down, and then stood looking at him in an extremely annoying fashion. Lucius sighed. He might as well live up to everyone's vulgar expectations.

He stepped to the side and ordered the men to return to the carriage. "Go back to Silchester and find your own meal," he told them brusquely. "You can return in a few hours." Damned but he hated the insinuation in their eyes. He may be a gentleman who — as his parents said — dirtied his hands by working, but that didn't mean he wasn't a *gentleman*.

Tess was waiting for him, kneeling on the bright red blanket and opening the basket. She seemed entirely happy. Likely a cheerful picnic was a much more pleasant idea for her than an excessive junket of sexual enthusiasm about which (Lucius was fairly certain) she knew nothing at all. In fact, he was being a damned thoughtful husband. Somehow the idea was unpleasing.

The willow was the silvery kind. Long tendrils draped themselves over the crimson blanket, and even Tess's hair, making it look tobacco brown in comparison. A glorious, velvety brown . . .

"Would you like to walk to the ruins first?" Lucius asked abruptly.

Tess looked up at him. She was beginning to think that she had married a very moody fellow. One couldn't tell from his face, of course. It was impossible to read anything from Lucius's face. But she could have sworn that he was looking *at* her in the coach, and then that he wasn't, and then she had decided . . . well, it was impossible to know. "Of course," she said, rising to her feet. "Let's go around this way, shall we?" To be honest, she had no particular desire to stumble again over the ruins of the Roman villa.

Rather than setting directly across the field toward the little uneven mounds in the near distance, Tess wandered off to the left. Beyond this hayfield was another one. And beyond that what looked to be a little straggling stone fence, and then a sycamore standing just on the mound of a little hill so that the sunlight turned its leaves golden.

"Look at that," she said softly. "Like the apples of Atlas."

"You're a font of classical knowledge," Lucius said with some surprise. "Did Atlas have a golden tree with a partridge in it?"

"No," she said, with a gurgle of laughter that delighted him. "Perseus found a garden with a golden tree that shaded golden apples. And —"

"I remember!" Lucius said. "He whipped out the head of Medusa and turned Atlas to stone, didn't he?"

"Exactly."

"So you and your sisters must have read as far as the O's then?"

"No. For a short time the local vicar paid some interest in our education, and it was he who introduced Ovid's *Metamorphoses*."

"That seems a very odd choice for a vicar."

"He was an odd vicar. Unfortunately, he began to have strong feelings for Annabel, and my father had to write the bishop and have him sent to another parish."

They had reached the golden tree now, which turned to a rather stately, but obviously unmetallic, sycamore up close. Nestled under the tree were two tip-tilted little graves. Tess immediately knelt down in the grass and rubbed the leaves and grimes off the headstone of the one.

"Emily Caudwell," she read softly. And: "Oh, Lucius, she was only sixteen years old. Poor thing. And here's William."

"The husband, one presumes," Lucius said, bending down to peer at the old stone.

"He didn't die for twenty-four years — or possibly twenty-five, I can't read it clearly."

She was pulling the weeds in front of Emily's tombstone and staining her gloves. Not that it mattered much, since Lucius had already decided to toss out every stitch of clothing belonging to his wife so that he could buy her new, from head to foot. Still, he bent down and pulled a weed or two from William's grave. The poor old sod.

"Don't pull that one," she said, putting a hand on his arm as he was about to jerk up a great clump of wildflowers.

"Why not?"

"It's heartsease. He must have planted it when she died. See — it's all over her grave, and has spread to his."

"Heartsease?" he repeated, looking down at the sprig of fragile-looking blossoms in his hand. They looked rather weedy, although the violet petals with lemon yellow hearts were charming.

"They can't have been married long, since she was only sixteen. Heartsease was a lovely thought on his part. It's also called Love-in-Idleness," she said.

"I prefer Love-in-Idleness," Lucius said, a smile playing around his lips. "Does it have any other names?" Strands of red-gold silk were beginning to fall from her poke bonnet, so, without thinking too much about it, he untied the ribbons under her chin and pulled it off.

More hair tumbled from the pins that held the heavy mass of it at her neck. He picked a tiny spray of yellow flowers and tucked it into her hair.

She was definitely blushing now. How many men were lucky enough to marry a bride who blushed?

"Another name?" he prompted.

"Kiss Her in the Buttery," not looking at him.

He picked three more sprays and tucked

them into her glowing hair. "Kiss Her in the Buttery. What about Kiss Her Under the Sycamore? I swear I've heard that name somewhere."

There was a smile trembling on her lips. "I suppose it *could* be a name."

He came to his knees before her; her lips were as silken as his feverish imagination had remembered them. He slipped his hands into the sleek hair, the perfect shape of her head making his fingers tremble, the little sigh of breath against his lips making him ache.

At first he kissed her as if she were a blushing bride and he an affectionate husband: gently, sweetly, and with an eye to innocence. But gradually the roaring in his blood began to beat back the gentleman in him, and he started to taste her rather than kiss her. And tasting her — tasting Tess, his wife, his own wife — that was like an intoxication in which every touch made him hungrier.

His fingers curled possessively into her sweet-smelling hair, and he bent his head, taking her mouth, that unbearably desirable mouth, with a growl that had nothing to do with gentlemanlike behavior.

If Tess had but known, her husband had just turned into one of those uncultivated men who rip their wife's clothes off their body, who fling themselves on the poor female in a carriage, in a garden . . . under a sycamore tree . . .

But she was drowning, her mind whirling. His mouth was hot on hers — *hot!* How could it be hot? She felt as if all her most important senses were lost, whirling around her so that all she could do was clutch his shoulders and hang on, fighting the strange sensations that kept sweeping over her body, making her knees tremble and an unwonted heat grow between her legs, and her forehead feel feverish — in fact, her whole body feel feverish.

It was alarming at the same time it was enthralling. It was frightening, as if some animal part of her wanted nothing more than to clutch Lucius by his neckcloth and pull him closer and closer. And yet they could hardly be closer; her body was pressed up against his in such a fashion that her breasts were positively squished by his chest, and she could feel — could feel —

Tess began to feel more than a little dizzy. Her hair was all down her back, and his hands were moving over her. When he was kissing her, she couldn't think, but then his lips moved to her throat, and suddenly her mind burst with questions.

"Lucius," she said, her voice quavering into the quiet heat of the afternoon. Nothing answered her but the song of a drowsy grasshopper. But she couldn't be mistaken. Everything that she and Annabel knew about men and women suggested that Lucius was planning to do more than kiss her under the sycamore tree.

"Lucius," she said again. And: "Lucius!" He was caressing her neck, whispering something against her skin, and his great hand was sweeping up her back, caressing her so tenderly that she began to tremble, and a bewildering sweep of heat broke over her body, following the track of his wandering hand, which was — which was —

"Mr. Felton!" she gasped.

He jerked away from her immediately. "Don't ever call me that!" he said, his voice a growl.

"Why not?" she said shakily, trying to concentrate on anything other than the hunger in his eyes and her violent wish to curl her fingers into his hair and pull him back to her.

"My name is Lucius," he said, standing up and helping her to her feet. "Shall we walk to the ruin now?"

It was just the surprise of his kisses that had her heart bumping in her chest like a drum, the shock that was making her feel desolate.

"Well, here we are," she said calmly, as they approached the tumbled-down walls. "What part of the ruin in particular so interested you that you wished to revisit it?"

Lucius could hardly say that there was nothing interesting about a pile of moss-covered rubble. Nor could he say that he'd instigated the picnic for one reason only: to provide a decoy so that his wife would think that he wasn't a ravening beast, wishing only to pull her into his bed.

Which he was.

"I found that bathing room extremely interesting," he answered calmly. "If you would not object, I would be glad to take a second look at the pipe system leading to the bath. I'm thinking of putting in a plunge-bath myself."

He carefully supported Tess down the fall of rocks in the corner. But the bathroom was manifestly uninteresting. After poking at the hole for a moment, he couldn't think how to carry on a pretense of interest.

"This must have led to a cistern," he said.

His wife was looking straight up into the sky, so he looked as well. A few drunken-looking birds were whirling and swooping after each other.

"From Latin, *cisterna*," she said agreeably, not taking her eyes from the starlings.

"Exactly," he said, rather taken aback. "You have some unusual bits of information, Tess." He tipped his head back to watch the birds in flight, as she was doing.

"They're mating," Tess said, turning to look at him. She was feeling suddenly daring, and older, and married.

"I doubt that, at this time of year," Lucius noted.

But Tess was having a rush of joy, and it was going to her head: a rush of joy that she'd married this big, dazzlingly elegant man who looked at her with such hunger. He didn't flatter. And he had none of Mayne's flummery.

The sky was high and blue, her husband was standing beside her looking confused and hungry, and she was married. *Married!* Married women could do anything! They could kiss under a sycamore and not lose their reputations. They could —

She turned slowly toward her husband.

They could do precisely as they wished. They didn't just observe life. They — they reached out and grabbed it.

For the rest of his life, Lucius Felton never forgot the next moment. His blushing, virginal bride disappeared. He found himself facing a woman whose mouth suddenly took on a tilt that could only be described as lustful. That smile was not that of an innocent . . .

She reached out to him, and he blinked, holding back.

"Lucius," she said. Her fingers curled into the hair at the nape of his neck, and she was on her tiptoes, must be on her tiptoes. "Lucius." And since he couldn't get his frozen body to move, she pulled his head toward hers and plastered her lips over his, and what she lacked in the way of experience, she made up for in raw, native talent.

He groaned, and the last threads of his control slipped away.

They were there, the two of them, in each other's arms in a place that may well have seen many an embracing Roman.

But, as Tess had noted during her first visit, the Romans were interested in more than grapes and aqueducts.

Chapter 28

In his adult life, Lucius had never given a second's thought to the idea of deflowering a bride. For one thing, he hadn't planned to have one. And for another, a cynical side of him had the idea that there weren't so many virgins waiting about anyway. And the whole idea of virgins was tedious. What could be more uninteresting than a woman who not only didn't know what she liked, and might well take a dislike to the whole business, but didn't know how to please you either?

No, virgins held no appeal.

Until now.

Because Tess was a virgin likely to win him to the sport in one fell swoop, except that he was quite aware that after making love to Tess, there was no second virgin possible.

She was cheerful, for one thing. Her voice was husky, desire-filled, joy-filled. She didn't tremble from fear, but from excitement. And her eyes weren't bright with terror, but with interest. Curiosity. And her curiosity! She had a wish to kiss the inside of his wrist, and then wondered what the inside of his elbow tasted like. He had to pull off his shirt to satisfy her curiosity, and then the feeling of her slender fingers running all up and down the furring on his chest was enough to undo him. There he was, an English gentleman, bare-chested in the outdoors. It was a curious feeling: rather liberating.

But he kept enough fragile control that he allowed her fingers to sing on his skin, but he didn't touch his breeches. And she, for all her shining eyes and laughter, didn't touch him below the waist.

They ended up, naturally enough, on the moss-covered bench that lined the room. At first they sat side by side. Then she found her way onto his lap.

He didn't know how long she sat there, the curve of her bottom against his legs, his arms tight around her, lips roving over her cheeks, and then returning to her mouth for more aching kisses. They were the kind of kisses from which there is no return. The kind of kisses that drive the blood into a muffled thrum that beats through the body and clouds the mind and finally makes the very idea of gentlemanly behavior an aberration. For wouldn't any man on God's earth, looking at Tess's eyes shining with sensual pleasure, understand that civility was rot? That the restrictions of genteel behavior were rot as well?

The only thing that mattered was making his new bride sigh as his hand shaped her breast. Sigh? Tess didn't sigh: she squeaked his name and closed her eyes, as if what she couldn't see wasn't really happening. But it *was*. They were both there, outdoors; he needed her eyes open, her — without a second's thought he wrenched her bodice down and curled his large hand around the soft weight of her breast.

Her eyes flew open, and she opened her mouth to protest. So he crushed his mouth against hers. It wasn't a gentle kiss, or a kind kiss, or a sweet kiss. It was a demand. The moment he pulled away she opened her mouth again, but:

"Your breast is exquisite," he told her, and whatever she meant to say was swallowed into a sharp cry as his thumb rubbed across her nipple, a cry that shuddered through her body and made her shift closer to him.

"Lucius," she said, and her voice quavered. He rubbed her nipple again, and she collapsed against his chest, eyes closed again.

Lucius couldn't look away from her, from the rosy cream of her lush breast in his hand and the way she arched into his touch, breathing so quickly that every breath was like a cry. He was on fire, every inch of him on fire, and yet some fugitive part of him kept noting that he hadn't crossed all the bounds of propriety yet.

Not yet. Not when he could pull her bodice back up at a second's notice, if he heard voices coming across the field. True, her hair tumbled like molten bronze down her back, and her lips were swollen from his kisses, and she was shuddering.

But it wasn't as if he were touching her below the waist. And then without conscious volition, his fingers were stealing under her skirts, over the weave of her stockings, finding the lump of her garter and stroking on, on to the sweet skin of her thighs, the rounded curve, dancing on her skin, dancing closer, dancing closer . . .

"Lucius Felton!" she said, and her eyes popped open now. "You mustn't — what are you doing?"

"Touching you," he said simply. "Touching my wife."

No one could see what he was doing, had there been anyone to see. There was merely his arm under her skirt, and she in the crook of his arm, her head thrown back so that he could capture her mouth when he wished it, his strong fingers shifting closer and closer . . . her breast lying open to the sunshine, a wanton invitation to pleasure.

She was quivering as his fingers slid closer, her eyes wide. "You mustn't!" she gasped again. He was almost there now. He felt a soft curl of hair against his finger; it sent a lightning stroke of pure lust to his groin.

"Why not?" he asked.

"It's *not* —" But she couldn't even bring into words all the things that this was not.

Lucius grinned at her. Blood was pounding through his body and pooling in his loins, but his brain was still functioning. Barely. "If we were Romans," he said to her, and only the lazy, husky tone of his voice betrayed that they weren't having a simple conversation, "we would both be unclothed."

"And there would be a roof!" she said, going rigid as he cupped her. "Lucius, I really don't think —"

But he couldn't let her finish that foolish protest. "Your body would be laid out before me like a feast," he said to her, his voice deepening even more. "The steam would make your skin slippery. I would probably lay you back on this bench" — he stopped to kiss her, to kiss her into silence — "I would lay you back, Tess, and I would kiss my way down your neck, and down your breast, and the curve of your stomach . . ."

Her eyes were dark as indigo ink. She didn't seem to be breathing, just waiting.

"I would kiss you *here*," he whispered, bending his head to her breast at the very same time he breached her thighs in a slow, dizzying lunge — an exploration, a delight, a curvaceous dance . . . His lips played the same wet dance with her breast, a rough caress that made her body quiver and shake under his touch, under his tongue.

All thought of footmen and picnics had fled Lucius's head, leaving only the sleepy song of the grasshoppers, together with the warm, dappled light that spilled into the Roman bath and made Tess's skin shimmer like diluted sunlight.

A moment, an hour later, he found himself on his knees, unwrapping his bride as if she were the most important present he'd ever received in his life. Under his shaking fingers, strings sang their way apart. Buttons fell apart as if they were never meant to fasten. It was the point of no return.

And at this crucial moment, Tess recovered her voice. It had deepened with desire to a huskier tone, a deeper hue, silken, wondering. "What are you doing now?" she wanted to know, when he pulled her gown over her head. "Are we playing Romans?"

"Undressing you," he said, with a hard kiss, pulling off her chemise as well. And then without waiting for her to catch breath, he scooped her onto his lap and let his hand drift where it longed to be, shaping her breast again and making her cry out in delicious surrender.

Her eyes drifted shut and she leaned against him with utter trust. Blood pounded in his ears and he could hear nothing more than the gentle hum of bees working in the daisies in the banks above them, that and her little gasps of breath when his thumb rubbed in a lazy circle.

But it seemed that he hadn't married a lady. Because she let out a hum of pleasure, a purring noise in her throat that didn't have a trace of self-conscious disapproval in it. Instead, her breast seemed to plump into his hand, a small nipple taut against his palm, a warm sound in her throat for every move of his hand . . .

Of course, this could not go where it showed every sign of going. The weight of her bottom was delicious on his lap. He shifted her back on the bench as if she were that Roman matron he talked of, but she wouldn't stay put. She sat up, all glowing skin, creamy pale curves that swelled to plump breasts, then the curve of her hips, a shy triangle of curls at her thighs.

"There were *two* Romans," she said. "And they were both unclothed."

His hands were wandering over her body with a harder stroke now, a possessive, take-no-prisoners kind of harshness that made her eyes lose their focus and her breath catch in her throat.

But: "You should have no clothing as well." And: "Lucius!"

So he stood up and pulled off his boots, and, his eyes never leaving her, wrenched off his breeches and his smalls.

Tess could feel cool moss under her bare bottom and cool moss at her back. She could hardly believe that her body wasn't burning an imprint. Lucius was all muscle: all smooth, hard lines, beautiful in the sunlight. He turned, and the long line of his flank looked like carved marble, and there in front —

She pressed back against the wall and a thrum of cowardice quivered in her heart. But there was something in his face she'd never seen there before. Was it joy? Desire. He looked free.

Perhaps all men had that wildness when they were — the very thought reminded her that she couldn't imagine a single gentleman of her acquaintance allowing himself to be unclothed in Mr. Jessop's field.

And yet, here was her husband. He was — magnificent. She reached out for him.

Throughout her entire life, Tess never forgot what it felt like when Lucius first snatched her off the bench and held her against his body, skin to skin, softness to muscle, man to woman.

There wasn't room on the bench for the two of them, so they lay on a little nest of clothing, and she explored him. He was rigid — all over.

"I just want you to know," he said, "that I won't actually take you here, Tess. I would never do that."

Her fingers stilled on the muscles of his flank. She had been thinking foggily that she would be more brave in touching him: after all, his fingers were *everywhere*.

So she slid her fingers there: over the clean smooth length of him, enjoying the hiss of breath from behind his clenched teeth, the involuntary jerk of his body.

But her skin longed for that feeling of him, so she came closer, until her breasts were against his chest, and he jerked again. She nuzzled his neck, and he made a rough sound in his throat; she ran her fingers over the muscles of his back, and her breasts rubbed against his chest again. He was shaking; she could feel his body shaking against hers.

Tess was the one grinning now. There is a great deal of pleasure in power, after all.

A second later she was flat on her back, and — the grin fled, like a dream in the night. One touch of his fingers, his lips at her breast, and she was crying out, twisting up toward him, lost in a fog of intoxicated sensation.

But Lucius was having a moment of clarity. "I can't do it, Tess," he gasped, stilling his fingers.

But she whimpered and bucked against him, so he answered her silent demand even though the slick welcome to his fingers turned his mind black, but still one thought caught. Her mother died years ago. She *had no mother.*

"It's not a question of breeding, Tess," he told her, trying to control his voice.

"The first time for women is painful. There's — there's blood. You wouldn't be comfortable here."

She blinked, and he saw she did know that. But the knowledge slid away instantly, replaced by a haze of desire, and she arched against him again, the softness of her inflaming him, the wantonness of her snapping his control.

He didn't seem to be able to stop touching her, his fingers taking a rhythm that they couldn't stop. Her full breasts rubbed against his chest and left streaks of fire, and she was twisting under him, moaning and crying, and suddenly she grabbed his shoulders. Her eyes flew open. "*This* hurts, Lucius," she said. "*This* hurts."

He let his fingers sink into her warmth.

"That doesn't hurt," she gasped, and then pulled his head down and kissed him — a kiss that was a moan, a touch and sound at once.

He let his hand fall away. It took nothing more than a delicious thought to poise himself against her. He was hungry for her, desperate for her.

A cry came from her throat — but it didn't speak of pain. Still . . . the blood. Every instinct told him that a gently raised female should experience something so distressing in her own bed, on clean sheets, in the dark preferably.

But Tess showed not the slightest wish to retreat into the shade.

She opened her eyes with a gasp and found her husband's dark eyes looking down at her. She couldn't help it, she laughed: a laugh and a gasp at once. "Don't be so serious, Lucius!"

"I feel you might regret —"

"Never," she interrupted. "You mustn't think we're the first to make love in Farmer Jessop's field."

"The Romans were long ago and as you say, they had a roof."

"Emily," she said, panting a little. "Emily and William. She was only sixteen — and why do you think he buried her under the sycamore tree?"

He was braced on his elbows above her and he just nudged her. A silent acknowledgment, an acknowledgment of Emily and her William.

"Do that again!"

He did, and a pleading sound flew from her lips.

"Again —"

She was arched toward him, thrown in erotic abandonment, crying with every touch. So he fell free suddenly, shook off thoughts of civility and white sheets and darkened rooms. What had that to do with his own wanton, ecstatic wife, her fingers digging into his shoulders?

He thrust.

Her eyes flew open and fixed on his face. He waited for her cry, for pain, for — for a gush of blood? He hardly knew what he was waiting for. It was as if the whole spun-sunshine silent world hung for a second, the blue sky holding its breath.

But her eyes were shining. "Go *on,*" she said in a husky whisper. "Or — or" — and now there was something like anguish in her eyes — "was that all?"

There, in the Roman baths, with swallows circling overhead, Mr. Lucius Felton threw back his head and laughed. And since his new wife took exception to his humor, he must needs soothe her vexed feelings.

So he thrust himself slowly into her again, and encountered nothing but joy. They experimented, until they found a rhythm that matched their passion.

The only thing pounding through Tess's mind was an urge to move. She understood, suddenly, with shocking clarity, crude stable jests about *riding* women. But was she being ridden? Or was she riding? Their bodies met each other with fierce strength. Lucius's breath was making a harsh sound, and he was clenching his teeth, braced on his arms, eyes shut.

Tess looked up at him and knew that she was losing control of the ride: her body was flying free on its own, riding him harder and higher. Suddenly she felt his hand rub across her nipple, a rough shaping of her breast with a hand that said, without words, this body is *mine*.

And she flung free, the heat exploding to the very ends of her fingertips, free with a cry that disappeared into the blue sky.

Chapter 29

Lucius's house was a Tudor collection of herringbone brick and tiny mullioned windows patched in rather higgledy-piggledy, with roofs sloping down in all directions. It looked as if Elizabethan ancestors had added on various chambers when they felt like it, and the whole had settled into the ground until it had a slightly crazed but comfortable look about it.

It wasn't nearly as large as Holbrook Court. It certainly wasn't a castle, as Annabel predicted, nor even a mansion. It was a large house, a large, charming, comfortable pile of a house.

Tess didn't realize just how much she was dreading becoming the Lady of the Castle until the carriage drew to a halt. "Is this it?" she breathed.

Lucius waved off his footman and helped her from the carriage. "Yes, this is Bramble Hill. Do you like it?"

She looked up at him, eyes glowing, and breathed, "Oh, Lucius, I adore it!" It wasn't until a few minutes later that she realized there was profound relief in his eyes.

"It's not as grand as Holbrook Court," he remarked.

They were walking up a wide sweeping circle of stairs to the large door. "I would dislike that very much," Tess said frankly. "I thought you would live in a castle."

"A castle?"

She nodded.

"I can buy you a castle if you'd wish."

"No, thank you."

Servants were spilling out of the entrance portico now, lining up on either side. Lucius might not live in a castle, but he certainly appeared to have enough staff for one.

"This is Mr. Gabthorne," Lucius said, introducing her to a round, cheerful-looking butler. "I am happy to say that Mrs. Gabthorne acts as a housekeeper for us, and does a wonderful job too. And this is . . ."

Introducing the servants — each of whose names Lucius recalled without difficulty — took over forty minutes. Afterward Lucius led her into a lofty-ceilinged sitting room that opened with huge arched windows to the gardens.

"Bramble Hill was redesigned two years

ago by John Nash, working with a landscape gardener," Lucius remarked. "All the main rooms have windows to the ground. From the drawing room, one can look west or south, either across the park, or past the conservatory and along the valley."

Tess turned around and around in the drawing room. The entrance to the garden was all entangled with ivy, honeysuckle, and jasmine. "It must be utterly beautiful in the summer."

"I'm fond of it," Lucius agreed.

She turned around and looked at him sharply. "I am surprised by all this —" She waved her hand at the graceful furniture and heavy silk rose fabric at the windows. The floor was strewn with rugs in faded jewel colors.

"Why?"

"I suppose because it's so — so homey. And yet it's not a family home, is it?"

Lucius strolled over to the mantelpiece and seemed absorbed in gathering a few fragrant chrysanthemum petals that had fallen from a bowl. "If you mean by that, did I grow up here, or was this house in my family when I was a child, no."

"Of course that's what I meant," Tess said. "You found this house yourself."

He nodded.

"And you furnished it so beautifully."

"I had help," he said mildly. "I travel a great deal, so it was no hardship to find pieces that I like and have them shipped here. I'm afraid you'll find, Tess, that I am rather set in my ways. All my houses look like this."

Her eyes widened. "Exactly like this?"

He laughed. "Not exactly."

And then, "*How* many houses are we talking about?"

He cocked his head, almost as if he were listening to the wind. "Four . . . five counting the hunting lodge."

Tess sat down suddenly. "And each is as beautifully appointed as Bramble Hill."

"I like to be surrounded by attractive things," he said, sitting down opposite her.

"Each has a full staff?"

"Naturally."

"It might as well be a castle," Tess said, blinking at him.

"I trust not."

"It's not the beauty of it that surprises me," Tess said, looking around again. "It's the way it looks, well, as if it had been here for a hundred years. As if you inherited it from a great-grandfather." She walked over to the wall and stood before a grand lady in an extremely starched ruff. The lady was clutching a fan, and looking down her nose, and altogether had the look of a rather ferocious ancestor.

"A portrait of an Elizabethan lady," Lucius said, walking over to her. "I bought it when the Lindley estate was sold off. Presumably she is a Lindley, although the sellers were unable to tell me her name."

Tess looked up at the fierce lady, nameless now and yet clearly so proud of her name. It seemed odd that Lucius had hung portraits that any reasonable person would assume to be his own ancestors, but she couldn't quite put her feeling into words without seeming critical, so she kept her tongue.

"I bought this painting at the same time," Lucius said, leading her across the room.

It was a girl, half-turned toward the room. For all its formality, her personality peeked through: she was wistful, yet there was a dimple in her cheek.

"That's lovely," Tess said. "I don't suppose you know who she is?"

"No idea. The painting was sold to me as a Vandyke, but I believe it's likely of the school, rather than the master himself."

Tess had no idea who Vandyke was, and she was conscious of a growing feeling of inadequacy. Lucius's house was so — so perfect. Perfectly appointed, even to the extent of ready-made ancestors. Perhaps this was common in England; *she* had never heard of hanging a portrait of an utterly unknown person. "Do you not have any representations from your own family?" she asked, and then could have bitten her tongue. Of course his family would not have given him any such thing.

But he answered easily enough. "None at all," and took her by the arm and led her through the gardens.

They were strolling through the rosebushes, all pollarded and stricken-looking, the poor things, when Tess asked: "And your house in London, is it as exquisite as this one?"

"I think so," Lucius said rather indifferently, poking a rock off the path with his cane.

"With similar portraits on the walls?"

He nodded. "I have a nice portrait of three children by William Dobson in the drawing room: I do know who those are. They were the children of a roundhead cavalier during the Civil Wars, whose name was Laslett."

"Are there still Lasletts in England?"

"I would expect they are somewhere,"

Lucius said. "I haven't the faintest idea. I've never met one, at any rate."

They turned down a path that led to a charming pergola. Tess admired the structure and thought about her husband.

It wouldn't do, that's all. It simply wouldn't do. Somehow she had to mend the fences between her husband and his parents, and then the first thing she would do after that would be to remove all these — these spurious relatives from the walls and give them back to whomever they belonged to. It wasn't right to have other people's family on one's walls. It was as if Lucius was trying to create a new family to replace the one that discarded him.

"Perhaps the Lasletts can't afford to buy the portrait back," Tess said, as they strolled back to the house.

"The Dobson portrait?" Lucius asked. He looked down at her, his dark eyes curious. "Likely not. I bought it for nearly a thousand pounds."

"There was a portrait of my mother that used to hang in her chamber," Tess said.

"I'll find it," Lucius said, before she had to continue.

"It might be difficult . . . it's been a very long time since my father —"

But Lucius was smiling. "I'll find it," he

repeated gently. "Now, may I show you the rest of the house? The lady's bower, for instance?"

There was something in his eyes that made Tess blush, and once they reached that bower, a perfect frenzy of rosebuds and ruffled silk, it was clear that Lucius's interest was less in playing guide than in . . . something else.

Naturally, there was a portrait of a lady hanging on the wall there too, just across from a beautiful rosewood writing desk. She was posed on a bench in the woods, leaning on one hand. Her eyes gazed at the viewer lazily, her other hand holding a book that she seemed too indolent to read. Tess moved quite close, trying to see the spine of her book.

"She's reading Shakespeare," Lucius said. "*Much Ado about Nothing*. Although I fear that the inestimable play seems to be sending her to sleep."

"Do you know who she is?" Tess asked.

"A Lady Boothby. I am not certain of her first name. The portrait is by Benjamin West and dates to the 1780s."

Tess blinked at Lady Boothby. "She's probably still *alive*," she pointed out.

"I quite like her," Lucius said.

"So do I," Tess agreed. "But I am not

quite certain that I wish to share my chambers with Lady Boothby."

"An odd way of thinking about it," Lucius said. "I have instructed my agents to buy any portrait that comes on the market by Benjamin West."

"Why do you have so many people spread about your houses?" she asked. "Portraits, I mean."

He tipped up her chin. "I'd much rather talk of *you* than Lady Boothby," he said, his lips brushing hers.

"But Lucius, I don't wish a portrait of a stranger in my intimate chamber," Tess said, trying to explain to him.

He shrugged. "Much ado about nothing, my dear. I'll have her removed to the attics immediately."

"The attics!" It seemed wrong to banish Lady Boothby to the attics.

Lucius had started kissing her neck, and his hands were drifting down her back.

He's distracting me, Tess thought. Clearly, he doesn't want to discuss Lady Boothby or any of those other portraits.

But that was the last clear thought she had for over an hour.

Chapter 30

October 1
Bramble Hill

Dearest Annabel and Josie,

I am writing this in my private sitting room, which sounds very grand but is precisely the same size as Mama's dressing room. As it turns out, Lucius does not own a castle. Bramble Hill is decorated with particular splendor, but truly, it is not much larger than our house in Scotland. The ground floor has a drawing room next to the dining room, where our library used to be; Lucius's study is to the back, overlooking the gardens, and there is a lovely salon between it and the dining room. I long to show you everything, and Lucius promises to bring you both here soon, perhaps as early as next week.

Is there any news of Imogen? Please do let me know as soon as she returns.

Lucius feels that she and Lord Maitland may take some time on their return trip. Since you will see her first, do give her my love.

I feel as if your questions are sounding in my ear as I write, Annabel. Lucius (perhaps I should refer to him as Mr. Felton, but he most dislikes that) is all that could be termed generous. He very much enjoys bestowing gifts on me. Yesterday he brought me a parrot with bright yellow feathers and a purplish beak. She is quite young and so cannot say a word, but apparently she will learn to speak if I apply myself. I spent a great deal of time this morning feeding her seeds in order to gain her confidence. She is dreadfully messy and enjoys flinging shells in every direction. The man who brought her to the house advised me to keep her with me as much as possible so that she will view me as a friend. She loves being out of her cage but finds her excitement difficult to control. It is fortunate that I am fond of bathing (and I leave you to ascertain the connotations of her excitement!).

I spent a good part of yesterday trying to come to an understanding of this household, only one of five houses Lucius owns. He works very long hours in his study, and I hesitate to interrupt him except for matters of the greatest importance, so it is a bit of a puzzle.

I shall write again after breakfasting tomorrow. Please do let me know by return post how you are both going on. I miss you.

Much love,
Your sister, Mrs. Felton
(I couldn't resist)

October 2
Bramble Hill

PRIVATE

Dear Annabel,

I am writing you this note privately because I feel that you are likely bursting with questions — none of which I intend to answer! Marriage is a very interesting state of affairs; I will tell you that.

Lucius is the sort of man who always knows precisely the most civilized response to any situation. I assure you that I shall soon be the most well mannered person in Christendom, simply by watching his example. He works far harder than Papa ever did; I shouldn't see him from morning to night if I didn't go to his study with occasional questions.

It has occurred to me that perhaps it would be good for Lucius if life were a bit more surprising. But this is, obviously, a matter for the future.

With love,
Tess

October 4
Bramble Hill

Dear Annabel and Josie,

I can imagine the two of you reading this together, probably curled up on Annabel's bed. I have named my parrot Chloe, although why I gave her such a refined name, I don't know. She does seem to have a liking to me, which she exhibits by pecking at my hair and squawking very loudly when I enter a room. The housekeeper, Mrs. Gabthorne, has taken a dislike to her. There was an unfortunate episode with a cup of tea, and I fear that Mrs. Gabthorne will never get over the shock of it.

I have to say that while one would

think it would be much easier to run a large house with the help of many servants, I am finding it quite a task. Mrs. Gabthorne is feuding with the head housemaid, Dapper. According to Mrs. Gabthorne, Dapper has an eye for one of the footmen who is at least five years her junior, and Mrs. Gabthorne worries (very righteously, you understand) that Dapper will attempt to corrupt the youth. Meanwhile Dapper tells me that Mrs. Gabthorne is "borrowing" tea and taking it to her sisters in the village. And how am I to ascertain the truth of that, pray? Of course, I daren't mention the footman to Dapper, either. In all, I find it more work to manage an establishment with servants than it was to manage a quite similar-sized house without servants.

The arrival of Lady Griselda's modiste is, indeed, a wonderful occurrence, and I naturally understand why you would rather remain at our guardian's house for the moment. I am not certain why you say that the scandal of Imogen's marriage is greatly lessened, however; in what manner and by what means? Do give Imogen a kiss from me when you see her this evening. I was so happy to have her note and hear that she and Lord Maitland are happily settled at Maitland House.

Love,
Tess

October 7
Bramble Hill

Dear Annabel and Josie,

This will be a very short note as I must dress for dinner. I have moved our evening meal forward as Lucius leaves for the city tonight. He plans to work during the day and return here the following evening, again traveling by night. I cannot feel this frantic motion is healthful. And of course, this means that he will not be able to join us for the races at Silchester tomorrow, but I shall see you there, Annabel.

I am utterly flummoxed to hear that my husband apparently saved Imogen from a Gretna Green marriage. He has mentioned nothing. One would think that marrying a man would give one insight into his character, but I seem to find Lucius more puzzling day by day. I am eager to hear all the details from Imogen when I see her at the races.

Josie, I shall miss you, but I do agree with Miss Flecknoe that dancing lessons are of great importance in a young lady's life. Annabel and Imogen will give you all my news from Silchester, and there will be many such races in the future.

My love to everyone,
Tess

Chapter 31

A half hour or so before their evening meal would be served Tess knocked on the connecting door that led to her husband's chambers. She wasn't sure of the etiquette of marriage: did one knock on one's husband's door? For some reason, it felt odd. Yet at the same time, if he were occupied in personal ablutions . . . she heard the deep sound of Lucius's voice saying something to his valet, and then his unhurried steps to the door.

"Good evening, my dear," he said.

The sight of him gave Tess the most peculiar sensation. He stood there with a look of inquiry on his face, and her knees grew weak, and the only thing she could think about was kissing him. She had the sudden sensation that her corset was too tight; she couldn't breathe properly. This reaction should have become familiar to her by now, but instead it seemed to grow stronger every moment.

The worst of it was that Lucius was clearly not similarly affected by her presence. He was unremittingly polite when they encountered each other in the breakfast room, at supper, or in a corridor. On those rare occasions that she ventured into his study, he never failed to offer his advice when it came to a knotty household problem. But he showed no wish to dally, or gaze in her eyes, or indulge in any manner of newlywed behavior.

This afternoon, for instance, when she entered his study to ask him a question about the diamond bracelet that suddenly appeared on her pillow, she had taken no more than a glance at the Empire-backed crimson settee in his study before a remarkably inflaming image appeared in her mind. But when she perched on his armchair and tried her best to entice him into neglecting his affairs — if only briefly — she had no success.

He moved away from her kisses and politely but firmly told her that he had work to do. She insisted on giving him a thank-you kiss; he insisted that she leave his study after the merest buss on her cheek. She gathered all her courage and melted against his chest, raising her face to his; he stepped backward so quickly that she almost toppled to the floor, after which he bowed her from the room.

It was only after Gussie had bathed and dressed her for night that Lucius would transform from friendly acquaintance to husband. And then, indeed, his eyes had a wicked shine, and he showed passionate interest in his wife.

Yet to all appearances, she was the only one who seemed afflicted during the day by thoughts of the evenings — and nights — they spent together.

For example, here he was, exquisitely dressed in a coat of somber blue, and all she could think of was the previous night and the way he nuzzled her stomach. And lower. She could feel her cheeks flaming.

"Tess," Lucius said. "Is there some way that I can aid you?"

"I am having some difficulty deciding which gown to wear tonight," Tess said, pulling herself together. "I am faced with a greater selection than I have had in my entire life. Do you think that I should wear this velvet gown, or that of sarsenet?" She indicated the two gowns placed on her bed.

He strolled over, and said, "Did *I* order that black velvet?"

"No, you did not," she said, nettled. "If my memory is correct, I ordered all the gowns in question. *You* merely lent me the benefit of your advice."

"You're not in full mourning," he said. "Wear the green. The black is a bit drab, don't you think?"

"No, the black is extremely elegant," Tess said, feeling a surge of stubbornness. Why *didn't* he ever show any signs of wishing to make love to her other than after twilight? Was he on a schedule of some sort?

"I prefer you in less drab clothing," he said, leaning against one of the posts of her bed.

"I believe I shall wear the black velvet," Tess said, just to be contrary. And then, to be even more contrary, she turned her back to him, and said, "If you would be so kind as to tighten my corset, Lucius. Gussie has gone to the kitchens on an errand."

"Of course," he murmured, walking over to her.

Tess couldn't help it; the very touch of his fingers gave her a peculiar physical sensation, like a melting in her lower stomach. Even the notion that he was standing just behind her — and now, lacing her corset in such a way that her breasts seemed to swell to at least twice their size. But it wasn't the corset that gave her the tingling sensation that her breasts were lush and — and desirous. That was the memory of last night. Her heart slammed against her ribs at the very thought.

Why should she allow her husband to think of her as a woman only at bedtime? And only when they were in her bedchamber? From which he discreetly departed at sometime during the night — and she didn't like that either, now she thought of it.

She walked away from him, feeling his eyes on her waist and allowing her hips to take on a sultry sway that she wouldn't even have understood only days before. After a few steps she glanced back at him over her shoulder. "If you would be so kind, Lucius," she said casually. "The gown."

A moment later the sweet smell of new velvet came over her head. Protecting her hair, she settled it over her shoulders. This was no drab mourning gown. It was cut extremely low, so low that the little sleeves fell down her shoulders and almost touched her elbows. It wasn't cut straight across either. The bodice dipped just at her cleavage. The best part of it, to Tess's mind, was the ermine trim, which nestled between her breasts and the glowing black velvet.

He still hadn't said a word. So she turned around quite slowly, and said, with every drop of casual interest she could muster, "Do I look unbearably drab, then, Lucius?"

He wasn't leaning against her bedpost any longer. His eyes had blackened to inky-dark, and he didn't look like a composed, perfect gentleman anymore.

Tess pulled up her skirts to reveal a slender ankle clad in silver silk that shimmered slightly in the candlelight.

He looked down obediently, and she arched her foot. "Do you suggest black slippers," she asked. "Or the shoes with the high heels? The shoes buckle on one side, like those of gentlemen, which is a rather amusing touch."

He stared at her feet for a moment, and then gave his sudden smile, the one he gave so rarely. It transformed his whole face. The power of it jolted down her legs like an electric shock. "I can only think that I am being punished," he observed. "Although I am uncertain of my transgression."

He knelt at her feet and slipped on the buckled high heels, his fingers sending shivers up her leg.

"Nonsense," she said, when he had finished, turning to her mirror and picking up a necklace of emeralds she had found on her breakfast plate two days ago. "Will you fasten this for me, Lucius?" And she bent her neck obediently and waited for his fingers to touch her there.

She seemed to spend a great deal of her day waiting for his fingers to touch her, now she thought about it.

He took the emeralds but let them slide back down to the dressing table.

"What would you like me to do, Tess?" he said. "Other than dress you?"

"Be impetuous," she whispered, her cheeks flaming with the boldness of it. But she met his eyes in the mirror and made herself relax back against his chest.

With a wild thrill of excitement she felt his fingers trace a delicious path from her throat to her collarbone, and then to the swell of her breasts.

"We are due at the table within the hour," Lucius said, turning her slightly and bending his head so that his lips could begin kissing the trail blazed by his fingers.

"Yes," Tess said weakly. She wanted to wrap her fingers into his hair. But she couldn't help him at all. Not at all. He had to make up his own mind. So she didn't reach out and —

"It's extremely ill bred to inconvenience the chef," Lucius observed. His lips had feasted on the delicate hollow of her collarbone and were sliding onto the plump slopes of her breasts.

"Yes," Tess said. Could she simply touch his shoulder? No. He had to make up his mind without her persuasion.

Suddenly, Lucius straightened and walked a few strides to the door. He opened it, and said briskly, "Why don't we enjoy a preprandial drink in the parlor?"

Tess stared at him in bewilderment. He had made up his mind — and he wanted to leave? To go to dinner?

He had made up his mind *incorrectly.*

And it was up to her, his wife, to inform him of that fact.

Of course, Lucius was standing in the doorway looking the very picture of domestic tranquillity. As if they'd been married some forty years! So Tess took matters into her own hands.

"I must say good-bye to Chloe," she said, turning toward the large cage in the corner. The moment she approached, Chloe squawked at her and tipped her head to one side in a charming greeting.

"That parrot has a rather annoying shriek," Lucius observed, walking over to the cage. “I had hoped that she would be company for you while I’m away, but her salutations may be more aggravating than cheering.”

“Do you travel often at night?” Tess asked, as she took Chloe from the cage. “It sounds so uncomfortable.”

“To London and back on a regular basis. If I travel at night, I lose no working time.”

“And do you see your parents when you are in London?” Tess carefully didn’t look at him. Chloe came out of the cage with an enthusiastic screech, clinging to Tess’s finger and waving her wings furiously to balance herself.

“Aren’t they supposed to be graceful birds?” Lucius said, stepping back as Chloe almost disbalanced. She flapped her wings so vigorously that a few small seeds flew into the air.

“Do you ever see your parents in London?” Tess repeated.

“Never. And they wouldn’t wish it,” he added.

There didn’t seem to be any way to ask further questions without seeming inquisitive, so Tess allowed Chloe to walk up her arm. Chloe leaned against Tess’s cheek for a moment and nibbled her ear affectionately. Tess scratched her head, and Chloe let out another shriek. She was getting more and more excited, shifting from leg to leg and squawking.

Lucius was staring at her with a raised eyebrow. "What a peculiar animal," he remarked. "Are you —"

But his voice broke off as Chloe succumbed to pure excitement.

"Damnation!" Lucius roared.

"Don't frighten her!" Tess said sharply, picking up Chloe and stowing her back into the cage. Chloe knew she'd done something wrong; she was making little squeaks that sounded somewhere between penitent and delinquent.

Typically, Lucius had moved from anger to practicality without another breath. "How are we going to get you out of this gown without risking your hair?"

Familiarity had not made Tess any happier with Chloe's bodily functions. "It has to go down, rather than up," Tess said. "Pull it down, if you please, Lucius."

"Down?" Lucius asked dubiously.

Tess pulled her arms through the tiny sleeves and yanked at her bodice. She gave a little wiggle. "It would be easier if you do it," she told him, carefully keeping her face bland.

So he carefully slid the close-fitting black

velvet down over her breasts, down her slender waist, with a tug over her hips, and, finally, she lifted her feet to allow him to pull it off.

"And my corset," Tess commanded, turning her back. "Please. I must bathe."

She felt his fingers at the ties on her corset and bit her lip so that she didn't smile.

Chloe was crooning hoarsely, obviously comforting herself. Tess silently promised her an extra helping of seeds in the morning.

The laces fell from her corset. Tess promptly pulled it forward and off of her body, and then pulled her chemise over her head as well, throwing it to the side. All she wore now were a pair of delicate lawn pantaloons — the very latest style, straight from Paris — her stockings, and her high heels.

"Lucius," she said, looking at him over her shoulder, "I'm afraid that I shall be lamentably late to dinner. The chef will be displeased."

She walked over and put one leg on the stool before her dressing chair, then bent over and began unbuckling her high heels.

A second later he was there, behind her. "I should be more impetuous, hmmm?" he said into her hair, but one large hand was curling around the curve of her bottom, and the other had pulled her snug against him. There was something in his voice that was both amused and potent, simmering from laughter into desire.

"Yes," she managed.

But that was all she managed, for at least a good hour, after which she said, rather drunkenly, "Again?" And then, with rather more interest, "Like that?"

Lucius must have been too tired to sneak away to London like a thief in the night. Because when Tess awoke in the early dawn, there was a large male body sprawled in the bed next to hers.

She bent over and asked: "London?"

"Not today," he said groggily.

She said one more word in his ear.

"Again?" he asked, but there was a smile in his voice. And later: "Like that, Tess?"

And finally: "God, but marriage is a surprise to me."

Chapter 32

Horse races are noisy affairs. The Cup itself wouldn't be run for two hours, but already the men crowding the railing were shouting and jostling amongst themselves, watching a group of two-year-olds tear around the back-stretch, heading for the starting gate. Eager bettors were howling at the jockeys, and then howling at each other. The grandstand shook as thirty-two or thirty-six hooves pounded by. One could smell dust and sweating horses, an odor as familiar to Tess as that of roses or baking bread.

Lucius took her arm and led her not to the grandstand, but to a small white structure just to its left.

"The royal box?" she asked.

"Not anymore," he answered. "It belonged to the Duke of York, who was very eager to give it up and even more eager for an influx of cash for his stables. I thought we might wish for a place of our own."

Tess thought, not for the first time, how very nice it was to be married to someone richer than a royal duke. The box was lovely: a proper room, with large open windows just on the track. It was furnished in a lavish manner that would suit the Duke of York: all hung with red velvet and gilded candelabras that looked rather tawdry in the sunlight.

Imogen and her husband were already settled at the windows. "How *are* you?" Tess asked her sister, giving her a delighted kiss. "I've missed you so; you can have no idea!"

"I am very well," Imogen said, smiling hugely. "How very nice to see you again, Mr. Felton. I understood you would be in London today."

"As it happened, I changed my mind," Lucius said, giving Tess a quick, wicked grin.

"I'm so sorry you arrived before us," Tess said, trying not to think about what had delayed them in bed that morning.

"We've been here since the warm-up rounds, of course, as Draven believes that he should be here from the very moment the books are opened. It's very important to know who the favorites are early."

"I — yes, I know," Tess said. How could she not? Had not Papa discoursed on the art of laying bets throughout virtually every meal they had shared in the last ten years?

"Annabel sends her heartfelt apologies," Imogen said. "Lady Griselda's *modiste* must return to London tomorrow, and Annabel has ordered so many gowns that she was needed for fittings all day. But she told me that she and Josie are coming to you within the week."

"She must be in seventh heaven," Tess said. "Are you ordering some clothing as well?"

Imogen shook her head. "Oh no, we —" But she broke off. "Josie is quite happy too. Her governess declared herself appalled by Josie's lack of etiquette, but they have struck a happy bargain according to which Josie submits to what she calls 'ladylike flummery' in the morning, and then she is allowed to read all she likes in the afternoon."

"Why aren't you ordering new clothing?" Tess persisted.

Imogen glanced at her husband, but he and Lucius were standing at the front of the box, watching a low-bodied, muscled horse sweep through the finish line. "I'm afraid that Draven lost a great deal of money at Lewes this week," she whispered to Tess.

"How much?" Tess asked bluntly.

"Twenty thousand pounds." And then, at Tess's expression, Imogen added hastily, "But trifles of this sort don't weigh heavily on a nature such as Draven's. He is in all things optimistic. But I do wish to do my part in keeping the household expenses down, of course. He was *so* crestfallen afterward."

"I can imagine," Tess said. All she had to do was picture her father's face.

They were interrupted by Draven, who wished to take Lucius to the stables so that they might supervise the dressing of some horse whose name Tess didn't catch. There was a roar of excitement from the crowd. Draven and Imogen rushed to the windows to find out what had happened. Lucius, quick as a wink, pulled her to her feet, backed her up a bit, put his hands on her face, and gave her one hard kiss.

Tess's mind blurred into an image that sprang to her mind from that morning: of him arched over her, his chest golden in the morning light, his face anything but expressionless — looking down at her, clenching his teeth, driving her higher and higher, watching her . . .

And now he had the same look in his eye, and all he was doing was rubbing her cheek with his thumb — his gloved thumb.

"How *do* you do that?" she asked.

"What?"

"Make me —" She stopped and pulled away, but her back was against the wall. Draven was leaning out of the box, howling at the racetrack. Tess could feel herself blushing. "*Think* of you," she whispered.

"I think of you," he said steadily, his eyes on hers. He wasn't even touching her, and her body was trembling. His eyes slid to the red velvet sofa that stood next to them, designed to support the Duke of York's not inconsiderable weight.

Tess could feel crimson spilling into her cheeks. But at the same time there was a welcoming pulse in her veins, in her heart.

Lucius put her hand down and strolled over to her sister and Draven. Tess leaned her head back against the wall and tried to think clearly. Without seeming to lift a finger, her husband was able to turn her — to entice her —

Suddenly she realized that Imogen was calling a cheerful good-bye, and Draven was ushering his wife out of the box, and Lucius was closing the door behind them. And locking it.

"You can't!" she whispered frantically.

"You mustn't even *think* such a thing!"

"Think what?" Lucius said. His eyes were lit with laughter as he strolled toward her. As she watched, he began deliberately pulling off his right glove, one finger at a time. She watched in fascinated horror as he tossed it onto the chair. It was followed by his left glove.

"I don't know what you're doing," Tess said with a gasp. But *she* knew perfectly well what he was doing. Her sensible, expressionless husband was removing his greatcoat, and there was an expression on his face that even a virgin wouldn't have mistaken. Her knees were trembling.

"This box is open," she pointed out. "Open to the public!"

"The windows look directly onto the track," he said agreeably. His voice had darkened to a timbre that she recognized. "The only people who might see us would have to be on the track itself."

What sounded like a herd of elephants thundered by on that track. "There are many people out there!" she whispered. He was unbuttoning his waistcoat. As she watched, he slipped free one button, and another, and another.

"Jockeys," he said. "Jockeys have better things to do than peer into windows. You wanted me to be more impetuous," he reminded her.

"I didn't mean this!" she gasped.

The waistcoat flew to the side in a flash of dark green. Despite herself, Tess's heart was beginning to pound.

A referee trotted past. He didn't look in their direction, but his striped shirt and small cap were as close to her as — "Don't you dare take your shirt off!" she cried.

Lucius started walking toward her now, his eyes gleaming. Tess felt like sinking back against the wall like a fainting heroine in a melodrama, but she forced herself to give him a minatory frown instead. "Anyone on a horse can see directly into this room," she pointed out.

"Mmmmm," he said, in an extremely unsatisfactory fashion. He tossed his hat onto the couch. Then all of a sudden, he was just in front of her, so close that his body breathed warmth against her and she suddenly smelled a spicy, out-of-door smell that was his alone. Her husband's.

"Oh, Lucius," she whispered, looking up at him. She knew her heart was in her eyes.

"Tess," he growled back. She was standing in the corner, his large body blocking her from anyone's view.

"They can't see you here," he said.

He was right. She could feel a smile forming on her lips, even as she tried to look stern and not — surely not — eager.

"That's irrelevant," she managed to say around the pounding in her throat. But he was pulling up her skirts.

"I have — to — touch — you," he said fiercely. "Do you hear me, Tess? I haven't been able to —"

But that large hand thrust between her legs before she could formulate an answer, and then she did act like a fainting heroine, melting toward him with a gasp. But he was there, a strong arm cradling her against his chest, his fingers sliding into her curls, into her warmth, and then, when she opened her mouth to protest, his mouth closed over hers. He held her against him, captive in his arms.

For a moment she struggled, but his mouth was hot on hers and his hand . . . his hand moved fluidly, made the blood course through her body and his lips were persuasive on hers, tender, asking, begging . . . Abruptly Tess stopped struggling and curled against him, curled into his kiss.

He said something, a hoarse word that she couldn't hear over the blood pounding in her ears. So he said it again: "*Please* . . . Tess?"

She gasped and looked at him, and the smile in her heart must have been in her eyes. Because his hands took up a different rhythm, stroking her more roughly now, and all she could do was cling to him, keeping her lips on his so that she couldn't possibly say no, as she ought to do.

Lucius looked down at her, and the stray thought came into his mind that he was not doing his best to demonstrate to his wife that she was no more than a fixture in his life, to be enjoyed at appropriate times and in appropriate places.

But there was no time for that. Tess was panting, little urgent pants that made him long to sweep her over to York's sofa and thrust into her warmth. But he couldn't do that. Someone might see us, he told himself. Her nails were biting into his shoulder.

"We really shouldn't do this," she panted.

"We're not doing anything," he soothed, but his hand never stopped stroking her. "Tip up your face, Tess." He was crooning it now, deep in his throat. "You're *mine,* my wife, my Tess, *my wife.*"

He tucked her head against his shoulder and kissed her with all the possession in his soul, with all the deep sense of gladness and rightness that came over him every time he looked at her, every time he thought those words, *my wife.*

She was shuddering against him; he kissed her harder, let his hand take a deeper stroke. She shook and cried out something, her fingers clutching his shirt convulsively.

He would have said it again, but there wasn't any need. She was his, she was his, and she was shuddering in his arms, and gulping air in the most endearing way he had ever seen. He clenched his teeth and held her against him, forcing away the desperate wish to rip open his trouser buttons, and —

This evening. That's what matrimonial beds were for. Rational activity. This wasn't rational.

She looked up at him, her eyes soft and unfocused, and her lips swollen from his kisses, and Lucius nearly threw rational thought to the winds. But instead he bent his head and kissed her gently, taking her cry into his heart. She slumped against him, as warm and boneless as a kitten. After a while, he said "Tess?"

"Hmmm," she said dreamily.

"I should probably put my waistcoat back on."

"Waistcoat," she said, rubbing her cheek against his chest.

"Exactly." He picked her up and put her on the couch, backing away quickly before he could give in to his baser urges. Particularly because Tess seemed to have thrown her scruples to the winds and was looking at him with an expression that invited him to join her.

He picked up his waistcoat and put it on, still looking at her, glorying, really, in the boneless way she lay against the back of the seat looking — looking — *carnal.* His wife. Desirous.

"Didn't you — don't you —" she said, her voice still as soft as melted butter.

"No!" he said sharply. He ran a hand through his hair. Miraculously, if you didn't look into her eyes, Tess looked as ladylike as she had in the beginning. It was enough to drive a man to distraction, thinking —

He stopped thinking about it and unbolted the door instead. One never knew when Tess's sister and her husband might return, although he'd given the bounder a thousand pounds and told him to put it on three races in a row. Maitland would undoubtedly have lost every penny.

The time with his wife was worth every cent.

"What a tiresome man your brother-in-law is," he said, finding his hat and putting it back on.

"Do you think so?" Tess said, grasping at the conversational tidbit so eagerly that he had to hide a grin. "I admit that I find him tedious in conversation myself." She stood up and walked to the front of the box, avoiding his eyes. He thought he caught a glimpse of something in her eyes — hurt? Mortification?

So he strolled up and stood just behind her and for a moment — a blissful moment — allowed himself to press against her delicious little bottom.

"Lucius!" she said in a stifled voice.

He stepped away and had to readjust his breeches for the fifteenth time. "I'm sorry, darling," he said. "I want you to know that I am on the edge of losing my control as a gentleman and throwing you onto that couch. And I can't do that. Of course."

She looked up at him quickly. The question was replaced by a smile; she reached up and adjusted his neckcloth.

It was such a wifely gesture that Lucius's normally inscrutable eyes — had Tess been looking at them, rather than fussing with his neckcloth — held an expression quite alien to their normal expression.

If forced to catalog it, Lucius would have called it desire. Oh, perhaps a stronger version — naked longing, perhaps. Proprietary. She was his wife.

Stronger than that?

Surely not.

He was kissing her when Draven Maitland opened the door to the box. It was all most shocking; kissing, in the open window.

"You might have been seen by any passing jockey," Imogen remarked, after the two husbands had taken themselves off to the stables. Draven was not the sort to stand around in a box when he could be brushing shoulders with the legs and finding out how the betting was weighing a favorite.

"I think the jockeys have better things to do," Tess said, suppressing a little grin.

Imogen looked at her sharply. "I see that you and Felton are behaving in a quite *newlywed* fashion."

"What do you mean by that?" Tess asked.

Her sister laughed. "You know precisely what I mean, Tess. Draven didn't say anything, but I'm certain that he felt as keenly as I did the shame of finding you two kissing behind a closed door, for all the world like a housemaid with the first footman."

"That is an unkind assessment," Tess said, a flush rising into her cheeks.

Imogen's eyes flashed. "If the shoe fits . . . You didn't get all that color in your cheeks from jostling amongst the legs and fielders in the stables, as Draven and I were doing. No, you were up here in your plush little birdcage, allowing yourself to be mauled by your rich husband. I wonder at you, Tess."

Tess looked at her. "And I at you, Imogen."

"At least I married for love," she snapped.

Tess could feel fury rising in her bosom. There was no one in the world who could make her as angry as her own sisters, and Imogen was doing an excellent job of deliberately provoking her. "Now you have gone from being unkind to coarse! In case you were unaware of the fact, I married quickly partly to quell the scandal caused by *your* marriage."

"Lady Griselda seems quite unperturbed by my sudden marriage," Imogen retorted, straightening her bonnet. "She tells me that marriage by special license is quite envied. Isn't this an utterly divine bonnet?

Lady Clarice gave it to me; she had only worn it two or three times and didn't care for it. Of course, *you* will never have to wear a hand-me-down again." This time there was pure spite in her tone.

"My understanding is that Lucius saved you from the scandal of a Gretna Green marriage," Tess said. "In fact, that he gave Lord Maitland the money to buy a special license."

Imogen waved her hand airily. "Naturally Draven does not carry hundreds of pounds with him at any given time. He's not a merchant, you know."

Tess's heart was beating so fast she could hear it in her ears. "Neither is Lucius. And I'm sorry if you find my choice of husband disagreeable."

"Oh, I don't! But it's sad to marry for love, and then have to watch one's sisters making matches based on a man's pocketbook."

"I didn't marry Lucius for that reason," Tess said, keeping her voice controlled with a severe effort.

"I know," Imogen said, "I heard about Mayne." For the first time there was a flash of genuine sympathy in her eyes. "I'm sorry about that, Tess."

Tess couldn't even think what Imogen

was talking about, and then remembered that she had been jilted by the earl.

"I don't mean to be so beastly," Imogen continued. "I can't think why I could be mean to you, of all people, for marrying under those circumstances. It's utterly loathsome of me!" She looked so dismayed that Tess felt her anger wane.

"It's all right," she said, giving Imogen a quick hug. "I *didn't* marry for love, and Lucius is terrifyingly rich. It's all true."

"Yes, I am quite lucky to have avoided that, aren't I?" Imogen said, and that savage little undertone was back in her voice.

Another group of horses pounded by their stand. "I must pay attention," Imogen said walking to the front of the box and sitting down. "Blue Peter will be up any moment. Lucius has all his hopes riding on him."

"What is he like?" Tess said, settling into a chair next to Imogen. She felt that an interlude of talking about horseflesh would be soothing for both of them.

"Blue Peter? You wouldn't like him," Imogen said.

"Is he unpleasant?"

"Very," Imogen said with feeling. "He tries to bite everything that comes within his reach, and he's too strong in the neck and shoulders. He'll be unridable soon. The boys are nervous and don't want to train him. The other day a ragamuffin threw a ginger-nut at him, and he almost kicked the fence down between himself and the boy."

"What a shame," Tess said. "How sad. How old is he?"

"That's it; he's only a yearling. Imagine what he'll be like as a two-year-old. But Draven loves the animal. He won't hear of his being cut." She was silent for a moment.

"Papa would have said he's too young to race. Perhaps the strain is too much for him."

"Papa had many antiquated ideas; Draven researches these things quite, quite carefully. They've been racing yearlings in England for years. Draven is far more educated than Papa ever was about these matters."

"I cannot see how a Cambridge degree would help him distinguish the effect on a horse of racing in its first year," Tess objected.

"Trust me," Imogen said loftily, "Draven is an entirely different sort of horseman from our father. For one thing, Papa never won, did he?"

Tess bit her lip. To her, the similarities between their father and Draven Maitland were obvious, and extended to the fact that Maitland had never (to the best of her knowledge) won a large cup, or indeed, managed to support himself without considerable help from his mother.

There was another howl; the race was already over.

"I missed that one entirely," Tess remarked, wishing that Lucius would return. There was something wrong with Imogen, and she wasn't certain how to talk to her about it. If only Annabel were here! Annabel was so good at finding out secrets.

"Races are getting shorter and shorter. Draven says that's because the legs are fixing most of the races by controlling the betting."

"I'm sure," Tess said. "But how are *you*, Imogen? Is marriage to Lord Maitland everything you dreamed it would be?"

"But I told you; he is all that is gracious and wonderful," Imogen said.

But Tess felt there was something wrong. Imogen's eyes didn't shine in the way they used to, before she married Draven. She kept saying that everything was wonderful, and yet —

"Are you quite certain?" she persisted.

"Of course I am!" Imogen said with a short laugh.

"Is it comfortable living with Lady Clarice?"

A shadow crossed Imogen's face. "I can see Annabel and Josie regularly. Every day, if I wish. But as soon as Draven wins his next golden cup, we shall move to our own establishment, naturally."

"That must be difficult," Tess said, putting a hand on Imogen's.

Imogen looked at her and grinned, and suddenly there was a flash of Tess's old, passionate sister. "Lady Clarice can be rather troublesome. But I find that since I began reading Catullus to her in the mornings, she has begun considering me *cultivated*, and that makes all the difference."

"I'm sure Miss Pythian-Adams would be happy to lend you a text or two," Tess said.

Imogen shuddered. "Miss Pythian-Adams is a very odd woman. Do you know, she actually thanked me for taking Draven off her hands? As if I could have had a greater wish in life than to marry my dearest husband!"

"Of course," Tess murmured.

But Imogen didn't seem to want to talk about her marriage anymore. "What is it like being married to Mr. Felton, Tess? Draven describes him as virtually the richest man in all England!"

"It's confusing. I find it quite mystifying, sometimes, to think where the day has gone, because it seems to take enormous amounts of time to do something as simple as talk to the housekeeper about meals, then there's the gardener, and the accounts — of course, I don't keep the accounts, but I try to look them over. In all, it's a tremendous amount of work."

"But you look happy," Imogen said. "Your eyes are *happy,* Tess." There was a moment's silence, then: "I think you must have fallen in love with your husband."

Tess froze for a second. "Perhaps someday." She caught sight of Lucius walking through the crowd toward her, with Draven at his side. "They are returning!"

The crowd moved aside as Lucius approached. Lord Maitland looked just as handsome, in a different sort of way: his eyes shining an audacious blue, gesticulating widely as he explained something to Lucius — something to do with Blue Peter, no doubt.

Watching him, Tess even felt a queer sort of affection. After all, Draven was family now. He was Imogen's husband, and though she could have wished Imogen had married a different sort of man, and in a different way, there was no overlooking that Imogen had wanted nothing but Draven from the moment she saw him.

She took Imogen's hand in her own and squeezed it. "I'm so glad that the two of you wed," she said impulsively. "I'm afraid that you would have suffered true unhappiness had things been different."

Imogen looked at her. "Yes, I likely should have done," she said. But there was something in her tone that made Tess frown again.

Lucius sat down beside Tess. Draven was still talking, something about the filly who would be running against Blue Peter and what a groom had told him about that filly's diet; he sat down next to Imogen and simply switched the flow of his conversation from Lucius to Imogen.

Lucius leaned close to her, and said, "I would say that the subject of oats and apples has been exhausted."

Tess smiled, but she felt sad for Imogen. Lucius's hand was just touching her back, but the very touch of his fingers made her body sing with the memory of what had happened a mere hour ago.

She looked up at him and knew they

were both thinking the same thing. "Shall we take a small stroll?" he asked. "I gather that Blue Peter will not race for an hour or so, and you have not so much as left the box."

Tess glanced at Imogen. Draven was describing a two-year-old filly with a white stripe on his nose and "that look, that calm, alert look, you know what I mean. I could take her to the Ascot, but my mother, dammit, I expect she won't —" Imogen was looking at him and nodding.

Tess turned away and took Lucius's arm. A moment later, they were threading their way through crowds that smelled of tobacco, spirits, and excitement. He put his arm around her, protecting her, possessive and warm, and Tess — who felt absolutely no need for protection, having practically grown up amongst crowds of jostling men of just this stripe — felt a streak of joy in her chest that was so sharp it almost hurt. She stopped. He stopped, perforce, and she looked up to his face and said, "Lucius."

"Hmm-hum?"

But what he saw in her eyes made amusement shine in his own, and he bent his head. "Did you wish to say something private, my dear?"

"Is your carriage in the vicinity?"

He answered her with a smile, then — regardless of the utter impropriety of the action, tipped up his wife's face and kissed her: swiftly, one hard, demanding kiss, so swift that no one really noticed, since their faces were trained to the track, and the horses pounding their way through the dust.

Only one person saw them, and that was Imogen, watching them from the box while Draven talked. "You see, when the group near the rail began to speed up," her husband was saying, "the filly pulled to the outside and shot ahead as if she were . . ."

Imogen saw that Lucius was looking down at Tess as if she were terribly, terribly precious, laughing at something now, his arm tight around her as if to keep the crowds from ever touching the precious Mrs. Felton.

"If only my mother understood a horse's investment potential," Draven was saying, as much to himself as her, because when that particular note of rage sounded in his voice it was always to do with his mother. And Imogen had learned quickly that there was nothing she could say that would better the business. Lady Clarice showed no signs whatsoever of loosening the purse strings now that her son was married. Indeed, as she told Imogen, not unkindly, it was for her own good.

"He puts every shilling I give him into his stables," she had told Imogen. "I don't begrudge him the money, but my dearest husband agreed with me that Draven does not have an eye for a winner."

"Draven has an excellent eye," Imogen had said stoutly. "It's only a matter of time until his stables are the finest in all England."

"I would be very happy for him," his mother had agreed, and then she had changed the subject.

"Draven," Imogen interrupted him now, "would you like to go for a walk?"

He leaped to his feet. "Of course you wish to see the filly, don't you? You can hardly help me talk my mother into releasing the funds unless you've seen her yourself, can you?" He hauled her to her feet with scant grace. "Good thought, Imogen."

At least he remembers my name, Imogen thought rather disconsolately.

Chapter 33

The footmen saw them coming, and this time Lucius didn't give a damn what they thought about what he was doing with his new wife in the carriage, given that the horses were unhitched and stabled for the afternoon. With one jerk of his head he sent them flying in different directions, not to return for at least an hour. He pulled open the door himself and let down the little steps.

On the top step, Tess turned and smiled at him over her shoulder. "You are coming with me, aren't you?" she asked, so throatily that he almost scooped up her perfect little rounded bottom and threw her in so he could slam the door behind them.

"I'm right behind you," he said.

It wasn't until she was lying back on the seat and he was sliding into her warmth, her head thrown back, one arm around his neck, the other over her head, that Lucius Felton realized — something.

Something important.

He couldn't put it into words, though. All he could do was drive into his wife, giving up any semblance of control he'd ever had over his emotions. She was under him, arching up, twisting under his hands as his fingers shaped her breasts, crying out . . . He could feel his own face changing, his teeth bared as he struggled to maintain control.

And then, suddenly, he realized that with Tess there would never be control.

He reached down and touched her slick, soft warmth and her eyes opened wider, wider . . .

"Lucius!" she cried.

And he gripped her hips, with the joy of a Bach hymn pouring through his soul, gripped her hips and pulled her higher and let go, let go, let go . . .

He could feel his face tightening and shaping itself in ungentlemanly ways, a guttural sound coming from his lips, a burst of noise, of pain, of *joy*.

She had one arm curled around his neck, and she was not lethargic now. She was boneless. Her hair spilled down the side of the seat; her lips were ruby red from kissing.

"What if you hadn't come to Rafe's house?" Lucius asked her suddenly. "What if you hadn't come?"

"Mmmm," Tess said. Then she sat up. "Imogen!"

Lucius sighed.

"Imogen is going to know instantly what we were doing," his wife said anxiously, trying to wind her hair into some sort of a pile on her head, presumably so that she could jam a bonnet on top of it.

Lucius grinned. "Your sister and her husband were passionate enough about each other that they actually eloped. I've no doubt but that they've stolen away an afternoon or two themselves."

There was a dim roar in the distance and a great pounding roar of hooves rounding the corner. Tess stopped trying to wind up her hair and lapsed back against Lucius's chest again. She didn't want to ever leave. She wanted to stay here with Lucius, in their little velvet-lined chamber, with her head on his shoulder and the wonderful melting feeling of delirium just past . . . she snuggled against him and listened to his heartbeat. It was steadier now, not galloping along.

"I don't think they talk very often," she said.

"Who?" He sounded sleepy.

"Imogen and her husband."

"*He* talks," Lucius said with some feeling. "He spent a good hour this afternoon talking up the points of some hellish animal he has running in the Cup. When we went to look at it, damned if the brute hadn't eaten a chunk of his stall. He was spitting wood chips in all directions. The stableboys are terrified of him."

"Imogen desperately wants him to win," Tess said, snuggling even closer and smelling the soap-clean smell of Lucius's chest. "Apparently Maitland lost twenty thousand pounds at Lewes last week."

"Silly chump," Lucius said, his hand tangling in her hair. "The jockey was trying to back out when we were down there, saying he was afraid the horse would pull his arms from his sockets. Maitland was threatening to race the horse himself; said he was bound to win."

"He can't do that," Tess said. "It sounds as if the horse is mad."

Lucius had pulled on his shirt but left it untucked when he sat down with her, so Tess slipped her hand under the white linen and slid them through over the rippled muscles of his chest. Under her ear, his heart beat steadily. "I'm so lucky," she whispered into his shirt.

But he heard her and smiled over her head.

* * *

Tess sat down next to Imogen, knowing without question that her cheeks were flushed rose, and her hair looked nothing as smooth as it had in the morning.

Imogen threw her a jaundiced look that said without words: *kissing behind the stables, were you?*

Draven had bounded to his feet the moment they opened the door. "Finally!" he said. "Since you're here now, I'll just check how Blue Peter is doing once more. I want to make sure the jockey understands how important this is. He was showing signs of being cowardly earlier."

"A yearling *and* a new stableboy," Lucius commented. "Perhaps you would do better to consider this a trial run."

But Draven shook his head with his customary intensity. "No, I've decided to take the purse from winning this race and buy that two-year-old filly that Farley's offering for sale. I must have her. She's a beauty, bone-deep, and she'll win the Ascot this year, I'm certain of it."

"I thought Blue Peter was going to win the Ascot," Tess said.

Draven nodded. "That's possible too. Very possible. Lovely horses, both of them. But the two-year-old has a bit more experience, and I fancy she has a slightly higher flank. A beauty, she is, and Imogen agrees with me. We went to the stables while you were walking — where were you?" he asked Lucius. "I looked all about for you because I wanted you to see the animal as well. Would be a lovely investment, but Imogen and I couldn't find you anywhere."

"We looked all over the grounds," Imogen put in, with a rather waspish note in her voice.

"Let me see how the race goes," Lucius said in a voice that quelled any further questions. "I'd be happy to think about the two-year-old, Maitland. Perhaps I could stroll with you to the stables?"

Draven's attention swung like a child's when offered a toy back to the important theme of the horse. "Good man! Let's be off, then. As I say, I'd wish to just check on that jockey and give him a last few words of advice. I'd love to be running Blue Peter myself, in all truth."

"You promised," Imogen said sharply.

He blinked and looked at Imogen as if he'd forgotten her very existence. "So I did," he answered. "It's just a matter of bracing up Bunts. He's being crotchety about it at the moment, but I'll have a word and all will be well." And he took himself out the door, obviously eager to chide the fearful Bunts.

Lucius looked down at Tess. He was wearing his noncommittal expression, but she could read him. Not that there was much interpretation needed in the way his hand touched her cheek and the back of her neck, a caress so fleeting that it burned her skin with its intensity.

"I shall return shortly," he said, inclining his head to Tess, and then bowing to Imogen.

Lucius had lovely manners, Tess thought to herself.

"I gather you didn't mind your husband making a cake of himself like that," Imogen said scornfully.

Tess straightened. "What do you mean?"

"Touching you in public," she said disdainfully. "Caressing you. I know we didn't grow up with a governess, Tess, but really, you must learn to tailor your behavior to that of proper society, or no one will wish to know you."

"Coming from someone who was saved from a Gretna Green marriage by my husband, your censure seems out of place," Tess said. "*You* certainly didn't consider tailoring your behavior, nor the effect that your elopement might have on Annabel's and Josie's future marriages!"

"Since Draven and I did not marry in Scotland, the question is moot," Imogen said icily.

"I fail to see what was so improper about Lucius's farewell," Tess said, trying to keep her temper. Imogen was unhappy. She wasn't sure why, but she could see it well enough.

"If you don't realize, I'm sure it's not my place to tell you."

"No, it isn't."

Imogen sniffed. She leaned forward out of the window, and said, "I'm almost certain that the Cup is about to begin. This box is all very well, but one can't hear any of the announcements."

Tess swallowed a violent desire to tell her sister to go stand at the rail if she didn't like the box.

Horses were pacing slowly toward the starting line. Tess always thought the jockeys looked so precariously small, perched on the great backs of the horses.

"I can't tell," Imogen said. "It might be the last race before the Cup. I don't see Draven's colors anywhere. What are Felton's colors?"

"I don't have any idea," Tess said, realizing that she'd visited Midnight Blossom, but ignored the rest of Lucius's stables. "He's running Something Wanton, though. Do you see him?"

They both squinted off toward the starting line, but it was well around the curve. The royal box was beautifully situated to see the end of a race, but not its beginning.

"I find it hard to believe that you don't even know your husband's colors," Imogen said. She could feel the meanness uncurling in her heart; it wasn't fair that Tess should marry a man who kissed her like that. In public, without a thought for what others thought. And who looked at her in such a way as if — as if — she shrugged away the thought.

"We haven't discussed his stables," Tess said.

"Well, if you want to have *that* sort of marriage," Imogen began.

But her sister cut her off. "To what sort of marriage do you refer?"

Imogen curled her lip. "The type in which the wife spends her day consulting with the housekeeper, which certainly appears to be your daily routine. The husband's wishes and deepest ambitions are never discussed. His true life happens outside the house, outside the marriage."

"My goodness you're dramatic," Tess said. She had a haughty, older sister expression that further inflamed Imogen's temper.

"I know every dream in Draven's heart!" Imogen said, knowing she should feel sorry that Tess had no real understanding of her husband. Their relationship was shallow. But it was hard to feel sorry when Lucius Felton looked at his wife that way. It wasn't *fair.*

There was a distant sound of a pistol shot, and they both glanced toward the starting line. The huge mass of colored horses were milling about, rearing in the air.

Tess could hear whickers from the horses and shouts from the jockeys. She certainly didn't know all the dreams in Lucius's heart. In fact, she doubted she knew any of them.

"A false start," Imogen said. "Draven says half of the false starts are because the legs are trying to exhaust a given horse and stop it from winning. Blue Peter would never be exhausted by such shabby tactics."

"I doubt Something Wanton would either," Tess said.

"Not that *you* would know. Have you even bothered to tell Mr. Felton about Something Wanton's likes and dislikes, so that he has the slightest chance of winning the race?"

"Likes? Dislikes?" Tess cried. "What does it matter? Something Wanton never won a race for Papa, for all the fact that he was so certain the horse liked apple-mash. And *no,* I haven't spent a moment discussing that horse with my husband."

"I forgot," Imogen said spitefully. "You need to discuss important matters like the linens and the household accounts."

"If I lived with my mother-in-law as you do, I undoubtedly wouldn't have to bother with the accounts," Tess snapped, finally exasperated beyond all measure. "What is the matter with you, Imogen?"

"Absolutely nothing," Imogen said primly, straightening her back and pretending to take a great interest in the horses pounding around the nearest curve on their first circle about the grounds.

Tess ground her teeth. "You told us repeatedly that you would expire if you weren't able to marry Maitland. And you did it. If you have rethought your position, there's no need to be rude to me."

Imogen bristled all over like a cat cornered by a terrier. "I have rethought nothing! I adore Draven. He is the very air I breathe!"

Tess stared at her. "I believe you. I simply begin to wonder whether breathing that air is poisoning your character."

"That is such an unpleasant thing to say," Imogen said slowly. So slowly that Tess had time to feel a pulse of heart-stopping guilt.

"You're right, and I'm sorry," she said in a rush.

Imogen was gripping the window ledge in front of her and staring blindly out at the horses rounding the curve for the second time in a dazzling sweep of pounding hooves and flashing colors. "I'm being a beast, Tess," she said. "And it's *not* because I regret marrying Draven. I love Draven."

She turned and Tess saw that truth raw in her eyes. "I adore him. I — well you know about me. I worship the ground he walks on. He . . . he doesn't feel precisely the same for me."

"Oh, dearest," Tess whispered.

"He cares for me," Imogen said. "It's just that he cares for his horses *more*." She said it fiercely, and when she looked up, her eyes were shiny with tears. "He talks about them in his sleep. He can't help talking about them all the time. He can't help it."

"I know," Tess said. "Papa was just the same."

"I thought of that," Imogen whispered. Her gloved fingers were clenching on the wood again and again. A light rain was beginning to splatter down on the track, dampening down the puffs of dust that blew in their direction. "But I don't think that Mama was unhappy, was she?"

"No," Tess said instantly. "She wasn't. I remember her quite well. She loved us, and she loved Papa. And I don't think she minded for a moment that she'd given up — well, the chance at a marriage in England, and the season, and all those gowns."

"I don't either," Imogen said. "I *don't either!*"

"Of course you don't —" Tess began but there was a sudden howl from the crowd, a primitive scream or moan that made both of their heads jerk back to the track.

"A horse is down," Imogen said, gloved hand to her mouth.

"Oh dear," Tess moaned. "I hate the racetrack, I hate it, I just hate it. Every time a horse goes down I think of all the horses that Papa lost, and how dearly he loved them, and the agony of putting them down . . ."

"I know just what you mean," Imogen said, reaching out and taking her hand tightly. "Remember how he wept when Highbrow had to be shot?"

Tess nodded. "He was never precisely the same again." People were rushing all over the racetrack. Horses were being led off. Clearly the accident had been a serious one. Tess had a terrible longing to rush out to Lucius's carriage and return to his house. Go back and check the linen and forget that the life of the track, with its glories and tragedies, ever existed.

"No, you're right," Imogen said. "Papa was never the same after Highbrow. All the money was gone, for one thing." She obviously remembered, suddenly, and glanced at Tess. "Not that *anyone* blamed you, Tess. He should never have listened to you in the first place. You were nothing more than a girl."

"Well, he never did listen to me again," Tess said woodenly.

The door opened and Lucius was standing there. Tess started up with a gladness that she couldn't conceal, but he was looking at her sister.

"Imogen," he said, and it was the first time he had used her first name.

Imogen rose from her seat. Her face had gone pale, but her voice was steady. "Draven?"

Lucius nodded.

"Was he riding?" And then, without waiting for an answer: "He was riding Blue Peter."

Lucius took her arm, and said, "We must go to him now." He looked at Tess, and she snatched Imogen's pelisse and bundled her into it, her hands trembling as she buttoned the front.

"He was riding Blue Peter," Imogen repeated, looking white about the lips. "But he's alive — isn't he alive?" she gripped Lucius's arm as he was opening the door.

"He's alive," Lucius said. "He wants to see you."

But Tess saw something in his dark eyes that Imogen wouldn't have recognized, and her heart sank.

The rain had stopped, leaving a clean smell in the air. The crowds were rapidly thinning. People rushed off, carriages jostling with gigs, fleeing in all directions to warm houses, sweltering pubs, cozy villages nearby.

They half walked, half ran through the

people strolling away, all of them talking of the accident.

"He went down like a log in a firestorm," one man said.

"The odds were eight to one against 'im," another voice said. "Why the devil would he risk his skin at odds like those?"

Imogen didn't look as if she could hear anything, to Tess's relief. She said in an oddly calm voice, "Where is he? Where have they taken him?"

"He's in the stables," Lucius said.

"Is he —" But she started running now, dropping Lucius's hand and picking up her skirts. With one look, they ran after her, Tess's bonnet falling off her head. Years later, the only thing she could remember of getting to the stables was her sharp sense that without her bonnet everyone would see her hair and know — know what?

The lost bonnet was irrelevant once they walked into the stables. Draven was lying on a cot, clearly the bed of one of the stable hands who guarded the stables at night.

He looked up at them with such a cheerful expression that Tess's heart bounded, and she turned to Lucius with delight. But when she grabbed his arm, he was looking at Imogen with such an expression of pity in his eyes that she looked at the cot again. Imogen had thrown herself on the ground beside her husband.

"I'll need a little nursing, I expect," Draven was saying, his voice feeble but jovial. "I know you want me off the racetrack."

Imogen touched him, her hands trembling. "Does it hurt? Has someone summoned a doctor? Do you have a broken limb, Draven?"

"A rib or two, I expect. Won't be the first ribs I've broken. And the pain is less now. I can bear it, Immie."

"You promised that you wouldn't ride Blue Peter," Imogen said, holding his hand tightly. "You promised, Draven, you promised!"

"I couldn't do it," he said, and his eyes fell away from hers. "I had to ride him, because Bunts wouldn't do the job."

Imogen realized she was crying because Draven's face blurred before her. Was he even whiter than he had been a moment ago? Why was he lying so still?

"Where is the doctor?" she cried up to Lucius.

He bent down beside her, and she met his eyes. "Call a doctor," she said, her voice faltering as she said it.

"The doctor saw him as soon as he fell," he said.

What she read in his eyes turned her heart to stone.

"It'll be all right," Draven said with something of his old jaunty confidence. "I'll need to mend for a while. The important thing is that Blue Peter is fine. I'll promise the little wife that I'll never jump on that horse again, how's that?"

"Nor any other dangerous animal," Imogen said, striving to smile at him as tears fell onto his cot.

"I didn't mean to ride," Draven told her. "You ask Felton. I was talking the jockey into doing it; he was an old woman to act as he did. I had him convinced, I did. And then he just lost heart at the last moment, and I couldn't bear it. I wanted to win, Imogen."

"I know you did." She clutched his hand against her cheek. "Oh sweetheart, I know you did."

"And it wasn't just to win either," he said, struggling almost as if he would sit up, but he lay back.

"Are you in pain?" she whispered. "Oh, Draven, does it hurt?"

But he shook his head. "That's how I know I'll be all right, Immie. I'll be all right. I was worried at first, because it hurt so much, but then the pain went away, and I knew I would live. I'll win next time, darling." He took his hand away from her and cupped her cheek. "I'll win a cup and we'll have a grand house in London, as grand as anything your sister has. And a royal box too."

"I don't want that," Imogen said, turning her face to kiss his hand. "I don't care, Draven. I only ever wanted to marry you. I always loved you, from the very moment I saw you."

"Silly girl," he said. He didn't seem to be able to raise his head anymore.

Imogen bent over him, putting her face against his chest. She could hear his heart beating, but it sounded a long way away. "I saw you coming across Papa's courtyard. You were so beautiful, so alive, so — yourself. Your horse had just won the Ardmore, do you remember?"

"Twenty-pound cup," he said. But he was blinking. "I can't see so well, Imogen."

A sob choked her voice, and she didn't answer immediately.

"I haven't — have I?" he asked.

Imogen raised her head and cupped her husband's face in her hands. "I love you, Draven Maitland. I *love you*."

Something in her face seemed to tell him the answer to his question. But he asked it again, his eyes fixed on her, "Immie. Do I really have to die?"

And when she didn't answer, just leaned down and kissed him on the lips, he merely said, "My Immie."

Draven was a reckless boy who'd grown into a gambling man. But he had never lacked courage, for all his recklessness. He had never been less than a man, for all his wildness. And he had never been less than the *wild thing* Imogen's papa used to call him, except for now. Because now he took what was clearly his last strength and reached for her hand.

"I love you, Immie."

Imogen couldn't answer. Sobs were tearing through her chest.

"I don't think I married you for the right reasons," he said, his voice lower now, and palpably thin. "I know I didn't. But I thank God I did it, Immie. It's the only good thing I've done in my life."

"Draven, don't —" she said. She bent her head onto his chest again. His hand was stroking her hair, slowly, so slowly. And she couldn't hear his heart. Could she?

"I'm not good at saying such things," he

said. "I'd better say them now. I married you, well, for who knows what reason. But I knew by nightfall, Immie, that it was the best thing I ever did. And what I've done since, it was all for you, even though I'm not good at saying those things."

Imogen came to kiss him. There was bright color at the edge of his lip. She dabbed it with her handkerchief, then realized to her horror that it was blood.

"Know that I love you," she whispered. "You were all I ever wanted in life. Being married to you was all I ever wanted."

"You deserve better," he whispered, squinting as if he was trying to see her better.

"There is *no one* better!" she said fiercely. *"No one!"*

"That's my Immie," he said. "Will you tell Mama that . . ." His voice trailed off.

"You love her," Imogen said. "I'll tell her, Draven. I'll tell her."

His hand had been on her shoulder, but it slipped back to the bed. There was a rustle behind her. Imogen didn't look until a man stooped at her side.

"I'm Reverend Straton. The doctor sent me," he said, kneeling next to Imogen with an utter lack of pompousness. He put his hand on Draven's forehead, and said in a deep voice, *"In thee, O Lord, do I put my trust . . ."*

Imogen put her hand on Draven's chest. She couldn't feel his heart. The priest was saying, *"verily I say unto you, He that heareth my word, and believeth on him that sent me, hath everlasting life, and shall not come into condemnation; but is passed from death unto life."*

Draven's eyes were closed, and he looked as if he were asleep and yet . . . and yet.

Then Tess was on her knees next to Imogen and hugging her, and Lucius brought them both to their feet. But Imogen tore herself away and fell down next to Draven again.

"It can't be true," she cried. All of a sudden she heard the sounds of the stable around her, a horse striking his hoof against the wood of his stable, someone walking at the far end of the corridor, the jingle of a bridle. It couldn't be that these things could continue without Draven.

"No!" she cried. "No!" She clutched him but he didn't open his eyes.

"Draven!" she cried. "Draven, it's not time, it's not time. Don't go, don't leave me, don't go!"

But he had gone. Anyone could see that. The Draven she had loved since the moment she saw him, walking across the courtyard laughing with the pure joy of winning — he was gone. His face was different, changed.

Tess pulled her into her arms, and whispered, "He's with God, Imogen. He's with Papa."

"Don't go!" Imogen cried again, and tried to twist out of Tess's arms. She felt crazed, as if the stables should crack open at the very sight of it, of Draven dead. "Come back!"

Then the priest was holding her, and saying something about God and heaven and places that were too far away to know about. But Imogen had gone deaf again; the only thing she could see was Draven's white face lying on the cot.

"We must take Draven home," Tess said to her, and that made sense. That was the only thing that made sense. They couldn't stay in the stable, around the horses. So she allowed Tess to draw her to her feet. She walked beside the bed and held his hand as they carried it, but his hand was limp, not like Draven's. Draven was always moving, always talking —

So she put down his hand, and they carried the bed into the sunshine.

He didn't open his eyes.

And then they went home.

And Draven came with them, in his own carriage.

Chapter 34

When they reached Lady Clarice's house, Rafe was there with Annabel and Josie; Lucius had sent a groom ahead to ask Rafe to tell Lady Clarice. Tess would have expected hysteria, tears, screams. . . . There was nothing. Lady Clarice sat like a statue in the sitting room. Her face was paper white, and she held a handkerchief, but she didn't use it. She and Imogen sat next to each other, but whereas Imogen kept crumpling sideways into Annabel's arms, sobbing so hard that she couldn't breathe, Lady Clarice just patted Imogen's hand and stared into space.

Tess sat next to Lucius, feeling as if she must *do* something, and yet — what was there to do? Rafe wandered around pouring doses of brandy into any unguarded teacup he found. They all sat about, and nothing much was said. And then nothing much was eaten at supper, and they retired. Imogen didn't feel she could go back to the chambers she had shared with

Draven, so Annabel and she went to a room together. Tess woke in the night, sobbing, Imogen's farewell to Draven somehow entangled in her mind with her own farewell to her father. Lucius kissed her wet cheeks and held her in the dark.

When Tess entered the drawing room in the morning, Imogen and Annabel were sitting together. Annabel was bending close to Imogen, saying something. Tess ran across the room and sat on Imogen's other side, winding an arm around her shoulders. "How are you, dearest?" she asked.

Imogen didn't look at her, just moved slightly, so that Tess's arm fell away. "I'm just fine," she said. She wasn't wringing her hands or crying.

"I've been telling Imogen that she must eat," Annabel said, in a rousing tone.

"Not at the moment," Imogen said.

Tess hesitated. There was something slightly . . . slightly unwelcoming about the way Imogen was leaning against Annabel. She would have thought that Imogen would be in *her* arms. Not that Annabel wasn't comforting, but after their mother died, she, Tess, had always —

Lucius entered the room, and she looked at him in relief, but as she turned back to

Imogen, she saw something in her eyes. A flash of pain?

Of course! Lucius's very presence must be painful to Imogen, since they married virtually at the same time, and Tess's husband was still alive. She rose and walked to Lucius. "May I see you privately for a moment?" she asked.

"Always," he replied, bowing to her sisters.

An hour later she returned, trying to ignore the fact that she didn't want Lucius to be on his way home without her. Yet her first loyalty was to Imogen.

But the moment she walked back in the room, Imogen looked up. Her face was white but for burning flags of color in her cheeks. "I would prefer to be alone."

Tess froze, staring at her.

"If you don't mind," Imogen added, leaning her head on Annabel's shoulder and closing her eyes.

Tess felt so shocked that it was as if she couldn't form words properly. "Of course. May I return with some refreshments?"

Imogen didn't look up. "If I wish for anything to eat, Annabel will summon the butler."

A moment later Tess was in the hallway, blinking at the wall and trying to remember whether she'd said something that might have offended her sister.

Rafe came down the stairs. "What's the matter, Tess?" he asked.

She looked at him, trying desperately not to cry. "Imogen . . . she didn't want me to be with her."

He led her away, into Lady Clarice's library. "She's grieving," he said. "Grief strikes everyone in different ways. Some wish to be alone, and others —"

"But she's with Annabel! She's not alone. And I've — I've —" Tess didn't even know how to describe the way she felt. "After our mother died, I practically raised all of them. How would Imogen . . . why?" The thoughts flew about her head like a little confused flock of birds. She wished desperately that she had not sent Lucius away.

"I'd offer you a drink," Rafe said with a sigh, "but it's too early."

Morning sun was creeping through the heavy curtains. Tess drew them and looked out at the courtyard. Perhaps Lucius would come riding back and take her with him. There was no sign of him, of course, so she sat on the edge of a chair, clasping her hands together so tightly that they hurt.

"Grief makes a person bloody-minded," Rafe said, throwing himself into a chair and stretching a leg so that he could kick a log on the fire, irrespective of the smudges on his boots. "After my brother died, I didn't say a civil word to anyone for over a year. Cursed the minister after the funeral service; I told him in no uncertain terms that Peter would have hated the whole damned affair. I wasn't myself."

The day continued in the same vein. Tess would enter a room, and Imogen would be shaking in Annabel's arms. Annabel would give Tess a look that said, unmistakably, *no.*

And then Tess would walk down the hallway and seek out Lady Clarice. To all appearances, Clarice had retreated behind a block of ice. She showed almost no reaction to anything said in her presence, and while she asked Tess to read the Bible to her, and appeared most appreciative, Tess didn't think she heard a word.

At some point in the afternoon, she found Rafe holding Imogen in a manner that anyone in polite society would find impolite. Imogen didn't even like Rafe! She was the one who said he was a drunk, and a slob, and lazy to boot. Yet if Tess came near her, Imogen froze and stopped crying. She answered in monosyllables. She looked away. If Tess hugged her, rather than Rafe or Annabel, Imogen's body was stiff.

Finally, she found the courage to ask Annabel, late at night, two days after Draven died. "Why?"

"She blames you," Annabel said. She was sitting in front of the fire in her bedchamber, sipping a glass of brandy. Annabel had apparently decided that Rafe's brandy was an excellent idea.

"Blames me? Blames me?" Tess repeated numbly.

"I didn't say it was logical."

Annabel looked exhausted. Her beautiful creamy skin was drawn and faintly sallow; her eyes were ringed with dark circles. Imogen cried all night, every night, and Annabel was always with her.

"How can she blame me?" Tess cried.

"Because the two of you were arguing when the race was happening," Annabel said heavily. "Or so she says. And she thinks that if she had been watching — if she had noticed that her husband was riding that devil of a horse . . ."

"She couldn't have done anything," Tess said, stunned. "It was already too late.

What could she have done?"

"I know it," Annabel said, taking another drink. "I've told her so. I think" — and she looked up at Tess, her eyes exhausted and sympathetic — "I think she simply can't bear the guilt of it herself."

"What guilt?" Tess whispered. "*He* chose to ride that horse. She made him promise not to do so!"

"Didn't he say that he'd done it all for her?"

Tess froze. He had said that, in the stables. "He didn't mean it that way!"

"She can't help thinking about it," Annabel said, turning the glass in her hand so that golden rays of light darted about the room. "Maitland said that he wanted to win so that she would have a house, so that Imogen didn't have to live with Lady Clarice any longer." There was a moment broken only by a log falling into two crashing, golden pieces in the fire. "I wish he hadn't said that," Annabel added.

"Oh, the poor sweetheart," Tess said. "I can't believe — he didn't mean that! I was there, I could tell her —"

"No," Annabel said sharply. "I've only just got her to sleep, and, Tess, she hasn't slept in two nights. *Please* don't wake her!"

"But I must tell her," Tess said, tears

snaking down her face. "Maitland didn't mean to cast blame on her, not in any sense. He was just telling her that he loved her more than his horses, that's all!"

"I'm sure he was. And her feelings don't make any sense. But blaming you is all she's hanging on to right now," Annabel said wearily. "Please don't take that away from her."

Tess was sobbing now. "How can you ask me such a thing? She's my sister, my little sister, and I love her! I would do anything for her! I want to be with her, help her."

Annabel was beside her then, arms around her, rocking her back and forth, and Tess had a pulse of guilt. The last thing Annabel needed was another person sobbing on her shoulder. "Hush," Annabel said, just as Tess had heard her say to Imogen, "hush."

So Tess wiped her eyes, and said, shakily, "Do you think I should leave?"

"I think you should go back to your husband," Annabel said, giving her a kiss. "Imogen will come around. She just can't face reality at the moment, and you're an easy target."

"I feel so responsible."

"Actually, what is probably best for her

right now is *you,*" Annabel said, going back to her chair. "She's so angry at you —"

"That angry?" Tess interjected, still disbelieving.

Annabel nodded. "Because of her rage at you, she hasn't had to think about life without her husband. And I don't think she's ready for that yet."

"How can she not want to be with me?" Tess said, a twinge clutching her heart. "How *can* she? Perhaps she just thinks that she doesn't want me, but she really does."

"She will need you later," Annabel said. "But right now, she's clinging to this foolish notion of blaming you, and it's keeping her sane, Tess. I honestly think you are doing the best thing for her, simply by allowing her to be angry at you."

Tess took a deep breath and scrubbed away a tear. "You will — you will send for me if she needs me? If she needs anything? If she changes her mind?"

Annabel nodded again. "Rafe is surprising me. Yesterday he even forgot to take a drink until well after sundown."

"You're not taking on his habits, are you?" Tess said, looking askance at Annabel's brandy.

"No," Annabel said with a sigh, coming

to her feet. "I'd better check on Imogen. Did Lady Clarice emerge from her bedchamber today?"

"Yes. But I don't think it's healthy that she never cries. And she never eats. I read to her all afternoon."

"Come to the house before the funeral," Annabel said, pausing in the door. "Perhaps Imogen will be able to greet you then."

Tess went back to her own bedchamber and cried. She thought about bursting into Imogen's room and demanding that she speak to her, then cried some more. And then — for it was quite the middle of the night, and her fire had burned down — she began to shiver and couldn't seem to stop.

Whenever she thought about Imogen, she thought about Lord Maitland. And whenever she thought about Maitland, she thought about Lucius.

So, in her muddled state, she decided that the only thing to be done was to go see her own husband. He wasn't far away, after all: he was at their house, a mere hour's ride.

She pulled on a pelisse over her nightrail and went downstairs. Somehow it wasn't very surprising to find Brinkley appearing from behind the baize door, looking tired but immaculate. "I hope I didn't wake you," she said, her voice echoing in the empty antechamber.

"Not in the least," he said gravely. And then, as if there was nothing odd in the least about a lady dressed in a nightrail and a pelisse, "Would you like me to summon your coach, madam?"

"Yes. Thank you, Brinkley."

She fell asleep waiting for her coach, nestled in her pelisse in the sitting room. She hardly noticed when Brinkley tucked blankets around her, and fell asleep again, jostling over the miles, going to Lucius. She was still asleep when the footmen opened the door of the carriage, peeked inside, and went for the master.

She began to wake up when strong arms closed around her and began to carry her toward the house. She was fuzzily aware that Lucius was carrying her up the stairs, as if she were featherlight. But she nestled her head against his chest and pretended to be asleep. He put her gently onto the bed, and she let her head fall slightly to one side, as if she were still sleeping. She felt his hand on her cheek for a second, then he went back to the door, and she heard him saying to someone — Mrs. Gabthorne — that they would just let her sleep.

And then, while Tess held her breath, she heard the door close. Had he stayed with her, or left the room when the servants crept away? For some reason it seemed a terribly important question. Lucius had probably left. He wouldn't sit around and stare at his wife when he could be sleeping peacefully in his own bedchamber.

The bed shifted as he sat down. "Are you ready to open your eyes yet, sleeping beauty?" he asked. His voice had that faint strain of amusement that Tess fancied only she could hear. Other people probably thought that he was making colorless conversation.

She didn't bother greeting him. She simply sat upright, pulled him against her, and pasted her mouth against his.

It wasn't, as kisses go, a very polished effort. She could feel how startled he was, but he did kiss her back, after a second or two.

But Tess didn't want just to kiss. She fell backward and pulled him with her so he ended up sprawled half-across her.

"Tess?" he said.

"I need you," she said fiercely. "I need you."

That was one thing — well, more than

one thing — that she loved about Lucius. He listened to her. His hands tangled in her hair, and he gave her a kiss so passionate, so sweet and so *alive* that tears came to her eyes.

She kissed him back so intently that it banished the steely coldness in her chest, the fear that he would die as well, that life was nothing more than a series of farewells.

His hand swept under her nightgown, and his knee was nudging between her legs. But Tess felt a deep, fierce wish to make love, not to be made love to, and so she managed to push him flat on the bed, pulling away his clothing, throwing his boots across the floor, covering his eyes when he threatened to laugh.

And then, when she had him before her like a feast, she told him to *stay still,* with all the command with which she spoke to her horse, Midnight Blossom.

And stay still he did, watching as she covered his body with kisses, her mouth flickering over every muscle, every sweat-dampened ridge and bone and even —

And even.

Lucius allowed it, knowing somehow that his wife needed to drive him half-mad with desire, that she relished each hoarse sound he made, each husky plea, each moan. She drew her hair over his flesh, sending him into near delirium until he judged she'd proved to herself that he was alive, every burning inch of him was alive.

So he rose with a motion so fluid and fast that she had no time to protest. Before she knew what was happening she was on her back, and he was holding her hips, lifting her, coming to her.

And again. And yet again, and again, and again.

There was no slaking for either of them; she thrust toward him as fiercely as he moved toward her. The primal dance of life on the earth's broad back . . .

Later, she collapsed into the bed, into the warmth of his arms, and broke into sobs.

"Poor sweetheart," he whispered into her hair. "There have been rather a lot of good-byes recently, haven't there?"

Tess woke with a burned-out feeling of clarity in her chest. She was tired of crying. In fact, she didn't want to cry again for at least a year or seven years, for that matter.

Lucius was lying on his stomach, great muscled shoulders spread across the pillow. In his sleep he didn't appear at all disciplined and contained. Instead he looked almost boyish, his hair tossed this way and that instead of ruthlessly swept back. He seemed — happy.

He needs his family to be truly happy, Tess thought. I'll approach his mother. She ran a finger down the sun-kissed skin of his neck, onto the honey gold skin of his shoulders. His skin was warm with sleep, all that lovely hard bone and muscle seemed soft, like a baby's touch. Her fingers wandered over him, over every little curve and ridge, not even knowing that a little hum had started in her throat.

Lucius knew. Lying utterly still and pretending to sleep — his turn at sleeping beauty — he heard that sweet little wandering hum and felt a bolt of lust that shocked him to the bottom of his toes. It took all his will not to roll over, to allow those small fingers their exploration. She was pulling down the sheet now, and her fingers more hesitantly slid up the ridge of his ass.

He didn't move. Couldn't move, pinned to the bed by the delicate flutter of her fingers, touching him where no woman had ever touched him, except in an abandoned frenzy. Her hum had deepened, grown more desirous to his mind. She was *caressing* him. The sheet fell back, onto his legs. Did she really think he was still asleep? She couldn't.

In one lithe, sweeping move he turned about, had her body in his arms, pinned her to the bed, his hard body not languid, not sleeping, fitting perfectly between her sweet thighs — and he drank her startled cry, kissed her so fiercely that she reared up against him, seeking him, quivering, crying —

Sure hands pushed her legs apart, and his hand was there —

A small scream broke from her lips, and she arched into his hand, soft, swollen, and wet, all that he could ever wish for. Ready.

"Tess," he said, and plunged into her warmth.

She looked up at him, dazed. All that sleepy warmth had transformed into hard muscle, braced above her, shoulders rigid, his weight turned from sleepy male to — to — he surged forward again, and she lost her thought, clutching his shoulders.

It was all too fast . . . she would never be able to — to — whatever it was called. She hadn't brushed her teeth. She hadn't *washed!* Anxiety poured over her even as her legs pulsed with a lick of fire.

"Tess," he whispered. She turned her mouth away. Her breath must be awful.

"I need to get up," she said, the sentence ending in a squeak as he rode higher and a fiery wave threatened to suck her under.

He was kissing her jawline, his body still, almost still, except every part of her noticed that he had moved — moved a bit.

She clutched his shoulders, let her hands trace an unsteady path down his chest and then said, "I must —"

"Now I need you," he said into her ear. His voice had none of the suave polish of its everyday lilt. He sounded hoarse.

Fire burst down her legs. He was moving again, hot against her, and it was clouding her brain, making her feel scorched, as if she were too close to some enormous fire.

"Don't stop, Tess. Don't leave." His voice was hoarse, dark with need.

She couldn't seem to get purchase in a spinning world. He pulled back, and she instinctively bent her legs and tried to follow him, up, up — Then he was gripping her about the waist, and she forgot about her teeth, about her breath, about washing, about anything but Lucius's dark eyes and the way every move of his hips made her —

Sent her —

She rolled her head, frantic, meeting his

every stroke, her eyes dark with desire and lust.

Lucius looked down, and in the very, very small portion of his brain that wasn't given over to pure desire, thought: "Damn. I've fallen in love with my wife."

But then her fingers slid down his back and fastened on his bottom and Lucius Felton — who never liked it when a woman touched him intimately — shuddered all over and lost every vestige of control, taking his wife with him, hard and fast, until she cried out —

And he cried out —

And fell on top of her —

And thought, *I love you*. But didn't say it.

Chapter 35

October 10
Maitland House

Dearest Tess,

I am so sorry to tell you that Imogen is not yet ready for a reconciliation with you, her dearest sister. Lady Clarice has inadvertently worsened the situation (not, of course, having any idea of Imogen's sense of guilt) by telling her that she chose Miss Pythian-Adams as a bride for her son precisely because Miss Pythian-Adams dislikes horses and presumably would keep Draven from the stables. Imogen now believes that if she had truly loved Draven, she would have allowed him to marry Miss Pythian-Adams, thereby saving his life. The lack of logic in this argument makes it hard to counter. Frankly, I'm worried about her. She does not seem fully to understand that Draven is gone, and sometimes talks as if she thinks he is merely out of sight, or traveling. She still does not sleep at night, but has taken to walking about the chambers they shared, talking to her husband (or rather, to his spirit, I suppose). She will not allow the bedding to be changed, nor his clothing to be removed. I am quite certain that she would refuse to move to your house, Tess, so I'm afraid we should give up our initial plan for the moment.

I think it would be best for Imogen if you continued to London with your husband rather than take us with you. Josie is well settled with her governess at Rafe's house; Lady Griselda has declared an intention to stay with them as long as she is needed. I am here with Imogen, and while I maintain a hope that I shall join you in London once the season begins, I certainly cannot leave Imogen at this time.

I know I will see you tomorrow at the burial, but I thought it best if you understood how it is with Imogen. I know it will give you pain if she is cold; please understand that she has only a frail command of her true circumstances at this moment.

Yours with all love,
Annabel

THE SILCHESTER DAILY TIMES

> Six outriders accompanied the hearse, blazoned with escutcheons of the Maitland family. Fourteen mourning coaches followed, every horse caparisoned in black velvet, bearing the arms of the Maitlands. Lord Maitland's lovely young wife and mother followed the deceased in the first mourning carriage; general distress was expressed by those who witnessed Lord Maitland's young bride enter St. Andrew's church for the burial. Some thirty private carriages followed the cavalcade. Among the mourners were the Duke of Holbrook, the Earl of Mayne, Earl Hawarden, and Sir Fibulous Hervey.

Burials of the very young are, by definition, heart-wrenching affairs. Tess couldn't help comparing Draven Maitland's funeral to that of her father. By the time her father died, he had had a full life with a wife, children, great successes, huge mistakes . . . Draven had only Imogen, and she had had him for under a month. Moreover, in the case of her father, those who loved him had accustomed themselves to the idea of his death.

She knew why Imogen refused to believe that Draven was dead. One moment her husband was there, and the next he was gone. *Gone*. Tess held Lucius's hand very tightly as she stared at the altar.

A bishop officiated, along with a dean and three or four priests. It was all very much grander than when Papa was buried; and yet it was all the same. They were both good-byes.

She glanced sideways at her husband. Lucius didn't really understand. He had never lost anyone; his friends were well and healthy, and his parents were alive.

That was one thing she understood, and he did not. If he did not reconcile with his mother before she died — and Lady Clarice had said she was ill — his good-bye would be terrible indeed. Imogen was distraught because she felt guilt. Imagine the guilt that Lucius must suffer if his mother died, longing to see him, and he had not entertained her wish.

He had to overcome his pride.

She glanced at the line of his jaw, at his shadowed eyes. He would never overcome his pride.

She had to do it for him. She made it into a silent vow, spoken in her heart and sealed with a press on her husband's hand.

She would effect a reconciliation between her husband and his parents, if it was the only good thing she did in her life. She would not allow him to be driven mad by guilt the way Imogen was.

The service passed like a miserable dream, broken only by the sound of sobs from about the church. There was no sound at all from the pew before Tess: Imogen and Lady Clarice now possessed precisely the same rigid, frozen silence.

The wind was cutting as they gathered around the door to the Maitland tomb. Tess could hardly hear; her black bonnet flapped around her face. There was a sudden break in the wind, and she heard the bishop say, *"henceforth blessed are the dead which die in the Lord: even so saith the Spirit: for they rest from their labors."*

It was hard to imagine Lord Maitland resting. He never rested: always rushing somewhere, in speech if not on his feet.

Tess swallowed and leaned against Lucius. He bent down and murmured in her ear, "Are you feeling faint? Would you like to walk to the side for a moment?

There was no particular reason she should remain at the grave. Imogen was holding Lady Clarice's arm. They were both staring at Draven's coffin. It was impossible to read their faces. Tess couldn't help Imogen; she couldn't help either of them.

She nodded to Lucius, and they slipped to the side, walking down a path through the small graveyard and stopping at an old stone bench. They sat down, and Lucius tucked the fold of his greatcoat around Tess, pulling her snugly against his body.

"A handkerchief?" he offered her.

"No," and then, because she had to say it aloud, "I feel dreadful for Imogen, and for his mother . . . but . . ." That was a tear running down her cheek, for all she had sworn not to cry ever again.

"I know," he said. "The grief for you is to be cast out by your sister."

She swallowed hard. "I just don't see why she doesn't need me," she whispered finally, her voice strangled in the back of her throat. "Why she doesn't — doesn't love me anymore. I didn't have anything to do with her husband's death!"

"I know," he said. "I know. Imogen will come about, Tess."

Lucius tucked her even closer under his arm as if she were a baby bird and he the mother. Then he bent his head and brushed a kiss on her lips. There was something infinitely sustaining about his touch.

"May I admit to being very happy that you are with me?" he said. He put a finger on her lips. "I know you wish you could be with your little sister, but Tess, I am glad you are with me instead."

A ghost of a smile touched her lips. He was so dear, trying to make her believe that she was necessary to him, when she knew perfectly well that Lucius was self-sustaining. He was peaceful in his solitude and happy in his study. He didn't need her. But it was perfectly *dear* of him to say so.

She leaned her head against his arm and watched a sparrow hop across the flagstones.

She could do that one thing for Lucius, the one thing that would make his solitude less stark. That would give him his own family portraits for the walls, and his own family around the table. He was only pretending to need her, but in fact he *did* need her. He needed her to give him his family back.

"Shall we go to London soon?" she asked.

"I do need to travel there, perhaps tomorrow," he said. "I dislike leaving you right now, but you needn't come with me if you don't wish it."

"I do wish it," she said.

They sat there together, she wrapped in the fold of his greatcoat, and he holding an unused linen handkerchief, until the bells of St. Andrew's began tolling again: one ring for each year of Draven's short life.

Chapter 36

Tess did not crane her head down St. James's Street when the carriage pulled to a halt. There was nothing to be gained from Lucius knowing of her curiosity about his parents' establishment; she had to be subtle about the whole business of family reunification. Lucius had that uncanny ability to close himself off so that she couldn't read what he was thinking at all. And Tess had an uneasy feeling that if he had the slightest idea what she had in mind, he would drive her out to whichever of his five houses was the farthest from London and leave her there.

She had asked whether he had sent word to his parents that they had married. And Lucius had said, "I am quite certain that my mother knew of our marriage before the ink was dry on the special license."

From that, Tess guessed that his mother longed for news of her son and had all her friends writing her with every detail they knew of his life.

Poor, poor woman.

So Tess glanced down the wide street lined with stately houses, but she didn't allow a flicker of curiosity to cross her face.

This time she wasn't surprised to find the drawing room hung with portraits of someone's ancestors. In place of pride over the mantelpiece was the portrait of three children Lucius had told her about. There were two girls and a boy, all dressed in the height of Elizabethan finery. The boy stood in the middle, his small hand resting on a rapier, his chin at an aggressive angle. His eyes were piggish and rather too close together. She was just as glad to know that that particular boy wasn't an ancestor.

"The portrait is quite lovely," she told Lucius.

But he knew her better now. He stood, eyes narrowed. "You don't like it, do you?" he asked.

"That boy is rather piggish," she said. "I'm glad he's *not* your great-grandfather, Lucius. Just imagine —" But the color surged into her face, and she fell silent.

He laughed. "You wouldn't want those eyes to show up in our children, is that it?"

"Naturally not," Tess said with dignity. "But anyone would come to the conclusion that these children are ancestors of yours, Lucius. Your family, to be exact."

"They're not ancestors," he said. "They're investments."

Tess managed not to roll her eyes. "Shall we have some tea?" she asked. "I declare, I am quite parched by the journey. And I should like to see my chambers, if you please."

The thought of showing Tess her new chambers distracted him.

His smile made her cheeks flush to an even deeper rose. *That* made him laugh. He walked over and tipped up her chin. "I seem to relinquish all claims to sane behavior around you."

"Are you saying that I bring out your worst?" Tess asked.

"Haven't you noticed men turning to satyrs in your presence before?"

"Is that what you meant?" A tiny smile curved her mouth. "Then, no. Around Annabel, of course. Everyone falls into love with Annabel. Papa was forever removing servants. Even the vicar had to be sent off to a faraway parish. But no one ever fell in love with me."

Everything Lucius could think of to say was too revealing. So he said nothing, and if Tess's face fell a little at his silence, he didn't notice because he was too busy sorting through the huge mound of invitations that Smiley brought in on a silver platter. "Of course, we can't do much until you are properly dressed," he said absently.

"I have the gowns we ordered in Silchester," Tess murmured.

"And I think we ought to get you a proper lady's maid as well."

Tess touched the nest of curls that Gussie had managed to put together that morning. It was true that Gussie wasn't the best lady's maid, but she would feel so —

Lucius caught her look. "We'll get you a dresser," he said. "Gussie? Is that her name?" And at Tess's nod: "Gussie can continue as your lady's maid."

Tess had discovered Lucius's response to any given problem was to hire a person to help. He seemed to think his house — houses, rather — could only be improved by hiring more and more servants.

"I would rather not hire a dresser," she stated. "Gussie's skills are improving."

He bowed. "As you wish. I must meet my secretary now, but I shall ask Madame Carême to visit you at her nearest convenience. Lady Griselda informs me that she is the *modiste* of choice at the moment. Will you find the time tedious if I retire to my study?"

Tess nodded. "Please don't give me a second thought, Lucius. I shall spend the morning with your housekeeper."

"*Our* housekeeper," he corrected her, coming over and putting his arms around her. "And as for telling me not to think of you" — he paused and gave her a swift, fierce kiss — "that's impossible, my dear."

A second later he was gone, while she stared at the closed door in a flush of dumbfound happiness.

"Mrs. Taine is ever so much nicer than Mrs. Gabthorne," Gussie reported that evening, dragging the brush through Tess's hair with rather more speed than kindness. "And I think she's a better housekeeper for it. She hasn't a mean thing to say of anyone, except the masters' parents. She was that kind when the third footman hadn't the time to sweep the front steps. Mrs. Gabthorne would have worked herself into a perfect frenzy, but Mrs. Taine just told him to make a point of it tomorrow."

"And what did she say about the master's parents?" Tess asked, pitching her voice to a casual key.

"Oh, Mrs. Felton is a bit of a tartar, by some accounts." Gussie put down the brush. "Would you like to bathe before bed, or shall I lay out a nightrail?"

But Tess picked up the brush and handed it back to her. "My nanny always said that one should brush one's hair five hundred times," she said. It was a bit of a fib, given their lack of a nanny, but Annabel had read the precept in a ladies' magazine.

"Oh," Gussie said, obviously taken aback. But she started vigorously brushing Tess's hair again.

"Mrs. Taine said?" Tess asked invitingly.

Gussie's eyes met hers in the mirror. "I'm not supposed to gossip. She made that quite clear to all of us."

"You're not gossiping," Tess said. "I am the mistress of the house." Never mind the fact that gossip was gossip, no matter who received it.

"*Well,*" Gussie said happily. "Mrs. Felton as lives two doors down suffers fearfully from megrims, or so the second housemaid Emma says. Emma is stepping out with the head groom over there. Mrs. Felton had a terrible attack when she heard of our master's marriage."

"Did she weep?" Tess asked, her heart

wringing at the very thought.

"Now that I don't know," Gussie said, giving the matter some thought. "Emma said that she was frisking about the house like a whirlwind: those were her exact words."

"She must have been distraught. Utterly distraught."

"But from what I've heard, madam, you're well shot of her. Emma says that she's up to her elbows in complaints, and even the shoeblack comes in for his share."

"Now *that* is gossip," Tess said. "The poor woman lives without a glimpse of her only son, other than what she can gather from acquaintances. I'm sure the pain of it must occasionally make her irritable."

Gussie put down the brush again. "I do think that must be five hundred strokes, madam, because my arm is fairly aching."

Tess sat at her dressing table for quite a while after Gussie left the room. How was she to approach Mrs. Felton — the other Mrs. Felton, as it were? And would Lucius be angry if she did so? Every time she tried to bring the subject up, he showed no signs of anger, but reiterated, "They have made their feelings clear." It was like talking to a brick wall.

Finally she decided that the best thing

would be to send Mrs. Felton a note. A properly reverential note from a daughter-in-law to a mother-in-law. Perhaps between the two of them they could patch up the chasm in the family.

She moved to her writing desk and began.

Dear Mrs. Felton,

I am persuaded that you must have as much interest as I in mending the —

No. Too blunt.

Dear Mrs. Felton,

I write to you with every hope that you are as happy as I to —

Too weak. Gussie's tales of Mrs. Felton's bad humor were worrisome.

Dear Mrs. Felton,

May I have the pleasure of greeting you tomorrow morning —

No. This would never work. The best thing would be to arrange it so that Lucius and she visited his parents together. Even if Lucius's mother *were* ill-humored, she could hardly behave so in front of her, a stranger and their new daughter-in-law. They all would behave with courtesy, and then it would be a short step to asking his parents to join them for dinner. And before they knew it, the family would be united. It would take small steps to heal such a terrible breach, Tess told herself.

Dear Mrs. Felton,

I take the liberty of requesting that Lucius and I pay you and Mr. Felton a call tomorrow morning, or another morning at your convenience. I am, naturally, eager to meet my husband's family.

Yours with all dutiful pleasure,
Teresa Felton

She had a return note the next morning at breakfast.

Mr. and Mrs. Felton will receive callers at two of the o'clock.

It wasn't precisely welcoming. She read it three times, and then looked at Lucius across the table. He was reading the *Times* and drinking coffee with all the concentration of a man who had a rather busy night (she caught back a smile).

"Lucius," she said, clearing her throat.

"Yes?" He didn't put down his paper.

"I have received a note from your mother."

He did put down his paper. But he didn't say a word, just stared at her with that searching gaze that always made her feel as if he could read her very soul.

"Isn't that lovely of her?" And when he didn't answer, "Your father and mother request that we visit them at our earliest convenience . . . in fact, she mentions this very afternoon, if you are free."

"Tess," he said, "what did you do?"

She widened her eyes to their most innocent. "It's natural that she should wish to meet me, Lucius. I *am* their daughter-in-law, after all."

"How did she know we were in residence?" he asked.

She casually let the note drop into her lap so that he couldn't read it. "Oh, I'm certain that the servants talk to each other," she said. "And we do live two doors apart, Lucius."

His eyes still hadn't left hers. But then he said, "Very well," and retreated behind his paper again.

It wasn't precisely a victory, Tess

thought to herself: it was more of a tactical retreat. But the important thing was that the first step of her campaign was in place.

Chapter 37

Mr. and Mrs. Felton awaited them in the drawing room. Whether by accident or by design, they were posed precisely like one of the Elizabethan portraits that Lucius hung on his walls.

Mrs. Felton was seated in a high-backed, ornately carved chair with a faint resemblance to a throne. She was very thin and sat very still, her face turned three-quarters toward the windows. She had a great quantity of hair intricately piled upon her head and rather fat hands that were at odds with her slender body. Each finger was so weighed down by rings that it looked stiff and even plumper.

It seemed that Lucius gained the beauty of his features from his father. Mr. Felton was smaller than Lucius and rather shriveled-looking, but the spare, angular beauty of his son's eyes and cheekbones were there. He must have been formidably handsome as a young man. Something about the way he rested one hand on the back of his wife's chair, waiting for her to speak before he greeted them, made Tess uneasy.

Lucius took her forward toward them. Finally, Mrs. Felton rose. The diamonds at her ears caught the light from the fire. She held out her hand, and Lucius bent to kiss it, quite as if he were greeting Queen Elizabeth herself.

"And you are my successor," Mrs. Felton said, turning to Tess. She smiled suddenly, and with the same abrupt charm that accompanied Lucius's rare smiles. "It is a true pleasure to meet you. I admit that I was losing hope that my son would marry at all."

Tess's heart lightened, and she smiled back, curtsying. "Thank you for your welcome," she said. "It is wonderful to meet my husband's family."

"I share your sentiments," Mrs. Felton said. "I have every hope that your marriage will be the catalyst to bring our beloved son" — she smiled at Lucius — "into our acquaintance again."

Lucius bowed. Tess felt a germ of irritation at his unsmiling face. Why didn't he tell his mother how glad he was that she was receiving him? Why wasn't he helping this reunion by saying something to signal his happiness?

"Do sit down," Mrs. Felton said. "Stilton, bring my son and his wife some tea, if you please. I shall have a glass of ratafia, and Mr. Felton shall have his normal repast." She suddenly seemed to think of something and turned her heavy, rather swollen-looking eyes to Tess for the first time. "Unless you would prefer a glass of ratafia? I was under the impression that you must be quite young, but now I see that you are more than old enough for spirits."

"Tea would be very welcome," Tess said.

"Splendid." Mrs. Felton waved the butler from the room. "Now, you must tell me about yourself, my dear. I never had a daughter, and I assure you that I am most, most delighted at the prospect. I understand that you are an orphan?"

Tess nodded. "My sisters and I are wards of the Duke of Holbrook."

Mrs. Felton's smile widened. "Ah, yes, my son's dearest friend. They met years ago at Eton. Of course, Holbrook was only a second son, as I'm sure you know. No one had any expectation that *he* would succeed to the title. Quite fortunate, really."

Tess thought that it depended on one's point of view; she knew without a moment's hesitation that Rafe would give his right arm to have his brother Peter alive. But she nodded.

"We have been quite pleased with our son's acquaintances," Mrs. Felton continued, as if neither her son nor husband were in the room at all. "You do realize that his circle includes the Earl of Mayne?"

"I have met the earl," Tess said cautiously, wondering whether Mrs. Felton would ever hear the tale of her near marriage to Mayne.

"Mr. Felton and I have never had the slightest concern about our son's intimate friendships. His godfather was kind enough to send him to Eton, and even as a boy Lucius associated himself only with the very best. I am certain that he has chosen you with equal care, my dear." She paused and smiled at Tess. "Since you are now a member of the Felton family, I deem it appropriate that I ask you questions rather more intimate than would be countenanced amongst strangers."

"Please, ask me any question that you wish," Tess replied. She hadn't really given much thought to being *a member of the Felton family*. Of course, one did gain a new family upon marriage.

"I ask this only because of your unfortunate circumstances," Mrs. Felton asked. "But . . . did you bring a dowry to the marriage?"

"A coarse question, Mother," Lucius said, "and unwarranted by our familial ties."

"Despite your avid interest in things financial, son, you forget that the great families arrange marriages for more reasons than an attractive face."

"We are not a great family," Lucius said. "And aren't you discussing things financial at the moment?"

"It is one thing to marry well and quite another to dirty one's hands with lucre," Mrs. Felton pronounced.

"I would be most happy to answer any questions that your mother asks, Lucius," Tess said with a frown at her husband.

"In that case," he remarked, "Tess did indeed bring a notable dowry to our marriage."

Tess blinked, and then folded her hands together. Only Lucius would label a horse a "notable" dowry.

"Good," Mrs. Felton said. "I trust you did not object to my question," she said to Tess. "One who is friends with the Duke of Holbrook and the Earl of Mayne might be expected to make a great marriage indeed." She sniffed. "It has been difficult to watch our son lower the tone of his acquaintance by proving mercantile in his daily life. One could not but worry that no worthy matron would wish to match her daughter with him."

"It is my understanding that your son was one of the most sought-after bachelors in all London," Tess noted.

"The daughters of shopkeepers, many of them," Mrs. Felton said, taking a slender glass of ratafia from the tray her butler held out. One of her rings knocked sharply against the delicate crystal.

Tess felt compelled to note that Lady Griselda's report had been quite the opposite. "I was informed that the daughter of the Duke of Surrey showed your son marked attention during the last season," she said gently.

"One had hopes, naturally." Mrs. Felton sighed. "But now my fears are in the past. I understand that you have some sort of a title in your background, and then there's the dowry." She gave Tess a measured smile.

Tess hoped to God that the truth of her equine dowry never found its way to the ears of any of Mrs. Felton's friends.

"My father, of course, was the Earl of

Devonshire," Mrs. Felton said, rearranging the rings on her left hand so that they caught the firelight and glimmered. "I rarely use my title, Lady Margery, as I prefer Mrs. Felton."

"Teresa's father was Viscount Brydone," Lucius put in.

"From the other side of the border? Then they have viscounts in those parts?" She smiled at Tess. "I always think it's so interesting how other countries mimic English customs. I suppose it's merely another sign of our supremacy throughout the world. I do hear that they even have some barons and some such in America."

Mr. Felton cleared his throat. "How are your stables?" he asked.

They all jumped slightly. It was clear to Tess that Mr. Felton spoke so infrequently that his wife hardly remembered his presence.

"Fine," Lucius said.

"Who will you run in the Ascot next year?"

Mrs. Felton laughed, and made a rueful gesture to Tess. "I'm afraid that I have a firm rule that Mr. Felton has perhaps forgotten: we do not speak of the stables in my presence. Otherwise, the conversation grows too, too tedious."

After a moment, Tess said, "How is your health, madam? Lady Clarice intimated that —"

"Please do not call me *madam*," Mrs. Felton said sweetly. "I'm afraid that I absolutely loathe the term. It has the smell of the shop, you know. The best people do not address each other in such a fashion, my dear."

"Oh," Tess said. "I am grateful for your advice."

Mrs. Felton lowered her chin in an approving nod. "Those whose titles are of recent creation," she advised Tess, "must always pay the closest attention to every nuance of the spoken language. My father's title reached back to the age of Elizabeth, and therefore I felt no such anxiety. For example, I married whom I pleased, and although my husband's birth is not equal to my own, I fancy my consequence has been unmarred."

Tess was beginning to feel slightly ill although there was nothing in Mrs. Felton's demeanor to suggest that she meant to offend. "The first Baron Brydone was given his title by King Edward I," she said, with a very credible show of carelessness.

"Really? Now who would have thought that there were such titles in Scotland in that date?" Mrs. Felton exclaimed. "Or that Edward found his way to such an outlandish place? I thought the country was full of *Picts* at that time. Warriors with blue paint on their faces."

"Actually, my father's title is English," Tess explained. "We were raised in Scotland, but King Henry VI granted the title of viscount."

"Very proper indeed, I am sure," Mrs. Felton said, her gaze seeming to warm slightly. "And I am truly happy to welcome you into the family. Dearest." She leaned toward her, again seeming to ignore the presence of her silent husband and son. "Perhaps between the two of us we can hatch up a plan to return my son to a place of respectability in the *ton*."

Tess blinked uncertainly.

"You are aware, are you not?" she said. "My son's activities have been the bane of my existence for years now." There was a distinct note of horror in her voice. "Stocks and so forth," she said, lowering her voice as if the very subject were indelicate. "Blood will tell. My father always said it, and he was right."

"Blood?" Tess repeated.

Mrs. Felton shook her head sadly, leaning even closer to Tess. "Surely you've noticed how seriously he takes commerce? As if it isn't good enough for a gentleman to live by rents, as has always been the case in my family. Why, if you believed my son, you'd think that Mr. Felton and I were dependent on his generosity."

"We *are* dependent on our son's generosity," said Mr. Felton.

Once again, they all jumped at the sound of his voice.

Mr. Felton was still standing behind his wife's chair. One hand was clenched on the back of her throne, and the other held a glass of liquor. He was looking straight at Lucius, ignoring his wife and daughter-in-law.

Mrs. Felton laughed, not bothering to turn her head and meet her husband's eyes. "That small unpleasantness, far in the past, has been made too much of, Mr. Felton."

"The unpleasantness, as you call it, continues month by month," her husband said, still looking at his son.

Tess was bewildered. Lucius was frowning at his father.

Mrs. Felton rose from her chair and turned to Tess with her charming smile. "May I show you the portraits of my ancestors, my dears? After all, this house will be yours someday. I have a magnificent portrait of the Earl of Devonshire with the countess, my mother."

"You allowed, Mrs. Felton, that subjects may be aired amongst us that are more intimate than might be discussed amongst strangers," her husband said.

"I'm afraid that we must leave," Lucius said. "I'm certain that Tess would be more than pleased to take up your invitation at some other time, Mother." Tess could tell from the wintry look in his eye that his father had seriously enraged him . . . somehow.

"As long as your wife understands our precise obligation to you," Mr. Felton said, still staring at his son. "I have allowed all of London to believe the worst of you, but I will not countenance a misunderstanding within the family."

"The merest trifle!" Mrs. Felton said, her affable voice taking on a shrill note. "A trifling assistance some years ago. And yet —"

Mr. Felton spoke over her, turning to Tess. "When Lucius — my son Lucius — was in his final year at Oxford, we came near to running aground. We were living above our means and that money from rents — well, there was nothing to rent anymore. No land."

Mrs. Felton was opening her mouth like a fish out of water.

"My son came down from Oxford for a matter of two months, and in that time he made so much money on the market that he paid my debts and financed the rest of his education."

"There was no need for recounting the past!" Mrs. Felton snapped. Her face was turning purplish.

"We would have been ruined," Mr. Felton continued, ignoring his wife. "Utterly bankrupt. Since then, Lucius has supported us. He paid the mortgages on our estate in the country. And how do we repay him?" He looked at his wife's head. She had turned away from him and was staring rigidly toward the windows. "All London knows of the breach between us."

"You exaggerate, as always, Mr. Felton. My husband," she said to Tess, "is far too sensitive for his own good. He is not a gentleman at heart. Those of our rank do not become ruined. That is something that occurs to commoners. *We* simply continue as we have always continued. The tradesmen are perfectly willing to wait for a time before they are paid, in return for the honor of our patronization."

Lucius held up a hand. He was taller than either of his parents, and far, far, more beautiful, Tess thought. He stood between them like a fine-grained version of his mother, her almost grotesque slenderness turned to his muscled grace; his father's shrunken prettiness become his masculine beauty.

"My wife and I are most grateful that you invited us to the house, Mother," he said, turning to her. "But I should not wish to outwear our welcome. I know that Tess will be most happy to return another day and take tea with you." He tucked Tess's hand under his arm.

She hadn't said anything for the last ten minutes and couldn't think what to say now, until his fingers tightened on her arm in a warning fashion. At which point, she dropped a curtsy, a bit lopsided due to Lucius's grasp, and managed to say that it had been a true pleasure.

Chapter 38

They didn't say a word on the way to their own house. Once inside the antechamber, when Smiley was taking Tess's pelisse and bonnet, Lucius bowed, and said, "If you will forgive me, I shall —"

"Oh, no!" Tess said, reaching out and grabbing his sleeve as he was about to melt away to his study.

Smiley prudently retired through the baize door, carrying their outer garments. Lucius raised an eyebrow. "Hasn't there been enough revelation for one day?"

Tess ignored this foolishness, opening the door to the drawing room and waiting for him to join her.

"I would rather not discuss my parents," he said, walking across the room away from her. "I am certain that you were able to gain a clear understanding of our relationship from our meeting this morning. I know that family is very important to you, Tess, and if you wish me to continue visiting them, I shall."

Tess watched his back. "But I would like to talk about your parents *now*," she said, perfectly agreeably. She was counting on Lucius's exquisite manners.

"Very well." He turned about and waited. He wasn't going to make this easy; his face was as expressionless as she had ever seen it.

"There are merely a few things that I would like to clarify," she said, perching on the armrest of a settee. "Your mother has an extraordinary interest in titles and matters of consequence, does she not?"

"Yes."

"I would guess that she owns a *Debrett's Peerage* and reads it regularly?"

"Of course."

"Then she already knew my father's title is both English and ancient," Tess said.

He bent his head. "Your surmise is quite likely correct. I'm afraid that my mother takes some pleasure in baiting visitors."

"One more question . . . I just want to make certain that my understanding is correct. You returned from Oxford and made the necessary funds to save your family from immediate destitution."

"That is an exaggeration," he said. "My mother is correct in that a gentleman's family can continue for some time with crippling debt."

"But without your contribution, there would have been no escape from that debt. Your father said there was no longer any land nor any rents. You would have had to leave university, for example."

"That is true."

"You saved your family's financial future, and in response, they disowned you publicly."

"Again, an exaggeration," he remarked. He turned and stared out the window. "My parents are simply disappointed that I continued to invest in the market after the most immediate necessity had passed."

She rose and ran over to him, standing at his elbow. "Lucius, you paid your family's debts, and then they threw you out *because of it?*"

His jaw was tight. "That casts their actions in an unpleasant light."

She slipped her hand into his. "Yes, it does."

He was silent. Then: "You must understand that from my mother's point of view, I could have done nothing more egregious. She lived with her parents' disapproval of her own marriage, which became a fear that my father's blood would show itself."

"So to her, it has," Tess said softly. "And since that date, you have continued to pay for your parents' maintenance?" No answer. "Lady Griselda mentioned that your family owned a large estate in the country."

She was shocked by the irritation in his eyes. "Does it matter where the estate came from, Tess? Of course they are happier with the land preserved."

She returned his gaze steadily. "Your mother's diamonds?"

He turned away again.

She pulled him to face her. "It's precisely the same thing you did for Imogen, and without even telling me. You saved Imogen's reputation by paying for a special license, didn't you?"

"That was nothing," he said, shrugging again.

"You didn't save merely Imogen's reputation. It was all of us."

"I told you before, Tess, money is simply not something that I care about very much. Remember?"

She did remember. He had told her that he would never care deeply for her, that he was incapable of strong feelings. Tess would — would *spit* before she believed that nonsense. He even loved his mother, for all she was a woman so obsessed with civility that she had discarded her only son like a worn garment. There was no other explanation for his buying a house on St. James's Square. And there was no other explanation for the portraits he sprinkled about the house. Not unless he missed his own family, unpleasant though they were.

"Lucius," she asked, looking up at him, "I have a question, and then I promise that I'll let you go back to work."

His eyes instantly lightened. "Anything you desire," he said.

"The morning when I was to marry Mayne," she said, gathering all her courage into the question, "I heard him come down the stairs. And then you left the room."

He seemed to have stiffened.

"What did you say to him?"

He stared down at her. She counted the seconds with the beats of her heart.

"I asked him to leave," he said finally.

Her heart leaped, but she still wanted to make certain. "Did you pay him to leave?"

A shadow crossed his face. "Is that what you think? That I use money as a stick to force people into compliance with my wishes?"

"No!" And: "Why did you ask Mayne to leave?"

"I wanted you," he said. "I wanted you myself."

"Then why didn't you ask me?" she said, and it was the most important question of all. "Why didn't you simply ask me?"

"I did ask —"

"Not then," Tess said. "We barely knew each other when you asked me at the Roman ruin. Why didn't you ask me again? Why did you allow Mayne to propose?"

He just stared down at her. "You deserve better than I. I'm not capable —"

But her eyes were glowing with some emotion that he couldn't quite define, and the words died in his mouth. She had turned his life upside down, thrown his reliance on civility to the wind as if those rules were no more than straw.

"I wanted you more than I could admit to myself," he finally said. "So I asked Mayne to leave."

"You fixed the problem," Tess said with satisfaction. "Just as you fixed the problem in your parents' finances and Imogen's elopement."

"No."

"No?"

"It wasn't the same, not at all." He reached out and brushed a lock of hair from her face. "I never wanted to fix anything as much as I wanted to fix your life, Tess. That was the frightening part. It was easy to make the money my father needed; I gambled on the market, and because I don't really care about money, it came easily. But I couldn't pay to fix your life. I could never buy you."

Her eyes were a little teary, but he thought it was with joy. And she was holding him very tightly.

"I care about you too much," he whispered, pulling her against him so that he didn't have to look in her eyes as he said it. "I fell in love with you, Tess. And now I love you more than — more than life itself. I know you'd rather be with Imogen, and that your family comes first in your heart —"

But she was shaking her head and pulling away from him. "I thought that . . . I thought that I was marrying for my family, and I thought that my heart would break when Imogen cast me out. And I was worried that your heart was destroyed by a similar event. But it's not, is it?"

"No," he said, searching her eyes.

"My heart *would* break if you ever left me," she whispered. "If you ever threw me out."

He pulled her back against his heart,

into his arms. “I would never leave you,” he said. “Never. I could no more throw you from my life than I could take my heart from my chest.”

She raised her eyes to see the love there, and it was so fierce that it burned into her heart, never to be doubted. Never to be questioned.

The words, “I love you, I love you” came from one pair of lips to the other, a rough whisper from one heart to the other, a promise from one soul to the other.

Epilogue

They were sitting for a family portrait. They had been sitting for it for the greater part of eight months, since Benjamin West was so old that his hands grew tired after an hour or so of wielding his brushes. But it seemed he was finally done. He lifted his head and nodded, signaling to his assistant to take his brushes. He was a delicate old gentleman, dressed in black velvet and high heels, wearing a powdered wig of the style of his youth.

"I believe that I am finished," he observed, standing up. He drifted away. "I shall leave you to contemplate yourselves in privacy." And with a wave of a lace handkerchief, he was gone.

"The only trouble," Tess said to her husband as they stood before the portrait on its easel, "is that Phin walks now, and he's pictured as a mere babe in white lace."

In Benjamin West's portrait, Phin was an angelic infant with no more than a tuft of hair and a sweetly sleepy expression. In fact, they all looked rather indolent, if exquisite; it seemed to be a marker of Mr. West's work.

The contrast to the real Phin was startling. For one thing, Phin was wearing nothing more than a little jacket and a nappy listing inelegantly in the direction of his chubby knees. For another, he had a mophead full of curls that stood out in all directions. The inelegance of his appearance was not helped by the fact that Chloe had taken up her favorite post, on his shoulder. Phin talked constantly, although no one understood what he said; likewise, Chloe squawked without forming intelligible words. The two of them made a cacophonous noise together.

Tess looked back at the portrait. Mr. West had depicted the three of them seated under a sycamore. Tess was the picture of slender elegance, dressed as if for a drawing room with the queen. Phineas was dozing in his mother's arms, while Tess looked up at her husband, posed just behind her with his hand on her chair. Lucius gazed at the viewer, sleepy-eyed and powerful.

"I like the way you're looking at me," Lucius said with some satisfaction.

She smiled. "I appear to love you, don't

I? Or perhaps if I wasn't quite so lazy, I might feel the emotion."

His arms wrapped around her, and a fierce voice said in her ear, *"might?"*

"All right, *do*." She laughed. And then, "Your arms won't reach about me if I grow any larger."

"I'm not worried," Lucius said, patting her belly with satisfaction.

She laughed again and turned in the circle of his arms so that she could look at the portrait again. "We just look so — so *idle!*"

"Love-in-idleness," he said into her hair.

"William's flower?" she said, remembering. "Heartsease."

"You are an ease to my heart," he told her.

She laid her head back against his shoulder and smiled at the three of them . . . the perfect family portrait.

Phin toddled by, swiping the leg of the pedestal as he did so. The portrait tottered, and the fate of the elegant, indolent family hung in the balance, until Lucius reached forward with a lightning grab and saved it.

Of course.

A Love Letter to Louisa May Alcott

The inspiration for this book, and indeed for my entire Sisters quartet, of which *Much Ado About You* is the first, came from novels written by Louisa May Alcott. Alcott is most famous for *Little Women*; some of you undoubtedly picked up the ancestral relation between my four squabbling, loving sisters and Alcott's little women. Yet a different Alcott novel served as a direct source for this particular book. Her *Rose in Bloom*, published in 1876, is a wonderful tale of a young orphan with eight male cousins. One of those cousins is very similar to my Draven, and Draven's wild ride on Blue Peter is modeled, to some extent, on my memories of weeping over *Rose in Bloom* as a young girl.

My husband is Italian, and we spend a great deal of time in that country. Last year we took our children to the island of Elba, where Napoleon was exiled after being tossed out of France. We dutifully toured Napoleon's villa and, on the way back to the beach where we were staying, we stumbled across a sign for a "Roman ruin." It was nothing more than that: a few tumbled rocks, a sunken room here or there. While the site was marked as such, no one was paying it much attention: apparently Romans loved Elba, and ruins of their various houses are to be found all over the island. So I just wanted to tell you that in case you wish to visit the ruined house that Lucius and Tess found so interesting, you'll have to travel to Italy, and then take a boat to Elba, and then rent a car and wind up into the hills . . . and the trip will be worth every penny.

Finally, the lovely poem by Catullus that both Tess and Lucius know by heart is called "How Many Kisses: For Lesbia." The translation that I quote here is by A. S. Kline and can be found in his *Catullus: The Poems*, available on-line at www.tonykline.co.uk/ (Poetry in Translation). The translation is glorious, and worth quoting in full:

Lesbia, you ask how many kisses of yours
would be enough and more to satisfy me.
As many as the grains of Libyan sand

that lie between hot Jupiter's oracle,
at Ammon, in resin-producing Cyrene
and old Battiades' sacred tomb:
or as many as the stars, when night is still,
gazing down on secret human desires:
as many of your kisses kissed
are enough, and more, for mad Catullus,
as can't be counted by spies
nor an evil tongue bewitch us.

Why Every Heroine Needs a Sister Just as Much as She Needs a Husband (Ooops! Did I Say More Than She Needs a Man?)

My editor says that I write romances that are partially about the heroine's love for a man, and partially about her love for her girlfriends. Well, of course. Too many novels depict a heroine sitting alone when the new sheriff rides in and she barely has time to think, *nice pecs,* before her life changes. I don't buy it. In real life, her best friend is propped on the barstool to her right, saying, "Honey, I never liked that fake tan look." And her sister is drinking her third cosmo and saying, "Definitely *not.*

Look how small his hands are. Do you suppose he wears that gun belt so low for a reason?" So, to the tune of wicked laughter, our heroine rolls her eyes at the sheriff and turns back to her friends. I have a sister *and* two best friends. In fact, it's a wonder I ever got married, considering the amount of commentary I received!

My little sister came along when I was one year old. It wasn't an unmixed blessing. She went through high school with long blonde hair, runner's legs, and a charming ability to get along with members of the opposite sex. *I* trotted through those same years in a plump body, with an afro perm of red curls (don't ask), and no ability for small talk whatsoever. By the time I went to college, I'd given up my perm and had a modified Farrah Fawcett do. I met my best friends in my freshman year. One was from San Francisco and talked of bands I'd never heard of. Another was from Boston, and had won the Latin prize in high school. Some twenty years later, we still talk on the phone several times a week. And as for my sister . . . she lives right down the road, and we see each other almost every day.

These three women have marked all the turning points, the afros, the perms, the summer of shaved head, great delights, and the seeming tragedies of my life and theirs. Together, we've had six children, several husbands, bad boyfriends and worse boyfriends, near death and illnesses. More to the point, we've saved one another from disaster more times than can be counted. Marion saved me from marrying a doctor by pointing out he discussed his mother more than his job. I saved Alissa from a fate worse than death by noting that the wonderful man she had just met had a pale circle around his finger. Bridget saved Marion from a drunken Bulgarian artist who threw fruit knives when enraged, by stressing his bald spot.

My last series was structured around female friendships, and in review was always being called a Regency *Sex and the City*. With my new series, which begins with *Much Ado About You*, I decided to write about sisters. Sisters who are girlfriends, best enemies, best friends, most beloved . . . all at one time. The heroine of *Much Ado* has three sisters: logical, plump Josie; sensual, witty Annabel; and passionate Imogen. She feuds with them as she falls in love with the hero. And she falls in love to the tune of their commentary. If I had to describe the book, I'd point to a mix between two great products of pop culture: *Sex and the City* meets *Little Women*.

The employees of Thorndike Press hope you have enjoyed this Large Print book. All our Thorndike and Wheeler Large Print titles are designed for easy reading, and all our books are made to last. Other Thorndike Press Large Print books are available at your library, through selected bookstores, or directly from us.

For information about titles, please call:

(800) 223-1244

or visit our Web site at:

www.gale.com/thorndike
www.gale.com/wheeler

To share your comments, please write:

Publisher
Thorndike Press
295 Kennedy Memorial Drive
Waterville, ME 04901